"[The] seductive antihero [is] at his swashbuckling best."
— *Publishers Weekly*

WHERE SERPENTS SLEEP

"C. S. Harris's attention to historical detail and sense of adventure combine to make a ripping read . . . captivated me to the final page."
— Will Thomas, author of the Barker & Llewelyn novels

"An intriguing mix of bloody murder, incest, and brutality. The author, who has done her historical homework, makes [the] fascinating focus of her book . . . Hero Jarvis, a young woman whose uncompromising independence puts her far ahead of her time."
— *The Washington Times*

"[Sebastian and Hero] are a perfect hardheaded match as they lead Harris's romping good story."
— *The New Orleans Times-Picayune*

"Harris does an excellent job of interweaving the mystery in this book with the larger story arc of the series . . . solidly written."
— *St. Petersburg Times*

"Outstanding. . . . Harris does a nice job of weaving the many plot strands together while exploring the complex character of her protagonist."
— *Publishers Weekly* (Starred Review)

WHY MERMAIDS SING

"A serial-killer thriller set two hundred years ago? . . . It works, thanks to Harris's pacing and fine eye for detail. A real plus: the murk and stench of the age only heighten the suspense."
— *Entertainment Weekly*

"Thoroughly enjoyable . . . moody and atmospheric, exposing the dark underside of Regency London . . . deliciously ghoulish . . . kept me enthralled."
— Deanna Raybourn, author of *The Dark Enquiry*

WHEN GODS DIE

"Like Georgette Heyer, Harris delves deep into the mores of Regency England, but hers is a darker, more dangerous place."
— *Kirkus Reviews* (Starred Review)

"Deftly combines political intrigue, cleverly concealed clues, and vivid characters . . . a fast-moving story that will have readers eagerly anticipating future volumes in the series."
— *Publishers Weekly* (Starred Review)

"Harris knows her English history and has a firm grasp of how a mystery novel is supposed to play out . . . a crescendo of suspense and surprise. . . . Fans of historicals, especially those set in Regency-era England, will snap up this triumph."
— *Library Journal* (Starred Review)

WHAT ANGELS FEAR

"Perfect reading. . . . Harris crafts her story with the threat of danger, hints of humor, vivid sex scenes, and a conclusion that will make your pulse race. Impressive."
— *The New Orleans Times-Picayune*

"A stunning debut novel filled with suspense, intrigue, and plot twists galore. C. S. Harris artfully re-creates the contradictory world of Regency England as her marvelous characters move between the glittering ballrooms and the treacherous back alleys of London. . . . Start this one early in the day—you won't be able to put it down!"
— Victoria Thompson, author of the Gaslight Mystery series

"Appealing characters, authentic historical details, and sound plotting make this an amazing debut historical."
— *Library Journal* (Starred Review)

"An absorbing and accomplished debut that displays a mastery of the Regency period in all its elegance and barbarity. . . . [It] will grip the reader from its first pages and compel to the finish."
— Stephanie Barron, author of the Jane Austen Mystery series

"The combined elements of historical fiction, romance, and mystery in this fog-enshrouded London puzzler will appeal to fans of Anne Perry." — *Booklist*

"A masterful blend of history and suspense, character and plot, imagination and classic mystery. A thoroughly intriguing, enjoyable read."
— Laura Joh Rowland, author of the Sano Ichirō Mystery series

BOOKS IN THE
SEBASTIAN ST. CYR MYSTERY SERIES

What Angels Fear
When Gods Die
Why Mermaids Sing
Where Serpents Sleep
What Remains of Heaven
Where Shadows Dance
When Maidens Mourn
What Darkness Brings

WHEN
MAIDENS
MOURN

A Sebastian St. Cyr Mystery

C. S. HARRIS

AN OBSIDIAN MYSTERY

OBSIDIAN
Published by New American Library, a division of
Penguin Group (USA) Inc., 375 Hudson Street,
New York, New York 10014, USA
Penguin Group (Canada), 90 Eglinton Avenue East, Suite 700, Toronto,
Ontario M4P 2Y3, Canada (a division of Pearson Penguin Canada Inc.)
Penguin Books Ltd., 80 Strand, London WC2R 0RL, England
Penguin Ireland, 25 St. Stephen's Green, Dublin 2,
Ireland (a division of Penguin Books Ltd.)
Penguin Group (Australia), 707 Collins Street, Melbourne, Victoria 3008,
Australia (a division of Pearson Australia Group Pty. Ltd.)
Penguin Books India Pvt. Ltd., 11 Community Centre, Panchsheel Park,
New Delhi–110 017, India
Penguin Group (NZ), 67 Apollo Drive, Rosedale, Auckland 0632,
New Zealand (a division of Pearson New Zealand Ltd.)
Penguin Books, Rosebank Office Park, 181 Jan Smuts Avenue,
Parktown North 2193, South Africa
Penguin China, B7 Jaiming Center, 27 East Third Ring Road North,
Chaoyang District, Beijing 100020, China

Penguin Books Ltd., Registered Offices:
80 Strand, London WC2R 0RL, England

First published by Obsidian, an imprint of New American Library, a division of
Penguin Group (USA) Inc. Previously published in an Obsidian hardcover edition.

First Mass Market Printing, March 2013
10 9 8 7 6 5 4 3 2 1

Copyright © The Two Talers, LLC, 2012
Excerpt from *What Darkness Brings* copyright © The Two Talers, LLC, 2013

PUBLISHER'S NOTE
This is a work of fiction. Names, characters, places, and incidents either are the
product of the author's imagination or are used fictitiously, and any resemblance
to actual persons, living or dead, business establishments, events, or locales is
entirely coincidental.
    The publisher does not have any control over and does not assume any responsibility for author or third-party Web sites or their content.

ALWAYS LEARNING   PEARSON

For my cousin
Kaitlyn Johnston

Out flew the web and floated wide;
The mirror crack'd from side to side;
"The curse is come upon me," cried
The Lady of Shalott.

—Alfred, Lord Tennyson (1809–1892),
"The Lady of Shalott"

✵

The place at which he stopped was no more than a
mound, partly surrounded by a ditch, from which it
derived the name of Camlet Moat. A few hewn
stones there were, which had escaped the fate of
many others . . . vestiges, just sufficient to show that
"here in former times the hand of man had been."

—Sir Walter Scott (1771–1832),
The Fortunes of Nigel

Chapter 1

Camlet Moat, Trent Place, England
Sunday, 2 August 1812

*T*essa Sawyer hummed a nervous tune beneath her breath as she pushed through the tangled brush and bracken edging the black waters of the ancient moat. She was very young—just sixteen at her next birthday. And though she tried to tell herself she was brave, she knew she wasn't. She could feel her heart pounding in her narrow chest, and her hands tingled as if she'd been sitting on them. When she'd left the village, the night sky above had been clear and bright with stars. But here, deep in the wood, all was darkness and shadow. From the murky, stagnant water beside her rose an eerie mist, thick and clammy.

It should have wafted cool against her cheek. Instead, she felt as if the heavy dampness were stealing her breath, suffocating her with an unnatural heat and a sick dread of the forbidden. She paused to swipe a shaky hand across her sweaty face and heard a rustling in the distance, the soft plop of something hitting the water.

Choking back a whimper, she spun about, ready to

run. But this was Lammas, a time sacred to the ancient goddess. They said that at midnight on this night, if a maiden dipped a cloth into the holy well that lay on the northern edge of the isle of Camlet Moat and then tied her offering to a branch of the rag tree that overhung the well, her prayer would be answered. Not only that, but maybe, just maybe, the White Lady herself would appear, to bless the maid and offer her the wisdom and guidance that a motherless girl such as Tessa yearned for with all her being.

No one knew exactly who the White Lady was. Father Clark insisted that if the lady existed at all—which he doubted—she could only be the Virgin Mary. But local legend said the White Lady was one of the grail maidens of old, a chaste virgin who'd guarded the sacred well since before the time of Arthur and Guinevere and the Knights of the Round Table. And then there were those who whispered that the lady was actually Guinevere, ever young, ever beautiful, ever glorious.

Forcing herself to go on, Tessa clenched her fist around the strip of white cloth she was bringing as an offering. She could see the prow of the small dinghy kept at the moat by Sir Stanley Winthrop, on whose land she trespassed. Its timbers old and cracked, its aged paint worn and faded, it rocked lightly at the water's edge as if touched by an unseen current.

It was not empty.

Tessa drew up short. A lady lay crumpled against the stern, her hair a dark cascade of curls around a pale, motionless face. She was young yet and slim, her gown an elegant flowing confection of gossamer muslin sashed with peach satin. She had her head tipped back, her neck arched; her eyes were open but sightless, her skin waxen.

And from a jagged rent high across her pale breast showed a dried rivulet of darkness where her life's blood had long since drained away.

Chapter 2

London
Monday, 3 August

*D*riven from his sleep by troublesome dreams, Sebastian St. Cyr, Viscount Devlin, leaned into his outstretched arms, fingers curling around the sill of his wife's open bedroom window. He'd learned long ago of the dangers that lurk in those quicksilver moments that come between darkness and the dawn. When the world hovers between night and day, a man could get lost in his own tortured memories of the past if he wasn't careful.

He drew a deep, shuddering breath into his lungs. But the dawn was unusually warm, the air too parched and dusty to bring any real relief. He was aware of a sheen of sweat coating his naked skin; a humming like bees working a hive droned behind his temples. The urge to wrap his hand around a cool glass of brandy was strong.

He resisted it.

Behind him, the woman who just four days before had become his Viscountess stirred in her bed. Their marriage was so recent—and the reasons behind it so complicated—that he sometimes found himself still thinking of her not as Hero Devlin but as "Miss Jarvis," formidable daughter of Charles, Lord Jarvis, the brilliant but ruthless cousin of the King who served as the acknowledged power behind the fragile regency of the Prince of Wales. Once, Jarvis had sworn to destroy Sebastian, however long it might take. Sebastian knew that his marriage to Jarvis's daughter had not changed that.

Looking over his shoulder, he watched now as Hero came slowly awake. She lay motionless for a moment. Then her eyelids fluttered open and she shifted her head against the pillow to stare at him from across a darkened room hung with blue silk and gilded mirrors and scented with lavender.

"Did I wake you?" he asked. "I am sorry."

"Don't be ridiculous."

Sebastian huffed a soft laugh. There was nothing either indulgent or coquettish about Hero.

She slipped from the bed, bringing with her the fine linen sheet to wrap around her nakedness as she crossed to him. In the darkness of the night, she could come to him without inhibition, a willing and passionate lover. But during the day . . .

During the day they remained in many ways essentially strangers to each other, two people who inhabited the same house yet were self-conscious and awkward when they chanced upon each other in the hall or met over breakfast. Only at night could they seem to put aside the wary distrust that had characterized their relationship from the beginning. Only in darkness could they forget the deep, dangerous antagonism that lay between his house and hers and come together as man and woman.

He was aware of the gray light of dawn stealing into the room. She hugged the sheet tighter around her.

"You never sleep," she said.

"I do. Sometimes."

She tipped her head to one side, her normally tidy

brown hair tangled by last night's lovemaking. "Have you always had such troublesome dreams, or only since marrying the daughter of your worst enemy?"

Smiling faintly, he reached out to draw her to him.

She came stiffly, her forearms resting on his naked chest, creating some distance between them. She was a tall woman, nearly as tall as Sebastian himself, with her powerful father's aquiline countenance and Lord Jarvis's famous, disconcerting intelligence.

He said, "I'm told it's not uncommon for men to dream of war after they've returned home."

Her shrewd gray eyes narrowed with thoughts he could only guess at. "That's what you dream of? The war?"

He hesitated. "Mainly."

That night, he had indeed been driven from his bed by the echoing *whomph* of cannonballs, by the squeals of injured horses and the despairing groans of dying men. Yet there were times when his dreams were troubled not by the haunting things he'd seen or the even more haunting things he'd done, but by a certain blue-eyed, dusky-haired actress named Kat Boleyn. It was an unintentional but nonetheless real betrayal of the woman he had taken to wife, and it troubled him. Yet the only certain way for a man to control his dreams was to avoid sleep.

The daylight in the room strengthened.

Hero said, "It's difficult for anyone to sleep in this heat."

He reached up to smooth the tangled hair away from her damp forehead. "Why not come with me to Hampshire? It would do us both good to get away from the noise and dirt of London for a few weeks." He'd been intending to pay a visit to his estate all summer, but the events of the past few months had made leaving London impossible. Now it was a responsibility that could be delayed no longer.

He watched her hesitate and knew exactly what she was thinking: that alone together in the country they would be thrown constantly into each other's company. It was, after all, the reason newlywed couples traditionally went away on a honeymoon—so that they might get to know each other better. But there was little that could be termed traditional about their days-old marriage.

He expected her to say no. Then an odd, crooked smile touched her lips and she surprised him by saying, "Why not?"

He let his gaze rove over the smooth planes of her cheeks, the strong line of her jaw, the downward sweep of lashes that now hid her eyes from his sight. She was a mystery to him in so many ways. He knew the formidable strength of her intellect, the power of her sense of justice, the unexpected passion his touch could ignite within her. But he knew little of the life she had lived before their worlds became intertwined, of the girl she had once been or the forces and events that had fashioned her into the kind of woman who could without hesitation or compunction shoot a highwayman in the face.

He said, "We can leave for Hampshire today."

She shook her head. "I'm to meet Gabrielle Tennyson up at Trent Place this morning. She's been consulting with Sir Stanley on the excavations of a site on his property called Camlet Moat, and she's promised to show me what they've discovered."

Sebastian found himself smiling. Hero's driving passion would always be her clearheaded, logical commitment to reforming the numerous unjust and cruel laws that both handicapped and tarnished their society. But lately she'd also developed a keen interest in the need to preserve the rapidly vanishing legacies of England's past.

He said, "They've discovered something of interest?"

"When you consider that 'Camlet' is a recent corruption of 'Camelot,' anything they find is intriguing."

He ran the backs of his fingers along her jawline and smiled when he saw her shiver in the heat. "If I remember my *Morte d'Arthur*, Sir Thomas Malory identified Camelot with what is now Winchester."

She wrapped her hand around his wrist, effectively ending the caress. "Gabrielle thinks Malory was wrong."

From the street below came the scent of fresh bread and the tinkling bell of the baker's boy crying, *"Hot buns."*

Sebastian said, "Tomorrow, then?"

By now, the golden light of morning flooded the room. Hero took a step back out of the circle of Sebastian's arms to hug the sheet tighter around her, as if already regretting her commitment. "All right. Tomorrow."

But it was barely an hour later when a constable from Bow Street arrived at the house on Brook Street with the information that Miss Gabrielle Tennyson had been found dead.

Murdered, at Camlet Moat.

Chapter 3

$\mathcal{A}$ small, middle-aged man with a balding pate and a serious demeanor stood at the base of the ancient earthen embankment. He had his hands clasped behind his back, his chin sunk into the folds of his modestly tied cravat. A weathered dinghy lay beside him where it had been hauled up onto the moat's bank. It was empty now, but a smear of blood still showed clearly along the edge of the gunwale.

Sir Henry Lovejoy, the newest of Bow Street's three stipendiary magistrates, found himself staring at that telltale streak of blood. He had been called to this murder scene some ten miles north of London by the local magistrate, who was only too eager to hand over his investigation to the Bow Street public office.

Lovejoy blew out a long, troubled sigh. On the streets of London, most murders were straightforward affairs: a drunken navvy choked the life out of his hapless wife; two mates fell out over a dice game or the sale of a horse; a footpad jumped some unwary passerby from the mouth of a fetid alley. But there was nothing ordinary about a murdered young gentlewoman found floating on an abandoned moat in the middle of nowhere.

Miss Gabrielle Tennyson had been just twenty-eight

years old. The daughter of a famous scholar, she'd been well on her way to earning a reputation as an antiquary in her own right—a decidedly unusual accomplishment for one of her sex. She lived with her brother, himself a well-known and respected barrister, in a fine house in the Adelphi Buildings overlooking the Thames. Her murder would send an unprecedented ripple of fear through the city, with ladies terrified to leave their homes and angry husbands and fathers demanding that Bow Street *do* something.

The problem was, Lovejoy had absolutely nothing to go on. Nothing at all.

He raised his gaze to where a line of constables moved along the moat's edge, their big boots churning through the murky water with muddy, sucking plops that seemed to echo in the unnatural stillness. He had never considered himself a fanciful man—far from it, in fact. Yet there was no denying that something about this place raised the hairs on the back of his neck. Perhaps it was the eerie way the light filtered down through the leaves of the thick stands of beech and hornbeam trees to bathe the scene in an unnatural green glow. Or perhaps it was a father's inevitable reaction to the sight of a beautiful, dead young woman—a sight that brought back a time of nearly unbearable heartbreak in Lovejoy's own life.

But he closed his mind to that.

He'd heard of this place, Camlet Moat. They said that once it had been the site of a medieval castle whose origins stretched back to the days of the Romans and beyond. But whatever fortified structures once stood here had long since been dismantled, their stones and mighty timbers carted away. All that remained was a deserted, overgrown square isle a few hundred feet across and the stagnant moat that had once protected it.

Now, as Lovejoy watched, one of the constables broke away from the others to come sloshing up to him.

"We've covered the entire bank, sir," said the man. "All the way around."

"And?" asked Lovejoy.

"We've found nothing, sir."

Lovejoy exhaled a long breath. "Then start on the island itself."

"Yes, sir."

A thunder of horses' hooves and the rattle of harness drew their attention to the narrow track that curled through the wood to the moat. A curricle and pair driven by an aristocratic young gentleman in a beaver hat and a caped driving coat drew up at the top of the embankment. The half-grown, scrappy-looking young groom in a striped waistcoat who clung to the rear perch immediately hopped down to race to the chestnuts' heads.

"It's Lord Devlin, sir," said the constable, staring slack-jawed as the Earl of Hendon's notorious son paused to confer with his tiger, then dropped lightly to the ground.

Lovejoy said, "That will be all, Constable."

The constable cast a last, curious glance toward the top of the slope, then ducked his head. "Yes, sir."

Lovejoy waited while the Viscount tossed his driving coat onto the curricle's high seat, then slid down the ancient embankment, the heels of his gleaming Hessian boots digging furrows in the soft leaf litter.

"Sir Henry," said the Viscount. "Good morning."

Lean and dark-haired, he was tall enough to tower over Lovejoy. But it was the man's eyes that tended to draw and hold a stranger's attention. Shading from amber to a feral yellow, they possessed an animallike ability to see great distances and in the dark. His hearing was exceptionally acute too, which could be disconcerting, even to those who knew him well.

The unusual friendship between the two men dated back some eighteen months, to a time when Devlin had been accused of murder and Lovejoy had been determined to bring him in. From those unlikely beginnings had grown respect as well as friendship. In Devlin, Lovejoy had found an ally with a rare passion for justice and a true genius for solving murders. But more important, Devlin also possessed something no Bow Street magistrate would ever have: an easy entrée at the highest levels of society and an innate understanding of the wealthy and wellborn who inevitably came under suspicion in a murder of this nature.

"My lord," said Lovejoy, giving a small, jerky bow. "I must apologize for intruding upon what should be for you and your new wife a time of joy and solitude. But when I learned of the victim's connection to Lady Devlin, I thought you would wish to know."

"You did the right thing," said Devlin. He let his gaze drift around the site, taking in the tangled growth of beech and oak, the green-scummed waters of the abandoned moat. "Where is she?"

Lovejoy cleared his throat uncomfortably. "We sent the remains to London an hour or so ago." Bodies did not keep well in the heat of August.

"To Gibson?"

"Yes, my lord." No one understood human anatomy or could read the secrets a body might have to reveal about its murderer better than Paul Gibson. Lovejoy nodded to the small boat beside them. "She was found in the dinghy—floating just at the edge of the moat here."

"You think this is where she was killed?" asked Devlin, hunkering down to study the blood-smeared gunwale.

"I think it probable she was stabbed in the dinghy, yes. But there were no footprints in the damp earth along this stretch of the bank, which leads me to suspect the boat simply drifted here from elsewhere—perhaps from the land bridge that crosses the moat on the eastern side

of the island. We understand that's where it's normally
kept moored. Unfortunately, there are so many footprints in that area that it's impossible to identify with
any certainty those that might belong to the killer."

Devlin was silent for a moment, his forehead fur-
rowed by a thoughtful frown as he continued to stare at
that ugly streak of blood. The Viscount could sometimes
be hesitant to commit to an investigation of murder. It
was a reluctance Lovejoy understood only too well.
More and more, it seemed to him that each death he
dealt with, each torn, shattered life with which he came
into contact, stole a piece of his own humanity and bled
away an irretrievable part of his joy in life.

But surely, Lovejoy reasoned, the connection between
this victim and his lordship's own wife would make it
impossible for the Viscount to refuse.

Lovejoy said, "A murder such as this—a young
woman brutally stabbed in a wood just north of
London—will inevitably cause a panic in the city. And
unfortunately, the impulse in these situations is all too
often to calm public outrage by identifying a culprit
quickly—at the cost of true justice."

"Are you asking for my help?"

Lovejoy met that strange, feral yellow stare, and held
it. "I am, my lord."

Devlin pushed to his feet, his gaze shifting across the
stretch of murky water to where the constables could be
seen poking around the piles of fresh earth that edged
Sir Stanley's series of exploratory trenches. In the misty,
ethereal light of morning, the mounds of raw earth bore
an unpleasant resemblance to rows of freshly dug graves.
Lovejoy watched Devlin's lips press into a thin line, his
nostrils flare on a painfully indrawn breath.

But the Viscount didn't say anything, and Lovejoy
knew him well enough to be patient.

And wait for Devlin's reply.

Chapter 4

Sebastian turned to walk along the crest of the ancient rampart that rose beside the stagnant moat. The shade here was deep and heavy, the blue sky above nearly obliterated by the leafy branches of the stands of old-growth timber that met overhead. A tangle of bracken and fern edged the quiet waters of the moat and filled the air with the scent of wet earth and humus and the buzz of insects.

He'd heard that once this wild tract of woodland to the north of London had been known as Enfield Chase, a royal hunting ground that rang with the clatter of noble hoofbeats, the shrill blast of the huntsman's horn, the baying of royal hounds. Through these lands had swept King Henry VIII and Queen Elizabeth and a host of glittering, bejeweled courtiers, their velvet cloaks swirling in the mist, their voices raised in hearty halloos.

But all that had ended long ago. Briars and underbrush had grown up to choke the forest floor, while commoners from the nearby village had carted away the last tumbled stones of whatever grand manor or castle had once stood here. A quiet hush had fallen over the site, unbroken until a beautiful, brilliant, independent-minded young woman with a boundless curiosity about the past had come searching for the origins of a legend—and died here.

He could remember meeting Miss Gabrielle Tennyson only once, a year or so earlier at a lecture on Roman London that he'd attended in the company of the Earl of Hendon. Sebastian recalled her as a striking, self-assured young woman with chestnut hair and an open, friendly smile. He hadn't been surprised to discover that she and Hero were friends. Despite their obvious differences, the two women were much alike. He found it difficult to think of such a strong, vital woman now lying on a surgeon's slab, robbed of her life and all the years of promise that had once stretched before her. Difficult to imagine the terror and despair that must have filled her eyes and congealed her heart when she looked her last on this quiet, secluded site.

He paused to stare again at the small wooded isle where a castle named Camelot had once stood. He was aware of Sir Henry Lovejoy drawing up beside him, his homely features pinched and tight, his hands clasped behind his back.

Sebastian glanced over at him. "You said she'd been stabbed?"

The magistrate nodded. "In the chest. Just once that I could see, although Dr. Gibson will be able to tell us with certainty once he's finished the postmortem."

"And the murder weapon?"

"Has yet to be found."

Sebastian eyed the murky water before them. If Gabrielle's murderer had thrown his knife into the moat, it might never be recovered.

Twisting around, he studied the narrow lane where his tiger, Tom, was walking the chestnuts up and down. "How the devil did she get out here? Any idea?"

Sir Henry shook his head. "We can only assume she must have arrived in the company of her killer."

"No one in the neighborhood saw anything?"

"Nothing they're willing to admit. But then, the nearest village is several miles away, and there are only a few isolated houses in the area. Tessa Sawyer—the village girl who found her—came upon the body quite by chance, shortly before midnight."

"And what was Tessa doing out in the middle of nowhere at night?"

"That is not entirely clear, I'm afraid, given the girl's garbled and rather evasive replies to our questions. However, I understand that yesterday was some sort of ancient pagan holy day—"

"Lammas."

"Yes, that's it," said Sir Henry. "Lammas. I'm told Camlet Moat has a reputation as a place of magic amongst the credulous. In addition to the apparition of a White Lady who is said to haunt the island, there's also the ghost of some unsavory Templar knight who is reputed to appear when provoked."

"I assume you've heard there's also a tradition that this may be the ancient site of King Arthur's Camelot?"

The magistrate sniffed. "A fanciful notion, no doubt. But yes, I understand Sir Stanley Winthrop became intrigued by the possibility after he purchased the estate last year and discovered Miss Tennyson's research on the history of the site."

"You think her murder could in some way be connected to the legends of the island's past?"

Sir Henry blew out a long, agitated breath. "I wish I knew. We're not even certain how long Miss Tennyson's body was lying here before it was discovered. Her brother, Mr. Hildeyard Tennyson, has been out of town for the better part of a fortnight. I've sent a constable to interview her servants, but I fear they may not be able tell us much of anything. Yesterday was Sunday, after all."

"Bloody hell," said Sebastian softly. "What does Sir Stanley Winthrop have to say about all this?"

"He claims he last saw Miss Tennyson when she left the excavations for home on Saturday afternoon."

Something in the magistrate's tone caught Sebastian's attention. "But you don't believe him?"

"I don't know what to believe. He tells us he can't imagine what she might have been doing up here yesterday. They don't work the excavations on Sundays."

Sebastian said, "Perhaps she came up to look around by herself."

Lovejoy frowned. "Yes, I suppose that's possible. She may well have surprised some trespasser, and in a panic, he killed her."

"And then stole her carriage and kidnapped her coachman?"

Lovejoy pulled a face. "There is that."

Sebastian adjusted the tilt of his beaver hat. "Her brother is still out of town?"

Lovejoy nodded. "We've sent word to his estate, but I doubt he'll make it back to London before nightfall at the earliest."

"Then I think I'll start with Sir Stanley Winthrop," said Sebastian, and turned back toward his curricle.

Lovejoy fell into step beside him. "Does this mean you're willing to assist Bow Street with the case?"

"Did you honestly think I would not?"

Sir Henry gave one of his rare half smiles, tucked his chin against his chest, and shook his head.

Chapter 5

"There you are, Jarvis," exclaimed the Prince Regent, his face flushed, his voice rising in a petulant whine as he clenched a sheet of cheap, ink-smeared paper in his fist. "Look at this!" He thumped the offending broadsheet with one plump, beringed hand. "Just look at it."

His Royal Highness George, Prince Regent of Great Britain and Ireland, lay beside the fireplace in his dressing room, his heavy legs draped off the edge of a gilt fainting couch contrived in the shape of a crocodile upholstered in scarlet velvet. Despite the heat of the day, a fire burned brightly on the hearth, for the Prince had a morbid fear of taking chill.

Having been stricken while still in the midst of his toilet, he wore only a pair of exquisitely fitted yellow unmentionables and a shirt ruffled with an extravagant cascade of lace. It was a style of linen that belonged more to the previous century, but the Prince still occasionally indulged his taste for it, perhaps because it reminded him of the golden years of his youth, when he'd been handsome and carefree and beloved by his people. These days, he needed a corset to contain his ever-increasing girth, the people who'd once cheered him now booed him openly in the streets, and shadowy radicals published seditious broadsheets bemoaning the lost days of Camelot and calling for King Arthur to return from the mists of Avalon and save Britain from the benighted rule of the House of Hanover.

So great had been the Prince's distress at the reading of this particular broadsheet that his valet had sent for the Prince's doctor. The doctor, in turn, took one look at the offending verbiage and requested the attendance of the Prince's powerful and infinitely wise cousin, Charles, Lord Jarvis.

"Calm yourself, Your Highness," said Jarvis, catching the eye of the Prince's doctor, who stood nearby. The doctor nodded discreetly and turned away.

"But have you seen this?" wailed the Prince. "They want Arthur to come back and get rid of me!"

Jarvis carefully loosed the broadsheet from the Regent's clutches. "I have seen it, Your Highness." Personally, Jarvis suspected the caricature accompanying the tract—which portrayed George as a grossly fat, drunken, overdressed buffoon with the ears of an ass—offended the Prince more than anything. But it was the implications of the appeal for Arthur's messianic return that concerned Jarvis. "Whoever is responsible for this will be dealt with."

The Prince's valet and doctor exchanged quick, furtive glances, then looked away. There was a reason Jarvis was feared from one end of the Kingdom to the other. His network of spies and informants gave him an eerie omnipotence, while those he "dealt with" were seldom seen again.

The doctor stepped forward with a glass of cloudy liquid on a silver tray. "Here, Your Highness; drink this. You'll feel much better."

"Who gave this broadsheet to the Prince?" Jarvis demanded in a harsh whisper to the Prince's valet as His Highness obediently gulped the doctor's brew.

The valet's plump, sweat-sheened face went pasty white. "I've no notion, my lord. In truth, I do not know!"

Frowning, Jarvis tucked the seditious literature into his coat and bowed himself out of the royal presence.

He was crossing the anteroom of the Prince's chambers when a pimply, half-grown page sidled up to him and bowed low, his mouth opening and closing as he struggled to speak. But all he succeeded in doing was pushing out a series of incoherent squeaks.

"For God's sake, boy, out with it," snapped Jarvis. "As it happens I've already eaten, so you needn't fear I'll have you for breakfast."

The boy's eyes bulged.

Jarvis suppressed a sigh. "Your message; say it."

The boy swallowed and tried again, the words tumbling out in a rush. "It's your daughter, my lord. Miss J—I mean, Lady Devlin. She desired me to tell you that she wishes to speak with you, my lord. She awaits you in your chambers."

※

No man in England was more powerful than Jarvis. His kinship with the King might be distant, but without Jarvis's ruthless brilliance and steady wisdom, the House of Hanover would have fallen long ago and the Hanovers knew it. Jarvis had dedicated his life to the preservation of the monarchy and the global extension of the might of England. Another man might have insisted on being named prime minister in return for his services. But Jarvis preferred to exercise his power from the shadows, unconstrained by either tradition or law. Prime ministers came and went.

Jarvis remained.

He found his daughter standing at the long window of the chambers reserved for his exclusive use overlooking Pall Mall. Once, Jarvis had possessed a son—an idealistic dreamer named David. But David had been lost years before to a watery grave. Now there was only Hero: brilliant, strong willed, and nearly as ruthless and enigmatic as Jarvis himself.

She wore a walking dress of dusky blue trimmed with moss green piping, and a jaunty hat with a broad brim turned up on one side and held in place with a silk posy. The sunlight streaming through the paned glass bathed her in a warm golden glow and touched her cheeks with color.

"You're looking good," he said, closing the door behind him. "Marriage seems to agree with you."

She turned to face him. "You're surprised?"

Rather than answer, he crossed the room to where a candlestick stood on a table beside a wing-back chair. The relationship between father and daughter had always been complicated. They were much alike, which meant she understood him as few others did. But that was not to say that she knew everything there was to know about him.

"What brings you here?" he asked, his attention seemingly all for the task of lighting the candle. He was aware of an air of constraint between them, for her recent marriage to Devlin had introduced a new element and subtly shifted the dynamic in a way neither had yet to confront or reveal.

"What makes you think I came for a purpose other than to see you?"

"Because if this were a gesture of familial affection, you wouldn't be at Carlton House. You would have come to Berkeley Square. Your mother is well, by the way—or perhaps I should say she is as well as she ever is. She's quite taken with the new companion you found for her."

Refusing to be distracted, Hero said, "Gabrielle Tennyson was discovered murdered this morning, at Camlet Moat." When he kept silent, she said, "You knew?"

He watched the wick of the candle catch, flare up bright. "There is little that happens in this Kingdom that I do not know about."

"There is also little that happens in this Kingdom that you don't control."

He glanced over at her. She stood with her back to the window, her hands curled so that her palms rested on the sill. Through the glass behind her he could see a heavy traffic of carriages, carts, and horses streaming up and down Pall Mall. He said, "Are you asking if I had her killed?"

"After what I overheard last Friday night, the thought naturally does occur to me." When Jarvis remained silent, she added impatiently, "Well? Did you?"

"I did not." He drew the broadsheet from his pocket and thrust it into the candle flame. It blackened and smoked for an instant, then caught fire. "Now the question becomes, do you believe me?"

She held herself quite still, her gaze on his face. "I don't know. I've never been able to tell when you're lying."

He tilted the paper as the flames took hold, then dropped it onto the cold, bare stones of the nearby hearth. "I take it Devlin has become involved in the investigation?"

"Lovejoy has asked for his assistance with the case, yes."

"And will you tell your husband that he should add me to his list of suspects, and why?"

She pushed away from the window, her nostrils flaring with a sharp intake of breath. "I am here because Gabrielle was my friend, not as Devlin's agent."

"Perhaps. But that doesn't exactly answer my question."

Their gazes met. They'd both known this day would come, when she'd find herself caught between what she felt she owed her own family and what she owed her new husband. Only, he hadn't expected it to come quite so soon.

She said, "I have no intention of betraying you . . . if you are telling me the truth."

He found himself smiling. "But then, in that case, you wouldn't actually be betraying me, now, would you?" He tipped his head to one side. "And how will your rather headstrong and passionate young Viscount react, I wonder, when he discovers that you have been less than forthcoming with him?"

"I must be true to myself and to what I believe is right. My marriage in no way negates that."

"And if he doesn't understand—or fails to agree?"

She turned toward the door. "Then we will disagree."

She said it evenly, in that way she had. He knew she had analyzed the situation and made her decision calmly and rationally. She was not the kind of woman to waste time agonizing or endlessly analyzing her choices. But that was not to say that the decision had been made lightly or that it would be without emotional consequences. For he had seen the troubled shadows that lurked in the depths of her fine gray eyes. And he knew an upsurge of renewed anger and resentment directed at Devlin, who had put them there.

After she left, he watched the broadsheet on the hearth burn itself out until nothing remained but a blackened ash. Then he went to stand where she had stood, his gaze on the courtyard below. He watched her exit the Palace, watched her climb the steps to her waiting carriage. He watched the carriage bowl away up Pall Mall toward the west, the clatter of her horses' hooves lost in the tumult of drivers' shouts and hawkers' cries and the rattle of iron-rimmed wheels over cobbles.

Turning, he rang for his clerk.

"Send Colonel Urquhart to me," he said curtly when the man appeared. "Now."

Chapter 6

The abandoned isle once known as Camelot lay on the northern edge of Trent Place, a relatively new estate dating only to late in the previous century, when the ancient royal chase had been broken up and sold to help pay for the first round of George III's wars. The properties thus created had proved popular with the newly wealthy merchants and bankers of the city. Sir Stanley, Trent Place's latest owner, was a prosperous banker granted a baronetcy by the King in reward for his assistance in financing the country's long struggle against Napoléon.

"One o' them constables was tellin' me this Sir Stanley already 'as a 'ouse in Golden Square what makes the Queen's Palace look like a cottage," said Sebastian's tiger, Tom, as they turned through massive new gates to a meticulously landscaped park. "So why'd he need to buy this place too, just a few miles from London?"

The boy was thirteen years old now, but still small and gap-toothed and scrappy, for he had been a homeless street urchin when Sebastian first discovered the lad's intense loyalty and sense of honor and natural affinity for horses. In a very real sense, Tom and Sebastian had saved each other. The ties that bound lord to servant and boy to man ran deep and strong.

Sebastian said, "The possession of an estate is the sine qua non for anyone aspiring to be a gentleman."

"The seenkwawhat?"

"Sine qua non. It's Latin for a condition without which something cannot be."

"You sayin' this Sir Stanley ain't always been a gentleman?"

"Something like that," said Sebastian, drawing up before what had once been a graceful Italianate villa but was now in the process of being transformed into something quite different by the addition of two vast wings and a new roofline. The pounding of hammers and the clatter of lumber filled the air; near a half-constructed wall, a tall, elegantly tailored gentleman in his early fifties could be seen conferring with a group of brickmasons.

"Keep your ears open around the stables," Sebastian told Tom as the tiger took the reins. "I'd be interested to hear what the servants are saying."

"Aye, gov'nor."

"Devlin," called Sir Stanley, leaving the bricklayers to stroll toward him.

He was a ruggedly handsome man, his chin square, his cheekbones prominent, his mouth wide and expressive. Despite his years, his body was still strong and powerful, and he had a head of thick, pale blond hair fading gradually to white, so that it formed a startling contrast to his unexpectedly sun-darkened features. The effect was more like what one would expect of a soldier or a nabob just returned from India than a banker.

They said the man had begun his career as a lowly clerk, the son of a poor vicar with sixteen children and no connections. Sebastian had heard that his rise to wealth, power, and influence had been both rapid and brutal and owed its success to his wily intelligence, his driving ambition, and a clear-sighted, unflinching ruthlessness.

"What brings you here?" asked Sir Stanley, pausing beside the curricle.

"I've just come from Camlet Moat," said Sebastian, dropping lightly to the ground.

"Ah. I see." The flesh of the man's face suddenly looked pinched, as if pulled too taut over the bones of his face. "Please," he said, stretching a hand to indicate the broad white marble stairs that led up to the central, original section of the house. "Come in."

"Thank you."

"I was with Squire John when he discovered the body," said Winthrop as they mounted the steps. "He's our local magistrate, you know. Seems some girl from the village showed up at the Grange in the middle of the night, babbling nonsense about white ladies and magic wells and a dead gentlewoman in the moat. The Squire was convinced it was all a hum—actually apologized for coming to me at the crack of dawn—but I said, 'No, no, let's go have a look.'" He paused in the entrance hall, a quiver passing over his tightly held features. "The last thing I expected was to find Gabrielle."

Sebastian let his gaze drift around the vast, marble-floored entrance hall, with its towering, gilt-framed canvases of pastoral landscapes by Constable and Turner, its ornately plastered ceiling picked out in pastel shades evocative of a plate of petit fours. In an age when it was not uncommon for husbands and wives to call each other by their surnames or titles, Winthrop had just referred to Miss Tennyson by her first name.

And Sebastian suspected the man was not even aware of his slip.

"I'd never seen someone who'd been murdered," the banker was saying. "I suppose you've had experience with it, but I haven't. I'm not ashamed to admit it was a shock."

"I'm not convinced anyone gets used to the sight of murder."

Sir Stanley nodded and turned toward the cavernous drawing room that opened to their left. "It may be frightfully early, but I could use a drink. How about you? May I offer you some wine?"

"Yes, thank you. Sir Henry Lovejoy tells me you don't work on the island's excavations on Sundays," said Sebastian as his host crossed to where a tray with a decanter and glasses waited on a gilded table beside a grouping of silk-covered settees.

Winthrop splashed wine into two glasses. "My wife believes the Sabbath should be a day of rest. On the seventh day, the Lord rested, and so should all of his children."

"Commendable," said Sebastian. Through a long bank of tall windows he could see an angular, bony woman he recognized as Lady Winthrop standing at the edge of an old-fashioned garden of box-edged parterres filled with roses. Despite the heat, she wore a long-sleeved sprigged muslin gown made high at the neck and trimmed with only a meager band of lace. She was younger than Winthrop by some fifteen or twenty years, a second wife as plain as her husband was handsome, her eyes small and protuberant and close set, her chin receding, her head thrust forward in a way that made her look forever inquisitive.

Or aggressive.

She was in the process of giving directions to a cluster of gardeners equipped with wheelbarrows and shovels. As Sebastian watched, she waved her arms in extravagant gestures as she delivered her instructions. Piles of rich dark earth and stacks of brick lay nearby; the Winthrops were obviously expanding their gardens as well as their new house. Watching her, Sebastian wondered if Lady Winthrop also referred to Miss Tennyson as "Gabrielle." Somehow, he doubted it.

Winthrop set aside the decanter to pick up the two glasses. "At first, in her naivety, my wife actually expected the brutes to be grateful. But she soon discovered how mistaken she was. All they do is grumble about being forced to go to church services."

"It's required?"

"Of course." Winthrop held out one of the glasses. "Religion is important to the order of society. It reconciles the lower classes to their lot in life and teaches them to respect their betters."

"So it does," said Sebastian, studying the banker's faintly smiling face as he took the wine handed him. But he was unable to decide whether Winthrop agreed with his wife or quietly mocked her. "So, tell me, do you honestly believe you've found King Arthur's Camelot?" He took a sip of the wine. It was smooth and mellow and undoubtedly French.

"Honestly?" The banker drained his own glass in two long pulls, then shook his head. "I don't know. But the site is intriguing, don't you agree? I mean, here we have a place long associated with the kings of England—a place whose name actually was Camelot. I'm told the word is of Celtic origin. It probably comes from 'Camulus,' the Celtic god of war. Of course, Miss Tennyson says—said," he amended hastily, correcting himself, "that it could also mean 'place of the crooked stream.' Personally, I prefer to think it is named after the god of war." Turning away to pour himself more wine, he raised the decanter in silent question to Sebastian.

Sebastian shook his head. He had taken only the one sip.

"The important thing," said Winthrop, refreshing his own drink, "is that we know the name dates back to well before the time of William the Conqueror. The corruption of 'Camelot' to 'Camlet' is quite recent, within the last hundred years or so."

Sebastian studied the older man's handsome features. His manner could only be described as affable, even likeable. But Sebastian couldn't get past the knowledge that the previous owner of Trent Place had been forced to sell the estate to Winthrop at a steep loss—and then blown his own brains out the next day.

Sebastian took another sip of his wine. "How did you meet Miss Tennyson?"

"By mere chance, actually, at a lecture presented by the Society of Antiquaries. She'd been doing research on the history of Camlet Moat and approached me when she learned I'd recently purchased the estate. Until then, I'd barely realized the moat existed. But the more I learned about it, the more intrigued I became."

"And you began the excavations—when?"

"A month ago now. We'd hoped to begin earlier, but the wet spring delayed things."

"Find anything interesting?"

"Far more than I'd anticipated, certainly. Foundations of stone walls five feet thick. Remnants of a forty-foot drawbridge. Even an underground dungeon complete with chains still hanging on the walls."

"Dating to when?"

"Judging from the coins and painted tiles we've come across, probably the thirteenth or fourteenth century, for most of it."

"I was under the impression King Arthur was supposed to have lived in the fifth or sixth century, after the Roman withdrawal from Britain—that is, if he lived at all."

"True." Winthrop turned away to reach for something, then held it out. "But look at this."

Sebastian found himself holding a corroded metal blade. "What is it?"

"A Roman dagger." Winthrop set aside his wine and went to open a large flat glass case framed in walnut that stood on its own table near the door. "And look at this."

He pointed with one blunt, long finger. "These pottery vessels are third- or fourth-century Roman. So is the glass vial. And see that coin? It's from the time of Claudius."

Sebastian studied the artifacts proudly displayed against a black velvet background. "You found all this at Camlet Moat?"

"We did. The drawbridge and dungeon probably date to the time of the de Mandevilles and their descendants, who held the castle for the Crown in the late Middle Ages. But the site itself is older—much older. There was obviously a fort or villa there in Roman times, which means that in all probability there was still something there during the days of Arthur, after the Romans pulled out."

Sebastian regarded the other man's flushed face and shining eyes. "Will you continue digging, now that Miss Tennyson is dead?"

All the excitement and animation seemed to drain out of Winthrop, leaving him pensive. "I don't see how we can. She's the one who knew what she was doing—and how to interpret what we were finding."

"You couldn't simply hire an antiquary through the British Museum?"

The banker gave a soft laugh. "Given that they all thought Miss Tennyson mad to be working with me on this, I can't see anyone of stature being willing to risk his reputation by following in her footsteps. And with harvesttime upon us, we were about to quit anyway."

"Any chance she could have come up yesterday to have a quiet look around the site by herself for some reason? Or perhaps to show it to someone?"

Sir Stanley appeared thoughtful. "I suppose it's possible, although she generally devoted her Sundays to activities with the boys."

Sebastian shook his head, not understanding. "What boys?"

"George and Alfred—sons of one of her cousins. I understand the mother's having a difficult confinement and the father isn't well himself, so Miss Tennyson invited the lads to spend the summer with her in London. They generally stayed home with their nurse when she came up to the island, but she liked to spend several days a week showing them around London. The Tower of London and the beasts at the Exchange—that sort of thing."

"So she didn't come every day when you were digging?"

"Not every day, no; she had some other research she was also pursuing. But she generally came three or four times a week, yes."

"How would she get here?"

"Sometimes in her brother's carriage, although she would frequently take the stage to Enfield and get someone at the livery there to drive her out to the moat. In that case, I always insisted she allow me to have one of the men drive her back to London in the afternoon."

It wasn't exactly unheard of for a gentlewoman to take the stage, especially for such a short, local trip. Maintaining a carriage, horses, and groom in London was prodigiously expensive; most families kept only one, if that.

"Her brother begrudged her the use of his carriage?"

"Quite the opposite, actually. It irked him to no end when she insisted on taking the common stage rather than using his carriage—said he was perfectly capable of taking a hackney or walking around London himself."

"But she didn't always listen?"

Winthrop's wide mouth curled into a soft smile that faded away into something sad as he shook his head. "She was like that."

"Like what?"

He went to stand at the long row of windows, his gaze

on the scene outside. A few puffy white clouds had appeared on the horizon, but the sun still drenched the beds of roses with a dazzling golden light. The workmen were now bent over their shovels; Lady Winthrop was nowhere to be seen. "She was an unusual woman," he said, watching the distant clouds. "Strong. Opinionated. Unafraid to challenge the conventions and assumptions of her world. And not given to suffering fools lightly."

"In other words," said Sebastian, "the kind of woman who could make enemies."

Winthrop nodded, his gaze still on the scene beyond the glass.

"Anyone you know of in particular?"

The banker drew a deep breath that expanded his chest. "It seems somehow wrong to be mentioning these things now, when the recollection of a few careless words uttered in anger could easily result in a man standing accused of murder."

"Are you saying Miss Tennyson quarreled with someone recently?"

"I don't know if I'd say they 'quarreled,' exactly."

"So what did happen?"

"Well, when I saw her on Saturday . . ."

"Yes?" prompted Sebastian when the man hesitated.

"I knew something was troubling her as soon as she arrived at the site. She seemed . . . strained. Jumpy. At first she tried to pass it off as nothing more than a melancholy mood, but I wasn't fooled."

"Was she given to melancholy moods?"

"She was a Tennyson. They're all melancholy, you know."

"No, I didn't know. Go on."

"She said she didn't want to talk about it. Perhaps I pressed her more than I should have, but in the end she admitted she was troubled by an encounter she'd had the previous day, on Friday. She tried to laugh it off—said it was nothing. But it was obviously considerably more than 'nothing.' I don't believe I'd ever seen her so upset."

The sound of a distant door opening echoed through the house.

"An encounter with whom?" asked Sebastian.

"I couldn't tell you his name. Some antiquary known for his work on the post-Roman period of English history."

"And this fellow disagreed with Miss Tennyson's belief that your Camlet Moat was the site of King Arthur's Camelot?"

Winthrop's jaw tightened in a way that caused the powerful muscles in his cheeks to bunch and flex. For the first time, Sebastian caught a glimpse of the steely ruthlessness that had enabled the banker to amass a fortune in the course of twenty years of war. "I gather he is of the opinion that King Arthur is a figment of the collective British imagination—a product of both our romantic wish for a glorious, heroic past and a yearning for a magical savior who will return to lead us once more to victory and glory."

"And was this disagreement the reason for Friday's 'encounter'?"

"She led me to believe so."

"But you suspect she was being less than open with you?"

"In a word? Yes."

Chapter 7

Quick footsteps sounded in the hall, and Winthrop turned as his wife entered the room. She drew up abruptly at the sight of Sebastian, her expression more one of haughty indignation than welcome. It was obvious she knew exactly why he was there.

"Ah, there you are, my dear," said the banker. "You've met Lord Devlin?"

"I have." She made no move to offer him her hand.

"We met at a dinner at Lord Liverpool's, I believe," said Sebastian, bowing. "Last spring."

"So we did." It was obvious Lady Winthrop had not found the encounter a pleasure. But then, Sebastian did have something of a reputation for dangerous and scandalous living. She said, "You're here because of the death of the Tennyson woman, are you? I told Sir Stanley no good would come of this Camelot nonsense."

Sebastian cast a glance at her husband, but Winthrop's face remained a pleasant mask. If he was embarrassed by his wife's boorish behavior, he gave no sign of it.

"I take it you don't share Sir Stanley's enthusiasm for the investigation of Camlet Moat?" said Sebastian, draining his wine.

"I do not."

Winthrop moved to close the lid on the glass case. "My wife is a God-fearing woman who worries that any interest in the island shown by their betters will merely increase the unfortunate predilection of the locals to fall victim to ancient and dangerous superstitions."

Lady Winthrop threw her husband a quick, veiled look.

"Have you visited the excavations yourself, Lady Winthrop?" Sebastian asked.

"I see no utility in poking about the rubbish of some long-vanished buildings. What's gone is gone. It's the fate of mankind that should concern us, not his past. Everything we need to know is written in the Good Lord's book or in the learned works of theology and morality penned by his inspired servants. It is his intentions that should be the object of our study, not some forgotten piles of stones and broken pots."

Winthrop said, his voice bland, "May I offer you some more wine, Lord Devlin?"

"Thank you, but no." Sebastian set aside his glass. "I must be going."

Neither his host nor his hostess urged him to stay. "I'll send a servant for your carriage," said Lady Winthrop.

"I'm sorry I couldn't have been of more assistance," said Winthrop a few moments later as he walked with Sebastian to the door and out into the blazing sunshine.

Sebastian paused at the top of the broad steps. "Tell me, Sir Stanley: Do you think it possible that Miss Tennyson's death could have something to do with your work at Camlet Moat?"

"I don't see how it could," said Winthrop, his face turned away, his gaze on the gravel sweep where Tom was just drawing up.

"Yet you are familiar with the legend that Arthur is only sleeping on the isle of Avalon, and that in England's gravest hour of need he will arise again to lead us to victory."

The two men walked down the steps. "I find legends endlessly fascinating; tales of noble heroes and beautiful maidens have entranced mankind through the ages. But as an inspiration to murder? I don't see it."

Sebastian leapt up to the curricle's high seat and gathered the reins. "Anything powerful can also be dangerous."

"Only to those who feel threatened by it." Winthrop took a step back. "Good day, my lord."

Sebastian waited until they were bowling away up the drive toward the park's gateway before glancing over at his tiger and saying, "Well? Anything?"

"It's a queer estate, this Trent Place," said Tom, who possessed a knack for inspiring other servants to gossip. "Seems like it changes owners nearly every other year."

"Not quite, but almost," said Sebastian. It was typical of new estates. Ancient manors could stay in the same family for centuries, but the new wealth of merchants and bankers frequently went as easily and quickly as it came. "And what is the servants' general opinion of the current owners?"

"There was some mutterin' and queer looks, but nobody was willin' to come out and say much o' anything. If ye ask me, they're afraid."

"Of Sir Stanley? Or his wife?"

"Maybe both."

"Interesting," said Sebastian. "And what do they think of the excavations at Camlet Moat?"

"That's a bit queer too. Some think it's excitin', but there's others see it as a sacra—sacra—" Tom struggled with the word.

"A sacrilege?"

"Aye, that's it."

"Interesting."

Sebastian guided the chestnuts through the park's massive new gateway, then dropped his hands; the horses leapt forward to eat up the miles back to London. He could see the heat haze roiling up from the hard-packed road, feel the sun blazing down hot on his shoulders. He was intensely aware of the fierce green of the chestnut trees shading a nearby brook, of the clear-noted poignancy of a lark's song floating on the warm breeze. And he found himself unable to stop thinking of the vibrant, intelligent young woman whose pallid corpse awaited him on Paul Gibson's cold granite slab, and to whom all the beauties of that morning—or any other morning—were forever lost.

By the time Sebastian drew up before Paul Gibson's surgery on Tower Hill, the chestnuts' coats were wet and dark with sweat.

"Take 'em home and baby 'em," he said, handing Tom the reins.

"Aye, gov'nor." Tom scrambled into the seat as Sebastian hopped down to the narrow footpath. "You want I should come back with the grays?"

Sebastian shook his head. "I'll send for you if I need you."

He stood for a moment, watching the lad expertly wind his way westward through the press of carts and coal wagons. Near the base of the hill, a ragged boy with a drum tapped a steady beat to attract customers to the street seller who stood beside him hawking fried fish. Nearby, a woman with a cart peddled eel jelly, while a thin man in a buff-colored coat watered a nondescript roan at an old fountain built against the wall of the corner house. Then, realizing he was only delaying the inevitable, Sebastian turned to cut through the noisome, high-walled passage that led to the unkempt yard behind Gibson's surgery.

At the base of the yard lay a small stone outbuilding used by the surgeon both for his official postmortems and for a series of surreptitious dissections performed on cadavers snatched from the city's graveyards under the cover of darkness by stealthy, dangerous men. As Sebastian neared the open door of the building, he could see the remains of a woman lying on the cold, hard granite slab in the center of the single, high-windowed room.

Even in death, Miss Gabrielle Tennyson was a handsome woman, her features gracefully molded, her mouth generous, her upper lip short and gently cleft, her chestnut hair thick and luxuriously wavy. He paused in the doorway, his gaze on her face.

"Ah, there you are," said Gibson, looking up. He set aside his scalpel with a clatter and reached for a rag to wipe his hands. "I thought I might be seeing you."

A slim man of medium height in his early thirties, Paul Gibson had dark hair and green eyes bright with an irrepressible glint of mischief that almost but not quite hid the dull ache of chronic pain lurking in their nuanced depths. Irish by birth, he had honed his craft on the battlefields of Europe, learning the secrets of life and death from an endless parade of bodies slashed open and torn asunder. Then a French cannonball had shattered his own lower left leg, leaving him with a painful stump and a weakness for the sweet relief to be found in an elixir of poppies. He now divided his time between teaching anatomy to the medical students at St. Thomas's Hospital and consulting with patients at his own private surgery here in the shadows of the Tower of London.

"Can you tell me anything yet?" asked Sebastian, looking pointedly away from what Gibson had been doing to the cadaver. Like Gibson, Sebastian had worn the King's colors, fighting for God and country from Italy to the West Indies to the Peninsula. But he had never become inured to the sight or smell of death.

"Not much, I'm afraid, although I'm only just getting started. I might have more for you in a wee bit." Gibson limped from behind the table, his peg leg tap-tapping on the uneven flagged flooring. He pointed to a jagged purple slit that marred the milky flesh of the body's left breast. "You can see where she was stabbed. The blade was perhaps eight or ten inches long and an inch wide. Either her killer knew what he was doing or he got lucky. He hit her heart with just one thrust."

"She died right away?"

"Almost instantly."

Sebastian dropped his gaze to the long, tapered fingers that lay curled beside the body's hips. The nails were carefully manicured and unbroken.

"No sign of a struggle?"

"None that I've found."

"So she may have known her attacker?"

"Perhaps." Gibson tossed the rag aside. "Lovejoy's constable said she was found drifting in a dinghy outside London?"

Sebastian nodded. "On an old moat near Enfield. Any idea how long she's been dead?"

"Roughly twenty-four hours, I'd say, perhaps a few hours more or a little less. But beyond that it's difficult to determine."

Sebastian studied the reddish purple discoloration along the visible portions of the body's flanks and back. He knew from his own experience on the battlefield that blood tended to pool in the lower portions of a cadaver. "Any chance she could have been killed someplace else and then put in that boat?"

"I haven't found anything to suggest it, no. The *livor mortis* is consistent with the position in which I'm told she was found."

Sebastian's gaze shifted to the half boots of peach-colored suede, the delicate stockings, the froth of white muslin neatly folded on a nearby shelf. "These are hers?"

"Yes."

He reached out to finger the dark reddish brown stain that stiffened the delicate lace edging of the bodice. Suddenly the dank, death-tinged air of the place seemed to reach out and wrap itself around him, smothering him. He dropped his hand to his side and went to stand outside in the yard, the buzz of insects loud in the rank grass of the neglected garden as he drew in a deep breath of fresh air.

He was aware of his friend coming to stand beside him. Gibson said, "Lovejoy tells me Miss Jar—I mean, Lady Devlin was acquainted with the victim."

"They were quite close, yes."

Sebastian stared up at the hot, brittle blue sky overhead. When the messenger from Bow Street arrived in Brook Street that morning, Sebastian thought he had never seen Hero more devastated. Yet she hadn't wept, and she had turned down his suggestion that she drive up to Camlet Moat with him. He did not understand why. But then, how much did he really know about the woman he had married?

Hero and this dead woman had shared so much in common—an enthusiasm for scholarship and research, a willingness to challenge societal expectations and prejudices, and a rejection of marriage and motherhood as the only acceptable choice for a woman. He could understand Hero's grief and anger at the loss of her friend. But he couldn't shake the uncomfortable sense that something else was going on with her, something he couldn't even begin to guess at.

Gibson said, "This must be difficult for her. Any leads yet on the two lads?"

Sebastian glanced over at him, not understanding. "What lads?"

"The two boys Miss Tennyson had spending the summer with her." Gibson must have read the confusion in Sebastian's face, because he added, "You mean to say you haven't heard?"

Sebastian could feel his heart beating in his ears like a thrumming of dread. "Heard what?"

"The news has been all over town this past hour or more. The children have vanished. No one's seen them since yesterday morning."

Chapter 8

*T*he Adelphi Terrace—or Royal Terrace, as it was some-times called—stretched along the bank of the Thames overlooking the vast Adelphi Wharves. A long block of elegant neoclassical town houses built by the Adams brothers late in the previous century, the address was popular with the city's rising gentry class, particularly with Harley Street physicians and successful barristers such as Gabrielle Tennyson's brother. As Sebastian rounded the corner from Adams Street, he found Sir Henry Lovejoy exiting the Tennysons' front door.

"You've heard about the missing children?" asked Sir Henry, his homely face troubled as he waited for Sebastian to come up to him.

"Just now, from Gibson."

Sir Henry blew out a long, painful breath. "I needn't scruple to tell you this adds a very troubling dimension to the case. A very troubling dimension indeed."

"You've found no trace of them?"

"Nothing. Nothing at all. Right now, we're hoping the children witnessed the murder and ran away to hide in the woods in fright. The alternative is . . . Well, it's not something I'm looking forward to dealing with."

They turned to walk along the terrace fronting onto

the wharves below. The fierce midday sun glinted off the broad surface of the river beside them and the air filled with the rough shouts of bargemen working the river and the rattle of carts on the coal wharf.

"We've had constables knocking on doors up and down the street," said Sir Henry, "in the hopes someone might be able to tell us what time Miss Tennyson and the children left the house, or perhaps even with whom. Unfortunately, the heat has driven most of the residents into the country, and of those who remain, no one recalls having seen anything."

"Any chance the children could have been snatched for ransom?"

"It's a possibility, I suppose, although I must confess I find it unlikely. I'm told the children's father is a simple, impoverished clergyman up in the wilds of Lincolnshire. And while the victim's brother, Mr. Hildeyard Tennyson, is a moderately successful barrister, he is not excessively wealthy." Sir Henry rubbed the bridge of his nose between one thumb and finger. "The elder boy, George, is just nine years old, while the younger, Alfred, is turning three. They were here with Miss Tennyson when the servants left yesterday morning, but as far as we've been able to tell, that's the last time any of them were seen." He hesitated, then added reluctantly, "Alive."

"And the servants never thought to raise the alarm when neither Miss Tennyson nor the children returned home last night?"

"They thought it not their place to presume to know their mistress's intentions."

"Yes, I can see that," said Sebastian. "And now they're so frightened of being blamed for the delay in launching a search that it's difficult to get much of anything out of them?"

"Exactly." Lovejoy sighed. "Although they may prove more willing to open up to you than to Bow Street." The warm breeze blowing off the water brought them the smell of brine and spawning fish and the freshness of the wide-open seas. His features pinched, Lovejoy paused to stare out across the barges and wherries filling the river. "I'm heading back up to Enfield now, to organize some men to drag the moat."

Sebastian said, "Any possibility the children could have been the killer's intended targets and Miss Tennyson simply got in the way?"

"Merciful heavens. Why would anyone want to kill two innocent children?" Lovejoy was silent a moment, his gaze still on the sun-spangled water, a bead of sweat rolling down one cheek. "But you're right; it is obviously a possibility. Dear God, what is the world coming to?" He narrowed his eyes against the glare coming off the water and said it again. "What is the world coming to?"

❧

The Tennysons' housekeeper was a small, plump woman named Mrs. O'Donnell. She had full cheeks and graying hair worn tucked neatly beneath a starched white cap, and she struck Sebastian as the type of woman who in happier times sported rosy cheeks and bustled about with brisk good cheer and a ready laugh. Now she sat crumpled beside the empty hearth in the servants' hall, a damp handkerchief clutched forlornly in one fist, her eyes red and swollen with tears, her cheeks ashen.

"If only the master had been home," she kept saying over and over again. "None of this would have happened."

"How long has Mr. Tennyson been gone?" asked Sebastian, settling onto a hard wooden bench opposite her.

"A fortnight, come Tuesday. He wanted Miss Tennyson and the lads to go into the country with him—get away from all the heat and dirt of the city. But she wouldn't leave that project of hers." Mrs. O'Donnell's nose wrinkled when she uttered the word "project," as if she spoke of something nasty and improper. It was obvious that for all her geniality, the housekeeper did not approve of Miss Tennyson's unorthodox interests.

Sebastian said, "I take it you're referring to the excavations up at Camlet Moat?"

Mrs. O'Donnell nodded and touched her handkerchief to the corner of one eye. "I know it's not my place to say such things, but, well . . . It's not *right*, if you ask me. Women belong in the home. And now look what's come of it! Her dead, and those poor lads gone missing. Such bright little fellows, they were. Quick-tempered and full of mischief, to be sure, but charming and winsome for all of that. Why, just yesterday morning before they left for church, Master George gave me a little poem he wrote all by himself." She pushed up from her seat and went to rummage amongst the litter of recipes and invoices, letters and broadsheets, that covered a nearby table. "It's here somewhere. . . ."

"That's the last time you saw them?" asked Sebastian. "Yesterday morning, when they were on their way to church?"

"It was, yes," she said, distracted by her search.

"Which church do they normally attend?"

"St. Martin's, usually."

"You think that's where they went yesterday?"

"I don't see why not, my lord."

"I'm told Miss Tennyson liked to take the boys on various outings several times a week, particularly on Sunday afternoons."

"Oh, yes. She was enjoying their visit ever so much. It was lovely to see her with them. Her face would light up and she'd laugh like she was a carefree girl again herself." A ghost of a smile animated the housekeeper's features, only to fade away into pinched sorrow. "Course, then there were the times I'd catch her watching them, and she'd go all still and quiet-like, and this look would come over her that was something painful to see."

"What sort of a look?"

"It was like a . . . like a *yearning*, if you know what I mean?"

"You think she regretted not having children of her own?"

"If she did, it was her choice, wasn't it? I mean, it's not like she didn't have plenty of offers. Turned them all down, she did." The housekeeper straightened, a tattered paper clenched in one hand. "Ah, here it is!" She thrust the page toward him.

Sebastian found himself staring at a single stanza of poetry written in a schoolboy's best copperplate. He read aloud:

> *Somewhere the sea, somewhere the sun*
> *Whisper of pain and love untold;*
> *Something that's done and more undone,*
> *Are only the dead so bold?*

He looked up. "George Tennyson wrote this?"

"He did. Oh, it's all great nonsense, to be sure. But it's still fine, wouldn't you say? And he but a boy of nine!"

"Do you mind if I keep it for a day or so? I'll see it's returned to you," he added when she looked hesitant.

"To be sure you may keep it, my lord. Only, I won't deny I would like to have it back."

"I understand." Sebastian tucked the boy's poem into his pocket. "Do you have any idea how Miss Tennyson and the children planned to spend yesterday afternoon?"

She looked thoughtful for a moment, then shook her head. "No, my lord; I don't know as I ever heard her mention it. We always lay out a cold collation for the family in the dining room, you see, before we leave for our half day. They eat when they come home from church, before they go out again. We left a lovely spread, with a side of beef and salmon in aspic and a chilled asparagus soup."

"And did Miss Tennyson and the children eat the meal you left for them on Sunday?"

"Oh, yes, my lord. In fact, the plate with Mrs. Reagan's oatmeal cookies was completely empty except for a few crumbs." She plopped back down in her chair, her hands wringing together so hard the fingers turned white. "Oh, if only Mr. Tennyson had been here!" she cried. "Then we'd have known for certain something was amiss when they didn't come home last night."

"What time did the servants return to the house?"

"The others were back by seven, although I'm afraid I myself wasn't in until nearly eight. I spent the day with my sister in Kent Town, you see; her husband's ever so sick, and Miss Tennyson told me not to worry if I was a bit late. She was that way, you know—so kind and generous. And now—" Her voice cracked and she turned her face away, her throat working silently.

Sebastian said, "Were you concerned when you arrived back and realized Miss Tennyson and the children hadn't returned themselves?"

"Well, of course I was! We all were. Margaret Campbell—she's the boys' nurse, you know—was all for going to the public office at once. She was convinced something must have happened to them. But we had no way of knowing that for certain, and who could ever have imagined that something like *this* had occurred? I mean, what if Miss Tennyson had simply decided to spend the night with some friends and forgot to tell us? Or she could have received bad news from the boys' parents and set off with the children for Lincolnshire. To tell the truth, I thought she might even have reconsidered staying in London and decided to join her brother in the country after all. I can tell you, she would not have thanked us if we'd raised a ruckus for naught."

Sebastian watched her twist her handkerchief around her fist. "Do you know of anyone who might have wanted to do either Miss Tennyson or the boys harm?"

Her puffy face crumpled. *"No,"* she cried. "None of this makes any sense. Why would anyone want to harm either her or those poor, poor lads? *Why*?"

Sebastian rested his hand on her shoulder. It was a useless, awkward gesture of comfort, but she looked up at him with pleading eyes, her plump, matronly form shuddering with need for a measure of understanding and reassurance he could not give.

Chapter 9

Leaving the servants' hall, Sebastian climbed the stairs to the nursery at the top of the Tennyson house.

It was a cheerful place, its walls newly covered in brightly sprigged paper and flooded with light from the rows of long windows overlooking the broad, sun-dappled expanse of the river. The two little boys might have only been visiting for the summer, but it was obvious that Gabrielle Tennyson had prepared for her young cousins' stay with loving care.

Pausing at the entrance to the schoolroom, Sebastian let his gaze drift over the armies of tin soldiers that marched in neat formations across the scrubbed floorboards. Cockhorses and drums and wooden boats littered the room; shelves of books beckoned with promises of endless hours spent vicariously adventuring in faraway lands. On the edge of a big, sturdy table near the door lay a cluster of small, disparate objects—a broken clay pipe bowl, a glowing brown chestnut, a blue and white ceramic bead—as if a boy had hurriedly emptied his pockets of their treasures and then never came back for them.

A woman's voice sounded behind him. "And who might you be, then?"

Turning, Sebastian found himself being regarded with a suspicious scowl by a bony woman with thick, dark red hair, gaunt cheeks, and pale gray eyes. "You must be the boys' nurse, Miss Campbell."

"I am." Her gaze swept him with obvious suspicion, her voice raspy with a thick northern brogue. "And you?"

"Lord Devlin."

She sniffed. "I heard them talking about you in the servants' hall." She pushed past him into the room and swung to face him, her thin frame rigid with hostility and what he suspected was a carefully controlled, intensely private grief. "Seems a queer thing for a lord to do, getting hisself mixed up in murder. But then, London folk is queer."

Sebastian found himself faintly smiling. "You came with the boys from Lincolnshire?"

"I did, yes. Been with Master George since he was born, I have, and little Master Alfred too."

"I understand the boys' father is a rector?"

"Aye." A wary light crept into her eyes.

Seeing it, Sebastian said, "Tell me about him."

"The Reverend Tennyson?" She folded her arms across her stomach, her hands clenched tight around her bony elbows. "What is there to tell? He's a brilliant man—for all he's so big and hulking and clumsy."

"I'm told he's not well. Nothing serious, I hope?"

The fingers gripping her elbows reminded him of claws clinging desperately to a shifting purchase. "He hasna been well for a long time now." She hesitated, then added, "A very long time." Lingering ill health was all too common in their society, frequently caused by consumption, but more often by some unknown debilitating affliction.

Sebastian wandered the room, his attention seemingly all for the scattered toys and books. "And the boys? Are they hale?"

"Ach, you'd be hard put to find two sturdier lads. To be sure, Master George can be a bit wild and hotheaded, but there's no malice in him."

It struck him as a profoundly strange thing for her to say. He paused beside a scattering of books on the window seat overlooking the river. They were the usual assortment of boys' adventure stories. Flipping open one of the covers, he found himself staring at the name *George Tennyson* written in the same round copperplate as the poem given him by the housekeeper.

Looking up, he said, "Do you know where Miss Tennyson planned to take her young cousins yesterday?"

The nursemaid shook her head. "No. She told them it was a surprise."

"Could she perhaps have intended to show them the excavations at Camlet Moat?"

"She could, I suppose. But how would that be a surprise? She'd taken them up there before."

"Perhaps she'd discovered something new she wanted to show them."

"I wouldn't know about that."

Sebastian studied the woman's plain, tensely held face. "What do you think has happened to them, Miss Campbell?"

She pressed her lips into a hard, straight line, her nostrils flaring on a quickly indrawn breath, her forehead creasing with a sudden upwelling of emotion she fought to suppress. It was a moment before she could speak. "I don't know," she said, shaking her head. "I just don't know. I keep thinking about those poor wee bairns out there somewhere, alone and afraid, with no one to care for them. Or—or—" But here her voice broke and she could only shake her head, unwilling to put her worst fears into words.

He said, "Did you ever hear Miss Tennyson mention the name of an antiquary with whom she had quarreled?"

Margaret cleared her throat and touched the back of her knuckles to her nostrils, her formidable composure slamming once more into place. "A what?"

"An antiquary. A scholar of antiquities. You never heard Miss Tennyson speak of any such person?"

"No."

"How about the children? Did they ever mention anyone? Anyone at all they might have met in London?"

She stared back at him, her face pale, her eyes wide.

Sebastian said, "There is someone. Tell me."

"I don't know his name. The lads always called him 'the Lieutenant.'"

"He's a lieutenant?"

"Aye." Her lip curled. "Some Frenchy."

"Where did the children meet this French lieutenant?"

"Miss Tennyson would oftentimes take the lads to the park of an evening. I think they'd see him there."

"They saw him often?"

"Aye. Him and his dog."

"The Lieutenant has a dog?"

"Aye. The lads are mad about dogs, you know."

"When did they first begin mentioning this lieutenant?"

"Ach, it must have been six weeks or more ago—not long after we first arrived in London, I'd say."

"That's all you can tell me about him? That he's a Frenchman and a lieutenant—and that he has a dog?"

"He may've been in the cavalry. I can't be certain, mind you, but it's only since we've come to London that Master George has suddenly been all agog to join the Army. He's forever galloping around the schoolroom slashing a wooden sword through the air and shouting, *Charge!* and, *At 'em, lads!*"

"Any idea where this lieutenant might have seen service?"

"To be honest, I didn't like to pay too much heed to young Master George when he'd start going on about it. Couldn't see any sense in encouraging the lad. The Reverend's already told him he's bound for Eton next year. Besides, it didn't seem right, somehow, him being so friendly with a Frenchy."

Sebastian said, "Many émigrés have fought valiantly against Napoléon."

"Whoever said he was an émigré?" She gave a scornful laugh. "A prisoner on his parole, he is. And only the good Lord knows how many brave Englishmen he sent to their graves before he was took prisoner."

⚜

Sebastian went to lean on the terrace railing overlooking the river. The tide was out, a damp, fecund odor rising from the expanse of mudflats exposed along the bank below as the sun began its downward arc toward the west. An aged Gypsy woman in a full purple skirt and yellow kerchief was telling fortunes beside a man with a painted cart selling hot sausages near the steps. Beyond them, a string of constables could be seen poking long probes into the mud, turning over logs and bits of flotsam left stranded by the receding water. At first Sebastian wondered what they were doing. Then he realized they must be searching for the children . . . or what was left of them.

He twisted around to stare back at the imposing row of eighteenth-century town houses that rose above the terrace. The disappearance of the two young children added both an urgency and a troubling new dimension to the murder of Gabrielle Tennyson. Had the boys, too, fallen victim to Gabrielle's killer? For the same reason? Or were the children simply in the wrong place at the wrong time? And if they hadn't suffered the same fate as their cousin, then where were they now?

Sebastian brought his gaze back to the top of the steps, his eyes narrowing as he studied the thin, drab-coated man buying a sausage from the cart.

It was the same man he'd seen earlier, at Tower Hill.

Bloody hell.

Pushing away from the railing, Sebastian strolled toward the sausage seller. Pocketing the drab-coated man's coin, the sausage seller handed the man a paper-wrapped sausage. Without seeming to glance in Sebastian's direction, the man took a bite of his sausage and began to walk away.

He was a tallish man, with thin shoulders and a round hat he wore pulled low on his face. Sebastian quickened his step.

He was still some ten feet away when the man tossed the sausage aside and broke into a run.

Chapter 10

*T*he man sprinted around the edge of the terrace and dropped out of sight.

Sebastian tore after him, down a crowded, steeply cobbled lane lined with taverns and narrow coffeehouses that emptied abruptly onto the sun-splashed waterfront below. A flock of white gulls rose, screeching, to wheel high above the broad, sparkling river.

The genteel houses of the Adelphi Terrace had been constructed over a warren of arch-fronted subterranean vaults built to span the slope between the Strand and the wharves along the river. Sebastian could hear the man's booted feet pounding over the weathered planking as he darted around towering pyramids of wine casks and dodged blue-smocked workmen unloading sacks of coal from a barge. Then the buff-coated man threw one quick look over his shoulder and dove under the nearest archway to disappear into the gloomy world beneath the terrace.

Hell and the devil confound it, thought Sebastian, swerving around a mule cart.

"Hey!" shouted a grizzled man in a cap and leather apron as the mule between the traces of his cart snorted and kicked. "What the bloody 'ell ye doin'?"

Sebastian kept running.

One behind the other, Sebastian and the drab-coated man raced through soaring, catacomblike arches, the bricks furred with soot and mold and perpetual dampness. They sprinted down dark tunnels of warehouses tenanted by wine sellers and coal merchants, and up dimly lit passages off which opened stables that reeked of manure and dirty straw, where cows lowed plaintively from out of the darkness.

"Who the hell are you?" Sebastian shouted as the man veered around a rotten water butt, toward the dark opening of a narrow staircase that wound steeply upward. *"Who?"*

Without faltering, the man clambered up the stairs, Sebastian at his heels. Round and round they went, only to erupt into a steeply sloping corridor paved with worn bricks and lined with milk cans.

Breathing hard and fast, the man careened from side to side, upending first one milk can, then another and another, the cans rattling and clattering as they bounced down the slope like giant bowling pins, filling the air with the hot splash of spilling milk.

"God damn it," swore Sebastian, dodging first one can, then the next. Then his boots hit the slick wet bricks and his feet shot out from under him. He went down hard, slamming his shoulder against a brick pier as he slid back down the slope and the next milk can bounced over his head.

He pushed up, the leather soles of his boots slipping so that he nearly went down again. He could hear the man's running footsteps disappearing around the bend up ahead.

Panting heavily now, Sebastian tore around the corner and out a low archway into the unexpected sunlight of the open air. He threw up one hand to shade his suddenly blinded eyes, his step faltering.

The lane stretched empty and silent before him.
The man was gone.

❧

After leaving Carlton House, Hero spent the next several hours at a bookseller's in Westminster, where she selected several items, one of which proved to be very old and rare. Then, sending her purchases home in the charge of a footman, she directed her coachman to the British Museum.

It was at an exhibition of Roman sarcophagi at the British Museum that Hero had first met Gabrielle Tennyson some six years before. Initially, their interaction had been marked more by politeness than by cordiality. Both might be gently born, well-educated women, but they belonged to vastly different worlds. For while the Jarvises were an ancient noble family with powerful connections, Gabrielle Tennyson came from a long line of barristers and middling churchmen—gentry rather than noble, comfortable rather than wealthy.

But with time had come respect and, eventually, true friendship. Their interests and ambitions had never exactly coincided: Gabrielle's passion had all been for the past, whereas Hero's main focus would always be the economic and social condition of her own age. Yet their shared willingness to challenge their society's narrow gender expectations and their determination never to marry had forged a unique and powerful bond between them.

Now Hero, much to her mingling bemusement and chagrin, had become Lady Devlin. While Gabrielle . . .

Gabrielle was dead.

The bells of the city's church towers were just striking three when Hero's coachman drew up outside the British Museum. She sat with one hand resting casually on the carriage strap, her gaze on the towering portal of the complex across the street as she listened to the great rolling clatter and dong of the bells swelling over the city.

Built of brick in the French style with rustic stone quoins and a slate mansard roof, the sprawling mansion had once served as the home of the Dukes of Montagu, its front courtyard flanked by long colonnaded wings and separated from Great Russell Street by a tall gateway surmounted by an octagonal lantern. She watched a man and a woman pause on the footpath before the entrance, confer for a moment, and go inside. Then two men deep in a heated discussion, neither of whom Hero recognized, exited the gateway and turned east.

One after another the bells of the city tapered off into stillness, until all were silent.

Hero frowned. She had come in search of an antiquary named Bevin Childe. Childe was known both for his formidable scholarship and for his fanatical adherence to a self-imposed schedule. Every Monday, Tuesday, and Thursday between the hours of ten and three he could be found in the Reading Room of the museum. At precisely three o'clock, he left the museum and crossed the street to a public house known as the Pied Piper, where he ate a plate of sliced roast beef and buttered bread washed down by a pint of good, stout ale. This was followed by a short constitutional around nearby Bedford Square, after which he returned to the Reading Room from four until six. But today, Childe was deviating from his prescribed pattern.

The minutes ticked past. "Bother," said Hero softly under her breath.

"My lady?" asked her footman, his hand on the open carriage door.

"Perhaps—" she began, then broke off as a stout man in his early thirties dressed in a slightly crumpled olive coat and a high-crowned beaver came barreling through the museum's gateway, his head down, a brass-headed walking stick tucked under one arm. He had the face of an overgrown cherub, his flesh as pink and white as a baby's, his small mouth pursed as if with annoyance at the realization that he was nearly ten minutes late for his nuncheon.

"Mr. Childe," called Hero, descending from the carriage, her furled parasol in hand. "What a fortunate encounter. There is something I wish to speak with you about. Do let's walk along for a ways."

Childe's head jerked up, his step faltering, a succession of transparent emotions flitting across his cherubic features as his desire to maintain his schedule warred with the need to appear accommodating to a woman whose father was the most powerful man in the Kingdom.

"Actually," he said, "I was just on my way to grab a bite—"

"It won't take but a moment." Hero opened her parasol and inexorably turned his steps toward the nearby square.

He twisted around to gaze longingly back at the Pied Piper, the exaggerated point of his high collar pressing into his full cheek. "But I generally prefer to take my constitutional *after* I eat—"

"I know. I do beg your pardon, but you have heard this morning's news about the death of Miss Tennyson and the disappearance of her young cousins?"

She watched as the pinkness drained from his face, leaving him pale. "How could I not? The news is all over town. Indeed, I can't seem to think of anything else. It was my intention to spend the day reviewing a collection of manor rolls from the twelfth century, but I've found it nearly impossible to focus my attention for more than a minute or two at a stretch."

"How . . . distressing for you," said Hero dryly.

The scholar nodded. "Most distressing."

The man might still be in his early thirties—not much older than Devlin, she realized with some surprise—but he had the demeanor and mannerisms of someone in his forties or fifties. She said, "I remember Miss Tennyson telling me once that you disagreed with her identification of Camlet Moat as the possible site of Camelot."

"I do. But then, you would be sorely pressed to find anyone of repute who does agree with her."

"You're saying her research was faulty?"

"Her research? No, one could hardly argue with the references to the site she discovered in various historical documents and maps. There is no doubt the area was indeed known as 'Camelot' for hundreds of years. Her interpretation of those findings, however, is another matter entirely."

"Was that the basis of your quarrel with her last Friday? Her interpretation?"

He gave a weak, startled laugh. "Quarrel? I had no quarrel with Miss Tennyson. Who could have told you such a thing?"

"Do you really want me to answer that question?"

Her implication was not lost on him. She watched, fascinated, as Childe's mobile features suddenly froze. He cleared his throat. "And your . . . your source did not also tell you the reason for our little . . . disagreement?"

"Not precisely; I was hoping you could explain it further."

His face hardened in a way she had not expected. "So you are here as the emissary of your husband, not your father."

"I am no one's emissary. I am here because Gabrielle Tennyson was my friend, and whoever killed her will have to answer to me for what they've done to her—to her and to her cousins."

If any woman other than Hero had made such a state-

ment, Childe might have smiled. But all of London knew
that less than a week before, three men had attempted to
kidnap Hero; she had personally stabbed one, shot the
next, and nearly decapitated the other.

"Well," he said with sudden, forced heartiness. "It was,
as you say, a difference of opinion over the interpretation of the historical evidence. That is all."

"Really?"

He stared back at her, as if daring her to challenge
him. "Yes."

They turned to walk along the far side of the square,
where a Punch professor competed with a hurdy-gurdy
player, and a barefoot, wan-faced girl in a ragged dress
sold watercress for a halfpenny a bunch from a worn
wooden tray suspended by a strap around her neck. A
cheap handbill tacked to a nearby lamppost bore a bold
headline that read in smudged ink, KING ARTHUR, THE
ONCE AND FUTURE KING!

Normally, the square would have been filled with children playing under the watchful eye of their nursemaids,
their shouts and laughter carrying on the warm breeze.
But today, the sunlit lawns and graveled walks lay silent
and empty. Gabrielle's murder and the mysterious disappearance of the two boys had obviously spooked the city.
Those mothers who could afford to do so were keeping
their children safely indoors under nervous, watchful eyes.

"I was wondering," said Hero, "where exactly were
you yesterday?"

If Childe's cheeks had been pale before, they now
flared red, his eyes wide with indignation, his pursed
mouth held tight. "If you mean to suggest that I could
possibly have anything to do with— That—that I—"

Hero returned his angry stare with a calculated look
of bland astonishment. "I wasn't suggesting anything, Mr.
Childe; I was merely hoping you might have some idea
about Miss Tennyson's plans for Sunday."

"Ah. Well . . . I'm afraid not. As it happens, I spend my Fridays, Saturdays, and Sundays at Gough Hall. The late Richard Gough left his books and papers to the Bodleian Library, you see, and I have volunteered to sort through and organize them. It's a prodigious undertaking."

She had heard of Richard Gough, the famous scholar and writer who had been director of the Society of Antiquaries for two decades and who had made the Arthurian legends one of his particular areas of interest. "Gough Hall is near Camlet Moat, is it not?"

"It is."

"I wonder, did you ever take advantage of the opportunity offered by that proximity to visit the excavations on the isle?"

"I wouldn't waste my time," said Childe loftily.

Hero tilted her head to one side, her gaze on his face, a coaxing smile on her lips. "So certain that Miss Tennyson was wrong about the island, are you?"

No answering smile touched the man's dour features. "If a real character known as Arthur ever existed—which is by no means certain—he was in all likelihood a barbaric warrior chieftain from the wilds of Wales whose dimly remembered reality was seized upon by a collection of maudlin French troubadours with no understanding of—or interest in—the world he actually inhabited."

"I take it you're not fond of medieval romances?"

She noticed he was staring, hard, at another handbill tacked up on the wall of the house at the corner. This one simply proclaimed, KING ARTHUR, SAVE US!

Hero said, "Who do you think killed her?"

Childe jerked his head around to look at her again, and for one unexpected moment, all the bombastic self-importance seemed to leach out of the man in a way that left him seeming unexpectedly vulnerable—and considerably more likeable. "Believe me when I say that if I could help you in any way, I would. Miss Tennyson was—" His voice quivered and he broke off, his features pinched with grief. He swallowed and tried again. "She was a most remarkable woman, brilliant and high-spirited and full of boundless energy, even if her enthusiasms did at times lead her astray. But she was also very good at keeping parts of her life—of herself—secret."

His words echoed so closely those of Hero's father that she felt a sudden, unexpected chill. "What sort of secrets are we talking about?"

"If I knew, they wouldn't be secrets, now, would they?" said Childe with a faintly condescending air.

Hero asked again, her voice more tart, "So who do you think killed her?"

Childe shook his head. "I don't know. But if I were intent on unmasking her killer, rather than focus on Miss Tennyson's associates and activities, I would instead ask myself, Who would benefit from the death of her young cousins?"

They had come full circle, so that they now stood on the footpath outside the Pied Piper. The door beside them opened, spilling voices and laughter and the yeasty scent of ale into the street as two gentlemen emerged blinking into the sunlight and crossed the street toward the museum.

"You mean, George and Arthur Tennyson?" said Hero.

She realized Childe was no longer looking at her but at something or someone beyond her. Throwing a quick glance over her shoulder, Hero found herself staring at the watercress girl from the square. The girl must have trailed behind them and now leaned wearily against a nearby lamppost, her wooden tray hanging heavy from its strap, a wilting bunch of greens clutched forlornly in one hand. She couldn't have been more than twelve or thirteen, with golden hair and large blue eyes in an elfin face. Already grown tall and leggy, she was still boy-thin, with only a hint of the breasts beginning to swell beneath the bodice of her ragged dress. And Childe was looking at her with his lips parted and his gray eyes hooded in a way that made Hero feel she was witnessing something unclean and obscene.

As if becoming aware of Hero's scrutiny, he brought his gaze back to her face and cleared his throat. "As I said. And now, Lady Devlin, you really must excuse me." Turning on his heel, he strode into the Pied Piper and shut the door behind him with a snap.

Hero stood for a moment, her gaze on the closed door. Then, digging her purse from her reticule, she walked over to the watercress girl. "How much for all your bunches?"

The girl straightened with a jerk, her mouth agape. "M'lady?"

"You heard me. You've what? A dozen? Tell me, do you always sell your watercress here, by the museum?"

The girl closed her mouth and swallowed. "Here, or at Bloomsbury Square."

Hero pressed three coins into the girl's palm. "There's a shilling for all your watercress and two more besides. But don't let me catch you around here again. Is that understood? From now on, you peddle your bundles only at Bloomsbury."

The girl dropped a frightened, confused curtsy. "Yes, m'lady."

"Go on. Get out of here."

The girl took to her heels and fled, the ragged skirt of her dress swirling around her ankles, her tray thumping against her thin body, her fist clenched about the coins in her hand. She did not look back.

Hero watched until the girl turned the corner and the receding patter of her bare feet was lost in the rumble of the passing carriages and carts, the shouts of the costermongers, the distant wail of the hurdy-gurdy player from the square.

But the uneasiness within her remained.

She was about to turn back toward her carriage when she heard a familiar low-pitched voice behind her say, "I suppose I shouldn't be surprised to find you here, but I must confess that I am."

Sebastian gave a startled laugh. "Is he?"

"Decidedly. As for what I know about him, I'm told his father is a Cambridge don. A doctor of divinity."

"I wouldn't have expected such a man to have much to do with Miss Tennyson."

He watched her brows draw together in a frown. "Meaning?" she asked.

"Meaning that however brilliant or accomplished she may have been, Miss Tennyson not only lacked a formal university education, but she was also female. And there's no need to scowl at me; I didn't say I *agreed* with that sort of prejudice, did I?"

"True. I beg your pardon."

"What about Childe himself? Is he a clergyman?"

"I believe he was once rather reluctantly destined for the church. But fortunately for Mr. Childe, a maternal uncle managed to acquire a fortune in India and then died without siring an heir. He left everything to Mr. Childe."

"Fortuitous, indeed—for both Mr. Childe and the church. How do you come to know so much about the gentleman?"

"From Gabrielle. Her brother was up at Cambridge with Childe, and the two men have remained friends ever since—much to Gabrielle's disgust, given that she has heartily detested the man since she was still in the schoolroom."

"Any particular reason why?"

"She said he was arrogant, opinionated, self-absorbed, pedantic, and—strange."

"'Strange'? Did she ever explain exactly what she meant by that?"

"No. I asked her once, but she just shrugged and said he made her uncomfortable."

"Interesting. And precisely how large of a fortune did the arrogant and pedantic Mr. Childe inherit?"

Chapter 11

Sebastian stood with one shoulder propped against the brick wall of the pub, his arms crossed at his chest, and watched his wife pivot slowly to face him. The hot sun fell full across a face unusually pale but flawlessly composed.

"Devlin," she said, adjusting the tilt of her parasol in a way that threw her features into shadow. "What brings you here?"

He pushed away from the wall. "I was hoping to find someone at the museum who could direct me to a certain unidentified antiquary who quarreled recently with Miss Tennyson. I take it that's the gentleman in question?"

"His name is Bevin Childe." She stood still and let him walk up to her. "Post-Roman England is his specialty."

"Ah, the Arthurian Age."

"Yes. But I wouldn't let Childe hear you call it that. I suspect you'd get an earful."

"Mr. Childe is not a fan of Camelot?"

"He is not."

"How much do you know about him?"

They turned to walk together toward her waiting carriage. "Apart from the fact that he's a pompous ass?" she said with unladylike frankness.

"A comfortable enough independence that he is now able to devote himself entirely to scholarship. I gather he currently divides his time between research here at the museum and a project he has undertaken for the Bodleian Library, which entails cataloging the library and collections of the late Richard Gough."

"That's significant," said Sebastian, studying her face. "Why?"

"Because amongst other things, Mr. Gough made a particular study of the Arthurian legends. And his home, Gough Hall, is near Enfield."

"And Camlet Moat?"

"Precisely."

Sebastian frowned. "So where does Mr. Childe live?"

"I believe he has rooms in St. James's Street."

"He's unmarried?"

"He is, yes. Gabrielle told me several weeks ago that he had become quite vocal in his disparagement of her conclusions about Camlet Moat. And Childe himself says that they quarreled over the issue again just last Friday. But he also made some rather vague references to Gabrielle's 'secrets' that I found disturbing."

"Secrets? What secrets?"

"He declined to elaborate."

They had reached her carriage. Sebastian shook his head at the footman who was about to spring forward; the man stepped back, and Sebastian opened the carriage door himself. "Any chance Childe could have been referring to a certain French prisoner of war with whom Miss Tennyson was apparently friendly?"

Hero turned to face him, her expression one of mingled surprise and puzzlement. "What French prisoner of war?"

"She never talked about him?" Pausing with one elbow resting on the carriage's open window, he gave her a brief summary of what he'd learned from the servants in the Tennyson household. "You're certain she never mentioned such a man to you?"

"Not that I recall, no."

Sebastian let his gaze rove over the shadowed features of her face, the smooth curve of her cheek, the strong, almost masculine angle of her jaw. Once, he would have said she was telling him the truth. But he knew her well enough by now to know that she was keeping something back from him.

He said, "When Bow Street brought word this morning of Gabrielle Tennyson's death, I was surprised that you had no wish to accompany me to Camlet Moat. In my naivety, I assumed it was because you knew Lovejoy would be discomfited by your presence. But you had another reason entirely, didn't you?"

She furled her parasol, her attention seemingly all for the task of securing the strap. Rather than answering him, she said, "We agreed when we married that we would respect each other's independence."

"We did. Yet your purpose in this is the same as mine, is it not? To discover what happened to Gabrielle Tennyson and her young cousins? Or is something else going on here of which I am not aware?"

She looked up at him, the light falling full on her face, and he saw there neither guile nor subterfuge, but only a tense concern. "You've heard the authorities discovered the boys are missing?"

Sebastian nodded silently.

"When I asked Childe who he thought killed Gabrielle, he said that rather than focusing on Gabrielle's associates, I ought to consider who would benefit from the elimination of the children."

Sebastian was silent for a moment, remembering a boy's flowing copperplate and armies of tin soldiers marching silently across a sunlit nursery floor. He refused to accept that the two little boys were dead too. But all he said was, "You've met them?"

"Her cousins? Several times, yes. I'm not one of those women who dote mindlessly on children, but George and Alfred are something special. They're so extraordinarily bright and curious and full of enthusiasm for learning about the world around them that they're a delight to be with. The thought that something might have happened to them too—" She broke off, and he saw the rare glaze of unshed tears in her eyes. Then she cleared her throat and looked away, as if embarrassed to be seen giving way to her emotions.

"'Something that's done and more undone,'" he quoted softly. "'Are only the dead so bold?'"

Hero shook her head, not understanding. "What?"

"It's from a poem George Tennyson wrote." He showed it to her. "Does it mean anything to you?"

She read through the short stanza. "No. But George was always writing disjointed scraps of poetry like that. I doubt it means anything."

"I'm told the boy's father has been ill for a long time. Do you have any idea with what?"

"No. But then, I don't know that much about Miss Tennyson's family. Her parents died before I knew her. Her brother is a pleasant enough chap, although rather typically preoccupied with his legal practice. He has a small estate down in Kent, which is where he is now. It has always been my understanding that he and Gabrielle were comfortably situated, although no more than that. Yet I believe there may be substantial wealth elsewhere in the family. Recent wealth."

"Good God," said Sebastian. "Was Miss Tennyson in some way related to Charles Tennyson d'Eyncourt?"

"I believe they are first cousins. You know him?"

"He was several years behind me at Eton."

His tone betrayed more than he'd intended it to. She smiled. "And you consider him a pretentious, toadying a—" She broke off to cast a rueful glance at the wooden faces of the waiting servants.

"Bore?" he suggested helpfully.

"That too."

For one unexpectedly intimate moment, their gazes met and they shared a private smile. Then Sebastian felt his smile begin to fade.

For the past fifteen months, d'Eyncourt had served as a member of Parliament from Lincolnshire. A fiercely reactionary Tory, he had quickly managed to ingratiate himself with the block of parliamentarians controlled by Hero's own father, Lord Jarvis.

Sebastian said, "Why do I keep getting the distinct impression there's something you're not telling me?"

She took his offered hand and climbed the step into the waiting carriage. "Would I do that?" she asked.

"Yes."

She gave a throaty chuckle and gracefully disposed the skirts of her dusky blue walking dress around her on the seat. "Will you tell the coachman to take me home, please?"

"Are you going home?"

"Are you?"

Smiling softly, he closed the door and nodded to the driver. He stood for a moment and watched as her carriage rounded the corner onto Tottenham Court. Then he went in search of the pretentious toadying bore who called himself Tennyson d'Eyncourt.

Chapter 12

Charles Tennyson d'Eyncourt was lounging comfortably in one of the leather tub chairs in the reading room of White's when Sebastian walked up to him.

The MP was considerably fairer than his cousin Gabrielle, slim and gracefully formed, with delicate features and high cheekbones and lips so thin as to appear nearly nonexistent. He had a glass of brandy on the table at his elbow and the latest copy of the conservative journal *The Courier* spread open before him. He glanced up, briefly, when Sebastian settled in the seat opposite him, then pointedly returned his attention to his reading.

"My condolences on the death of your cousin, Miss Gabrielle Tennyson," said Sebastian.

"I take it Bow Street has involved you in the investigation of this unfortunate incident, have they?" asked d'Eyncourt without looking up again.

"If by 'unfortunate incident' you mean the murder of Miss Tennyson and the disappearance of the young children in her care, then the answer is yes."

D'Eyncourt reached, deliberately, for his brandy, took a sip, and returned to his journal.

"I'm curious," said Sebastian, signaling a passing

waiter for a drink. "How close is the relationship between you and Miss Tennyson?"

"We are—or I suppose I should say *were*—first cousins."

"So the two missing boys are . . . ?"

"My nephews."

"Your brother's sons?"

"That is correct."

"I must confess that, under the circumstances, I am rather surprised to find you lounging in your club calmly reading a journal."

D'Eyncourt looked up at that, his thin nose quivering. "Indeed? And what would you have me do instead, I wonder? Go charging into the countryside to thrash the underbrush of Enfield Chase like a beater hoping to flush game?"

"You think that's where the children are liable to be found? At Camlet Moat?"

"How the devil would I know?" snapped d'Eyncourt and returned once more to his reading.

Sebastian studied the other man's pinched profile. He couldn't recall many of the younger boys at Eton, but Sebastian remembered d'Eyncourt. As a lad, d'Eyncourt had been one of those ostentatiously earnest scholars who combined shameless toadying with nauseating displays of false enthusiasm to curry favor with the dons. But to his fellow students he was ruthless and vindictive, and quickly acquired a well-deserved reputation as someone who would do anything—and say anything—to get what he wanted.

In those days he'd simply been called "Tennyson," the same as his cousin and missing nephews. But several years ago he had successfully petitioned the Home Secretary to have his name changed to the more aristocratic d'Eyncourt, the extinct patronym of one of his mother's ancestors, to which his claims were, to say the least, dubious. It was well-known that his ambition was to be made Lord d'Eyncourt before he was forty.

"You seem oddly unconcerned about their fates," said Sebastian.

"It is the stuff of tragedy, to be sure. However, none of it alters the fact that my brother and I have never been close. His life is narrowly focused on his benefices in Somersby, whereas I live most of the year in London, where I take my duties at Parliament very seriously indeed. I doubt I would recognize his children if I passed them in the street."

"Is that why they've been staying with Miss Tennyson, their cousin, rather than with you, their uncle?"

D'Eyncourt sniffed. "My wife is not fond of London and chooses to remain in Lincolnshire. I do currently have my sister Mary with me, but I could hardly ask her to undertake the management of two wild, poorly brought-up boys, now, could I?"

"*Are* they wild and poorly bought up?"

"They could hardly be otherwise, given their parentage."

"Really?" Sebastian settled more comfortably in his seat. "Tell me about the boys' father—your brother. I hear he's not well. Nothing serious, I hope?"

A curious hint of color touched the other man's high cheekbones. "I fear my brother's health has never been particularly robust."

"Can you think of anyone who might benefit from the death or disappearance of his sons?"

"Good heavens; what a ridiculous notion! I told you: My brother is a rector. He holds two livings, which together provide him with a respectable income. But he has always been a hopeless spendthrift, and the foolish woman he married is even worse, with the result that my father is forever being forced to tow them out of the river tick."

D'Eyncourt's father was a notorious figure known irreverently as "the Old Man of the Wolds," thanks to his extensive landholdings in the Wolds, an area of hills and wide-open valleys in the northeast of England. His fortune, while of recent origins, was reportedly huge, deriving largely from a series of astute land purchases and the old man's ruthless manipulation of anyone unfortunate enough to drift into his orbit.

Sebastian said, "You are your father's sole heir?"

D'Eyncourt's thin nostrils flared with indignation. "I am. And may I take leave to tell you that I resent the inference inherent in that question? I resent it very much."

"Oh, you have my leave to tell me anything you wish," said Sebastian, stretching to his feet. "Just one more question: Can you think of anyone who might have wished Miss Tennyson harm?"

D'Eyncourt opened his mouth as if to say something, then closed it and shook his head.

"You do know of someone," said Sebastian, watching him closely. "Who is it?"

"Well . . ." D'Eyncourt licked his thin lips. "You are aware, of course, that my cousin fancied herself something of a bluestocking?"

"I would have said she could more accurately be described as a respected antiquary rather than as a bluestocking, but, yes, I am aware of her scholarly activities. Why?"

D'Eyncourt pulled a face. "Most women who indulge in such unsuitable activities have enough regard for the reputations of their families to adopt a male nom de plume and keep their true identities a secret. But not Gabrielle."

"My wife also chooses to publish under her own name," said Sebastian evenly.

D'Eyncourt gave an uncomfortable titter and looked faintly unwell. "So she does. No offense intended, I'm sure."

Sebastian said, "Are you suggesting that Miss Tennyson's investigations into the history of Camlet Moat might have contributed in some way to her death?"

D'Eyncourt gave a dismissive wave of his hand. "I know nothing of this latest start of hers. I was referring to a project she undertook some two or three months ago; something to do with tracing the original line of London's old Roman walls or some such nonsense. Whatever it was, it involved venturing into several of the more unsavory districts of the city. Not at all the proper sort of undertaking for a lady."

"You say this was two or three months ago?"

"Something like that, yes."

"So what makes you think it could have anything to do with her recent death?"

"Last week—Thursday, to be precise—I was on my way to meet with a colleague in the Strand when I happened to see Gabrielle arguing with a very rough customer near the York Steps. Thinking her in some sort of difficulty, I naturally approached with the intention of intervening. Much to my astonishment, she was not at all appreciative of my attempts on her behalf. Indeed, she was quite curt. Insisted there was no need for me to concern myself—that the individual I had seen her with was someone she had encountered when she discovered that the foundations of his tavern incorporated some extensive vestiges of the city's original Roman walls."

"Did you happen to catch the man's name?"

D'Eyncourt shook his head. "Sorry. But it shouldn't be that difficult to discover. I believe she said the tavern was called the Devil's Head or the Devil's Tower or some such thing. The man was a most unsavory-looking character—tall, with dark hair and sun-darkened skin, and dressed all in black except for his shirt. I thought at the time he reminded me of someone I know, but I couldn't quite place the resemblance."

"What makes you think he was a threat to her?"

"Because of what I heard him say, just before they noticed me walking up to them. He said"—d'Eyncourt roughened his voice in a crude imitation of the man's accent—"'Meddle in this and you'll be sorry. Be a shame to see something happen to a pretty young lady such as yourself.'"

Chapter 13

Sebastian was silent for a moment, trying to fit this incident into everything else he'd been told.

"Of course she tried to deny it," said d'Eyncourt. "Claimed he'd said no such thing. But I know what I heard. And it was obvious she was more than a little discomfited to be seen talking to this individual."

Sebastian studied the other man's narrow, effete features. But d'Eyncourt had spent a lifetime twisting incidents and conversations to serve his own purposes; his face was a bland mask.

Sebastian said, "What do you think it was about?"

D'Eyncourt closed his journal and rose to his feet. "I've no notion. You're the one who dabbles in murder, not I. I have far more important tasks with which to concern myself." He tucked *The Courier* beneath his arm. "And now you must excuse me; I've a meeting scheduled at Carlton House." He gave a short bow nicely calculated to convey just a hint of irony and contempt. Then he strolled languidly away, leaving Sebastian staring after him.

"Your drink, my lord?"

The waiter standing at Sebastian's elbow needed to repeat himself twice before Sebastian turned toward him.

"Thank you," he said, taking the brandy from the waiter's silver tray and downing it in one long, burning pull.

It was when he was leaving White's that Sebastian came face-to-face with a familiar barrel-chested, white-haired man in his late sixties. At the sight of Sebastian, the Earl of Hendon paused, his face going slack.

For twenty-nine years Sebastian had called this man father, had struggled to understand Hendon's strangely conflicted love and anger, pride and resentment. But though the world still believed Sebastian to be the Earl's son, Sebastian, at least, now knew the truth.

Sebastian gave a slow, polite bow. "My lord."

"Devlin," said Hendon, his voice gruff with emotion. "You . . . you are well?"

"I am, yes." Sebastian hesitated, then added with painful correctness, "Thank you. And you?"

Hendon's jaw tightened. "As always, yes, thank you."

Hendon had always been a bear of a man. Through all his growing years and well into his twenties, Sebastian had been aware of Hendon towering over him in both height and breadth. But as the moment stretched out and became something painful, Sebastian suddenly realized that with increasing age, Hendon was shrinking. He was now the same height as Sebastian, perhaps even shorter. When had that happened? he wondered. And he felt an unwelcome pang at the realization that this man who had played such a vital role in his life was growing older, more frail, less formidable.

For one long, intense moment, the Earl's fiercely blue St. Cyr eyes met Sebastian's hard yellow gaze. Then the two men passed.

Neither looked back.

⁂

Sebastian found Hero seated at the table in his library, a pile of books scattered over the surface.

She had changed into a simple gown of figured muslin with a sapphire blue sash and had her head bent over some notes she was making. He paused for a moment in the doorway and watched as she caught her lower lip between her teeth in that way she had when she was concentrating. He'd often come upon her thus, surrounded by books and documents at the heavy old library table in her father's Berkeley Square house. And for some reason he could not have named, seeing her here at work in the library of their Brook Street home made their marriage seem suddenly more real—and more intimate—than the long hours of passion they'd shared in the darkness of the night. He found himself smiling at the thought.

Then she looked up and saw him.

He said, "So you did come home."

She leaned back in her chair, her pen resting idle in her hand. "I did. And did you find Mr. d'Eyncourt?"

"At White's." He went to rest his palms on the surface of the table and lean into them, his gaze on her face. "I need to know the route of London's old Roman walls. Can you trace me a map, with references to existing streets and landmarks?"

"Roughly, yes."

He handed her a fresh sheet of paper. "Roughly will do."

She dipped her pen in the ink. "What is this about?"

As she began to sketch, he told her of his interview with Gabrielle's cousin. "Do you have any idea what d'Eyncourt may have been talking about?"

"I do, actually. Several months ago, Gabrielle undertook to trace the remnants of the old city walls for a volume on the history of London being compiled by Dr. Littleton."

Sebastian frowned. "Isn't that the same volume you've been working on?"

"It is. Although I have been looking into the surviving vestiges of London's monastic houses." She finished her diagram and slid it across to him. "How exactly do you intend to go about finding this tavern owner?"

He stood for a moment, studying her sketch. She'd actually drawn two wall circuits, one older and smaller than the other. The northern stretch of the oldest wall had run roughly along the course of Cornhill and Leadenhall Street, then down along Mark Lane before turning east to Thames Street and Walbrook. The later, larger circuit ran from the Tower to Aldgate and Bishopsgate, before turning westward to St. Giles churchyard and then veering south to Falcon Square. He traced the line to Aldersgate and Giltspur Street, angling over to Ludgate and the Thames, then eastward back toward the Tower again.

"That's a lot of wall," he said, folding the map. "I'll give it to Tom and see what he can find."

"You do realize that Gabrielle could have told her cousin a lie to put him off. I don't think they were exactly close."

"She may have. But I wouldn't be surprised if the part about the tavern and the Roman wall, at least, was true." He nodded to the books scattered across the table's surface. "What is all this?"

"I've been brushing up on my knowledge of King Arthur and Guinevere and the Knights of the Round Table."

He reached for the nearest book, a slim, aged volume covered in faded blue leather, and read the title embossed in gold on the spine. "*La donna di Scalotta.*" He looked up. "What is it?"

"An Italian novella about the Lady of Shalott."

He shook his head. "Never heard of it."

"I wasn't familiar with it, either. But I remembered Gabrielle telling me she was working on a translation."

He leafed through the volume's aged pages and frowned. "I certainly wouldn't want to try to translate it." Sebastian's Italian had come largely from the soldiers, partisans, and bandits he'd encountered during the war and had little in common with the volume's archaic, stylized language. "When was it originally written?"

"The thirteenth century, I believe."

"Do you think it might somehow be related to the excavations at Camlet Moat?"

"I don't believe so, no. Gabrielle was interested in all aspects of the Arthurian legend; this is a relatively unknown part of it." She turned her head as the sound of the front doorbell echoed through the house. "Are you expecting someone?" she asked, just as Sebastian's majordomo, Morey, appeared in the doorway.

"A Mr. Hildeyard Tennyson to see you, my lord. He says he is the brother of Miss Gabrielle Tennyson. I have taken the liberty of showing him to the drawing room."

Chapter 14

*H*ildeyard Tennyson wore the haggard, stunned expression of a man whose world has suddenly collapsed upon him, leaving him shattered and numb.

Dressed in riding breeches and dusty boots that told of a long, hard ride back to town, he stood beside the front windows overlooking the street, his hat in his hands, his back held painfully straight. Of above-average height, with his sister's thick chestnut hair and chiseled features, he looked to be in his early thirties. He turned as Sebastian and Hero entered the room, displaying a pale and grief-ravaged face. "My apologies for coming to you in all my dirt," he said, bowing. "I've just ridden in from Kent."

"Please, sit down, Mr. Tennyson," said Hero gently. "I can't tell you how sorry we are for your loss."

He nodded and swallowed hard, as if temporarily bereft of speech. "Thank you. I can't stay. I'm on my way up to Enfield to hire some men to help extend the search for the children into the woods and surrounding countryside. But I heard from one of the magistrates at Bow Street that you've offered to do what you can to help with the investigation, so I've come to thank you . . . and, I must confess, in the hopes that you might have found something—anything at all—that might make sense of what has happened." He fixed Sebastian with a look of desperation that was painful to see.

Sebastian went to pour brandy into two glasses. "Sit down," he said in the voice that had once commanded soldiers into battle. "It will be getting dark soon. If you'll take my advice, you'll go home, rest, and give some thought as to where and how your energies can be most efficiently exerted in the morning."

Tennyson sank into a chair beside the empty hearth and swiped a shaky hand over his face. "I suppose you're right. It's just—" He paused to blow out a harsh breath. "It feels so damnably wrong—begging your pardon, Lady Devlin—not to be doing *something*. I blame myself. I should have insisted Gabrielle and the boys come with me to Kent."

"From what I know of Gabrielle," said Hero, taking the chair opposite him, "I'm not convinced you would have succeeded even if you had tried to insist."

Gabrielle's brother gave a ghost of a smile. "You may be right. Not even our father could compel Gabrielle to do something she didn't wish to do. She was always far more headstrong than I, despite being four years my junior."

"There were only the two of you?" asked Sebastian.

Tennyson nodded. "We had several younger brothers who died when we were children. Gabrielle was quite close to them and took their deaths hard. I've often wondered if it wasn't one of the reasons she was so eager to have George and Alfred come stay with her this summer."

Sebastian handed him the brandy. "Would you say you and your sister were close?"

"I would have said so, yes."

"You don't sound so certain."

Tennyson stared down at the glass in his hand. "Gabrielle was always a very private person. Lately I've had the sense that our lives were diverging. But I suppose that's inevitable."

Sebastian went to stand beside the cold hearth, one arm resting along the mantel. "Do you know if she had any romantic connections?"

"Gabrielle?" Tennyson shook his head. "No. She's never had any interest in marriage. I remember once when I was up at Cambridge and very full of myself, I warned her that if she didn't get her nose out of books no man would ever want to marry her. She laughed and said that suited her just fine—that a husband would only get in the way of her studies."

"So you wouldn't happen to know the name of a French lieutenant she had befriended?"

"A Frenchman? You mean an émigré?"

"No. I mean a paroled French officer. She never mentioned such a man?"

Tennyson stared at him blankly. "Good heavens. No. Are you suggesting she was somehow involved with this person?"

Sebastian took a slow sip of his own brandy. "I don't know."

"There must be some mistake."

"That's very possible."

Tennyson scrubbed a hand over his eyes and down his face. When he looked up, his features were contorted with agony. "Who could do something like this? To kill a woman and two children . . ."

"Your young cousins may still be alive," said Sebastian. "We don't know yet."

Tennyson nodded, his entire upper body rocking back and forth with the motion. "Yes, yes; I keep trying to cling to that, but . . ." He raised his glass to drink, his hand shaking badly, and Sebastian thought that the man looked stretched to the breaking point.

"Can you think of anyone who might have wished either your sister or the children harm?"

"No. Why would anyone want to hurt a woman like Gabrielle—or two little boys?"

"Some enemy of the boys' father, perhaps?"

Tennyson considered this, then shook his head. "My cousin is a simple clergyman in Lincolnshire. I'd be surprised if he knows anyone in London."

Hero said, "Would you mind if I were to have a look at Gabrielle's research materials, on the off chance there might be some connection between her death and her work at Camlet Moat? I could come to the Adelphi myself in the morning."

He frowned, as if the possible relevance of his sister's scholarship to her death escaped him. "Of course; if you wish. I'll be leaving for Enfield at first light, but I'll direct the servants to provide you with any assistance you may require. You can box it all up and simply take it, if that would help."

"It would, yes. Thank you."

Tennyson set aside his glass and rose to his feet with a bow. "You have both been most kind. Please don't bother ringing; I can see myself out."

"I'll walk down with you," said Sebastian, aware of Hero's narrowed gaze following them as they left the room.

"It occurs to me there may be something else you felt reluctant to mention in front of Lady Devlin," Sebastian said as they descended the stairs.

Tennyson looked vaguely confused. "No, nothing."

"Any possibility someone could be seeking to hurt you by striking at those you love?"

"I can't think of anyone," he said slowly as they reached the ground hall. "Although in my profession one never—" He broke off, his eyes widening. "Merciful heavens. Emily."

"Emily?" said Sebastian.

A faint suggestion of color touched the barrister's pale cheeks. "Miss Emily Goodwin—the daughter of one of my colleagues. She has recently done me the honor of agreeing to become my wife, although the death of her paternal grandmother has perforce delayed the formal announcement of our betrothal."

"You may count on my discretion."

"Yes, but do you think she could be in danger?"

"I see no reason to alarm her unnecessarily, especially given that the particulars of your betrothal are not known." Sebastian nodded to Morey, who opened the front door. "But it might be a good idea to suggest that she take care."

"I will, yes; thank you."

Sebastian stood in the open doorway and watched the man hurry away into the hot night. Then he went back upstairs to his wife.

"And what precisely was that about?" she asked, one eyebrow raised, as he walked into the room.

Sebastian found himself smiling. "I thought there might be something he was reluctant to discuss in front of such a delicate lady as yourself."

"Really. And was there?"

"No. Only that it seems he's formed an attachment to some Miss Goodwin, the daughter of one of his colleagues, and now he's hysterical with the fear that his sister's killer might strike against her next. I suspect it's a fear shared by virtually every father, husband, and brother out there."

"You think it's possible Gabrielle's death could have something to do with her brother's legal affairs?"

"At this point, almost anything seems possible."

※

Tom squinted down at Hero's map, his lips pursing as he traced the dotted line of London's old Roman walls, which she had superimposed on her sketch of the city's modern streets.

"Can you follow it?" asked Sebastian, watching him. He knew that someone at some point had taught Tom to read, before the death of the boy's father had driven the family into desperation.

"Aye. I think maybe I even know the place yer lookin' for. There's a tavern called the Black Devil about 'ere—" He tapped one slightly grubby finger just off Bishopsgate. "It's owned by a fellow named Jamie Knox."

Sebastian looked at his tiger in surprise. "You know him?"

Tom shook his head. "Never seen the fellow meself. But I've 'eard tales o' him. 'E's a weery rum customer. A weery rum customer indeed. They say 'e dresses all in black, like the devil."

"A somewhat dramatic affectation." It wasn't unusual for gentlemen in formal evening dress to wear a black coat and black knee breeches. But the severity of the attire was always leavened by a white waistcoat, white silk stockings, and of course a white cravat.

"Not sure what that means," said Tom, "but I do know folks say 'e musta sold 'is soul to the devil, for 'e's got the devil's own luck. They say 'e 'as the reflexes of a cat. *And* the eyes and ears of—"

"What?" prodded Sebastian when the boy broke off.

Tom swallowed. "They say 'e 'as the eyes and ears of a cat, too. Yellow eyes."

Chapter 15

The Black Devil lay in a narrow cobbled lane just off Bishopsgate.

Sebastian walked down gloomy streets lit haphazardly by an occasional sputtering oil lamp or flaring torch thrust into a sconce high on an ancient wall. The houses here dated back to the time of the Tudors and the Stuarts, for this was a part of London that had escaped the ravages of the Great Fire. Once home to courtiers attached to the court of James I, the area had been in a long downward slide for the past century. The elaborately carved fronts overhanging the paving were sagging and worn; the great twisting chimneys leaned precariously as they poked up into the murky night sky.

By day, this was a district of small tradesmen: leather workers and chandlers, clock makers and tailors. But now the shops were all shuttered for the night, the streets given over to the patrons of the grog shops and taverns that spilled golden rectangles of light and boisterous laughter into the night.

He paused across the street from the Black Devil, in the shadows cast by the deep doorway of a calico printer's shop. He let his gaze rove over the public house's gable-ended facade and old-fashioned, diamond-paned windows. Suspended from a beam over the door hung a cracked wooden sign painted with the image of a horned black devil, his yellow-eyed head and barbed tail silhouetted against a roaring orange and red fire. As Sebastian watched, the sign creaked softly on its chains, touched by an unexpected gust of hot wind.

Crossing the narrow lane, he pushed through the door into a noisy, low-ceilinged public room with a sunken stone-flagged floor and oak-paneled walls turned black by centuries of smoke. The air was thick with the smell of tobacco and ale and unwashed, hardworking male bodies. The men crowded up to the bar and clustered around the tables glanced over at him, then went back to their pints and their bonesticks and their draughts.

"Help ye, there?" called a young woman from behind the bar, her almond-shaped eyes narrowing with shrewd appraisal. She looked to be somewhere in her early twenties, dark haired and winsome, with a wide red mouth and soft white breasts that swelled voluptuously above the low-cut bodice of her crimson satin gown.

Sebastian pushed his way through the crowd to stand half turned so that he still faced the room. In this gathering of tradesmen and laborers, costermongers and petty thieves, his doeskin breeches, clean white cravat, and exquisitely tailored coat of Bath superfine all marked him as a creature from another world. The other men at the bar shifted subtly, clearing a space around him.

"A go of Cork," he said, then waited until she set the measure of gin on the boards in front of him to add, "I'm looking for Jamie Knox; is he here?"

The woman behind the bar wiped her hands on the apron tied high around her waist, but her gaze never left his face. "And who might ye be, then?"

"Devlin. Viscount Devlin."

She stood for a moment with her hands still wrapped in the cloth of her apron. Then she jerked her head toward the rear. "He's out the back, unloading a delivery. There's an alley runs along the side of the tavern. The court opens off that."

Sebastian laid a coin on the scarred surface of the bar. "Thank you."

The alley was dark and ripe with the stench of rotting offal and fish heads and urine. The ancient walls looming high above him on either side bulged out ominously, so that someone had put in stout timber braces to keep the masonry from collapsing. As he drew nearer, he realized the tavern backed onto the churchyard of St. Helen's Bishopsgate, a relic of a now-vanished priory of Benedictine nuns. He could see the church's ancient wooden tower rising over a swelling burial ground where great elms moaned softly with the growing wind.

He paused just outside the entrance to the tavern yard. The courtyard looked to be even older than the tavern itself, its cobbles undulating and sunken, with one unexpectedly high wall of coursed flint blocks bonded with rows of red tile. Sebastian could understand why a woman with Gabrielle Tennyson's interests would find the site fascinating.

Someone had set a horn lantern atop an old flat stone beside a mule-drawn cart filled with hogsheads. The mules stood with their heads down, feet splayed. At the rear of the tavern the wooden flaps of the cellar had been thrown open to reveal a worn flight of stone steps that disappeared downward. As Sebastian watched, the grizzled head and husky shoulders of a man appeared, his footfalls echoing in the wind-tossed night.

Sebastian leaned against the stone jamb of the gateway. He had one hand in his pocket, where a small double-barreled pistol, primed and loaded, partially spoiled the line of his fashionable coat. A sheath in his boot concealed the dagger he was rarely without. He waited until the man had crossed to the cart, then said, "Mr. Jamie Knox?"

The man froze with his hands grasping a cask, his head turning toward the sound of Sebastian's voice. He appeared wary but not surprised, and it occurred to Sebastian that the comely young woman behind the bar must have run to warn her master to expect a visitor. "Aye. And who might ye be?"

"Devlin. Lord Devlin."

The man sniffed. Somewhere in his mid-thirties, he had a compact, muscular body that belied the heavy sprinkling of gray in his thick, curly head of hair. Far from being dressed all in black, he wore buff-colored trousers and a brown coat that looked in serious need of a good brushing and mending. His face was broad and sun darkened, with a long scar that ran down one cheek. Sebastian had seen scars like that before, left by a saber slash.

The man paused for only an instant. Then he hefted the hogshead and headed back to the stairs. "I'm a busy man. What ye want?"

The accent surprised Sebastian; it was West Country rather than London or Middlesex. He said, "I understand you knew a woman named Miss Tennyson."

The man grunted. "Met her. Came sniffin' around here a while back, she did, prattlin' about Roman walls and pictures made of little colored bits and a bunch of other nonsense. Why ye ask?"

"She's dead."

"Aye. So we heard." The man disappeared down the cellar steps.

Sebastian waited until he reemerged. "When was the last time you saw her?"

"I told ye, 'twere a while back. Two, maybe three months ago."

"That's curious. You see, someone saw you speaking

to her just a few days ago. Last Thursday, to be precise. At the York Steps."

The man grasped another hogshead and turned back toward the cellar. "Who'er told ye that didn't know what he was talkin' about."

"It's possible, I suppose."

The man grunted and started down the steep stairs again. He was breathing heavily by the time he came back up. He paused to lean against the cellar door and swipe his sweaty forehead against the shoulder of his coat.

"You were a soldier?" said Sebastian.

"What makes ye think that?"

"It left you with a rather distinctive face."

The man pushed away from the cellar. "I was here all day Thursday. Ask any o' the lads in the public room; they'll tell ye. Ye gonna call 'em all liars?"

Sebastian said, "I'm told Jamie Knox has yellow eyes. So why are yours brown?"

The man gave a startled laugh. "It's dark. Ye can't see what color a man's eyes are in the dark."

"I can."

"Huh." The tavern owner sniffed. "They only say that about me eyes because of the sign. Ye did see the sign, didn't ye? They also like t'say I only wear black. Next thing ye know, they'll be whisperin' that I've got a tail tucked into me breeches."

Sebastian let his gaze drift around the ancient yard. The massive flint and tile rampart that ran along the side of the court was distinctly different from the wall that separated the yard from the burial ground at its rear. No more than seven feet high and topped by a row of iron spikes designed to discourage body snatchers, that part of the wall lay deep in the heavy shadows cast by the sprawling limbs of the graveyard's leafy elms. And in the fork of one of those trees crouched a lean man dressed all in black except for the white of his shirt. He balanced there easily, the stock of his rifle resting against his thigh.

To anyone else, the rifleman would have been invisible.

Sebastian said, "When he comes down out of his tree, tell Mr. Knox he can either talk to me, or he can talk to Bow Street. I suppose his choice will depend on exactly what's in his cellars."

The stocky man's scarred face split into a nasty grin. "I don't need to tell him. He can hear ye. Has the eyes and ears of a cat, he does."

Sebastian turned toward the gateway. The stocky man put out a hand to stop him.

Sebastian stared pointedly at the grimy fingers clenching his sleeve. The hand was withdrawn.

The man licked his lower lip. "He could've shot out both yer eyes from where he's sittin'. And I'll tell ye somethin' else: He looks enough like ye t'be yer brother. Ye think about that. Ye think about that real hard." He paused a moment, then added mockingly, *Me lord.*

Chapter 16

Sebastian walked down Cheapside, his hands thrust deep into the pockets of his coat, the hot wind eddying the flames of the streetlamps to send leaping shadows over the shuttered shop fronts and dusty, rubbish-strewn cobbles.

Once, he had been the youngest of three brothers, the fourth child born to the Earl of Hendon and his beautiful, vivacious countess, Sophie. If there had ever been a time in his parents' marriage that was pleasant, Sebastian couldn't remember it. They had lived essentially separate lives, the Earl devoting himself to affairs of state while the Countess lost herself in a gay whirl of balls and routs and visits to country houses. The few occasions when husband and wife came together had been characterized by stony silences punctuated all too often with stormy bouts of tears and voices raised in anger.

Yet Sebastian's childhood had not been an entirely unhappy one. In his memories, Sophie's touch was always soft and loving, and her laughter—when her husband was not around—came frequently. Her four children had never doubted her love for them. Though unlike each other in many ways and separated in age, the three brothers had been unusually close. Only Amanda, the eldest child, had held herself aloof. "Sometimes I think Amanda was born angry with the world," Sophie had once said, her thoughtful, worried gaze following her daughter when Amanda stormed off from a game of battledore and shuttlecock.

It would be years before Sebastian understood the true source of Amanda's anger.

He paused to look out over the gray, sunken tombs and rank nettles choking St. Paul's churchyard, his thoughts still lost in the past.

In contrast to his gay, demonstrative wife, the Earl of Hendon had been a stern, demanding father preoccupied with affairs of state. But he'd still found the time to teach his sons to ride and shoot and fence, and he took a gruff pride in their prowess. An intensely private man, he had remained a distant figure, detached and remote — especially from his youngest child, the child so unlike him in looks and temperament and talents.

Then had come a series of tragedies. Sebastian's oldest brother, Richard, was the first to die, caught in a vicious riptide while swimming off the coast of Cornwall near the Earl's principal residence. Then, one dreadful summer when the clouds of war swept across Europe and the fabric of society as they'd always known it seemed forever rent by revolution and violence, Cecil had sickened and died too.

Once the proud father of three healthy sons, Hendon found himself left with only the youngest, Sebastian. Sebastian, the son most unlike his father; the son on whom the Earl's wrath always fell the hardest, the son who had always known himself to be a disappointment in every way to the brusque, barrel-chested man with the piercingly blue St. Cyr eyes that were so noticeably lacking in his new heir.

That same summer, when Sebastian was eleven, Hendon's countess sailed away for a day's pleasure cruise, never to return. *Lost at sea,* they'd said. Even at the time, Sebastian hadn't believed it. For months he'd climbed the cliffs overlooking the endless choppy waters of the Channel, convinced that if she were in truth dead, he'd somehow know it; he'd feel it.

Odd, he thought now as he pushed away from the churchyard's rusted railing and turned his feet toward the noisy, brightly lit hells off St. James's Street, how he could have been so right about that and so wrong about almost everything else.

⁂

Lying alone in her bed, Hero heard the wind begin to pick up just before midnight. Hot gusts billowed the curtains at her open window and filled the bedroom with the smell of dust and all the ripe odors of a city in summer. She listened to the charlie cry one o'clock, then two. And still she lay awake, listening to the wind and endlessly analyzing and reassessing all that she had learned so far of the grinding, inexorable sequence of shadowy, half-understood events and forces that had led to Gabrielle's death and the disappearance of her two little cousins. But as the hours dragged on, it gradually dawned on Hero that her sleeplessness had as much to do with the empty bed beside her as anything else.

It was a realization that both startled and chagrined her. Her motives for entering into this marriage had been complicated and confused and not entirely understood by anyone, least of all herself. She was not a woman much given to introspection or prolonged, agonized examination of her motives. She had always seen this characteristic as something admirable, something to be secretly proud of. Now she found herself wondering if perhaps in that she had erred. For who could be more foolish than a woman who doesn't know her own heart?

A loose shutter banged somewhere in the night for

what seemed like the thousandth time. Thrusting aside the covers with a soft exclamation of exasperation, she crossed the room to slam down the sash. Then she paused with one hand on the latch, her gaze on the elegant, solitary figure strolling down the street toward the house.

The night was dark, the wind having blown out most of the streetlights and both oil lamps mounted high on either side of the entrance. But Hero had no difficulty recognizing Devlin's long stride or the lean line of his body as he turned to mount the front steps.

She knew a wash of relief, although she had been unwilling to acknowledge until now the growing concern his long absence had aroused. Then her hand tightened on the drapery beside her.

They were strangers to each other in many ways, their marriage one born of necessity and characterized by wary distrust leavened by a powerful current of passion, a grudging respect, and a playful kind of rivalry. Yet she knew him well enough to recognize the brittle set of his shoulders and the glitteringly dangerous precision of each graceful movement.

Eleven months before, something had happened in Devlin's life, something that had driven him from his longtime mistress Kat Boleyn and created a bitter estrangement between the Viscount and his father, the Earl. She did not know precisely what had occurred; she knew only that whatever it was, it had plunged Devlin into a months-long brandy-soaked spiral of self-destruction from which he had only recently emerged.

But now, as she listened to his footsteps climb the stairs to the second floor and heard the distant click of his bedroom door closing quietly behind him, she knew a deep disquiet . . .

And an unexpected welling of an emotion so fierce that it caught her breath and left her wondrous and shaken and oddly, uncharacteristically frightened.

❦

Tuesday, 4 August

"My lord?"

Sebastian opened one eye, saw his valet's cheerful, fine-boned face, then squeezed the eye shut again when the room lurched unpleasantly. "Go away."

Jules Calhoun's voice sounded irritatingly hearty. "Sir Henry Lovejoy is here to see you, my lord."

"Tell him I'm not here. Tell him I'm dead. I don't care what the hell you tell him. Just go away."

There was a moment's pause. Then Calhoun said, "Unfortunately, Lady Devlin went out early this morning, so she is unable to receive the magistrate in your stead."

"Early, you say? Where has she gone?" He opened both eyes and sat up quickly—not a wise thing to do under the circumstances. *"Bloody hell,"* he yelped, bowing his head and pressing one splayed hand to his pounding forehead.

"She did not say. Here, my lord; drink this."

Sebastian felt a hot mug thrust into his free hand. "Not more of your damned milk thistle."

"There is nothing better to cleanse the liver, my lord."

"My liver is just fine," growled Sebastian, and heard the valet laugh.

Calhoun went to jerk back the drapes at the windows. "Shall I have Morey tell Sir Henry you'll join him in fifteen minutes?"

Sebastian swung his legs over the side of the bed and groaned again. "Make it twenty."

❦

Sebastian found the magistrate munching on a tray of cucumber and brown bread and butter sandwiches washed down with tea.

"Sir Henry," said Sebastian, entering the room with a quick step. "My apologies for keeping you waiting."

The magistrate surged to his feet and dabbed at his lips with a napkin. "Your majordomo has most kindly provided me with some much-needed sustenance. I've been up at Camlet Moat since dawn."

"Please, sit down," said Sebastian, going to sprawl in the chair opposite him. "Any sign yet of the missing children?"

"None, I'm afraid. And that's despite the hundreds of men now beating through the wood and surrounding countryside in search of them. Unfortunately, Miss Tennyson's brother has offered a reward for the children—he's even set up an office in the Fleet, staffed by a solicitor, to handle any information that may be received."

"Why do you say 'unfortunately'?"

"Because the result is likely to be chaos. I've seen it happen before. A child is lost; with the best of intentions, the grieving family offers a reward, and suddenly you have scores of wretched children—sometimes even hundreds—being offered to the authorities as the 'lost' child."

"Good God," said Sebastian. "Still, I can understand why he is doing it."

"I suppose so, yes." Lovejoy blew out a harsh breath. "Although I fear it is only a matter of time until their bodies are discovered. If the children had merely been frightened by what they saw and run off to hide, they would have been found by now."

"I suppose you must be right." Sebastian considered pouring himself a cup of tea, then decided against it.

What he needed was a tankard of good strong ale. "Still, it's strange that if they are dead, their bodies weren't found beside Miss Tennyson's."

"I fear there is much about this case that is strange. I've spoken to the rector at St. Martin's, who confirms that Miss Tennyson and the two children did indeed attend services this past Sunday, as usual. He even conversed with them for a few moments afterward—although not, unfortunately, about their plans for the afternoon."

"At least it helps to narrow the time of her death."

"Slightly, yes. We've also checked with the stages running between London and Enfield, and with the liveries in Enfield, but so far we've been unable to locate anyone who recalls seeing Miss Tennyson on Sunday."

"In other words, Miss Tennyson and the children must have driven out to Camlet Moat with her killer."

"So it appears. There is one disturbing piece of information that has come to light," said Lovejoy, helping himself to another sandwich triangle. "We've discovered that Miss Tennyson was actually seen up at the moat a week ago on Sunday in the company of the children and an unidentified gentleman."

"A gentleman? Not a driver?"

"Oh, most definitely a gentleman. I'm told he walked with a limp and had an accent that may have been French."

For a gentlewoman to drive in the country in the company of a gentleman hinted at a degree of friendship, of intimacy even, that was quite telling. For their drive to have taken Gabrielle Tennyson and her French friend to Camlet Moat seemed even more ominous. Sebastian said, "I've heard she had befriended a French prisoner of war on his parole."

"Have you? Good heavens; who is he?"

"I don't know. I've yet to find anyone who can give me a name."

Lovejoy swallowed the last of his sandwich and pushed to his feet. "If you should discover his identity, I would be most interested to know it. I've no need to tell you how this latest development is likely to be received. Sales of blunderbusses and pistols have already skyrocketed across the city, with women afraid to walk to market alone or allow their children to play outside. The Prime Minister's office is putting pressure on Bow Street to solve this, quickly. But if people learn a Frenchman was involved! Well, we'll likely have mass hysteria."

Sebastian rose with his friend, aware of a profound sense of unease. He knew from personal experience that whenever Downing Street or the Palace troubled itself with the course of a murder investigation, they tended to be more interested in quieting public hysteria than in seeing justice done. The result, all too often, was the sacrifice of a convenient scapegoat.

Eighteen months before, Sebastian had come perilously close to being such a scapegoat himself. And the man who had pushed for his quick and convenient death was his new father-in-law.

Charles, Lord Jarvis.

Chapter 17

*A*fter the magistrate's departure, Sebastian poured himself a tankard of ale and went to stand before the empty hearth, one boot resting on the cold fender.

He stood for a long time, running through all he knew about Gabrielle Tennyson's last days, and all he still needed to learn. Then he sent for his valet.

"My lord?" asked Calhoun, bowing gracefully.

To all appearances, Jules Calhoun was the perfect gentleman's gentleman, elegant and urbane and polished. But the truth was that the valet had begun life in one of the most notorious flash houses in London, a background that gave him some interesting skills and a plethora of useful contacts.

"Ever hear of a man named Jamie Knox?" Sebastian asked, drawing on his gloves. "He owns a tavern in Bishopsgate called the Black Devil."

"I have heard of him, my lord. But only by repute. It is my understanding he arrived in London some two or three years ago."

"See what else you can find out about him."

"Yes, my lord."

Sebastian settled his hat at a rakish angle and turned toward the door. Then he paused with one hand on the jamb to glance back and add, "This might be delicate, Calhoun."

The valet bowed again, his dark eyes bright with intelligence, his features flawlessly composed. "I shall be the soul of discretion, my lord."

Hero had begun the morning with a visit to the Adelphi Terrace.

She found Mr. Hildeyard Tennyson already out organizing the search for his missing cousins. But he had left clear instructions with his servants, and with the aid of a footman she spent several hours bundling up Gabrielle's research materials and notes. Having dispatched the boxes to Brook Street, she started to leave. Then she paused to turn and run up the stairs to her friend's bedroom.

She stood for a long moment in the center of the room, her hands clenched before her. She had called Gabrielle friend for six years. But although they had been close in many ways, Hero realized now just how compartmentalized their friendship had been. They had talked of history and art, of philosophy and poetry. Hero knew the pain Gabrielle had suffered at the early loss of her mother and her lingering grief over the brothers who died so young; she knew her friend's fondness for children. But she did not know Gabrielle's reason for turning away from marriage and any possibility of bearing children of her own.

It occurred to Hero that she had simply assumed her friend's reasons mirrored her own. But she knew that assumption was without basis. Gabrielle had challenged the typical role of women in their society by her own enthusiasm for scholarship and her determination to openly pursue her interests. Yet she had never been one to crusade for the kind of changes Hero championed.

When Hero spoke of a future when women would be allowed to attend Oxford or to sit in Parliament, Gabrielle would only smile and faintly shake her head, as if convinced these things would never be—and perhaps never should be.

She had certainly never spoken of her friendship with some mysterious French lieutenant. But then, Hero had never mentioned to Gabrielle her own strange, conflicted attraction to a certain dark-haired, amber-eyed viscount. And Hero found herself wondering now what Gabrielle had thought of her friend's sudden, seemingly inexplicable wedding. They'd never had the opportunity to discuss it.

There were so many things the two friends had needed to discuss—had intended to discuss that morning Hero was to drive up to Camlet Moat. Now Hero was left with only questions and an inescapable measure of guilt.

"What happened to you?" she said softly as she let her gaze drift around her friend's room to linger on the high tester bed and primrose coverlet, the mirrored dressing table and scattering of silver boxes and crystal vials. The chamber was, essentially, as Gabrielle had left it when she went off on Sunday, not knowing she would never return. Yet Hero could feel no lingering presence here, no whispered essence of the woman whose laughter and dreams and fears this place had once witnessed. There was only a profound, yawning stillness that brought a pricking to Hero's eyelids and swelled her throat.

Leaving the house, she directed her coachman to the Park Lane home of a certain member of Parliament from the Wolds of Lincolnshire. Only then, as her carriage rocked through the streets of London, did Hero lean back against the soft velvet squabs, and for the first time since she'd learned of Gabrielle's death, she allowed the tears to fall.

❧

A few carefully worded inquiries at the War Office, the Alien Office, and the Admiralty provided Sebastian with the information that there were literally thousands of paroled French and allied officers in Britain. Most captured enemy officers were scattered across the land in fifty so-called parole towns. But some were billeted in London itself.

Prisoners of war from the ranks were typically thrown into what were known as "the hulls." Rotting, demasted ships deemed too unseaworthy to set sail, the hulls were essentially floating prisons. By day, the men were organized into chained gangs and marched off to labor on the docks and in the surrounding area's workshops. At night they were locked fast in the airless, vermin-ridden, pestilence-infested darkness belowdecks. Their death rate was atrocious.

But the officers were traditionally treated differently. Being gentlemen, they were credited with possessing that most gentlemanly of characteristics: honor. Thus, a French officer could be allowed his freedom with only a few restrictions as long as he gave his word of honor as a gentleman—his parole—that he would not escape.

"That's the theory, at least," grumbled the plump, graying functionary with whom Sebastian spoke at the Admiralty. "Problem is, too many of these damned Frog officers are *not* gentlemen. They raise them up from the ranks, you see—which is why we've had over two hundred of the bastards run off just this year alone." He leaned forward as if to underscore his point. "No honor."

"Two hundred?"

"Two hundred and thirty-seven, to be precise. Nearly seven hundred in the past three years. These Frenchies may be officers, but too many of them are still scum. Vermin, swept up out of the gutters of Paris and lifted far above their proper station. That's what happens, you see, when civilization is turned upside down and those who were born to serve start thinking themselves as good as their betters." The very thought of this topsy-turvy world aroused such ire in the functionary's ample breast that he was practically spitting.

"Yet some of the best French officers have come up through the ranks," said Sebastian. "Joachim Murat, for example. And Michel Ney—"

"Pshaw." The functionary waved away these examples of ungentlemanly success with the dismissive flap of one pudgy hand. "It is obvious you know nothing of the Army, sir. Nothing!"

Sebastian laughed and started to turn away.

"You could try checking with Mr. Abel McPherson— he's the agent appointed by the Transport Board of the Admiralty to administer the paroled prisoners in the area."

"And where would I find him?" asked Sebastian, pausing to look back at the clerk.

"I believe he's in Norfolk at the moment. I've no doubt he left someone as his deputy, but I can't rightly tell you who."

"And who might have that information?"

"Sorry. Can't help you. But McPherson should be back in a fortnight."

※

Hero was received at the Mayflower house of the honorable Charles d'Eyncourt by the MP's married sister, a dour woman in her mid-thirties named Mary Bourne.

Mrs. Bourne had never met Hero and was all aflutter with the honor of a visit from Lord Jarvis's daughter. She received Hero in a stately drawing room hung with blond satin and crammed with an assortment of gilded crocodile-legged tables and colorful Chinese vases that would have delighted the Prince Regent himself. After begging "dear Lady Devlin" to please, pray be seated, she sent her servants flying for tea and cakes served on a silver tray so heavy the poor butler staggered beneath its weight. She then proceeded, seemingly without stopping for breath, to prattle endlessly about everything from her Bible study at the Savoy Chapel to her dear Mr. Bourne's concerns for her remaining in the metropolis with such a ruthless murderer on the loose, and followed that up with an endless description of a recent family wedding at which fandangos and the new waltz had been danced, and the carriages decked out in good white satin. "At a shilling a yard, no less!" she whispered, leaning forward confidingly. "No expense was spared, believe me, my dear Lady Devlin."

Smiling benignly, Hero sipped her tea and encouraged her hostess to prattle on. Mary Bourne bragged (in the most humble way possible, of course) about the morning and evening prayers that all servants in her own household at Dalby near Somersby were required to attend daily. She hinted (broadly) that she was the pseudonymous author of a popular denunciation of the modern interest in Druidism, and from there allowed herself to be led ever so subtly, ever so unsuspectingly, to the subject Hero had come to learn more about: the precise nature of the relationship between Charles d'Eyncourt and his brother, George Tennyson, the father of the two missing little boys.

※

Charles, Lord Jarvis lounged at his ease in a comfortable chair beside the empty hearth in his chambers in Carlton House. Moving deliberately, he withdrew an enameled gold snuffbox from his pocket and flicked it open with practiced grace. He lifted a delicate pinch between one thumb and forefinger and inhaled, his hard gaze never leaving the sweating pink and white face of the

stout man who stood opposite him. "Well?" demanded
Jarvis.

"This c-complicates things," stammered Bevin Childe.
"You must see that. It's not going to be easy to—"

"How you accomplish your task is not my problem.
You already know the consequences if you fail."

The antiquary's soft mouth sagged open, his eyes widening. Then he swallowed hard and gave a jerky, panicky
bow. "Yes, my lord," he said, and then jumped when Jarvis's clerk tapped discreetly on the door behind him.

"What is it?" demanded Jarvis.

"Colonel Urquhart to see you, my lord."

"Show him in," said Jarvis. He closed his snuffbox
with a snap, his gaze returning to the now-pale antiquary.
"Why are you still here? Get out of my sight."

Hat in hand, the antiquary backed out of the room as
if exiting from a royal presence. He was still backing
when Colonel Jasper Urquhart swept through the door
and sketched an elegant bow.

"You wished to see me, my lord?"

The Colonel was a tall man, as were all the former
military men in Jarvis's employ, tall and broad-
shouldered, with fair hair and pale gray eyes and a ruddy
complexion. A former rifleman, he had served Jarvis for
two years now. Until today, he hadn't disappointed.

"Yesterday," said Jarvis, pushing to his feet, "I asked
you to assign one of your best men to a certain task."

"Yes, my lord. I can explain."

Jarvis sniffed and tucked his snuffbox back into his
pocket. "Please don't. I trust the individual in question is
no longer in my employ?"

"Correct, my lord."

"You relieve me. See that his replacement does not
similarly disappoint."

The Colonel's thin nostrils quivered. "Yes, my lord."

"Good. That will be all."

Sebastian spent three frustrating hours prowling the rooming houses, taverns, and coffeehouses known to be frequented by officers on their parole. But the questions he asked were of necessity vague and the answers he received less than helpful. Without knowing the French lieutenant's name, how the devil was he to find one paroled French officer amongst so many?

He was standing beside the Serpentine and watching a drilling of the troops from the Hyde Park barracks when he noticed a young, painfully thin man limping toward him. A scruffy brown and black mutt with a white nose and chest padded contentedly at his heels, one ear up, the other folded half over as if in a state of perpetual astonishment. The man's coat was threadbare and his breeches mended, but his linen was white and clean, his worn-out boots polished to a careful luster, the set of his shoulders and upright carriage marking him unmistakably as a military man. His pallid complexion contrasted starkly with his brown hair and spoke of months of illness and convalescence.

He paused uncertainly some feet away, the dog drawing up beside him, pink tongue hanging out as it panted happily. "*Monsieur le vicomte?*" he asked.

"Yes." Sebastian turned slowly to face him. "And you, I take it, must be Miss Tennyson's mysterious unnamed French lieutenant?"

The man brought his heels together and swept an elegant bow. This particular French officer was, obviously, not one of those who had been raised through the ranks from the gutters of Paris. "I have a name," he said in very good English. "Lieutenant Philippe Arceneaux, of the Twenty-second Chasseurs à Cheval."

Chapter 18

"We met last May in the Reading Room of the British Museum," said Arceneaux as he and Sebastian walked along the placid waters of the Serpentine. The dog frisked happily ahead, nose to the ground, tail wagging. "She was having difficulty with the archaic Italian of a novella she was attempting to translate, and I offered to help."

"So you're a scholar."

"I was trained to be, yes. But France has little use for scholars these days. Only soldiers." He gazed out across the park's open fields, to where His Majesty's finest were drilling in the fierce sunshine. "One of the consolations of being a prisoner of war has been the opportunity to continue my studies."

"This novella you mentioned; what was it?"

"A now obscure elaboration of a part of the Arthurian legend called *La donna di Scalotta*."

"*The Lady of Shalott*," said Sebastian thoughtfully.

The Frenchman brought his gaze back to Sebastian's face. "You know it?" he said in surprise.

"I have heard of it, but that's about it."

"It's a tragic tale, of a beautiful maiden who dies for the love of a handsome knight."

"Sir Lancelot?"

"Yes."

"Convenient, isn't it, the way Camelot, Lancelot, and Shalott all happen to rhyme?"

Arceneaux laughed out loud. "Very convenient."

Sebastian said, "Were you in love with her?"

The laughter died on the Frenchman's lips as he lifted his shoulders in a shrug that could have meant anything, and looked away. It occurred to Sebastian, watching him, that the Lieutenant appeared young because he was— probably no more than twenty-four or -five, which would make him several years younger than Gabrielle.

"Well? Were you?"

They walked along in silence, the sun warm on their backs, the golden light of the afternoon drenching the green of the grass and trees around them. Just when Sebastian had decided the Frenchman wasn't going to answer, he said softly, "Of course I was. At least a little. Who wouldn't be? She was a very beautiful woman, brilliant and courageous and overflowing with a zest for life. While I—" His voice broke and he had to swallow hard before he could continue. "I have been very lonely, here in England."

"Was she in love with you?"

"Oh, no. There was nothing like that between us. We were friends—fellow scholars. Nothing more."

Sebastian studied the Frenchman's lean profile. He had softly curling brown hair and a sprinkling of cinnamon-colored freckles high across his cheeks that gave him something of the look of a schoolboy. At the moment, the freckles were underlaid by a faint, betraying flush.

"When did you last see her?" Sebastian asked.

"Wednesday evening, I believe it was. She used to bring her young cousins here, to the park, to sail their boats on the Serpentine. I would meet them sometimes. The boys liked to play with Chien."

Sebastian glanced over at the brown and black mongrel, now loping methodically from tree to tree in a good-natured effort to mark all of Hyde Park as his own personal territory. "Chien? That's his name?" "*Chien*" was simply the French word for "dog."

"I thought if I gave him a name, I might become too attached to him."

The dog came bounding back to the young lieutenant, tail wagging, brown eyes luminous with adoration, and the Lieutenant hunkered down to ruffle the fur around his neck. The dog licked his wrist and then trotted off again happily.

"Looks as if that's working out well," observed Sebastian.

Arceneaux laughed again and pushed to his feet. "He used to live in the wasteland near that new bridge they're building. I go there sometimes to sit at the end overlooking the river and watch the tide roll in and out. He would come sit beside me. And then one day just before curfew, when I got up to leave, he came too. Unfortunately, he has a sad taste for the low life—particularly Gypsies. And a shocking tendency to steal hams. George used to say I should have called him 'Rom,' because he is a Gypsy at heart."

The Lieutenant watched the dog roll in the grass near the water's edge and his features hardened into grim lines. After a moment, he said, "Do you think George and Alfred are dead too?"

"They may be. Or they could simply have been frightened by what happened to their cousin and run away to hide."

"But the authorities are looking for them, yes? And Gabrielle's brother has offered a reward. If that were true, why have they not been found?"

Sebastian could think of several explanations that made perfect sense, although he wasn't inclined to voice them. Small boys were a valuable commodity in England, frequently sold as climbing boys by the parish workhouses or even by their own impoverished parents. The chimney sweeps were in constant need of new boys, for the work was brutal and dangerous. Even boys who survived eventually outgrew the task. It wasn't unknown for small children to be snatched from their front gardens and sold to sweeps. Very few of those children ever made it home again.

But the chimney sweeps weren't the only ones who preyed on young children; girls and boys both were exploited for sexual purposes the very thought of which made Sebastian's stomach clench. He suspected the trade in children was a contributing factor to Tennyson's decision to ignore the concerns of the magistrates and post a reward for the boys' return. Then he noticed the way the Lieutenant's jaw had tightened, and he knew the Frenchman's thoughts were probably running in the same direction.

Sebastian breathed in the warm, stagnant aroma of the canal, the sunbaked earth, the sweet scent of the lilies blooming near the shadows of the trees. He said, "Did Miss Tennyson seem troubled in any way the last time you saw her?"

"Troubled? No."

"Would you by any chance know how she planned to spend this past Sunday afternoon?"

"Sorry, no."

Sebastian glanced over at him. "She didn't speak of it?"

"Not that I recall, no."

"Yet you did sometimes see her on Sundays, did you not?"

Arceneaux was silent for a moment, obviously considering his answer with care. He decided to go with honesty. "Sometimes, yes."

"Where would you go?"

A muscle worked along the Frenchman's jaw as he

stared out over the undulating parkland and shrugged. "Here and there."

"You went up to Camlet Moat a week ago last Sunday, didn't you?"

Arceneaux kept his face half averted, but Sebastian saw his throat work as he swallowed.

One of the conditions of a prisoner's parole was the requirement that he not withdraw beyond certain narrowly prescribed boundaries. By traveling up to Camlet Moat, the Frenchman had violated his parole. Sebastian wondered why he had taken such a risk. But he also understood how frustration could sometimes lead a man to do foolish things.

"I have no intention of reporting you to the Admiralty, if that's what you're worried about," said Sebastian.

"I didn't kill her," said Arceneaux suddenly, his voice rough with emotion. "You must believe me. I had no reason to kill any of them."

Some might consider unrequited love a very common motive for murder. But Sebastian kept that observation to himself. "Who do you think would have a reason to kill them?"

Arceneaux hesitated, the wind ruffling the soft brown curls around his face. He said, "How much do you know about Camlet Moat?"

"I know that Miss Tennyson believed it the lost location of Arthur's Camelot. Do you?"

"I will admit that when I first heard the suggestion, it seemed laughable. But in the end I found her arguments profoundly compelling. The thing is, you see, our image of Camelot has been molded by the writings of the troubadours. We picture it as a fairy-tale place—a grand medieval castle and great city of grace and beauty. But the real Camelot—if it existed at all—would have been far less grand and magnificent. There is no denying that Camlet Moat's name is indeed a recent corruption of

Camelot. And it is an ancient site with royal connections that remained important down through the ages."

"One wouldn't think so to look at the island today."

"That's because the medieval castle that once stood there was completely razed by the Earl of Essex in the fifteenth century, its stones and timbers sold to help finance repairs to the Earl's family seat at Hertford."

Sebastian frowned. "I thought the site belonged to the Crown."

"It has, off and on. But it was for several centuries in the possession of the descendants of Sir Geoffrey de Mandeville."

Every schoolboy in England was familiar with Sir Geoffrey de Mandeville, one of the most notorious of the robber barons spawned by the chaos of the twelfth century, when William the Conqueror's grandchildren Matilda and Stephen did their best to turn England into a wasteland in their battle for the throne. Accumulating a band of black knights, de Mandeville pillaged and looted from Cambridge to Ely to the Abbey of Ramsey; the treasure he amassed in the course of his bloody career—a king's ransom in gold and coins and precious gems—had reportedly never been found.

"There is a legend," said Arceneaux, "that de Mandeville buried his treasure at Camlet Moat. They say that when he was attained for high treason, he hid on the island in a hollow oak tree overhanging a well. The tree broke beneath his weight, and he fell into the well and drowned. Now his ghost haunts the island, guarding his treasure and reappearing to bring death to anyone who would dare lay hands upon it."

"Don't tell me you believe this nonsense?"

Arceneaux smiled. "No. But that doesn't mean that other people don't."

"Are you suggesting Gabrielle Tennyson might have been killed by a treasure hunter?"

"I know they had difficulty with someone digging at the site during the night and on Sundays too. The workmen would frequently arrive in the morning to find great gaping holes at various points around the island. She was particularly disturbed by some damage she discovered last week. She suspected the man behind it was Winthrop's own foreman—a big, redheaded rogue named Rory Forster. But she had no proof."

"She thought whoever was digging at the site was looking for Mandeville's treasure?"

The Frenchman nodded. "My fear is that if she and the lads did decide to go up there again last Sunday, they may have chanced upon someone looking for Mandeville's treasure. Someone who . . ." His voice trailed away, his features pinched tight with the pain of his thoughts.

"When you went with Miss Tennyson to the site, how did you get there?"

"But I didn't—" he began, only to have Sebastian cut him off.

"All right, let's put it this way: If you had visited the site last Sunday, how would you have traveled there?"

The Frenchman gave a wry grin. "In a hired gig. Why?"

"Because it's one of the more puzzling aspects of this murder—Bow Street has yet to discover how Miss Tennyson traveled up to the moat the day she was killed. You have no ideas?"

Arceneaux shook his head. "I assumed she must have gone there in the company of whoever killed her."

As she did with you, Sebastian thought. Aloud, he said, "I'm curious: Why bring this tale to me? Why not take what you know to Bow Street?"

A humorless smile twisted Arceneaux's lips. "Have you seen today's papers? They're suggesting Gabrielle and the boys were killed by a Frenchman. Just this morning, two of my fellow officers were attacked by a mob calling them child murderers. They might well have been killed if a troop of the Third Volunteers hadn't chanced to come along and rescue them."

They drew up at the gate, where Tom was waiting with the curricle. Sebastian said, "What makes you so certain I won't simply turn around and give your name to the authorities?"

"I am told you are a man of honor and justice."

"Who told you that?"

The Frenchman's cheeks hollowed and he looked away.

Sebastian said, "You took a risk, approaching me; why?"

Arceneaux brought his gaze back to Sebastian's face. He no longer looked like a young scholar but like a soldier who had fought and seen men die, and who had doubtless also killed. "Because I want whoever did this dead. It's as simple as that."

The two men's gazes met and held. They had served under different flags, perhaps even unknowingly faced each other on some field of battle. But they had more in common with each other than with those who had never held the bloodied, shattered bodies of their dying comrades in their arms, who had never felt the thrum of bloodlust coursing through their own veins, who had never known the fierce rush of bowel-loosening fear or the calm courage that can come from the simple, unshrugging acceptance of fate.

"The authorities will figure out who you are eventually," said Sebastian.

"Yes. But it won't matter if you catch the man who actually did kill them, first." The Frenchman bowed, one hand going to his hip as if to rest on the hilt of a sword that was no longer there. "My lord."

Sebastian stood beside his curricle and watched the Frenchman limp away toward the river, the scruffy brown and black dog trotting contentedly at his side.

Sebastian's first inclination was to dismiss the man's tale of ghosts, robber barons, and buried treasure as just so much nonsense. But he had a vague memory of Lovejoy saying something about a local legend linking some ancient Templar knight to the moat.

"Was that the Frog ye been lookin' for, gov'nor?" asked Tom.

Sebastian leapt up into the curricle's high seat. "He says he is."

"Ye don't believe 'im?"

"When it comes to murder, I'm not inclined to believe anyone." Sebastian gathered his reins, then paused to look over at his tiger. "Do you believe in ghosts, Tom?"

"Me? Get on wit ye, gov'nor." The boy showed a gap-toothed grin. "Ye sayin' that Frog is a ghost?"

"No. But I'm told some people do believe Camlet Moat is haunted."

"By the lady what got 'erself killed there?"

"By a twelfth-century black knight."

Tom was silent for a moment. Then he said, "Do you believe in ghosts, gov'nor?"

"No." Sebastian turned the chestnuts' heads toward the road north. "But I think it's time we took another look at Camelot."

Chapter 19

*A*listair St. Cyr, Earl of Hendon and Chancellor of the Exchequer, slammed his palm down on the pile of crude broadsheets on the table before him. "I don't like this. I don't like it at all. These bloody things are all over town. And I tell you, they're having more of an effect than one could ever have imagined. Why, just this morning I overheard two of my housemaids whispering about King Arthur. Housemaids! We've heard this nonsense before, about how the time has come for the 'once and future king' to return from the mists of bloody Avalon and save England from both Boney and the House of Hanover. But this is different. This is more than just a few yokels fantasizing over their pints down at the local. Someone is behind this, and if you ask me, it's Napoléon's agents."

Jarvis drew his snuffbox from his pocket and calmly flipped it open with one practiced finger. "Of course it's the work of Napoléon's agents."

Hendon looked at him from beneath heavy brows. "Do you know who they are?"

"I believe so." Jarvis lifted a pinch of snuff to one nostril and sniffed. "But at this point, it's more than a matter of simply closing down some basement printing press.

The damage has been done; this appeal to a messianic hero from our glorious past has resonated with the people and taken on a life of its own."

"How the bloody hell could something like this have aroused such a popular fervor?"

"I suppose one could with justification blame the success of the pulpit. When people fervently believe the Son of God will return someday to save them, it makes it easier to believe the same of King Arthur."

"That's blasphemy."

"I'm not talking about religion. I'm talking about credulity and habits of thought."

Hendon swung away to go stand beside the window and stare down at the Mall. "I'll confess that at first I found it difficult to credit that there are people alive today who could actually believe that Arthur will return, *literally*. I had supposed these pamphlets were simply tapping into the population's yearning for an Arthur-like figure to appear and save England. But an appalling number of people do seem to genuinely believe Arthur is out there right now on the Isle of Avalon, just waiting for the right moment to come back."

Jarvis raised another pinch of snuff and inhaled with a sniff. "I fear the concept of metaphor is rather above the capacity of the hoi polloi."

Hendon turned to look at him over one shoulder. "So what is to be done?"

Jarvis closed his snuffbox and tucked it away with a bland smile. "We're working on that."

꽃

Sebastian had expected to find the moat overrun with parties of searchers eager for the chance to collect the reward posted by Gabrielle Tennyson's brother. Instead, he reined in beneath the thick, leafy canopy at the top of

the ancient embankment to look out over an oddly deserted scene, the stagnant water disturbed only by a quick
splash and the disappearing ripples left in the wake of
some unseen creature. He could hear the searchers, but
only faintly, the thickness of the wood muffling the distant baying of hounds and the halloos of the men beating the surrounding countryside. Here, all was quiet in
the August heat.

"Gor," whispered Tom. "This place gives me the
goosies, it does."

"I thought you didn't believe in ghosts."

"This place could change a body's mind, it could."

Smiling, Sebastian handed his tiger the reins and
jumped down. "Walk them."

"Aye, gov'nor."

A distinct scuffing noise, as of a shovel biting dirt, carried on the breeze. Sebastian turned toward the sound.
The site was obviously not as deserted as it had first appeared.

The land bridge to the island lay on the eastern side
of the moat. He crossed it warily, one hand on the pistol
in his pocket. Sir Stanley had run his excavation trenches
at right angles on the far side of the bridge, where at one
time a drawbridge might have protected the approach to
the now vanished castle.

The rushing sound of cascading dirt cut through the
stillness, followed again by the scrape of a shovel biting
deep into loose earth. Sebastian could see him now, a
big, thickly muscled man with golden red hair worn
long, so that it framed his face like a lion's mane. He
had the sleeves of his smock rolled up to expose
bronzed, brawny arms, and rough trousers tucked into
boots planted wide as he worked shoveling dirt back
into the farthest trench.

He caught sight of Sebastian and paused, his chest

rising and falling with his hard breathing. He was a star-tlingly good-looking man, with even features and two dimples that slashed his cheeks when he squinted into the sun. He swiped the back of one sinewy arm across his sweaty face and his gaze locked with Sebastian's.

"You Rory Forster?" Sebastian asked.

The man slammed his shovel into the dirt pile and wrenched it sideways, sending a slide of dark loam over the edge into the trench. "I am."

"I take it Sir Stanley has decided to end the excavations?"

The man had a head built like a battering ram, with a thick neck and a high forehead, his eyes pale blue and thickly lashed and set wide apart. "'Pears that way, don't it?" he said without looking up again.

Sebastian let his gaze drift around the otherwise deserted site. "Where's the rest of your crew?"

"Sir Stanley told 'em they could go look fer them nippers."

"You're not interested in the reward?"

Rory Forster hawked up a mouthful of phlegm and spat. "'Tain't nobody gonna find them nippers."

"So certain?"

"Ye think they're out there, why ain't ye joinin' the search?"

"I am, in my own fashion."

Forster grunted and kept shoveling.

Sebastian wandered between the trenches, his gaze slowly discerning the uncovered remnants of massively thick foundations of what must once have been mighty walls. Pausing beside a mound of rubble, he found himself staring at a broken red tile decorated with a charging knight picked out in white.

He reached for the tile fragment, aware of Forster's eyes watching him. "Did you come out here this past Sunday?" asked Sebastian, straightening.

Forster went back to filling his trench. "We don't work on Sundays."

"No one stays to guard the site?"

"Why would they?"

"I heard rumors you've had trouble with treasure hunters."

Forster paused with his shovel idle in his hands. "I wouldn't know nothin' 'bout that."

Sebastian kept a wary eye on the man's shovel. "I've also heard you and Miss Tennyson didn't exactly get along."

"Who said that?"

"Does it matter?"

Forster set his jaw and put his back into his digging again, the dirt flying through the air. Sebastian breathed in the scent of damp earth and decay and a foul, dark smell that was like a breath from an old grave. He said, "I can understand how it might get under a man's skin, having to take orders from a woman."

Forster scraped the last of the dirt into the trench with the edge of his shovel, his attention seemingly all for his task. "I'm a good overseer, I am. Sir Stanley wouldn't have kept me on if'n I wasn't."

Sebastian watched Rory Forster move on to the next trench. The man's very name—Forster, a corruption of "forester"—harkened back to the days when this wood had been part of a vast royal hunting park. His ancestors would have been the kings' foresters, charged with husbanding the royal game and protecting them from the encroachments of poachers. But those days were long gone, lost in the misty past.

Sebastian said, "Did Miss Tennyson tell Sir Stanley she suspected you were the one vandalizing the site in search of treasure?"

Forster straightened slowly, the outer corner of one eye twitching as if with a tic, the rough cloth of his smock dark with sweat across his shoulders and chest and under his arms. "Ye ain't gonna pin this murder on me. Ye hear me?" he said, raising one beefy arm to stab a pointed finger at Sebastian. "I was home with me wife all that night. Never left the house, I didn't."

"Possibly," said Sebastian. "However, we don't know precisely when Miss Tennyson was murdered. She may well have met her death in the afternoon."

The twitch beside the man's eye intensified. "What ye want from me?"

"The truth."

"The truth?" Forster gave a harsh laugh. "Ye don't want the truth."

"Try me."

"Huh. Ye think I'm a fool?"

Sebastian studied the man's handsome, dirt-streaked face. "You can say what you have to say to me, in confidence. Or you can tell your tale to Bow Street. The choice is yours."

Forster licked his lower lip, then gave Sebastian a sly, sideways look. "Ye claim it was me what told ye, and I'll deny it."

"Fair enough. Now, tell me."

Forster sniffed. "To my way o' thinkin', them Bow Street magistrates ought to be lookin' into Sir Stanley's lady."

"You mean Lady Winthrop?"

"Aye. Come out here Saturday about noon, she did. In a real pelter."

Sebastian frowned. Lady Winthrop had told him she'd never visited her husband's controversial excavations. "Was Sir Stanley here?"

"Nah. He'd gone off by then. Somethin' about a prize mare what was near her time. But Miss Tennyson was still here. She's the one her ladyship come to see. A right royal row they had, and ye don't haveta take me word for it. Ask any o' the lads workin' the trenches that day; they'll tell ye."

"What was the argument about?"

"I couldn't catch the sense o' most o' it. Her ladyship asked to speak to Miss Tennyson in private and they walked off a ways, just there." Forster nodded toward the northeastern edge of the island, where a faint path could be seen winding through the thicket of bushes and brambles.

"But you did hear something," said Sebastian.

"Aye. Heard enough to know it was Sir Stanley they was fightin' about. And as she was leavin', I heard her ladyship say, 'Cross me, young woman, and ye'll be sorry!'"

Chapter 20

"You're certain you heard her right?" asked Sebastian.

The foreman sniffed. "Ye don't believe me, ask some of the lads what was here that day. Or better yet, ask her ladyship herself. But like I said, if ye let on 'twas me what told ye, I'll deny it. I'll deny it to yer face."

"Who are you afraid of?" asked Sebastian. "Sir Stanley? Or his wife?"

Forster huffed a scornful laugh. "Anybody ain't afraid of them two is a fool. Oh, they're grand and respectable, ain't they? Livin' in that big house and hobnobbin' wit' the King hisself. But I hear tell Sir Stanley, he started out as some clerk with little more'n a sixpence to scratch hisself with. How ye think he got all that money? Mmm? And how many bodies ye think he walked over to get it?"

"And Lady Winthrop?"

"She's worse'n him, any day o' the week. Sir Stanley, he'll leave ye alone as long as yer not standin' between him and somethin' he wants. But Lady Winthrop, she'd destroy a man out o' spite, just 'cause she's mean."

❧

Some twenty minutes later, Sebastian's knock at Trent House's massive doors was answered by a stately, ruddy-faced butler of ample proportions who bowed and intoned with sepulchral detachment, "I fear Sir Stanley is not at present at home, my lord."

"Actually, I'm here to see Lady Winthrop. And there's no point in telling me she's not at home either," said Sebastian cheerfully when the butler opened his mouth to do just that, "because I spotted her in the gardens when I drove up. And I'm perfectly willing to do something vulgar like cut around the outside of the house and accost her directly, if you're too timid to announce me."

The butler's nostrils quivered with righteous indignation. Then he bowed again and said, "This way, my lord."

Lady Winthrop stood at the edge of the far terrace, the remnants of last night's wind flapping the figured silks of her high-necked gown. She had been watching over the activities of the band of workmen tearing out the old wall of the terrace. But at Sebastian's approach she turned, one hand coming up to straighten her plain, broad-brimmed hat as she shot the butler a tight-jawed glare that warned of dire future consequences.

"Don't blame him," said Sebastian, intercepting the look. "He denied you with commendable aplomb. But short of bowling me over, there really was no stopping me."

She brought her icy gaze back to Sebastian's face and said evenly to the red-faced butler, "Thank you, Huckabee; that will be all."

The butler gave another of his flawless bows and withdrew.

"My husband is out with the men from the estate searching for the missing Tennyson children," she said, her fingers still gripping the brim of her hat. "He'll be sorry he missed you. And now you really must excuse me—"

"Why don't you show me your gardens, Lady Winthrop?" said Sebastian when she would have turned away. "No need to allow the interesting details of our conversation to distract these men from their work."

She froze, then forced a stiff laugh. "Of course. Since you are here."

She waited until they were out of earshot before saying evenly, "I resent the implication that I have something to hide from my servants."

"Don't you? You told me yesterday that you never visited the excavations at the moat. Except you did, just last Saturday. In fact, you had what's been described as a 'right royal row' with Miss Tennyson herself."

Lady Winthrop's lips tightened into a disdainful smile. "I fear you misunderstood me, Lord Devlin. I said I did not make it a practice of visiting the site; I did not say I had never done so."

Sebastian studied her proud, faintly contemptuous face, the weak chin pulled back against her neck in a scowl. As the plain but extraordinarily well-dowered only daughter of a wealthy merchant, she had married not once, but twice. Her first, brief marriage to a successful banker ended when her husband broke his neck on the hunting field and left his considerable holdings to her; her second marriage a few years later to Sir Stanley united two vast fortunes. But this second union, like her first, had remained childless, an economic merger without affection or shared interests or any real meeting of the minds.

It must be difficult, Sebastian thought, *to be a wealthy but plain, dull woman married to a handsome, virile, charismatic man.* And he understood then just how much this woman must have hated Gabrielle Tennyson, who was everything she, Lady Winthrop, was not: not only young and beautiful, but also brilliant and well educated and courageous enough to defy so many of the conventions that normally held her sisters in check.

He said, "And your argument?"

She drew her brows together in a pantomime of confusion. "Did we argue? Frankly, I don't recall it. Have you been speaking to some of the workmen? You know how these yokels exaggerate."

"Doing it a bit too brown, there, Lady Winthrop."

Angry color mottled her cheeks. "I take it that must be one of those vulgar cant expressions gentlemen are so fond of affecting these days. Personally I find the tendency to model one's speech on that of the lower orders beyond reprehensible."

Sebastian let out his breath in a huff of laughter. "So why did you visit Camlet Moat last Saturday?"

"Years before the light of our Lord was shown upon this land, England was given over to a terrible superstition dominated by a caste of evil men bound in an unholy pact with the forces of darkness."

"By which I take it you mean the Druids."

She inclined her head. "I do. Unfortunately, there are those in our age who in their folly have romanticized the benighted days of the past. Rather than seek salvation through our Lord and wisdom in his word, they choose to dabble in the rituals and tarnished traditions of the ignorant."

Sebastian stared off down the hill, to where a doe could be seen grazing beside a stretch of ornamental water. "I've heard that the locals consider the island to be a sacred site."

"They do. Which is why I chose to visit Camlet Moat last Saturday. My concern was that the recent focus of attention on the area might inspire the ignorant to hold some bizarre ritual on the island."

"Because Lammas began Saturday night at sunset?"

Again, the regal inclination of the head. "Precisely."

"So why approach Miss Tennyson? Why not Sir Stanley?"

"I fear I have not made myself clear. I went to the site in search of my husband. But when I found him absent, I thought to mention my concerns to Miss Tennyson."

The thin lips pinched into a tight downward curve. "Her response was predictably rude and arrogant."

Those were two words Sebastian had yet to hear applied to Miss Tennyson. But he had been told she didn't suffer fools lightly, and he suspected she might well have perceived Lady Winthrop as a very vain and foolish woman. He said, "She didn't think you had anything to worry about?"

"On the contrary. She said she believed the island was a profoundly spiritual place of ancient significance."

"Is that when you quarreled?"

She fixed him with an icy stare full of all the moral outrage of a woman long practiced in the art of self-deception, who had already comfortably convinced herself that the confrontation with Gabrielle had never occurred. "We did not quarrel," she said evenly.

There were any number of things he could have said. But none of them would have penetrated that shield of righteous indignation, so he simply bowed and took his leave.

He did not believe for a moment that she had overcome her distaste for her husband's excavations in order to drive out to the moat and have a conversation that could just as easily have been held over the breakfast table. Instead, she had deliberately chosen a time when she knew Sir Stanley to be elsewhere.

Jealousy could be a powerful motive for murder. He could imagine Lady Winthrop killing Gabrielle in a rage of jealousy and religious zeal. But he could not imagine her then murdering two children and disposing of their bodies somewhere in the wilds of the chase.

Yet as he drove away, he was aware of her standing at the edge of her garden watching him.

And he wondered why.

※

Sebastian was standing in the middle of his library and studying the new boxes of books and papers that had appeared since that morning when he heard the peal of the front bell. A moment later, Morey paused in the library's entrance to clear his throat.

"Yes?" prompted Sebastian when the majordomo seemed temporarily at a loss for words.

"A personage to see you, my lord."

"A personage?"

"Yes, my lord. I have taken the liberty of putting him in the drawing room."

Sebastian studied the majordomo's painfully wooden face. Morey normally left "personages" cooling their heels in the hall.

"I'll be right up," he said.

※

The man who stood before the empty fireplace was dressed all in black: black breeches, black coat, black waistcoat, black cravat. Only his shirt was white. He stood with his dark head tilted back as he stared up at the portrait of the Countess of Hendon that hung over the mantel. With the grace of a dancer or fencer, he pivoted slowly when Sebastian entered the room to pause just inside the doorway.

"So we meet," said Sebastian, and carefully closed the door behind him.

Chapter 21

$\mathcal{T}$he man called Jamie Knox was built tall and lean, taller even than Sebastian, with wavy, almost black hair and the yellow eyes of a wolf or feral cat.

Sebastian had been told once that he had his father's eyes—his *real* father's eyes. But he'd always thought he looked like his mother. Now, as he stared at the face of the man who stood across the room from him, he wondered if it was his imagination that traced a resemblance in the tavern owner's high-boned cheeks and gently curving mouth.

Then he remembered Morey's strange reaction and knew it was not his imagination.

He crossed to where a decanter and glasses rested on a side table. "May I offer you a brandy?"

"Yes, thank you."

The inflections were similar to that of the curly-headed man of the night before. The accent was not that of a gentleman.

"Where are you from?" asked Sebastian, splashing brandy into two glasses.

"Shropshire, by way of a rifle regiment."

"You're a rifleman?"

"I was."

Sebastian held out one of the glasses. After the briefest of hesitations, the man took it.

"I fought beside riflemen in Italy and the Peninsula," said Sebastian. "I've often thought it will be Napoléon's insistence on arming his men with only muskets that will ultimately cause his downfall."

"You may be right. Only, don't go telling the French bugger himself, hmm?" Knox took a deep drink of his brandy, his intense yellow gaze never leaving Sebastian's face. "You don't look much like your da, the Earl, do you?"

"I'm told I resemble my mother."

Jamie Knox jerked his chin toward the portrait over the mantel. "That her?"

"Yes."

He took another sip. "I never knew my father. My mother said he was a cavalry captain. Your father ever in the cavalry?"

"Not to my knowledge."

A faint gleam of amusement lit up the other man's eyes. He drained his brandy with the offhand carelessness of a man well accustomed to hard drinking, then shook his head when Sebastian offered him another.

"You came around asking about my conversation with Gabrielle Tennyson last week."

"So you don't deny the confrontation occurred."

"Why should I? She heard I'd uncovered one of those old picture pavements in my cellars, and she kept pestering me to let her take a look at it."

"You mean, a Roman mosaic?"

"That's it. Picture of a naked fat man holding a bunch of grapes in one hand and riding a dolphin."

"You expect me to believe you threatened a woman over a mosaic?"

Knox's lips curved into a smile, but the glitter in his eyes had become hard and dangerous. He looked to be a few years older than Sebastian, perhaps as much as thirty-three or -four. "I didn't threaten to kill her. I just told her she'd be sorry if she didn't back off. Last thing I need is some bloody bluestocking sniffing around the place. Not good for business."

"Especially if she's sniffing around your cellars."

Knox laughed. "Something like that, yes."

The rifleman let his gaze drift around Sebastian's drawing room, the amusement slowly dying out of his expression. By Mayfair's standards, the Brook Street house was not large; the furnishings were elegant but neither lavish nor opulent. Yet as Sebastian watched Knox's assessing eyes take in the room's satin hangings, the delicate cane chairs near the bow window overlooking the street, the gently faded carpet, the white Carrara marble of the mantelpiece, he had no doubt that the room must appear quite differently to a rifleman from the wilds of Shropshire than it did to Sebastian, who was raised in the sprawling splendor of Hendon House in Grosvenor Square and the halls and manors of the Earl's various estates across Britain.

"Nice place you got here," said Knox, his accent unusually pronounced.

"Thank you."

"I hear you got married just last week."

"I did, yes."

"Married the daughter of Lord Jarvis himself."

"Yes."

The two men's gazes met, and held.

"Congratulations," said Knox. Setting aside his empty glass, he reached for the black hat he had rested on a nearby table and settled it on his head at a rakish angle. Then he gave a faintly mocking bow. "My lord."

Sebastian stood at the bowed front windows of his drawing room and watched Jamie Knox descend the front steps and stroll off down the street. It was like watching a shadowy doppelganger of himself.

Or a brother.

☘

Sebastian was still standing at the window some moments later when a familiar yellow-bodied carriage drew up. He watched Hero descend the coach steps with her usual grace and then enter the house.

She came into the room pulling off a pair of soft yellow kid gloves that she tossed on one of the cane chairs. "Ah, good," she said. "You're finally up."

"I do generally try to make it out of bed before nightfall," he said.

He was rewarded with a soft huff of laughter.

Today she wore an elegant carriage gown of emerald satin trimmed with rows of pintucks down the skirt and a spray of delicate yellow roses embroidered on each sleeve. She yanked at the emerald ribbons that tied her velvet hat beneath her chin and tossed the hat onto the chair with her gloves. "I've just come from an interesting conversation with Mary Bourne."

"Who?"

"Mrs. Bourne. She's sister to both Charles Tennyson d'Eyncourt and the Reverend Tennyson, the father of the two missing boys."

Sebastian frowned. He had a vague recollection of d'Eyncourt mentioning a sister staying with him. "Is she like her brother d'Eyncourt?"

"Oh, no; she's far worse. She's a saint, you know."

Sebastian laughed out loud.

"No, it's true; I mean that quite literally. She's a Calvinist. You can have no notion of the misery it brings her, knowing that she alone can look forward to the joys awaiting her in heaven whilst the vast majority of her family is doomed to suffer the everlasting torments of hell."

"She actually told you that?"

"She did. Personally, I suspect she derives enormous satisfaction from the comfortable conviction that she is one of the chosen elite while everyone around her is doomed to burn. But then, self-perception is not one of her strong suits."

Sebastian leaned back against the windowsill, his arms crossed at his chest, his gaze on his wife's face. Her eyes were sparkling and a faint flush rode high on her cheekbones. He found himself smiling. "So why did you go see her? Or were you looking for d'Eyncourt?"

"No. I knew d'Eyncourt would be at Westminster. I wanted to talk to Mary Bourne alone. You see, I've been puzzled by the arithmetic." Hero sank into one of the chairs beside the empty hearth. "D'Eyncourt told you he is his father's heir, right? Except, d'Eyncourt is only twenty-eight, while little George Tennyson—the elder of the missing boys—is nine years old. That means that if d'Eyncourt's brother were indeed a younger son, he would need to have sired his own son at the tender age of seventeen. Obviously possible, but unlikely, given that he is in holy orders."

"So what did you discover?"

"That the boys' father is actually thirty-four years old."

Sebastian pushed away from the window. "You're certain?"

"Are you suggesting the woman might have mistaken the ages of her own brothers? D'Eyncourt is the baby of the family. He's younger than his brother by a full six years."

⁂

The bells of the abbey were tolling seven when d'Eyncourt emerged from Westminster Hall and turned toward Parliament Street. The setting sun soaked the ancient buildings with a rich tea-colored light and cast long shadows across the paving.

Sebastian fell into step beside him.

The MP cast a quick look at Sebastian, then glanced away without slackening his pace. There was neither surprise nor puzzlement on his smoothly handsome features. "I've just received a note from my sister Mary, telling me she enjoyed a visit from Lady Devlin this afternoon. My sister is an earnest but guileless woman. As such she is frequently slow to see the subterfuge in others. It wasn't until some time after Lady Devlin's departure that my sister began to ponder the direction their conversation had taken."

Sebastian showed his teeth in a smile. "Ah, yes; Lady Devlin is quite practiced in the arts of guile and subterfuge, is she not?"

D'Eyncourt pressed his lips together and kept walking.

Sebastian said, "And once Mrs. Bourne realized the indiscretions of her talkative tongue, she immediately sat down and dashed off a note to her baby brother warning him— What, exactly? That you were about to be caught out in a very telling lie?"

D'Eyncourt drew up at the edge of the Privy Gardens and turned to face him, a slim, elegant man with a smug air of self-assurance. "I never claimed to be my father's firstborn. I simply told you that I am his heir. And that is the truth."

"His only heir?"

"Yes."

"How can that be?"

D'Eyncourt's thin nostrils quivered with indignation. "That is none of your affair."

Sebastian advanced on him, backing the dandified parliamentarian up until his shoulders slammed against the rough stone wall behind him. "Gabrielle Tennyson's death made it my affair, you god damned, pompous, self-congratulatory son of a bitch. A woman is dead and two innocent little boys are missing. If you know anything—*anything*—that can help make sense of what has happened to them—"

"I am not afraid of you," said d'Eyncourt, his Adam's apple bobbing up and down as he swallowed.

"You should be."

"You can't accost me in the streets! What are you imagining? That those two children stand between me and my father's wealth? Well, you are wrong. My father disinherited my older brother and made me his sole heir when I was six years old. Why else do you suppose my brother took holy orders and now serves as a rector? Because that is his future! Everything my father owns—the estates, the investments—all will in due time pass to me."

"I can think of only one reason for a man to disinherit his twelve-year-old son and make his youngest child his sole heir."

Two bright spots of color appeared on d'Eyncourt's cheeks. "If you are suggesting that my brother was disinherited because he is ... because he is *not* my brother, then let me tell you right now that you are sadly mistaken. My brother was disinherited because by the time he reached the beginnings of puberty it had become obvious to our father that his health and temperament were totally unsuited for the position which would be required of him."

"But not unsuited to his becoming a rector?"

D'Eyncourt stared back at him. "The requirements of the two callings are utterly dissimilar."

"So tell me," said Sebastian, "how has your brother adjusted to having a fortune of some half a million pounds wrested from his grasp?"

"He was, naturally, somewhat aggrieved—"

"Aggrieved?"

"Aggrieved. But he has with time grown more accustomed to his situation."

"As an impoverished rector at Somersby?"

"Just so."

Sebastian took a step back.

D'Eyncourt made a show of adjusting his cravat and straightening the set of his coat. "I can understand how it might be difficult for someone of your background to understand, but you must remember that my family's wealth—while substantial—is only recently acquired. Hence the rules of primogeniture do not apply. My father is free to leave his property as he sees fit."

"True," said Sebastian. "But it occurs to me that if your father could change his will once, he is obviously free to do so again—in favor of his two grandsons, this time."

D'Eyncourt stiffened. "If you mean to suggest—"

"The suggestion is there, whether it is put into words or not," said Sebastian, and turned away.

❧

Sebastian arrived back at Brook Street to be told that Lady Devlin had already departed for a musical evening in the company of her mother, Lady Jarvis.

"However," said Morey, bowing slightly, "I believe Calhoun has been most particular to have a word with you."

"Has he? Then send him up," said Sebastian, heading for the stairs.

"Well?" asked Sebastian when Calhoun slipped into the dressing room a few minutes later. "Find anything?"

"Not as much as I had hoped, my lord," said Calhoun, going to lay out Sebastian's evening dress. "From what I have been able to ascertain, Mr. Knox arrived in London just three years ago. He used to be with the 145th Rifles but was discharged when his unit was reduced after Corunna."

"So he actually was a rifleman."

"He was, my lord. In fact, he's famous for having killed some bigwig Frenchy by shooting the man off his horse at some seven hundred yards. And I'm told he can shoot the head off a running rabbit at more than three hundred yards." Calhoun paused a moment, then added, "In the dark."

Sebastian looked up from unbuttoning his shirt. "How did he end up in possession of the Black Devil?"

"Reports differ. Some say he took to the High Toby for a time before he either won the tavern at the roll of the dice or killed the previous owner." "Taking to the High Toby" was slang for becoming a highwayman. "Or perhaps both."

"He seems very sensitive about his cellars."

"That's not surprising, given the nature of some of his associates."

"Oh? And who might they be?"

"The name that came up most frequently was Yates. Russell Yates."

Chapter 22

Sebastian waited beyond the light cast by the flickering oil lamp at the head of the lane. The theater was still closed for the summer, but rehearsals for the upcoming season were already under way. The dark street rang with the laughter of the departing troupe.

He kept his gaze on the stage door.

The night was warm, the wind a soft caress scented by oranges and a thousand bittersweet memories. He heard the stage door open, watched a woman and two men walk toward the street. The woman paused for a moment beneath the streetlight, caught up in conversation with her fellow players. The dancing flame from the oil lamp glinted on the auburn highlights in her thick, dark hair and flickered seductively over the familiar, beloved planes of her face. She had her head thrown back, lost in laughter at one of her friends' remarks. Then she stilled suddenly, her head turning, her eyes widening in a useless attempt to probe the darkness. And Sebastian knew she had sensed his presence and that the bond between them that had existed all these years, while weakened, had not broken.

Her name was Kat Boleyn, and she was the most celebrated actress of the London stage. Once, she had been the love of Sebastian's life. Once, he had thought to grow old with her at his side, and to hell with the shocked mutterings of society and the outraged opposition of his father—*of the Earl of Hendon,* he reminded himself. Then an ugly tangle of lies and an even uglier truth had intervened. Now Kat was married to a flamboyant ex-privateer named Russell Yates, a man with a secret, forbidden passion for his own gender and shadowy ties to the smugglers and agents who plied the channel between England and Napoléon's France.

Sebastian watched her say good night to her friends and walk up to him. She wore an ivory silk cloak thrown over her shoulders, the hood thrust back in a way that framed her face. He said, "You shouldn't walk alone at night."

"Because of these latest murders, you mean?" She turned to stroll beside him up Hart Street. The pavement was crowded with richly harnessed horses and elegant carriages, their swaying lamps filling the air with the scent of hot oil. "Gibson tells me you have involved yourself in the investigation." He watched her eyebrows pinch together in a worried frown as she said it, for she knew him well. She knew the price he paid with each descent into the dark world of fear and hatred, greed and despair, that inevitably swirled around a murder. Yet even though she knew, intellectually, what drove him to it, she could never quite understand his need to do what he did.

He said, "Don't worry about me."

A smile lit her eyes. "Yet you are free to worry about me?" The smile faded as she paused to turn toward him, her gaze searching. She had deeply set eyes, thickly lashed and of a uniquely intense blue that she had inherited from her natural father, the Earl of Hendon. And every time he looked into them, he knew a searing pain that was like a dagger thrust to the heart.

She said, "You're not here for the sake of auld lang syne, Sebastian; what is it?"

"I'm told Yates has dealings with a tavern owner named Jamie Knox."

She sucked in a quick breath that jerked her chest. It was an unusual betrayal for an actress who could normally control her every look, every tone, her every word and movement.

He said, "Obviously, you know Knox as well. What can you tell me about him?"

"Very little, actually. He is an intensely private person, cold and dangerous. Most people who know him are afraid of him. It's an aura he cultivates."

"You met him through Yates?"

"Yes." She hesitated, then asked, "He is involved in this murder? How?"

"He was seen arguing with Gabrielle Tennyson several days before she was killed. He claims it was over a Roman mosaic."

"You don't believe him?"

"No. But I don't understand how he fits into anything else I've learned, either."

"I'll see what I can find out." The door to a tavern near the corner opened, spilling light and voices and laughter into the street. "Has Knox seen you?"

"Why do you ask?"

Her gaze met his. "You know why."

They had reached the arch where her carriage awaited. Sebastian said, "A few weeks ago, I met a man in Chelsea who told me I reminded him of a highwayman who'd once held up his carriage on Hounslow Heath."

"You believe that was Knox?"

"I'm told he took to the High Toby for a time after he left the Rifles. I wouldn't want to think there are *three* of us walking around."

He said it lightly, but his words drew no answering smile from her. She said, "I know you've had men on the Continent, searching for your mother. Have they found her?"

"No."

"You can't simply ... let it go, Sebastian?"

He searched her pale, beloved face. "All those years when you didn't know the identity of your father, if you thought you had the truth within reach, could you have ... let it go?"

"Yes." She did smile then, a sweet, sad smile. "But then, my demons are different from yours." Reaching up on tiptoe, she brushed her lips against his cheek, then turned away. "Good night, Sebastian. Keep yourself safe."

He walked down increasingly empty streets. The sky above was dark and starless, the air close; the oil lamps mounted high on the dark, looming walls of the tightly packed, grimy brick houses and shops flickered with his passing. At one point he was aware of two men falling into step behind him. He tightened his grip on the walking stick he carried tucked beneath one arm. But they melted away down a noisome side alley, their footfalls echoing softly into the night.

He walked on, rounding the corner toward Long Street. He could hear the thin, reedy wail of a babe somewhere in the distance, the jingle of an off-tune piano, the rattle of carriage wheels passing in the next block. And from the murky shadows of a narrow passageway up ahead came a soft whisper.

"C'est lui."

He drew up just as the same two men burst from the passage and fanned out to take up positions, one in front of him, the other to his rear. Whirling, Sebastian saw the glint of a knife in the hand of one; the other, a big, fair-haired man in dark trousers and high leather boots, carried a cudgel he slapped tauntingly against his left palm.

"Watch!" shouted Sebastian as the man raised the club over his head. "Watch, I say!"

Before the man could bring the club down, Sebastian rushed him, the walking stick whistling through the air toward the assailant's head. The man threw up his left arm, blocking Sebastian's blow at the last instant. The impact shattered the ebony shaft of the walking stick, shearing it off some eight inches from Sebastian's fist. But the shock of the unexpected counterattack was enough to send the man staggering back. He lost his footing and went down.

His companion growled, *"Bâtard!"*

"Watch!" shouted Sebastian again, swinging around just as the second man—smaller, leaner, darker than his companion—lunged, his knife held in an underhanded grip.

Sebastian tried to parry the man's thrust with the broken shaft of the walking stick and felt the blade slip off the wood to slice along his forearm. Then the man on the ground closed his hands around Sebastian's ankle and yanked.

Lurching backward, Sebastian stumbled over the fallen man and went down, bruising his hip on a loose cobblestone as he rolled. Swearing long and hard, he grabbed the cobblestone as he surged up onto his knees.

The man with the cudgel took a swipe. Sebastian ducked, then came up to smash the stone into the side of his attacker's head with a bone crushing *twunk*. The man reeled back, eyes rolling up, the side of his face a sheet of gore. Panting hard, Sebastian reached into his boot and yanked his own dagger from its hidden sheath.

The knife clenched in one hand, the bloody rock still gripped in the other, he rose into a low crouch. "Come on, you bastard," he spat, his gaze locking with that of his remaining assailant.

The man was clean-shaven and relatively young, no more than thirty, his coat worn but clean, his cravat simply but neatly tied. He licked his lower lip, his gaze flicking from Sebastian to the still figure lying between them in a spreading pool of blood.

His nostrils flared on a quickly indrawn breath.

"Well?" said Sebastian.

The man turned and ran.

Sebastian slumped back against the brick wall, his injured arm cradled against his chest, his blood thrumming in his ears, his gaze on the dead man beside him.

Chapter 23

"*G*hastly," said Sir Henry Lovejoy, peering down at the gory head of the dead man sprawled on the pavement at their feet. The watch had arrived, panting, only moments after the attack on the Viscount, who sent the man running to Bow Street, just blocks away. Now Sir Henry shifted his glance to Lord Devlin. "Who is he? Do you know?"

"Never saw him before," said Devlin, stripping off his cravat to wind around his bleeding arm.

"And his companion who fled?"

"Was also unfamiliar to me."

Lovejoy forced himself to look more closely at the dead man. "I suppose they could have been common footpads after your pocketbook."

"They could have been."

"But you don't think so. I must confess, he does not exactly have the look of a footpad."

"He's also French."

"French? Oh, dear; I don't like the sound of that. Do you think there could be some connection between this incident and the Tennyson murders?"

"If there is, I'll be damned if I can see it." Devlin looked up from wrapping his arm. "Have you found the children's bodies, then?"

"What? Oh, no. Not yet. But with each passing day, it becomes increasingly difficult to believe that they could still be alive." Lovejoy nodded to the men from the dead house who had arrived with a shell, then stood watching them shift the body. "We've begun to look into the backgrounds of the various men involved in the excavations up at the moat. Some disturbing things are coming to light about this man Rory Forster."

Devlin finished tying off the ends of his makeshift bandage. "Such as?"

"He's said to have quite a temper, for one thing. And he's not above using his fists on women."

"That doesn't surprise me."

"Of course, his wife backs up his claim that he was home with her Sunday afternoon and evening. But I wouldn't put it beyond him to bully her into saying it. The problem is, I don't see how he could possibly be the killer."

Devlin flexed the hand of his injured arm, testing it. "Why's that?"

"Because if he is, how did the Tennysons get up to the moat in the first place? The logical conclusion is they could only have driven up there in the company of their murderer."

"The same could be said of Sir Stanley Winthrop. If he is the killer, then how the devil did the Tennysons get to Enfield?"

Lovejoy cleared his throat. "My colleagues at Bow Street are of the opinion that it is ridiculous even to suggest that Sir Stanley might be involved in any way."

Devlin laughed. "There's no doubt it would negatively impact the nation's war effort, to have one of the King's leading bankers arrested for murder."

Lovejoy studied the blood seeping through the Viscount's makeshift bandage. "Don't you think you should perhaps have that properly attended to, my lord?"

Devlin glanced down and frowned. "I suppose you're right. Although I fear the coat is beyond help."

🌿

"You're certain you heard them speaking French?" asked Paul Gibson, his attention all for the row of stitches he was laying along the gash in Sebastian's arm.

"I'm certain." Sebastian sat on a table in the front room of Gibson's surgery. He was stripped to the waist, a basin of bloody water and cloths set nearby.

Gibson tied off his stitches and straightened. "I suppose it could have been a ruse to mislead you."

"Somehow I don't think the intent was to allow me to live long enough to be misled. I suspect my questions are making someone nervous."

Gibson reached for a roll of bandages. "Someone French, obviously."

"Or someone involved with the French."

"There is that."

"Of course," said Sebastian, watching his friend work, "just because my questions are making someone nervous doesn't necessarily mean that particular someone is the killer. He could simply have something to hide."

"Yet it does tell you this 'someone' isn't afraid to kill to keep his secrets."

"Powerful men usually do have a lot of secrets . . . and there are several powerful men whose names seem to keep coming up in this."

Gibson tied off the bandage and frowned. "Who else besides d'Eyncourt and Sir Stanley?"

Lord Jarvis, Sebastian thought, although he didn't say it. He slipped off the table and reached for his shirt. "Isn't that enough?" He pulled the shirt on over his head. "Have you finished the autopsy of Miss Tennyson's body?"

"I have. But I'm afraid there's not much more I can tell you. She was stabbed through the heart sometime Sunday.

No other sign of injury. Whoever killed her made no attempt to force himself on her."

"Well, at least the poor woman didn't need to suffer that."

Gibson scratched behind his ear. "There is one thing I noticed that may or may not prove relevant."

Something in his voice caused Sebastian to look up from buttoning his shirt. "Oh? What's that?"

"I said she wasn't forced before her death. But then, neither was she a maiden."

❧

Sebastian expected Hero to have long since retired for the night. Instead, she was sitting cross-legged on the library floor surrounded by a jumbled sea of books and papers. She had her head bent over some manuscript pages; a smudge of ink showed along the edge of her chin, and she was so intent on what she was doing that he suspected she hadn't even heard him come in.

"I thought you had planned a musical evening with your mother," he said, pausing in the doorway.

She looked up, the brace of candles burning on a nearby table throwing a soft golden light over her profile and shoulders. "That finished hours ago. I decided I might as well get started looking at Gabrielle's research materials. I can't help but think that the key to what happened to her and the boys is here somewhere." Her eyes narrowed at the sight of his arm reposing in a sling. "You're hurt."

"Nothing serious. Two men jumped me in Covent Garden and tried to kill me."

"And you consider that not serious?"

He went to sprawl in a chair beside the empty hearth. "The attempt to kill me was definitely serious. The wound to my arm is not."

"Who were they?"

"I don't know for certain about the one I killed, but the one who got away was swearing at me in French."

She was silent for a moment, lost in thoughts he could only guess at. She was far too good at hiding away bits of herself. Then she pushed up from the floor and went to pour a glass of brandy that she held out to him, her gaze on his face. "There's something else that you're not telling me," she said. "What is it?"

He took the brandy. "Am I so transparent?"

"At times."

She sank into the chair opposite and looked at him expectantly. He was aware of the lateness of the hour, of the quiet darkness of the house around them, and of the absurd hesitation he felt in speaking to his own wife about the sexuality of her dead friend.

"Well?" she prompted.

"Paul Gibson finished the postmortem of Miss Tennyson's body. He says she was not a virgin."

He watched her lips part, her chest rise on a sudden intake of breath. He said, "You didn't know?"

"No. But then, we never discussed such things."

"Yet the knowledge still surprises you."

"It does, yes. She was so determined never to marry."

"She may have been involved in a youthful passion long forgotten."

Hero tipped her head to one side, her gaze on his face. "Are such youthful passions ever forgotten?"

"Perhaps not."

She rose to her feet, and for a moment he thought he caught a glimpse of the soft swelling of her belly beneath the fine muslin of her gown. Then he realized it was probably an illusion, a trick of the light or the drift of his own thoughts. For it was the child growing in her belly—conceived in a moment of fear and weakness when together they had faced what they'd thought was certain death—that had brought them here, to this moment, as husband and wife.

She went to pick up the papers she'd been reading, including a notebook whose pages showed signs of much crossing and reworking. He said, "What is that?"

"Gabrielle's translation of *The Lady of Shalott*."

"Ah. I've discovered the identity of the Frenchman she befriended, by the way. He's a cavalry officer named Philippe Arceneaux."

She looked around at him. "You found him?"

"I'd like to take credit for it, but the truth is, he found me. He says they met in the Reading Room of the British Museum. He was helping her with the translation."

Hero stood very still, the notebook in her hand forgotten. "Do you think he could have been her lover?"

"He says no. But he admits he was at least half in love with her. He seems to have made a practice of timing his walks in the park to coincide with when she took the boys to sail their boats on the Serpentine. And a week ago last Sunday, he drove up to Camlet Moat with her to see the site—although he'll never admit it since it was a flagrant violation of his parole."

She fell silent, her gaze fixed on something far, far away.

"What is it?" he asked, watching her.

She shook her head. "I was just thinking about something Gabrielle told me once, perhaps a month or more ago."

"What's that?"

"She asked if I ever had the sense that I was missing something—something important in life—by choosing to devote myself to research and writing, rather than marrying. She said lately she'd begun to feel as if she were simply watching life, rather than actually living it. She said it was as if she spent her days staring at the pale shadows of other people's lives reflected in a mirror— entertaining at first, perhaps, but ultimately empty and unsatisfying. And then she said . . ."

"Yes?"

"She said, 'Lately, I find I've grown half sick of shadows.'"

Her gaze met his. He was aware, again, of the stillness of the night around them. And he found himself thinking of the exquisite softness of her skin, the silken caress of her heavy dark hair sliding across his belly, the way her eyes widened in wonder and delight when he entered her. He gazed deep into her wide, dark eyes, saw her lips part, and knew her thoughts mirrored his own.

Yet the latent distrust that had always been there between them now loomed infinitely larger, fed by the unknown currents swirling around Gabrielle Tennyson's death and the lingering poisons of Jarvis's unabated malevolence and Sebastian's own tangled, sordid past. They had come to this marriage as two wary strangers united only by the child they had made and the passion they had finally admitted they shared. Now it seemed they were losing even that. Except . . .

Except that wasn't quite right, either. The passion was still there. It was their ability to surrender to it that was slipping away.

He said, his voice oddly husky, "And what did you tell her, when Gabrielle asked if you ever had the sense you were missing something in life?"

A ghost of a smile touched her lips. "I lied. I said no."

He thought for one aching moment that she would come to him. Then she said, "Good night, Devlin," and turned away.

❧

The next morning, a constable from Bow Street arrived to tell Sebastian that one of his Covent Garden attackers had been identified. The dead man's name was Gaston Colbert, and he was a French prisoner of war free on his parole.

Chapter 24

Jarvis was at his breakfast table when he heard the distant peal of the bell. A moment later, Hero entered the room wearing a shako-styled hat and a walking dress of Prussian blue fashioned à la hussar with epaulettes and double rows of brass buttons up the bodice. She yanked off her gloves as she walked.

"Good morning," Jarvis said, calmly cutting a piece of steak. "You're looking decidedly martial today."

She came to flatten her palms on the table and lean into them, her gaze hard on his face. "Last night, two men tried to kill Devlin. Do you know anything about that?"

He laid his knife along the top edge of his plate. "It is my understanding that the assailant whom Devlin dispatched with his typically lethal efficiency was a French officer on his parole. What makes you think the incident has anything to do with me?"

"Because I know you."

Jarvis took a bite of steak, chewed, and swallowed. "I confess I would not be sorry to see someone remove your husband from the landscape. But am I actively attempting to put a period to his existence? Not at the present moment."

She held herself very still, her gaze still searching his face. "Do you know who is?"

"No. Although I could speculate."

She drew out the nearest chair and sat. "So speculate."

Jarvis carved another slice of meat. "You've noticed the broadsheets that have appeared around town of late, calling for King Arthur to return from Avalon and lead England in its hour of need?"

"Do you know who's behind them?"

"Napoléon's agents, of course."

"And are you suggesting these agents have set someone after Devlin? Why?"

"Those who make it a habit of poking sticks into nests of vipers shouldn't be surprised when one of those vipers strikes back."

"You think that if Devlin finds whoever is behind the broadsheets, he'll find Gabrielle's killer?"

Jarvis reached for his ale and took a deep swallow. "It might be interesting."

"And convenient for you—if Devlin should manage to eliminate them."

He smiled. "There is that."

She collected her gloves and rose to her feet.

Jarvis said, "Have you told Devlin of my interaction with Miss Tennyson last Friday evening?"

Hero paused at the door to look back at him. "No."

Her answer surprised and pleased him, and yet somehow also vaguely troubled him. He let his gaze drift over his daughter's face. There was a bloom of color in her cheeks, an inner glow that told its own story. He said suddenly, "You do realize I know why you married him."

Her lips parted on a sudden intake of breath, but otherwise she remained remarkably calm and cool. "I can't imagine what you mean."

"Your former abigail confessed her observations on

your condition before she was killed." When Hero only continued to stare at him, he said, "Is the child Devlin's?"

Her pupils flared with indignation. "It is."

"Did he force himself upon you?"

"He did not."

"I see. Interesting."

She said, "The situation is . . . complicated."

"So it seems." He reached for his snuffbox. "And the child is due—when?"

"February."

Jarvis flipped open the snuffbox, then simply held it, half forgotten. "You will take care of yourself, Hero."

Her eyes danced with quiet amusement. "As much as ever."

He gave her no answering smile. "If anything happens to you, I'll kill him."

"Nothing is going to happen to me," she said. "Good day, Papa."

After she had gone, he sat for a time, lost in thought, the snuffbox still open in his hand. Then he shut it with a snap and closed his fist around the delicate metal hard enough that he heard it crunch.

※

Lieutenant Philippe Arceneaux was playing chess with a hulking mustachioed hussar in a coffee shop near Wych Street when Sebastian paused beside his table and said, "Walk with me for a moment, Lieutenant?"

The black and brown dog at Arceneaux's feet raised his head and woofed in anticipation.

"*Monsieur!*" protested the mustachioed Frenchman, glaring up at him. "The game! You interrupt!"

The hussar still wore the tight Hungarian riding breeches and heavily decorated but faded dark blue dolman of his regiment. At each temple dangled braided love knots known as *cadenettes*, with another braid behind each ear. The *cadenettes* were kept straight by the weight of a gold coin tied at the end of each braid, for Napoléon's hussars were as known for their meticulous, flamboyant appearance as for their ruthlessness as bandits on horseback.

"It's all right," said Arceneaux in French, raising both hands in rueful surrender as he pushed back his chair and rose to his feet. "I concede. You have thoroughly trounced me already. My situation is beyond hope."

Sebastian was aware of the hussar's scowl following them to the coffee shop's door.

"Who's your friend?" Sebastian asked as they turned to stroll toward the nearby church of St. Clements, the dog trotting happily at their heels.

"Pelletier? Don't mind him. He has a foul disposition and a worse temper, but there's no real harm in him."

"Interesting choice of words," said Sebastian, "given that two of your fellow officers tried to kill me in Covent Garden last night."

Arceneaux's smile slipped. "I had heard of the attack upon you." He nodded to the arm Sebastian held resting in a sling. "You were wounded?"

"Not badly. Yet I now find myself wondering, why would two French officers on their parole want to kill me?"

Arceneaux stared at him, eyes wide. "You think I know?"

"In a word? Yes."

Chien let out a soft whine and Arceneaux paused to hunker down and ruffle the animal's ears. After a moment, he said, "I make a living teaching French to small boys and working as a translator for a Fleet Street publisher. It earns me enough to keep a garret room in a lodging house, just there." He nodded to a nearby lane. "My father is able to send money from time to time. But his life is hard too. He owns a small vineyard near Saint-Malo. His best customers were always the English. War has not been good for business."

"What exactly are you saying?"

Arceneaux pushed to his feet. "Only that men whose profession is war can sometimes find that their most lucrative employment involves using their . . . professional skills."

"For whom?"

The Frenchman shook his head. "That I do not know." They continued walking, the dog frisking ahead. Arceneaux watched him a moment, then said, "There's something I didn't tell you about before—something I think may explain what happened to you last night. When I said I last saw Gabrielle on Wednesday, I was not being exactly truthful. I also saw her Friday evening. She was . . . very distressed."

"Go on."

"She said she had discovered something . . . something that both angered and frightened her."

"What sort of 'thing' are we talking about here?"

"A forgery or deception of some sort. She warned me that it was for my own protection that she not tell me more. All I know is that it was connected to the Arthurian legend in some way."

"A forgery?"

"Yes."

"And why the devil didn't you tell me this before?"

Arceneaux's face had grown so pale as to appear almost white. "She said it was more than a simple forgery. The motive behind it was not monetary."

"Did she say who was involved?"

"There was some antiquary she had quarreled with over it, but I believe he was only a pawn. Someone else was behind the scheme—someone she was afraid of. Which surprised me, because Gabrielle was not the kind of woman to be easily frightened."

"This antiquary—did she tell you his name?"

Arceneaux shook his head.

But it didn't matter. Sebastian knew who it was.

Chapter 25

*I*t took a while, but Sebastian finally traced Bevin Childe to an exhibition of ancient Greek pottery being held at the Middle Temple in a small hall just off Fountain Court.

He was bent over with his plump face pressed close to the glass of a cabinet containing an exquisite redware kylix. Then he looked up to see Sebastian regarding him steadily from a few feet away and his mouth gaped. He jerked upright, his gaze darting right and left as if seeking some avenue of escape.

"No," said Sebastian with a soft, mean smile. "You can't run away from me."

The antiquary gave a weak, sick laugh. Then his jaw hardened. "I have no intention of running. I have heard about you, Lord Devlin. My conversation with your wife was bad enough. I am staying right here. You can't hurt me in a hall full of people."

"True. But do you really want them to hear what I have to say?"

Childe stiffened. "If you expect me to understand what you mean by that rather mystifying pronouncement, I fear you are doomed to disappointment."

Sebastian nodded to the ceremonial cup before them.

"Lovely piece, isn't it? It certainly looks authentic. Yet I knew a man with a workshop outside of Naples who could turn out a dozen of these in a week. Forgeries, of course, but—"

Childe hissed. "*Shhh!* Keep your voice down." He cast another quick look around. A fat man with a protuberant mouth and full lips was staring at them over his spectacles. "Perhaps," said Childe, "it would be better after all if we were to continue this conversation outside."

⁂

They walked along Middle Temple Lane, toward the broad expanse of the Temple gardens edging the Thames. Once the precinct of the Knights Templar, the Inner and Middle Temples now served as two of the city's Inns of Court, those professional associations to which every barrister in England and Wales belonged. The morning sun soaked the upper reaches of the medieval walls around them with a rich golden light. But here, in the shadows of the closely packed buildings, the air was still cool.

Sebastian said, "I've discovered that your argument with Miss Tennyson last Friday had nothing to do with the location of Camelot. It was over a forgery. And don't even attempt to deny it," he added when Childe shook his head and took a deep breath.

Childe closed his mouth, his fingers playing with the chain that dangled from his watch pocket. His small gray eyes were darting this way and that again, as his frightened brain worked feverishly to analyze what Sebastian knew and how he might have come to know it. With every dart of those frantic eyeballs, Sebastian suspected the man was revising and editing what he was about to say.

"What forgery?" Sebastian asked.

Childe chewed the inside of his cheek.

"God *damn* you; a woman is dead and two little boys missing. What forgery?"

Childe cleared his throat. "Are you familiar with the discovery of the bodies of King Arthur and Guinevere in Glastonbury Abbey in 1191?"

"Not really."

Childe nodded as if to say he had expected this ignorance. "According to the medieval chronicler Gerald of Wales, King Henry the Second learned the location of Arthur's last resting place from a mysterious Welsh bard. The King was old and frail at the time, but before his death, he relayed the bard's information to the monks of Glastonbury Abbey. Following the King's instructions, the monks dug down between two ancient pyramids in their churchyard. Sixteen feet below the surface they came upon a split, hollowed-out log containing the bodies of a man and a woman. Above the coffins lay a stone slab, attached to the bottom of which was an iron cross. The cross bore the Latin inscription 'Here lies buried the renowned King Arthur with Guinevere his second wife, in the Isle of Avalon.'"

"Convenient," said Sebastian. "Almost as if those who buried him looked into the future a few hundred years and knew that someday those monks would be digging up good King Arthur, so they made certain to include in their engraving all the information anyone might need to make the identification complete."

"Just so," said Childe with a slight bow. "Needless to say, the monks collected the newly discovered bones and reburied them, first in the abbey's Lady Chapel, then beneath the high altar in a marble coffin provided by King Edward in 1278."

"Along with the cross?"

"Of course. It was attached to the top of the sepulchre. But when the abbey was destroyed in the suppression of the monasteries under Henry the Eighth, the bones of King Arthur and his Queen disappeared. For a time, the cross was reportedly kept in the parish church of St. John the Baptist. But it, too, eventually disappeared, probably during the time of Cromwell."

"And what precisely does any of this have to do with Miss Tennyson?"

Childe cleared his throat. "As you know, I have been occupied in cataloging the library and collection of the late Richard Gough. Amongst his possessions I discovered an ancient leaden cross inscribed with the words '*Hic Iacet Sepultus Inclitus Rex Arturius in Insula Avalonia.*'"

"Nothing about Guinevere?"

Childe gave another of his little bows. "Just so. Reports on the exact inscription have always varied slightly."

"How large a cross are we talking about here?"

"Approximately one foot in length."

"Where the devil did it come from?"

"That I do not know. As far as I have been able to ascertain, the cross came into Gough's possession—interestingly enough, along with a box of ancient bones—in the last days of his life, when he was unfortunately too ill to give them the attention they deserved. However, Gough apparently believed the cross to be that which the monks discovered in the twelfth century."

"And Gough believed the bones were those of Arthur and Guinevere? You can't be serious."

"I am only reporting on the conclusions reached by Gough himself. There is no more respected name amongst antiquaries."

"I take it Miss Tennyson did not agree with Gough's conclusions?"

Childe sighed. "She did not. Last Friday, she drove out to Gough Hall to view the cross and the bones. The bones are undeniably of great antiquity, but she instantly dismissed the cross as a modern forgery. When I begged to differ with her—"

"You did? I was under the impression you considered Arthur a wishful figment of the collective British imagination."

Childe puffed out his chest. "I may personally doubt the validity of the various tales which have grown up around some obscure figure who may or may not have actually lived. However, I have nothing but respect for the scholarship of Mr. Richard Gough, and I would consider it unprofessional to cavalierly dismiss the relic out of hand, simply because it does not conform to my preconceived notions."

"So what happened with Miss Tennyson?"

"We argued. Heatedly, I'm afraid. Miss Tennyson became so incensed that she seized the cross from my hands and hurled it into the lake."

"You were walking beside a lake? Carrying a foot-long iron cross?"

Childe stared at him owlishly. "We were, yes. You could hardly expect Miss Tennyson to enter the house to view the artifact. I may have known her since she was in pigtails, but it still would not have been at all proper. So we chose instead to walk in the park. Gough Hall has a lovely—and unfortunately very deep—ornamental lake."

"Unfortunate, indeed."

"Needless to say, her intemperance in positively flinging the cross into the lake enraged me. I fear I flew into quite a passion myself. Heated words were exchanged, and she departed in high dudgeon. I never saw her again."

Sebastian studied the stout man's flushed, self-satisfied face. He was obviously quite pleased with the tale he had concocted. But where the actual truth lay was impossible for Sebastian to guess. He said, "I assume the servants at Gough Hall can corroborate your story?"

"There is only an elderly caretaker and his wife in residence at the moment, but I have no doubt they will vouch for me, yes. Old Bentley even helped me drag a grappling hook along the edges of the lake. But we gave it up after an hour or so. I fear the cross is lost—this time forever."

"You believe it was genuine?"

"I believe it was the cross presented to the world by the monks of Glastonbury in 1191, yes."

Which was not, Sebastian noted, precisely the same thing.

He watched a cluster of legal students hurry across the gardens, their black robes flapping in the hot wind. "You say Miss Tennyson was angry?"

"She was, yes. It's a very choleric family, you know."

"And melancholy."

"Melancholy, yes."

From here they could see the broad expanse of the sun-dazzled river, the massive bulk of the bridge, and the warehouses and wharves of the opposite bank. Sebastian said, "There's just one thing I don't understand."

"Oh?"

"What in the incident you describe could possibly have made her afraid?"

Childe's smug smile slipped. "Afraid?"

"Afraid."

Childe shook his head. "I never said anything about her being afraid."

"That's because you left out the part about the dangerous forces with a nonmonetary motive."

A sudden gust of hot wind stirred the branches of the beeches overhead, letting through a shaft of golden sunlight that cut across Childe's face when he turned to stare blankly at Sebastian. "I'm sorry; I don't have the slightest idea what you're talking about."

"You don't?"

"No." Childe cleared his throat and nodded to the arm Sebastian still had resting in a sling. "You injured yourself?"

"Actually, someone tried to kill me last night; do you have any ideas about that?"

Childe's jaw went slack. *"Kill you?"*

"Mmm. Someone who doesn't like the questions I'm asking. Which tells me that Gabrielle Tennyson had good reason to be afraid. Whatever is going on here is dangerous. Very dangerous. It's not over yet, and it looks to me as if you're right in the middle of it. You might want to consider that, next time you're tempted to lie to me."

The antiquary had turned a sickly shade of yellow.

Sebastian touched his good hand to his hat and smiled. "Good day, Mr. Childe. Enjoy the rest of your pottery exhibition."

Chapter 26

*T*wenty minutes later, Sebastian turned his curricle into Bow Street to find the lane ahead clogged by a raucous, tattered mob that spilled out of the public office to overflow the footpath and completely block the narrow carriageway. Ragged men and gaunt-cheeked women clutching an assortment of howling, filthy, malnourished children jostled and shoved one another in a frantic melee swirling around a small, bespectacled magistrate endeavoring to push his way through the motley crowd.

"Lord Devlin!" called Sir Henry Lovejoy, determinedly turning his steps toward the curricle.

"What the devil is all this?" asked Sebastian as Tom jumped down to run to the frightened chestnuts' tossing heads.

Lovejoy staggered against the side of the carriage, buffeted by the surging crowd. "It's been like this since yesterday. We've been positively besieged by parents offering up their children for Mr. Tennyson's reward—everything from babes in arms to sturdy lads of twelve and fourteen. Even girls. And this is only the overflow. Tennyson has hired a solicitor with chambers near Fleet Street to whom anyone with information is supposed to apply."

"My God," said Sebastian, his gaze traveling over the desperate, starving mass. "No indication yet of what actually happened to the Tennyson children?"

Lovejoy blew out a long, tired breath and shook his head. "It's as if they simply vanished off the face of the earth."

The magistrate gave a lurch and almost fell as a wild-eyed, pock-scarred woman clutching what looked like a dead child careened into him. He righted himself with difficulty. The crowd was becoming dangerous. "Have you discovered anything of interest?"

"Not yet," said Sebastian. As much as he trusted Sir Henry, when it came to murder investigations, Sebastian had learned to play his cards close to his chest. "I was wondering if you could provide me with the direction of the girl who found Miss Tennyson's body."

"You mean, Tessa Sawyer? She lives with her father a few miles to the southwest of the moat in a village called Cockfosters. I believe the mother is dead, while the father is something of a layabout. Why do you ask?"

"I have some questions I thought she might be able to answer."

Sebastian was aware of the magistrate giving him a long, steady look. But Lovejoy only nodded and took a step back into the shouting, jostling crowd.

※

Cockfosters proved to be a tiny village consisting largely of a church, an aged inn, and a few villas and scattered cottages lying to the west of Camlet Moat.

Following directions given by the curate at the village church, Sebastian drove up a rutted track to a tumble-down thatched cottage of whitewashed, rough-coursed stone that lay on the far edge of the hamlet. A young girl of some fifteen or sixteen years of age was in the dusty, sunbaked yard pegging up clothes on a line stretched between a corner of the house and a half-dead mulberry tree. A slim, tiny thing with baby-fine brown hair and eyes that looked too big for her face, she hummed a fey, haunting tune as she worked, so lost in her own world that she seemed oblivious to the elegant curricle drawing up outside her gate.

Sebastian jumped down into the dusty lane and felt a shooting jolt of pain in his arm, for he had dispensed with the sling on the drive out to Enfield. He paused a brief moment to catch his breath, then said, "Excuse me, miss; are you Tessa Sawyer?"

"Oh!" The girl jerked, her hands clenching the wet shirt she held to her chest, her nostrils flaring in alarm. "Ye startled me, ye did."

"I beg your pardon." Sebastian paused with one hand on the gate's rusty latch. "May I come in?"

The girl dropped a nervous curtsy, her eyes widening as she glanced from Sebastian to the carriage waiting in the sun-soaked lane, its high-bred chestnuts flicking their tails at the flies. "Oh, yes, sir. But if yer lookin' fer me da, he's not here. He's out helpin' search for the bodies of them dead boys, he is."

Sebastian had to whack his hip against the gate to get it to open. "Actually, you're the one I wished to speak to. What makes you think the boys are dead, Tessa?"

Tessa shook her head in some confusion. "It's what everyone's sayin', isn't it? I mean, it stands to reason, don't it?"

Sebastian let his gaze drift around the yard. A few scrawny chickens pecked halfheartedly at the bare earth, while a brown goat with a bell around its neck nuzzled a pile of rubbish beside the remnants of an old stone shed. If there had ever been any glass in the cottage's windows, it was long gone, the unpainted shutters hanging at drunken angles. From the looks of the worn, moldy thatch, Sebastian had no doubt the roof leaked when it rained.

He said, "Did you see any sign of the children when you were at the moat Sunday night?"

Tessa shook her head. "No, sir. I didn't see nor hear nothin' 'cept a little splash. And I can't rightly say what that was. It coulda been a water rat, or maybe a frog."

"Had you ever seen the lady in the boat before?"

Tessa swallowed, her face becoming pinched. "Just once."

"Really? When was that?"

"Last week, sometime. I think maybe it was Sunday."

"You mean, this past Sunday?"

"No. The Sunday before."

"You saw her at the island?"

"Oh, no, sir. She came here, she did—to Cockfosters."

Sebastian knew a flicker of surprise. "Do you know why?"

Tessa sucked her lower lip between her teeth and bit down on it, her gaze drifting away.

"Tell me," said Sebastian.

She drew in a quick breath. "She come here lookin' fer Rory Forster. Lit into him somethin' fierce, she did, just outside the smithy's."

"Forster lives in the village?"

"On a farm, to the east of here. Didn't ye know?" Sebastian's ignorance obviously shocked her. "Most o' the men doin' the diggin' at the moat come from Trent Place. But Sir Stanley hired Rory on account of how he once worked for some famous gentleman down in Salisbury."

"You mean, Sir Richard Colt Hoare? At Stonehenge?"

The girl looked at him blankly. "I wouldn't know about that."

"And what precisely was Miss Tennyson's interest in Forster?"

Tessa turned away and began pegging up the shirt. "I weren't there for most of it."

"But you did hear about it afterward, didn't you? Didn't you?" Sebastian prodded when the girl remained mute.

Tessa smoothed her hands down over the worn cloth. "Folks say she was mad at Forster for tearin' out the linin' of the island's well. They say somebody turned it into a muddy mess."

"A well?"

She nodded, her face hardening. "He shouldn't have done that. It's a special place."

"Special in what way?"

She threw him a quick, sideways glance. "You know what it's like when you sit in a really old church and you're all alone, and it's quiet and the sun's streamin' through the stained-glass windows and you just feel this . . . this kind of peace and joy settle over you? That's what it's like at the White Lady's well."

"What White Lady?"

"The White Lady. I've never seen her meself, but others have. She guards the well. She always has."

Sebastian studied the girl's fine-boned face, the wistful look in her big hazel eyes, and resisted the urge to point out that the White Lady of Camlet Moat had obviously failed to guard her well from some treasure hunter's shovel. He'd heard of the well maidens, ancient nature spirits said to guard the sacred wells and springs of Britain and Ireland. Although belief in the well maidens predated Christianity, it had never completely disappeared, and small shrines to the well maidens could still be found scattered across the countryside. Somehow, it seemed all of a piece with everything else he'd learned about the island that it should have a sacred well too. He realized Miss Tennyson must have come upon the destruction when she visited the island in the company of Arceneaux and the children.

He said, "Did she drive to the village in a gig? With a man and two children?"

"Yes, sir."

"Where would I find Forster?"

Tessa sniffed and jerked her head back toward the crossroads. "He married the Widow Clark just last year. Her farm's on the edge of the old chase."

Sebastian touched his hat and swept the girl an elegant bow. "Thank you, Miss Sawyer. Good day."

Turning away, he was reaching for the gate's latch when Tessa said suddenly, "You know, I did hear the last part of what Miss Tennyson said to Rory."

Sebastian swung to face her. "Oh? And what was that?"

"She told him she was going to ask Sir Stanley to fire him."

"And did you hear Rory's response?"

"Aye. He said that weren't a good idea. And when she asked him if he was a-threatenin' her, he said—" Tessa broke off, all color leaching from her cheeks.

"What did he say?"

The girl swallowed. "He said yes."

Chapter 27

Sebastian found Rory Forster clearing rocks from a grassy field edged by a small stream.

Reining in beneath the shade cast by a spreading elm, Sebastian paused to watch as the man heaved a watermelon-sized stone up onto the pile in the bed of the low cart beside him. The cart's brown mule stood placidly in the afternoon heat, ears twitching as Sebastian left the curricle in Tom's care and climbed over the stile.

"Good afternoon," Sebastian called.

Straightening with another large gray stone clutched in both hands, Forster threw a quizzing glance at Sebastian, then dropped the rock into the cart. "Wot ye doin' here? Didn't ye hear? The diggin' at Camlet Moat is finished. I don't work fer Sir Stanley no more and I got nothin' else to say to ye."

Sebastian brushed away a fly buzzing about his face. "When we spoke the other day, you forgot to mention your confrontation with Miss Tennyson a week ago last Sunday. Here, in Cockfosters. Outside the smithy's."

"Me brother's the smithy—like our da was before him."

"Which I suppose explains how Miss Tennyson knew where to find you."

Forster turned away to stoop down and grasp another rock.

Sebastian said, "The incident was witnessed by half the village."

Forster grunted. "Aye. She were a feisty thing, that woman. She could squawk all she wanted, but I knew that in the end she wasna gonna go to Sir Stanley. She'd no proof of anything."

"Maybe she recently discovered something. Maybe that's why you killed her."

Forster heaved another rock up and over the side of the cart. "I told ye and the magistrate both: I was home with me wife Sunday."

Sebastian stared off to where the field sloped gently toward a line of chestnuts growing along a small watershed to the west. The air was hot, the pasture a bright emerald green and scattered with small daisies. The scene was deceptively peaceful, with an air of bucolic innocence that seemed to have no place for passion and greed. Or murder.

He said, "Do you believe Sir Geoffrey de Mandeville hid his treasure on the island?"

Forster glanced over at him and smiled, the dimple-like slashes appearing in his tanned cheeks. "De Mandeville? Nah. But did ye never hear of Dick Turpin?"

"Dick Turpin? You mean, the highwayman?"

"Aye. Him as once worked Finchley Common. Used to hide out at the island, he did. His uncle Nott owned the Rose and Crown by the Brook, across the chase at Clay Hill. Seems to me, if there's treasure on that island, it's more likely Dick Turpin's than some old knight what's been dead and gone for who knows how many hundreds of years."

"Is that what you were looking for? A highwayman's gold?"

Forster reached for his mule's reins. "Never claimed it

were me. All I'm sayin' is, Turpin's story is well-known about here. Coulda been anyone lookin' for what he mighta hid."

"So why did Miss Tennyson accuse you?"

Forster urged the mule forward a few feet, then stopped to reach for another stone. "She didn't like me much. Never did."

"And you didn't like her," said Sebastian, keeping his eyes on the hefty rock in Forster's hands.

"I won't deny that. She threatened to tell Sir Stanley I was the one who tore apart the well. But she had no proof and she knew it."

"So why did you threaten her?"

"I didn't. Anyone who tells you different is either makin' stuff up or jist repeatin' crazy talk he heard." Forster slammed the rock down on the growing pile, then paused with his fists propped on his lean hips, his breath coming hard, his handsome, sun-browned face and neck glistening with perspiration. "I been doin' me some thinkin'. And it occurs to me that meybe Sir Stanley has more to do with what happened to the lady than I first suspicioned."

"Odd, given that yesterday you seemed more intent on casting suspicion on Sir Stanley's wife, Lady Winthrop, than on Sir Stanley himself."

"I told ye, I been doing me some thinkin'. It occurs to me this might all have somethin' to do with the way Sir Stanley likes to fancy himself one of them ancient Druids."

"A Druid," said Sebastian.

"That's right. Dresses up in white robes and holds heathen rituals out at the island. I know for a fact Miss Tennyson seen him doin' it just the other day. He coulda been afraid she'd give away his secret."

"Couldn't have been much of a secret if you knew about it."

Forster's eyes narrowed with unexpected amusement. He laid a finger beside his nose and winked, then turned away to stoop for another stone.

Sebastian said, "And how precisely do you know that Miss Tennyson saw Sir Stanley enacting these rituals?"

Forster hawked up a mouthful of phlegm and spit it into the grass. "Because I was there meself. Last Saturday evening, it was, long after we'd finished work for the day. Sir Stanley was at the island in his robes when Miss Tennyson comes back—"

"How?" interjected Sebastian.

"What do ye mean, 'how'?"

"You said Miss Tennyson came back. So was she walking? In a gig? Who was driving her?"

"She come in a gig, drivin' herself."

It was the first Sebastian had heard of Gabrielle Tennyson driving herself. It was not unusual for a woman to drive in the country without a groom. But Gabrielle would have driven out from London, which was something else entirely. He said, "Did she do that often? Drive herself, I mean."

"Sometimes."

"So you're saying she arrived at the island and found Sir Stanley about to engage in some sort of ancient ritual?"

"That's right. Just before sunset, it was."

"Did either of them know you were there?"

"Nah. I was hid behind some bushes."

"And what precisely were you doing at the island?"

"I'd forgot me pipe."

"Your pipe."

Forster stared at Sebastian owlishly, as if daring Sebastian to doubt him. "That's right. Went back for it, I did. Only then I seen Sir Stanley in his strange getup, so I hid in the bushes to see what was goin' on."

"And you were still hiding in the bushes when you saw Miss Tennyson drive up?"

"I was, yes." Forster turned away to reach down for a big, jagged rock. "I couldn't hear what they was sayin'. But there's no doubt in me mind she seen him and that rig he was wearin'."

"And then what happened?"

"I don't know. I left."

"So you're suggesting—what, precisely? That Sir Stanley was so chagrined by Miss Tennyson's discovery of his rather unorthodox behavior and belief system that he lured her back to the island on Sunday and killed her?"

"I ain't suggestin' nothing. Just tellin' ye what happened, that's all."

"I see. And have you told anyone else about this encounter?"

"No. Why would I?"

"Why, indeed?" Sebastian started to turn away, then paused as a thought occurred to him. "One more question: Did you discover anything unusual or interesting in the course of the excavations at the island last Saturday?"

Forster frowned. "No. Why?"

"I'm just wondering why Miss Tennyson would return to the island, first on Saturday evening, then again on Sunday."

"That I couldn't say."

"You've no idea at all?"

"No." Forster reached for his mule's reins.

"What precisely did you discover Saturday?"

"Just an area of old cobblestones—like a courtyard or somethin'."

"That's all?"

"Ain't nothin' to kill a body over, is it? Well, is it?"

"I wouldn't have thought so," said Sebastian. "Except for one thing."

Forster wrapped the reins around his fists. "What's that?"

"Miss Tennyson is dead."

"And them two nippers," said Forster.

"Are they dead?" Sebastian asked, his gaze hard on the countryman's beard-shadowed face.

"They ain't been found, have they?"

"No," said Sebastian. "No, they have not."

※

"Ye think 'e's tellin' the truth?" Tom asked as Sebastian leapt up into the curricle's high seat.

Sebastian glanced back at his tiger. "How much did you hear?"

"Most o' it."

Sebastian gathered his reins. "To be frank, I'm not convinced Forster has the imagination required to invent such a tale entirely out of whole cloth. But do I believe him? Hardly. I suspect he went out to the island that night on a treasure-hunting expedition. But he may indeed have seen something." He turned the horses' heads toward Enfield Chase. "I think I'd like to take a look at this sacred well."

※

The island lay deserted, the afternoon sun filtering down through the leafy canopy of old-growth elms and beech to dapple the dark waters of the moat with rare glints of light.

"Ain't nobody 'ere," whispered Tom as Sebastian drew up at the top of Camlet Moat's ancient embankment. "I thought they was still lookin' for them two boys."

"They are. But I suspect they've given up hope of finding any trace of them around here," said Sebastian, his voice also low. Like Tom, he knew a reluctance to disturb the solemn peace of the site.

Without the scuffing sounds from Forster's shovel or the distant shouts of the searchers they'd heard the day before, the silence of the place was as complete as if they had strayed deep into a forgotten, enchanted forest. Sebastian handed his reins to the tiger and jumped lightly to the ground, his boots sinking into the soft leaf mold beside the track. One of the chestnuts nickered, and he reached out to caress the horse's soft muzzle. "Walk 'em a bit. I shouldn't be long."

"Aye, gov'nor."

He crossed to the island by way of the narrow land bridge. The trenches dug by Sir Stanley's workmen had all been filled in, leaving long, narrow rows of mounded dark earth that struck Sebastian as bearing an unpleasant resemblance to the poor holes of churchyards. But he knew that in a year or so, the grass and brush of the island would cover them again, and it would be as if no one had ever disturbed the site.

Sebastian paused for a moment, his gaze drifting around the abandoned clearing. One of the more troublesome aspects of this murder had always been the question of how Gabrielle Tennyson—and presumably her cousins—had traveled up to the moat that fateful Sunday. The discovery that Gabrielle sometimes drove herself here in a gig opened up a host of new possibilities.

It was an unorthodox thing for a young woman to do, to drive herself into the countryside from London. Perhaps she thought that at the age of twenty-eight she was beyond those restrictions. Or perhaps she considered the presence of her nine-year-old cousin and his brother a sufficient sop to the proprieties. But if the Tennysons had driven themselves here that fatal day, the question then became, What the bloody hell happened to the horse and gig? And why had no liveryman come forward to say he had hired the equipment to them?

Sebastian turned to follow the path he'd noticed before, a faint trail that snaked through the brambles and brush to the northeastern corner of the island. It was there, in a small clearing not far from the moat's edge, that he found what was left of the old well.

Once neatly lined with dressed sandstone blocks, the well now looked like a dirty, sunken wound. Ripped from the earth, the old lining stones lay jumbled together with wet clay and shattered tiles in a heap at the base of a gnarled hawthorn that spread its bleached branches over the muddy hole. From the tree's branches fluttered dozens of strips of tattered cloth.

Sebastian drew up in surprise. They called them rag trees or, sometimes, clootie trees. Relics of an ancient belief whose origins were lost in the mists of time, the trees could be found at sacred places to which suppliants with a problem—be it an illness, grief, hardship, or unrequited love—came to whisper a prayer and leave a strip of cloth as a token offering that they tied to the branches of the tree. As the cloths rotted in the wind and sun and rain, the suppliants believed their prayers would be answered, their illnesses cured, their problems solved. Rag trees were typically found beside sacred wells or springs, for dipping the cloth in holy water was said to increase the power of the charm.

He understood now why Tessa had ventured out to Camlet Moat by moonlight.

He watched as a hot breeze gusted up, flapping the worn, weathered strips of cloth. And he found himself wondering how many other villagers came here to visit the island's sacred well.

Quite a few, from the look of things.

He went to hunker down beside the pile of muddy stones. The desecration of the well had obviously occurred quite recently. But it was impossible to tell if the man—or men—who'd done this had found what they were looking for.

A faint sound drew Sebastian's head around as his acute hearing distinguished the distant clatter of approaching hooves, coming fast. He listened as the unseen horse and rider drew nearer, then checked. A man's low voice, asking a question, drifted across the water, followed by Tom's high-pitched reply.

Sebastian stayed where he was and let the current owner of Camelot come to him.

Chapter 28

Dressed in the supple doeskin breeches and well-cut riding coat of a prosperous country gentleman, Sir Stanley Winthrop paused at the edge of the clearing, his riding crop dangling from one hand. "Lord Devlin. What brings you here?"

Sebastian pushed to his feet. "You didn't tell me the island was the site of a rag tree."

"I suppose I didn't consider it relevant. Surely you don't think it could have something to do with Gabrielle's death?"

Sebastian turned to let his gaze rove over the ancient hawthorn with its tattered, weathered offerings. "It's an interesting superstition."

"You consider it a superstition?"

Sebastian brought his gaze back to the banker's face. "You don't?"

"I think there are many things on this earth we don't understand, and the power of the human will is one of them."

Sebastian nodded to the pile of muddy stones at his feet. "When did this happen?"

"Gabrielle found it this way when she came up here a

week ago. There's an old legend that Geoffrey de Mandeville buried his treasure beneath the well."

"Any idea who's responsible?"

"Some ignorant fool, I'm afraid. Obviously searching
for gold."

"Mandeville's gold? Or Dick Turpin's?"

"Ah, you've heard the stories about Turpin as well,
have you?" Winthrop stared down at the muddy mess,
and Sebastian caught a flash of the steely rage he'd
glimpsed briefly once before. "Unfortunately, both have
become associated with the island."

"Did Miss Tennyson tell you who she thought had
done it?"

"She told me that she had her suspicions. But when I
pressed her to elaborate, she said she had no real proof
and was therefore hesitant to actually accuse anyone."

"She never said she suspected your foreman, Rory
Forster?"

"She suspected Rory? No, she didn't tell me. How very
disturbing."

Sebastian studied the other man's face. But Winthrop
once more had his emotions carefully under control; the
even features gave nothing away. Sebastian said, "Why
didn't you tell me Miss Tennyson returned to the island
the evening before she died? Or that you were here that
evening too?"

Winthrop was silent for a moment, as if tempted to
deny it. Then he pursed his lips and shrugged. "If you
know we were here, am I to take it you also know why?"

"I'm told you have an interest in Druidism. That you
came here last Saturday dressed in white robes to enact
a pagan ritual in observance of Lammas. Is that true?"

A faint glimmer of amusement shone in the other
man's eyes. "What precisely are you imagining, Lord
Devlin? That Gabrielle came upon me by chance and I

was so horrified to be discovered that I murdered her to keep her quiet?"

"It has been suggested."

"Really? By whom?"

"You know I can't answer that."

"No, I suppose you can't."

"*Are* you interested in Druidism?"

"Does it shock you that I should have an interest in the religions of the past?"

"No."

Winthrop raised an eyebrow in surprise. "In that you are unusual. Believe me."

Sebastian said, "And did Miss Tennyson share your interest in the religion of our ancestors?"

"She shared my interest, yes. I can't, however, say she shared my belief."

"Do you believe?"

Again that faint gleam of amusement flickered in the banker's light gray eyes. "I believe there are many paths to wisdom and understanding. Most people are content to find the answers to life's questions in the formal dogmas and hierarchies of organized religion. They find comfort in being told what to believe and how to worship."

"And you?"

"Me? I find my peace and sense of meaning in ancient places such as this"—Winthrop spread his arms wide, his palms lifted to the sky—"with the trees and the water and the air. The exact beliefs of our ancestors may be lost, but the essence of their wisdom is still here—if you listen to the whispers on the wind and open your heart to our kinship with the earth and all her creatures."

"Is Lady Winthrop aware of your beliefs?"

Winthrop's hands dropped back to his sides. "She is aware of my interest."

Which was not, as Winthrop himself had pointed out,

the same thing at all. Sebastian said, "I gather Lady Winthrop's own religious beliefs are rather . . . orthodox." *And rigid,* he thought, although he didn't say it.

"We must each follow our own individual paths."

Sebastian studied the older man's craggy face, the chiseled line of his strong jaw, the fashionably cut flaxen hair mixing gracefully with white. He found it difficult if not impossible to reconcile this talk of spiritualism and harmony with what he knew of the hard-driven banker who had amassed a fortune by financing war and ruthlessly crushing anyone who stood in his way.

As if sensing Sebastian's doubt, Winthrop said, "You're skeptical, of course."

"Do you blame me?"

"Not really. It's no secret that my life has been spent in the pursuit of money and power. But men can change."

"They can. Although it's rare."

Winthrop went to stand beside the dark waters of the moat, his back to Sebastian, the tip of his riding crop tapping against his thigh as he stared across at the opposite bank. "I once had five children; did you know? Three girls and two boys, born to me by my first wife. They were beautiful children, with their mother's blue eyes and blond curls and winsome ways. And then, one by one, they died. We lost Peter first, to a fever. Then Mary and Jane, to measles. I sometimes think it was grief that killed my wife. It was as if she just faded away. She died less than a month after Jane."

"I'm sorry," said Sebastian softly.

Winthrop nodded, his lips pressed together tightly. "I married again, of course—a most brilliant alliance to the widow of a late colleague. I knew she was likely to prove barren since she'd never given my colleague children, but what did it matter? I still had two children. When I bought Trent Place last year, I believed I'd finally achieved everything I'd ever wanted. Then my last two children died within weeks of each other. Elizabeth caught a putrid sore throat; then James fell and broke his neck jumping his hack over a ditch. There are just too many ways children can die. And when I buried James . . ." Winthrop's voice cracked. He paused and shook his head. "When I buried James, I realized I'd dedicated my life to amassing a fortune, and for what? So that I could build my family the most elaborate monument in the churchyard?"

Sebastian remained silent.

After a moment, Winthrop gave a ragged laugh. "The current Lady Winthrop is of the opinion that my grief over the loss of my children has affected the balance of my mind. Perhaps she is right. All I know is that I find neither peace nor comfort in the righteous dogmas of her church, whereas in a place like this—" He blew out a long, painful breath. "In a place like this, I find, if not peace, then at least a path to understanding and a way to come to grips with what once seemed unbearable."

"And Miss Tennyson? Did she come to Camlet Moat at sunset last Saturday to participate in . . . whatever it was you were here to do?"

"Participate?" Winthrop shook his head. "No. But she was interested in observing. I may feel no compulsion to advertise my spiritual beliefs, but neither am I ashamed of them. So you see, if you are imagining that I killed Miss Tennyson because she discovered my interest in Druidism, you are wrong."

Sebastian said, "Were you romantically involved with her?"

Winthrop looked genuinely startled by the suggestion. "Good God, no! I'm practically old enough to have been her father."

Sebastian shrugged. "It happens."

"Not in this instance. There was nothing of that nature between us. We were friends; I respected her intelligence and knowledge and the strength of her will. If

my own daughters had lived, I like to think they would
have grown up to be like her. But that is how I thought
of her—as a daughter."

From what Sebastian had learned of Miss Tennyson,
she was the kind of woman who tended to intimidate
and alarm most men, rather than inspire them to admiration. But there were always exceptions.

He said, "I'm told Miss Tennyson sometimes drove
herself out here in a gig. Is that true?"

"Sometimes, yes. She didn't do it often, though." Winthrop gave a soft smile that faded rapidly. "When her
brother complained about her habit of taking the stage,
she said she always threatened to take to driving herself
instead."

"But she did drive herself out here Saturday evening?"

"She did, yes."

"Do you think it is possible she drove herself out here
Sunday, as well?"

"I suppose it's possible."

The wind gusted up again, fluttering the weathered
strips of cloth on the rag tree. Sebastian said, "What else
can you tell me about Sir Geoffrey de Mandeville?"

Winthrop frowned. "Mandeville?" The sudden shift in
topic seemed to confuse him.

"I understand he's said to haunt the island."

"He is, yes. Although the local legend that claims he
drowned in this well is nonsense. He was killed by an arrow
to the head at the siege of Burwell Castle—miles from here."

"Where is he buried?"

"At the Temple, in London."

Sebastian knew a flicker of surprise. "So he was a
Knight Templar."

"The association is murky, I'm afraid. They say that
the Knights Templar came to him when he lay dying and
flung their mantle over him, so that he might die with the
red cross on his breast."

"Why?"

"That is not recorded. All we know is that the Templars put Mandeville's body in a lead casket and carried him off to London, where his coffin hung in an apple tree near the Temple for something like twenty years."

"A lead coffin? In a tree?"

"That's the tale. He'd been excommunicated, which meant the Templars couldn't bury him in their churchyard. Those were dark times, but there's no denying Mandeville was an exceptionally nasty piece of work."

"'Those were the days when men said openly that Christ slept and his saints wept,'" said Sebastian softly, quoting the old chroniclers.

Winthrop nodded. "In the end, the Pope relented. The edict of excommunication was lifted and the Knights Templar were allowed to bury him. You can still see his effigy on the floor of the Temple today, you know."

"Unusual," said Sebastian, "if he wasn't actually a Templar."

"It is, yes."

"And the belief that his treasure lay at the bottom of this well?"

Winthrop was silent for a moment, his gaze on the muddy hole the well had now become. "Tales of great treasure often become associated with sacred sites," he said. "The memory of a place's importance can linger long after the true nature of its value has been forgotten. Then those who come later, in their ignorance and greed, imagine the place as a repository of earthly treasures."

"You think that's what happened here?"

"Unfortunately, there's no way of knowing, is there? But the association of Camelot, the Templars, and the tales of lost treasure is definitely intriguing."

"Intriguing?" said Sebastian. "Or deadly?"

Sir Stanley looked troubled. "Perhaps both."

❦

Hero spent the rest of the morning sorting through the stacks of Gabrielle Tennyson's books and papers, looking for something—anything—that might explain her friend's death.

She couldn't shake the conviction that the key to Gabrielle's murder lay here, in the piles of notes and translations the woman had been working on. But Gabrielle's interests had been so wide-ranging, reaching from the little-known centuries before the Celts through the time of the Romans to the dark ages that befell Britain following the collapse of the Empire, that wading through her research was a formidable undertaking.

It was when Hero was studying Gabrielle's notes on *The Lady of Shalott* that a loose sheet of paper fluttered to the floor. Reaching down to pick it up, she found herself staring at a handwritten poem.

> *Bid me to weep, and I will weep*
> *While I have eyes to see:*
> *And having none, yet I will keep*
> *A heart to weep for thee.*
>
> *Bid me despair and I'll despair,*
> *Under that cypress tree:*
> *Or bid me die, and I will dare*
> *E'en Death, to die for thee.*
>
> *Thou art my life, my love, my heart*
> *The very eyes of me,*
> *And hast command of every part,*
> *To live and die for thee.*

Hero leaned back in her seat, her hand tightening on the paper, the breath leaving her lungs in a rush as a new and totally unexpected possibility occurred to her.

Chapter 29

*H*ero was curled up in an armchair beside the library's empty hearth, a volume of seventeenth-century poetry open in her lap, when Devlin came to stand in the doorway. He brought with him the scent of sunshine and fresh air and the open countryside.

"What happened to your sling?" she asked, looking up at him.

"It was in my way."

"Now, there's a good reason to stop wearing it."

He huffed a soft laugh and went to pour himself a glass of wine. "Did Gabrielle ever mention an interest in Druidism to you?"

"Druidism? Good heavens, no. Why on earth do you ask?"

He came to stand with his back to the empty fireplace. "Because it turns out that she went back out to Camlet Moat at sunset the night before she died, to watch Sir Stanley enact some pagan ritual at an ancient sacred well on the island. *Drove herself* there, in fact, in a gig."

"You can't be serious."

"I wish I wasn't. But Rory Forster saw her there, and Sir Stanley himself admits as much."

"What was Forster doing at the island at sunset?"

"According to Rory? Retrieving a forgotten pipe—
and hiding in the bushes. Although I suspect it far more
likely that he went there with the intent of digging for
buried treasure and was perplexed to discover he wasn't
going to have the island to himself that night."

"Treasure?"

"Mmm. Buried by either Dick Turpin or a Knight Templar, depending upon which version one believes. Exactly
a week before she was killed, Miss Tennyson stormed into
Cockfosters and publicly accused Rory of ripping out the
lining of the island's sacred well."

"In search of this treasure?"

Devlin nodded. "According to the legend, Sir Geoffrey de Mandeville hid his ill-gotten gains beneath the
bottom of the well, and his spirit is supposed to appear
to frighten away anyone who attempts to remove it. But
his ghost must have been asleep on the job, because I
checked, and someone recently made a right sorry mess
of the thing."

"You say she confronted Rory a week ago Sunday?"

He drained his wine. "The timing is interesting, isn't
it? That's the day she was out there with Arceneaux.
Then, just a few days later, she drove out to Gough Hall
and had a stormy argument with Bevin Childe. She was
a very confrontational and contentious young woman,
your friend."

Hero smoothed a hand down over her skirt. "So you
spoke to Bevin Childe?"

"I did. He claims to have discovered something called
the Glastonbury Cross amongst Richard Gough's collections. I'm told it's the cross that was said to have marked
the graves of King Arthur and Guinevere at the abbey.
Have you ever heard of it?"

"Yes."

"Well, it seems Miss Tennyson was convinced the
cross was a modern forgery, and in the midst of a rather

violent argument with Childe, she seized the cross and threw it in a lake."

She was aware of him watching her intently. "What a . . . strange thing to do," she said, keeping her voice level with effort.

He frowned and came to take the seat opposite her. "Are you all right, Hero?"

"Yes, of course; just tired."

"Perhaps, under the circumstances, you're doing too much." He said it awkwardly; the coming babe, despite being the reason for their marriage, was something they never discussed.

She made an inelegant sound of derision. "If by 'the circumstances' you are referring to the fact that I am with child, let me remind you that gestation is a natural occurrence, not a dread debilitating disease."

"True. Yet I do take special care of my mares when they are with foal."

At that, she laughed out loud. "I don't know if I should be flattered or insulted by the comparison."

The corners of his eyes crinkled with amusement. "Oh, flattered, definitely."

Their gazes met, and the moment stretched out and became something intimate and unexpected.

She felt her cheeks grow warm, and looked away. "How did you come to learn of Gabrielle's confrontation with Childe over the cross?"

"Lieutenant Arceneaux told me."

"Arceneaux? Now, that's interesting." She picked up the sheet of parchment she'd discovered and held it out to him. "I found this with Gabrielle's papers."

"'Bid me to weep, and I will weep,'" he read, "'while I have eyes to see.'" He looked up at her. "You know the poem?"

"No. But it does sound familiar, doesn't it? I believe it may be from one of the Cavalier poets." She closed the poetry book and set it aside. "But so far I haven't been able to find it."

"It's the last three stanzas from Robert Herrick's 'To Anthea, Who May Command Him Anything.'"

Her eyes widened. "You know it?"

He smiled. "That surprises you, does it? Did you imagine I spent all my time riding to hounds and drinking brandy and trying to pop a hit over Gentleman Jackson's guard?"

She felt an answering smile tug at her lips. "Something like that."

"Huh." He pushed up and went to compare the bold hand of the poem to the flowing copperplate that filled Gabrielle Tennyson's notebooks. "This doesn't look like her writing," he said after a moment.

"It's not."

He glanced over at her. "You know whose it is?"

She came to extract one of the notebooks from the pile. "Here. Look at the translation of *The Lady of Shalott* Gabrielle was working on; you'll see the handwriting of the poem matches that of the alterations and notations someone else made in the margins of her work. I think the poem was given to her by Philippe Arceneaux."

Devlin studied the notations, his lips pressing into a tight line.

Hero said, "Do you think the Lieutenant was more in love with her than he led you to believe?"

"'Thou art my life, my heart, my love,'" he quoted, setting the translation aside. "It rather sounds that way, does it not? Not only that, but I'd say Miss Tennyson was in love with him too."

Hero shook her head. "How can you be so certain?"

He looked down at the creased sheet he still held in his hand. "Because she kept this."

❧

Lieutenant Philippe Arceneaux and his scruffy little dog were watching a cricket match at Marylebone Park Fields on the northern outskirts of the city when Sebastian came to stand beside him.

A warm sun washed the grass of the nearby hills with a golden green. They could hear the lowing of cows, see a hawk circling lazily above the stand of oaks edging the field. The batsman scored a run and a murmur of approval rippled through the crowd of spectators.

Sebastian said, "You've acquired a fondness for cricket, have you? You must be one of the few Frenchmen ever to do so."

Arceneaux huffed a low laugh. "Most of my fellow officers consider it incomprehensible, but yes, I have."

"I gather you've also acquired a fondness for our Cavalier poets."

"Pardon?"

"'A heart as soft, a heart as kind, / A heart as sound and free / As in the whole world thou canst find / That heart I'll give to thee,'" quoted Sebastian softly as the bowler delivered the ball toward the batsman.

"A lovely piece of poetry," said Arceneaux, his attention seemingly all for the bowler. "Should I recognize it?"

"It's from a poem by Robert Herrick."

"No ball," called the umpire.

The relentless August sun beat down on the open field, filling the air with the scent of dust and hot grass. Arceneaux held himself very still, his features wooden, his gaze on the fielders.

Sebastian said, "The same poem you copied out and gave to Miss Tennyson."

The Frenchman's throat worked as he swallowed. A sheen of perspiration covered his newly sun-reddened face. "You found it, did you?"

"Lady Devlin did."

"How did you guess it was from me?"

"The handwriting matches the notations you made on Miss Tennyson's translation of *The Lady of Shalott*."

"Ah. Of course."

They turned to walk away from the crowd and take the lane that curled toward the rolling countryside stretching away to the north. The dog trotted on ahead, tongue lolling happily, tail wagging. Sebastian said, "I hope you don't intend to insult my intelligence by attempting to continue denying the truth."

Arceneaux shook his head, his gaze on the herd of cows grazing placidly in the grassy, sunbaked pasture beside them. At the top of the slope, a stand of chestnuts drooped in the airless heat, their motionless leaves a vivid green swath against an achingly clear, forget-me-not blue sky. "You want the truth, my lord? The truth is, I fell in love with Gabrielle the first time I saw her. I was in the Reading Room at the museum going over some old manuscripts, and I just happened to look up and . . . there she was. She was standing beneath the high windows of the Reading Room, waiting for an attendant to hand her the book she wanted, and . . . I was lost."

"She returned your affections?"

He gave an odd smile. "She didn't fall in love with me at first sight, if that's what you're asking. But we quickly became good friends. We'd go for walks around the gardens of the museum and argue passionately about the competing visions of love in the two sections of the *Roman de la rose* or the reliability of the various medieval chroniclers. She was several years older than I, you know. She used to tease me about it, call me a little boy. I suspect that if I'd been her own age or older, she would never have allowed our friendship to progress the way it did. But as it was, she felt . . . safe with me. She told me later she'd fallen in love with me before she'd even realized what was happening."

"Did you ask her to marry you?"

"How could I? Situated as I am, a prisoner of war?" He pointed to the mile marker in the grass beside the road. "See that boundary? Under the terms of my parole, I am allowed to go no farther."

"Yet you did venture beyond it, the day you and Gabrielle went up to Camlet Moat."

Sebastian expected the man to deny it again. Instead, he gave a halfhearted shrug and said, "Sometimes . . . sometimes men succumb to mad impulses, I suppose, of frustration and despair and a foolish kind of bravado. But . . . how could I ask her to be my wife? How could I ask any woman to share such a circumscribed life, perhaps forever?"

"Yet some paroled French officers do marry here."

"They do. But they don't marry women like Gabrielle Tennyson. I loved her too much to ask her to live in a garret with me."

"She had no independence of her own?"

The Frenchman swung to face him. "Good God. Even if she had, what do you take me for?"

"You would hardly be the first man to live on his wife's income."

"I am not a fortune hunter!"

"I never said you were." Sebastian studied the other man's boyish, tightly held face and asked again, "Did you ask her to marry you?"

"I did not."

Arceneaux turned away, his gaze following the dog, who now had his nose to the ground, tail flying high as he tracked some fascinating scent to the prickly edge of the hedgerow, then sat down and let out a woof of disappointment and frustration.

Sebastian said, "I think you're still lying to me, Lieutenant."

Arceneaux gave a ragged laugh. "Oh? And would you blame me if I were?" He flung his arm in an expansive arc that took in the vast urban sprawl stretching away to the south. "You know the mood of hysteria that has swept over the city. Tell all those people Gabrielle Tennyson had a French lover and see what sort of conclusions they leap to. They'd hang me before nightfall."

"Were you lovers? And I mean that in every sense of the word."

"*Monsieur!*" Arceneaux held his head high, his nostrils flaring with indignation, his hands curling into fists at his sides.

"I should tell you that a postmortem has been performed on Miss Tennyson's remains." Sebastian hesitated. "We know she was no maid."

"Why, you—"

Sebastian flung up a forearm to block the punch Arceneaux threw at his jaw.

"*Bâtard!*" spat Arceneaux when Sebastian grabbed his wrist and held it.

Sebastian tightened his grip, his lips peeling away from his teeth as he leaned in close, enunciating his words with careful precision. "God damn it. Cut line, Lieutenant. Whose honor do you imagine I've insulted? Yours?" To suggest that a gentleman had seduced a woman he was unable or unwilling to marry was indeed a grave insult. "Because this isn't about you, Lieutenant—"

"If you think I care about that—"

"And it isn't about Gabrielle Tennyson's honor, either," Sebastian continued, ignoring the interruption. "It's about finding the man—or woman—who killed her, and who probably killed those two little boys with her. So tell me, what do you know of Miss Tennyson's interactions with Sir Stanley?"

"For the love of God, what are you suggesting now?" Arceneaux jerked back hard against Sebastian's hold.

Sebastian let him go. "Take a damper, would you? I'm

asking because when an attractive young woman and an older but still virile man are thrown often into each other's company, people talk."

"Who?" Arceneaux's fists clenched again. "Who is suggesting there was anything between them?"

"Lady Winthrop, for one. The woman was obviously more than a little jealous of the time Miss Tennyson spent with her husband."

The Frenchman spat in distain. "Lady Winthrop is a fool."

"Is she?"

"She lost her husband long ago, only not to Gabrielle. She lost him to his grief over his dead children, and to his passion for the past, and to the whispered wisdom of the Druids."

"So Miss Tennyson knew about Sir Stanley's interest in the Druids, did she?"

"She did. I told you, they were friends—good friends. But nothing more."

Sebastian studied the French officer's fine-boned, scholarly face. "And you had no concerns about the woman you loved spending so much time in another man's company?"

"I did not. Does that surprise you? Was it not your William Shakespeare who wrote of the 'marriage of true minds'?"

"'If this be error and upon me proved,'" quoted Sebastian, "'I never writ . . .'"

"'Nor no man ever loved.'" Arceneaux straightened his cravat and smoothed the front of his worn coat with painful dignity. "I loved Gabrielle, and I knew she loved me. I never doubted her. Not for a moment."

"And you know of no other man in her life?"

"No!"

"Do you know anything about her previous suitors?"

Arceneaux frowned as he watched Chien prance contentedly toward them, ears cocked. "I know there was one man—a suitor who pressed her repeatedly to marry him. Nothing she said seemed to dissuade the man. It was very odd."

"Who was this?"

"She didn't tell me his name, although I gathered he was a friend of the family."

"So her brother would likely know him?"

"I should think so, yes. The man was quite open in his pursuit of her. She told me he'd been dangling after her for years—even used to send her sweets and collections of love poems when she was still in the schoolroom."

"That sounds rather . . . distasteful."

"She found it so, yes."

Chien ran one happy, panting circle around them, then dashed off again after a sparrow chirping on the branch of a nearby rambling rose.

Sebastian said, "Did Miss Tennyson ever tell you why she was so determined never to wed?"

Arceneaux watched the sparrow take flight, chattering in annoyance. Chien paused with his tail up, ears on the prick. "It is not so unusual, is it, amongst women who have decided to devote themselves to scholarship?"

Chien came trotting back to stick his cold wet nose under Sebastian's hand. Sebastian let his hand drift down the dog's back. There had been a time when Hero, too, had sworn never to wed. She had only agreed to become his wife because she'd discovered she carried his child—and even then he'd had the devil's own time convincing her. He thought he could understand Miss Tennyson sticking resolutely to her choice.

Yet the sense that the Frenchman was lying remained with him.

Chapter 30

Jarvis stood at the edge of the terrace, a glass of champagne balanced in one hand as he let his gaze drift over the sweating men in tails and snowy cravats who chatted in desultory tones with gaily laughing ladies wearing filmy muslins and wide-brimmed hats. The sun was devilishly hot, the champagne warm. Normally Jarvis avoided such affairs. But this particular al fresco party was being hosted by Lady Elcott, the Prince's latest flirt, and Jarvis was here in attendance on the Prince.

A faint apprehensive fluttering amongst the crowd drew Jarvis's attention to a tall, familiar figure working her way across the terrace toward him. She wore a striking gown of cream silk trimmed in black and a black velvet hat with a cockade with black and cream feathers. She was not in any sense the most beautiful woman present, but she still managed to draw every eye.

"And here I thought you'd given up the frivolous amusements of society in order to join your husband in his sordid passion for murder investigations," said Jarvis as Hero paused beside him.

"I told you my involvement in this has nothing to do with Devlin. Gabrielle Tennyson was my friend, and whoever killed her will have to answer to me." She let her gaze, like his, slide over the ladies and gentlemen scattered across the lawn below. "Apart from which, I see no reason to view the two pursuits as mutually exclusive."

"Society and murder, you mean? You have a point. If truth were told, I suspect you'd probably find that Lady Elcott numbers more murderers amongst her guests than you'd be likely to find down at the corner pub . . . although I doubt any of these worthies will ever find themselves in the dock for their crimes."

She brought her gaze back to his face. "You do realize I now know about the Glastonbury Cross."

"Do you?" He took a slow sip of his champagne. "And what, precisely, do you 'know' of it?"

His response was obviously not what she had hoped for. Her eyes narrowed, but she covered her disappointment by taking a sip of her lemonade.

He smiled. "You learned this game from me, remember? And I'm still better at it than you. Shall I tell you precisely what you know? You know that amongst the late Richard Gough's collections, Bevin Childe found a box of ancient bones and a graven artifact he identified as the Glastonbury Cross. You also know that Miss Tennyson, when she heard of Childe's discovery, dismissed the cross as a modern forgery and and—in a rather alarming fit of unbridled choler—threw the item in question into the lake."

Hero returned his smile with one of her own. "Actually, I've figured out a bit more than that. I've been looking into those broadsheets you were telling me about—the ones expressing a longing for the 'once and future king' to return and lead the English to victory by ridding us of the unsatisfactory usurpers currently on the throne." She glanced over to where the Prince Regent, red-faced and sweating, his coat of Bath superfine straining across his back, had his face and shoulders hunched over a mounded plate of buttered crab. "I can see how the expression of such sentiments might be causing distress in certain cir-

cles, even if, as you intimated, the broadsheets were originally the work of French agents. These things can sometimes
take on a life of their own. And while we like to think our
own age too sophisticated to give heed to such legends,
the truth is that far too many people out there are still
both ignorant and woefully credulous—and all too ready
to believe in a miraculous savior."

"How true."

A warm wind gusted up, shifting the spreading
branches of an elm overhead and casting dancing patterns
of light and shadow across the strong features of her face.
She said, "Some six hundred years ago, Henry the Second
was also troubled by restless subjects who yearned for Arthur to return from the dead and save them. Fortunately
for him, the monks of Glastonbury Abbey stepped into
the breach with their well-timed discovery of what they
claimed were King Arthur and Guinevere's bones."

"Most fortuitous, was it not?" said Jarvis with a smile.

"Mmm. And how injudicious of good old King Henry
the Eighth to lose such a valuable national treasure in
his scramble to take over the wealth of the church, thus
allowing all those nasty rumors to start up again."

"Shockingly careless of him," agreed Jarvis, consign-
ing his champagne glass to a passing waiter.

"Yet history does sometimes have a way of repeating
itself . . . or should I say, rather, that it can be made to
repeat itself? Particularly if a certain courageous young
woman who threatens to get in the way is removed."

Jarvis drew a figured gold snuffbox from his pocket
and flipped it open with one finger.

Hero watched him, her gaze on his face. "Gabrielle
was not the type of woman to frighten easily. Yet before
she died, she was afraid of someone. Someone powerful.
I think she was afraid of you."

He raised a pinch of snuff to one nostril and sniffed.
"She had a unique way of showing it, wouldn't you say?"

Hero leaned into him, the polite society smile still curving her lips, her voice low. "I think Gabrielle was right: That cross is a forgery. I think you somehow coerced Childe into claiming he had discovered the fake cross amongst Gough's collections, in the hopes that news of its recovery would help dampen these dangerous murmurs calling for King Arthur's return. After all, if it worked for the Plantagenets a few hundred years ago, why shouldn't it work now?"

"Why not, indeed?"

"The one thing I haven't figured out yet is how you convinced Childe to cooperate."

"Really, Hero; perhaps you should consider giving up this budding interest in murder investigations and turn your hand instead to writing lurid romances." He saw something he couldn't quite read flicker in her eyes, and closed his snuffbox with a snap. "I told you, I did not kill your troublesome friend."

When she remained silent, he gave a soft laugh. "You don't believe me, do you?"

"Almost. But not entirely." She tilted her head to one side. "If you considered it necessary, would you have killed her—even knowing she was my friend?"

"Without hesitation."

"And would you tell me?"

"Before, yes. Now . . . I'm not so certain."

"Because of Devlin, you mean?"

"Yes." He let his gaze drift once more across the assembly of hot aristocrats. "And are you regretting it? Your decision to be less than forthcoming with your new husband, I mean?"

"No."

He brought his gaze back to her face. "So sure, Hero?" he asked, and saw her color deepen.

She said, "I don't believe you deliberately had Gabrielle killed. But can you be so certain you are not indirectly responsible?"

Father's and daughter's gazes locked, and held.

"Darling!"

Hero turned as Lady Elcott fluttered up to them trailing a cloud of filmy lime organza and yards of cream satin ribbon. She rested the tips of her exquisitely manicured fingers on Hero's arm and arched her overplucked brows. "You came! What a delight! Did you bring that wicked husband of yours with you?"

"Not this time," said Hero.

"Excuse me," said Jarvis with a bow, moving adroitly to the Prince's side in time to prevent him from starting on a second plate of crab.

When he looked back toward the edge of the terrace, Hero had managed to escape their hostess's clutches and disappear.

※

Sebastian found Paul Gibson leaning over the stone platform in the center of the outbuilding behind his surgery. He whistled softly as he worked, his arms plunged up to the elbows in the gory distended abdomen of a cadaver so bloated and discolored and ripe that it made Sebastian gag.

"Good God," he said, his eyes watering as the full force of the foul stench engulfed him. "Where the devil did they find that one?"

"Pulled him out of Fleet Ditch, at West Street. Caught up under the bridge, he was, and from the look of things, he was there a good long while."

"And no one smelled him?"

"There's an abattoir at the corner. I suppose the odors just sort of . . . mingled." The surgeon grinned and reached for a rag to wipe his hands and arms. "So what can I do for you, then? And please don't tell me you're sending me another corpse, because I've already got two more to deal with when I'm through with this one."

"No more corpses." Retreating to the sun-blasted

yard, Sebastian stood hunched over with his hands braced on his thighs as he sucked fresh air into his lungs. "Just a question, about Gabrielle Tennyson. You said she was no longer a maid. Any chance she could have been with child?"

"No trace of it that I saw."

"Would you be able to tell for certain? I mean, even if she wasn't very far along?"

"Let's put it this way: If she was far enough along to know it, I'd know it."

Sebastian straightened, then swallowed quickly as another whiff of the cadaver hit him. "Bloody hell. I don't know how you stand it."

Gibson gave a soft chuckle. "After a while, you don't notice the smell." He thought about it a moment, then added, "Usually."

"I wasn't talking about just the smell."

"Ah." The Irishman's gaze met Sebastian's, the merriment now gone from his face. "The thing of it is, you see, by the time I get them, they're just so much tissue and bone, and that's what I focus on—that's the mystery I need to unravel. I don't need to dwell on the fear and pain they must have experienced during whatever happened that landed them on my table. I don't need to pry into whatever betrayal and hurt, or anger and despair was in their lives. That's what you do. And to tell you the truth, Devlin, I don't know how *you* do it."

When Sebastian remained silent, Gibson rested a hand on his shoulder, then turned back toward the stone outbuilding and its bloated, decaying occupant.

"Was he murdered?" Sebastian called after him. "The man on your table in there, I mean."

Gibson paused in the open doorway to look back at him. "Not this one. Tumbled into the water drunk and drowned, most likely. I doubt he even knew what hit him—which is probably not a bad way to go, if you've got to go."

"I suppose it does beat some of the alternatives."

Gibson grunted. "You think Gabrielle Tennyson and her young cousins were killed by a man who was afraid he'd planted a babe in her belly?"

Sebastian started to remind him that no one knew for certain yet that either Alfred or George Tennyson was dead. Then he let it go. Surely it was only a matter of time before one of the search parties or some farmer out walking with his dog came upon the children's small bodies half submerged in a ditch or hidden beneath the leaf mold in a hollow left by a downed tree?

He shook his head. "I don't know. At this point, anything's possible."

"Poor girl," said Gibson with a sigh. "Poor, poor girl."

The setting sun was painting purple and orange streaks low on the western horizon by the time Sebastian reached the Adelphi Buildings overlooking the Thames. He was mounting the steps to the Tennyson town house when he heard his name called.

"Lord Devlin."

Turning, he saw Gabrielle's brother striding across the street toward him. "Have you some news?" asked Hildeyard Tennyson, his strained features suffused with an agonized hope.

"I'm sorry; no."

Tennyson's lips parted with the pain of disappointment. He'd obviously been out again looking for the children; dust layered his coat and top boots, and his face was slick with sweat and tinged red by too many hours spent beneath a hot sun.

"You're still searching the chase?" asked Sebastian as they turned to walk along the terrace overlooking the Thames.

"The woodland and the surrounding farms and fields,

yes. But so far, we've found nothing. Not a trace. It's as if the children vanished into the mist." The barrister blew out a long, ragged breath. "Simply . . . vanished."

Sebastian stared off over the river, where the sinking sun spilled a wash of gold across the water. Barges loaded with coal rode low and dark in the water; a wherryman rowing his fare across to Lambeth plied his oars. The splash of his wooden panels threw up arcs of droplets that glistened like diamonds in the dying light.

Tennyson followed Sebastian's gaze, the circles beneath his eyes dark as he watched the wherryman's progress across the river. "I know everyone, from the magistrates and constables to the farmers and workmen I've hired, thinks the boys must be dead. I hear them speaking amongst themselves. They all think they're looking for a shallow grave. But they don't let on to me."

Sebastian kept his gaze on the water.

After a moment, Tennyson said, "My cousin—the boys' father—is on his way down from Lincolnshire. He's not well, you know. I just hope to God the journey doesn't kill him." He hesitated, then added, "Or the inevitable grief."

Sebastian found it difficult to meet the other man's strained, desperate eyes. "You told me the other day your sister had no interest in marriage."

"She didn't, no," said the barrister slowly, obviously struggling to follow Sebastian's train of thought. "She quite fixed her mind against it at an early age. Our father blamed her attitude on the influence of the likes of the Misses Berry and Catherine Talbot. But the truth is, Gabrielle was far more interested in Roman ruins and the inscriptions on medieval tombstones than in bride clothes or layettes."

"Nevertheless, she must have attracted some suitors over the years."

"Some, yes. But without encouragement, few stayed around for long."

"Do you remember any who were more persistent than the others?"

Tennyson thought about it a moment. "Well, I suppose Childe held out longer than most. But— Good God; no one could suspect him of such a deed."

"Childe? You mean, Bevin Childe?"

"Yes. You know him? Frankly, I would have thought if anyone had a chance with Gabrielle, it would be Childe. I mean, the man has both a comfortable independence and a passion for antiquities that matched her own. She'd known him since she was still in the schoolroom—indeed, he claims he first fell in love with her when she was little more than a child in pigtails and a torn flounce. But she would have none of him."

"How did he take her rejection of his suit?"

A touch of amusement lit up the barrister's haggard features. "Frankly? With incredulity. No one could ever accuse Childe of having a low opinion of himself. At first he was convinced she was merely displaying what he called 'a becoming degree of maidenly modesty.' Then, when he was finally brought to understand that she was not so much shy as merely disinterested, he credited her lack of enthusiasm to an imperfect understanding of his worth. I'd never before realized what an insufferable bore the man could be. I'm afraid he made quite a cake of himself."

"When did he finally get the hint?"

"That his suit was hopeless? I'm not certain he ever did. She was complaining about him shortly before I left for Kent."

"Complaining about his disparagement of her theories about Camlet Moat, you mean?"

"No. About his continued refusal to accept her rejection of his suit as final."

Chapter 31

*B*evin Childe was feeling his way down the unlit stairs from his rooms in St. James's Street when Sebastian stepped out of the shadows of the landing to grab the scholar by the back of his coat with both fists and swing him around to slam him face-first against the wall.

"Merciful heavens," bleated the antiquary as his protuberant belly *thwumped* into the paneling. "Oh dear, oh dear, oh dear. My purse is in the inner pocket of my coat. You're welcome to it, sir, although I must warn you that you will find there scant reward for this brutish act of violence upon my person."

"I am not interested in your bloody purse," growled Sebastian.

"Devlin?" The antiquary went limp with relief. "Is that you?" He attempted to twist around but found himself frustrated when Sebastian tightened his grip. "Good God; I imagined you a cutpurse." He stiffened with gathering outrage. "What is the meaning of this?"

Sebastian kept his voice low and deadly calm. "I should perhaps have warned you that when it comes to murder, I am not a patient man. And you, Mr. Childe, are sorely trying my patience."

"There are laws in this country, you know. You can't

simply go around accosting gentlemen in their lodgings. It's not legal. It's not right. It's not—not the done thing!"

Sebastian resisted the urge to laugh out loud. Instead, he leaned into the antiquary until the man's plump face was squished sideways against the elegantly paneled wainscoting. "You didn't tell me you were a suitor for Miss Tennyson's hand. A disgruntled and annoyingly persistent suitor."

"Well, it's not the sort of thing a gentleman does go around talking about, now, is it? I mean, a man has his pride, don't you know?"

"So you're saying your pride was offended by Miss Tennyson's rejection of your suit?"

Childe quivered, as if suddenly becoming aware of the pit yawning at his feet. "I don't know if I'd say that, exactly."

"Then what would you say? *Exactly?*"

"Women such as Miss Tennyson must be delicately wooed. But I'm a persistent man. I've no doubt my suit would eventually have prospered."

"You've no doubt."

"None." Childe's voice had grown in confidence to the point of sounding smug.

"So you would have me believe you didn't know she'd recently fallen in love with a dashing young cavalry officer she met at the British Museum?"

"What?" Childe tried again to twist around, but Sebastian held him fast. "I don't believe it! Who? Who is this man? This is nonsense. You're making that up. It's impossible."

"You'd better hope I don't discover that you did know."

Childe blanched. "What does that mean?"

"It means," said Sebastian, shifting his grip, "that there is a certain kind of man who doesn't take kindly to the realization that the woman he's decided to honor by making her his wife has scorned his courtship not because she was shy and needed to be 'delicately wooed,' but because she quite frankly preferred another man to him. What does it take to drive a man like you to violence, Childe? Hmm? A threat to your scholarly reputation? Or an affront to your manhood? How would you react, I wonder, if the very same woman who'd humiliated you as a suitor then threatened to destroy your credibility as an antiquary? Would that be enough to compel you to murder?"

Perspiration glistened on the man's forehead and clustered in droplets on the end of his nose. A foul odor of sweat and fear rose from his person, and his voice, when he spoke, was a high-pitched crack. "This is madness. Miss Tennyson and I disagreed about the authenticity of the cross in Gough's collection; that is all. My credibility as an antiquary was never threatened in any way."

"Then why—"

Sebastian broke off at the sound of the street door opening below. Men's voices, slurred by drink, echoed up the stairwell. He loosed his hold on the antiquary and took a step back.

"I'm not through with you. When I find out more, I'll be back. And if I discover you've been lying to me, I can guarantee you're going to regret it."

※

Sebastian returned to Brook Street to find Hero perusing an improving pamphlet written by one Ezekiel Smyth and entitled *Satan, Druidism, and the Path to Everlasting Damnation.*

"Good God," he said. "What are you reading?"

She laughed and cast it aside. "Believe it or not, this piece of sanctimonious drivel was written by George and Alfred Tennyson's aunt, Mary Bourne."

"You can't be serious."

"Oh, but I am. She also attends a weekly Bible study class with one Reverend Samuel at the Savoy Chapel. Another member of the study group is none other than Lady Winthrop."

He reached for the pamphlet and flipped through it. "Now, that's interesting."

"It is, isn't it?" She looked over at him, her eyes narrowing. "You've split the shoulder seam of your coat; what have you been doing?"

He glanced down at his coat. "Ah. I hadn't noticed. It could have been when Lieutenant Arceneaux tried to draw my cork for insulting the honor of the woman he loved—"

"How did you do that?"

"By asking if he lay with her. He says he did not, incidentally."

"Do you believe him?"

"No. He did, however, provide me with one bit of information which proved to be valuable: It seems Mr. Bevin Childe was a suitor for Miss Tennyson's hand—an annoying suitor who refused to take no for an answer. According to Hildeyard, the man has been in love with Gabrielle since she was a child."

Hero stared at him. "Did you say, since she was a child?"

"Yes; why?"

But she simply shook her head and refused to be drawn any further.

*

Thursday, 6 August

By 9:50 the next morning, Hero was seated in her carriage outside the British Museum, a sketch pad open on her lap and her pencils sharpened and at the ready.

She had no illusions about her artistic abilities. She was able to draw a fairly credible, easily recognizable likeness of an individual. But her sketches were competent, nothing more. If she were a true artist, she could have sketched Bevin Childe from memory. As it was, that was beyond her.

And so she waited in the cool morning shade cast by the tall fronts of the town houses lining Great Russell Street. At exactly 9:58, a hackney pulled up outside the Pied Piper. His movements slow and ponderous in that stately way of his, Mr. Bevin Childe descended from the carriage, then stood on the flagway to pay his fare.

He cast one disinterested glance at the yellow-bodied carriage waiting near the museum, then strode across the street, his brass-handled walking stick tucked up under one arm.

Within the shadows of her carriage, Hero's pencil scratched furiously, capturing in bold strokes the essence of his likeness.

As if somehow aware of her intense scrutiny, he paused for a moment outside the museum's gatehouse, the high points of his shirt collar digging into his plump cheeks as he turned his head to glance around. Then he disappeared from her view.

She spent the next ten minutes refining her sketch, adding details and nuances. Then she ordered her coachman to drive to Covent Garden.

The man's jaw sagged. "I beg your pardon, m'lady, but did you say 'Covent Garden'?"

"I did."

He bowed. "Yes, m'lady."

Chapter 32

*S*ebastian was alone at his breakfast table reading the latest reports on the Americans' invasion of Canada when a knock sounded at the entrance. He heard his majordomo, Morey, cross to open the front door; then a dog's enthusiastic barking echoed in the hall.

Sebastian raised his head.

"Chien! No!" someone shouted. "Come back!"

Morey hissed. "Sir! I really must insist that you control your— Oh, merciful heavens."

A scrambling clatter of nails sounded on the marble floor in the hall, and a familiar black and brown mongrel burst into the room, tail wagging and tongue lolling in confident expectation of an enthusiastic reception.

"So you're proud of yourself, are you?" said Sebastian, setting aside his paper.

"Chien!" Lieutenant Philippe Arceneaux appeared in the doorway. "I do most profusely beg your pardon, my lord. *Chien*, heel!"

"It's all right," Sebastian told the anxious majordomo hovering behind the French officer. "The Lieutenant and his ill-mannered hound are both known to me. And no, you are not to take that as an invitation to further liberties," he warned as the dog pawed at his gleaming Hessians. "Mar the shine on my boots, and Calhoun will nail your hide to the stable door. And if you think that an idle threat, you have obviously not yet made the acquaintance of my valet."

"He might be more inclined to believe you," observed Arceneaux with a smile, "if you were not pulling his ears."

"Perhaps. Do come in and sit down, Lieutenant. May I offer you some breakfast? And no, that question was not addressed to you, you hell-born hound, so you can cease eyeing my ham with such soulful intent."

"Thank you, my lord, but I have already eaten—we have *both* eaten," he added, frowning at the dog. "Shame on you, Chien; you have the manners of a tatterdemalion. Come away from there."

The dog settled on his hindquarters beside Sebastian's chair and whined.

"Obedient too, I see," observed Sebastian, draining his tankard.

"He likes you."

"He likes my ham."

Arceneaux laughed. Then his smile faded. "I have brought him with me because I have a request to make of you."

Sebastian looked up from scratching behind the dog's ears. "Oh?"

"It seems to me that if I could take Chien up to Camlet Moat, there's a good possibility he might pick up some trace of Alfred and George, something to tell us where they've gone or what has happened to them. Something the authorities have missed. He was very fond of the children."

Sebastian was silent for a moment, considering the implications of the request. "Sounds like a reasonable idea. But why come to me?"

"Because I am not allowed to journey more than a

mile beyond the boundaries of the city. But if you were to square it with the authorities and go with us . . ."

Sebastian studied Arceneaux's fine-boned, earnest face, with its boyish scattering of freckles and wide, sky blue eyes. "Why not? It's worth a try." He pushed to his feet. "See what you can do to keep your faithful hound out of the ham while I order my curricle brought round."

⁂

A bored clerk at the Admiralty, the government department in charge of all prisoners of war, grudgingly granted permission for Arceneaux to leave London in Sebastian's custody. As they left the crowded streets of the city behind, Sebastian let his hands drop; the chestnuts leapt forward, and Chien scrambled upright on the seat between the two men, his nose lifted and eyes half closed in blissful appreciation of the rushing wind.

Sebastian eyed the mongrel with a healthy dose of skepticism. "Personally, I wouldn't have said he numbered any bloodhounds amongst his diverse and doubtless disreputable ancestry."

Arceneaux looped an arm over the happy animal's shoulders. "Perhaps not. But the boys used to play hide-and-seek with him, and he was always very good at finding them."

Sebastian steadied his horses. "When you drove Miss Tennyson and the lads out to the moat last week, did you take Chien with you?"

"I never said I—"

"Just answer the bloody question."

Arceneaux let out a huff of resignation. "We did, yes." A faint smile of remembrance lightened his features. "Chien leapt into the moat after a duck and then rolled around in the loose dirt beside the trenches. Gabrielle told him he was not welcome up there ever again."

The Frenchman fell silent, his grip on the dog tightening as he stared off across the sun-drenched fields, his own thoughts doubtless lost in the past. It wasn't until they had reached the overgrown woods of the chase that he said, "I've been thinking and thinking, trying to come up with some reason for her to have taken the boys there again this past Sunday." He shook his head. "But I can't."

"Did you know that Bevin Childe had in his possession a lead cross that was said to have come from the graves of King Arthur and Guinevere?"

"*Mon dieu.* You can't mean the Glastonbury Cross?"

"That's it. Childe claims to have found it along with a box of old bones amongst the collections he's been cataloging at Gough Hall. But Miss Tennyson was convinced it was a recent forgery."

"Is that what she was talking about? But . . . if that's all it was, why wouldn't she have told me?"

"I was hoping perhaps you could help explain that. I gather the controversy surrounding the discovery of Arthur's grave in the twelfth century is considerable?"

Arceneaux nodded. "The problem is, it all seems just a shade too tidy. At the time, the Anglo-Norman kings were facing considerable opposition to their attempts to conquer Wales, and much of that resistance used Arthur as a rallying cry. The country people still believed in the old legends—that Arthur had never really died and would one day return from the mystical Isle of Avalon to expel the forces of evil."

"With the Normans and the Plantagenet kings being identified as the forces of evil?"

"Basically, yes. The thing of it was, you see, there was no grave anyone could point to and say, 'Here lies King Arthur, dead and buried.' That made it easy for people to believe that he hadn't actually died—and could therefore someday return. So the grave's discovery was a true boon to the Plantagenets. They could then say, 'See, Arthur is dead. Here is his grave. He's not coming back. We are his rightful heirs.'"

"Why Glastonbury Abbey?"

"Well, at one time the site of Glastonbury actually was a misty island surrounded by marshland, which helps give some credibility to the association with Avalon. But what makes the monks' discovery particularly suspect is that at the time they claimed to have found Arthur's grave, the abbey church had just burned down and their chief patron and benefactor—Henry the Second himself—had died. They needed money, and what better way to increase their pilgrim traffic than with the discovery of the burial site of King Arthur and his queen?"

"In other words, it was all a hoax."

"It's tempting to see it that way. The problem is, if it was simply a scheme to increase the abbey's revenue, then the monks didn't do a very good job of advertising their find. And the way the burial was described—sixteen feet down, in a hollowed-out log—sounds oddly appropriate to a sixth-century burial. One would have thought that if they were manufacturing a hoax, the monks in their ignorance would have come up with something a bit more . . ." He hesitated, searching for the right word.

"Regal?" suggested Sebastian, guiding his horses onto the narrow track that led to the moat.

"Yes."

"I'm told the cross disappeared during the Commonwealth."

"It did, although it was reportedly seen early in the last century."

"In other words, Bevin Childe could conceivably have found the Glastonbury Cross amongst the collection he's been cataloging—leaving aside the question of whether it was actually manufactured in the twelfth century or the sixth."

"Theoretically, I suppose he could have."

"So why was Miss Tennyson convinced it was a recent forgery?"

Arceneaux looked out over the shady glade surrounding the moat. "I don't know. I gather Childe believes the cross to be genuine—at least to the twelfth century?"

"So he claims."

"Where is it? Would it be possible for me to see it?"

Sebastian drew up near the land bridge to the island, the horses snorting and sidling nervously. Tom jumped down and ran to their heads.

"Unfortunately, no. Childe claims Miss Tennyson threw it into Gough Hall's ornamental lake the Friday before she died."

"She did what?"

Sebastian dropped to the ground, his boots sinking into the soft earth. "I gather she had something of a temper?"

"She did, yes." Arceneaux climbed down more carefully, the dog bounding after him. "But it still seems a strange thing to have done."

Sebastian started to say, "Maybe she—" Then he broke off, his gaze caught by a dark, motionless shape floating at the edge of the moat's stagnant green waters. The dog stopped in his tracks, the fur on his back rising as his lips pulled away from his teeth and a deep, throaty growl rumbled in his chest.

Arceneaux rested a hand on Chien's head, his own voice a whisper. "What is it?"

"Stay here," said Sebastian, sliding down the embankment to the water's edge.

The man's body floated facedown in the algae-scummed water, arms flung stiffly to its sides. Splashing into the murky shallows, Sebastian fisted his hand around the collar of the brown corduroy coat and hauled the body up onto the bank, the bracken and ferns crushing beneath his boot heels and the dead man's sodden, squelching weight.

"Is he dead?" Arceneaux asked, holding the dog at the top of the ancient earthen works. "Who is it?"

Sebastian hesitated a moment, his breath coming uncomfortably hard. The man's clothes were rough, his boots worn, his golden red hair worn a bit too long. Hunkering down beside the body, Sebastian slowly rolled it over.

The man flopped onto his back with a sodden plop, arms flailing outward, to reveal a pale, dripping face and blankly staring eyes. A water-blurred stain discolored the torn, charred front of his leather jerkin and smock.

Sebastian sank back on his heels, one hand coming up to adjust his hat lower over his eyes as he blew out a long breath. "It's Rory Forster."

Chapter 33

*T*he local magistrate proved to be a foul-tempered, heavy-featured squire named John Richards.

Well into middle age and running comfortably to fat, Squire John was far more interested in his hounds and the joint his cook was preparing for his dinner than in all the sordid, tedious requirements of a murder investigation. When Tom—upon discovering that Sir Stanley and his lady had removed to London for a few days—carried Sebastian's message to the Squire, the tiger had a hard time convincing the man to leave his cow pasture.

The Squire now stood on the shady bank of the moat, one beefy hand sliding over his ruddy, sagging jowls as he stared down at the waterlogged body at his feet. "Well, hell," he muttered, his brows beetling into a fierce scowl. "Truth be told, I was more than half convinced your tiger was making up the whole tale when he came to me. I mean, two bodies found floating in Camlet Moat in one week? Impossible, I'd have said. But here's another one, all right."

"At least this one's local," observed Sebastian.

The Squire drew a handkerchief from his pocket and wiped his bulbous nose. "But that's the worst part of it, you see. Can't imagine Bow Street interesting themselves in the murder of some blacksmith's son from Cockfosters." A hopeful gleam crept into his watery gray eyes. "Unless, of course, you think this might have something to do with that young gentlewoman we found here last Sunday?"

"I wouldn't be surprised but what it does."

The Squire brightened. "I'll send one of the lads off to London right away." A flicker of movement drew his attention across the moat, to where Philippe Arceneaux was methodically crisscrossing the island with Chien bounding enthusiastically at his side. The Squire wiped his nose again, his eyes narrowing with suspicion. "Who did you say that fellow was?"

"My dog handler."

"That's your dog?"

"It is."

"Huh. Fellow's got a Frenchy look about him, if you ask me. They're saying it was a Frenchman who killed that gentlewoman, you know. What is this fellow doing with that dog, exactly?"

"I was hoping the dog might pick up some trace of the missing Tennyson children."

When the Squire still looked doubtful, Sebastian added, "It's a . . . a Strand hound. They're famous for their ability to track missing persons. This one is particularly well trained and talented."

"Well trained, you say?" asked the Squire, just as Chien flushed up a rabbit and tore off after it through the underbrush.

Behind him, Arceneaux shouted, "Chien! *À moi. Imbécile.*"

"He is sometimes distracted by the local fauna," Sebastian admitted.

The Squire sniffed. "Best keep him away from Forster here. Don't reckon Bow Street would fancy dog prints all over the place."

Sebastian hunkered down again to study the dead man's charred clothing and gaping raw wound. The flies were already busy, and he brushed them away with his hand. He didn't need Gibson to tell him that the man had been shot—and at close quarters. But whatever other secrets the dead man had to reveal would need to wait for the anatomist's examination. After a moment, Sebastian said, "I'm told Forster married a local widow this past year."

"That's right. Rachel Clark, of Hollyhock Farm. I sent one of the lads over there to warn her, just in case what your tiger was telling me turned out to be true." The Squire sniffed again. "She could've done a sight better, if you ask me. Very prosperous property, Hollyhock Farm. But then, there's no denying Forster was a handsome man. And when it comes to good-looking men, it's a rare woman who doesn't make a fool of herself." The Squire's lips pursed as he shifted his brooding gaze to Sebastian. "Course, it's even worse when they deck themselves out like a Bond Street beau and drive a fancy sporting carriage."

Sebastian cleared his throat and pushed to his feet. "Yes, well . . . I'd best remove my Strand hound and his handler before they contaminate the scene." He motioned to Arceneaux, who dragged Chien from where he was now intently following the hopping progress of a toad and hauled the reluctant canine off toward the curricle.

For one moment, Sebastian considered as a courtesy telling the Squire of his intention to visit the twice-widowed Rachel of Hollyhock Farm. Then the Squire added darkly, "And a title, of course. Just let a man have looks and a title, and when it comes to the ladies, it doesn't matter what sort of a dastardly reputation the sot might have."

Sebastian touched his hat and bowed. "Squire John."

As they drove away, he was aware of the Squire still standing at the water's edge, the shade of the ancient grove pooling heavily around him, one meaty hand swiping the air before his face as he batted at the thickening cloud of flies.

※

"I would like to apologize," said Arceneaux stiffly, one hand resting around the damp, happy dog as they drove toward Hollyhock Farm. "I put you through all this, and for what? Chien found no trace of the boys. Nothing."

Sebastian glanced over at him. "It was worth a try."

The Frenchman stared straight ahead, his face troubled. "None of this makes any sense. What could have happened to them? How could they have simply disappeared like this? And why?"

But it was a question Sebastian could not begin to answer.

※

Hero found the area around Covent Garden's vast square crowded with a swarm of fruit and vegetable sellers. Vendors' cries of "Ripe cher-ries, sixpence a pound" and "Buy my primroses, two bunches a penny" echoed through the narrow streets; the scent of freshly cut flowers and damp earth and unwashed, closely packed bodies hung heavily in the air. As they pushed their way closer to the market, the coachman was forced to check his horses to a crawl.

She kept her gaze focused straight ahead, ignoring the pleading cries of the urchins who leapt up to press their faces against her carriage windows and the roar of laughter from the ragged crowd gathered around a Punch and Judy show on the church steps. By day, the classical piazza laid out before St. Paul's by Inigo Jones was the site of London's largest produce market. But later, when the shadows of evening stretched across the cobblestones and the square's motley collection of stalls and lean-tos closed for the night, willing ladies in tawdry satins with plunging necklines and husky crooning voices would emerge to loiter beneath the colonnades and soaring porticos and hiss their lewd invitations to passersby.

Slowly inching through the throng, the carriage finally swung onto King Street and then drew up before a once grand mansion now divided into lodgings. Hero lowered her hat's veil and waited while her footman knocked on the house's warped, cracked door. It wasn't until the door was opened and the large, familiar form of Molly O'Keefe, the house's mistress, filled the entrance that the footman came to let down the carriage steps.

The two women had come to know each other months earlier, when Hero was researching a theory on the economic causes of the recent explosion in the number of prostitutes in the city. Clucking at the sight of her, Molly whisked Hero into a dilapidated hall with stained, once grand paneling and a broken chandelier that dangled precariously overhead, then slammed the door in the faces of her gawking neighbors. "Yer ladyship! Sakes alive, I ne'er thought to be seeing ye again."

"Molly, I need your help," said Hero, and drew the portrait of Bevin Childe from her sketch pad.

Chapter 34

*T*rue to its name, Hollyhock Farm proved to be a rambling brick cottage with a low slate roof and white-painted windows surrounded by a riot of hollyhocks and lavender and fat pink cabbage roses as big as Sebastian's fist. At the edge of the garden curled a lazy stream spanned by an old, honeysuckle-draped wooden bridge. A flock of white geese waddling along the stream's banks looked up, the warm wind ruffling their feathers, their necks arching in alarm as Chien stood up on the curricle's seat and let out a woof in their direction.

"Do try to keep that hell-born hound out of the geese, will you?" said Sebastian, dropping lightly to the gravel verge outside the garden.

"Chien," whispered Arceneaux, pulling the dog's head around. "Behave."

Sebastian had expected to find the widow of Hollyhock Farm surrounded in her grief by family and neighbors. But she was alone in her garden, her arms wrapped across her chest, the skirts of her simple muslin gown brushing the trailing plantings of lady's mantle and alyssum as she paced the cottage's flagstone paths. She was obviously past the first blush of youth, perhaps even a year or two older than her dead husband, but still slim and attractive, with softly waving golden hair and a sweet, heart-shaped face.

"Mrs. Forster," said Sebastian, drawing up a few feet away from her. "If I might have a word with you?"

The face she turned to him was dry-eyed, a pale mask of shock and grief and something else—something that looked suspiciously like relief, as if she were slowly wakening from a seductive nightmare. She nodded and swallowed hard, her throat cording with the effort. "They're saying Rory might be dead. That his body was found by some London lord out at Camlet Moat. Is it true, then?"

"It is, yes. I'm sorry. Please allow me to offer my condolences on the loss of your husband."

She sucked in a deep breath that shuddered her chest. But otherwise she struck him as remarkably composed. "Thank you."

"I know the timing is awkward, but would you mind if I asked a few questions?"

She shook her head and drew in another of those shaky breaths. "No. Although I don't know what I can tell you that would be of any use to you. I didn't even know Rory was going out to the moat this morning. He said he was planning to work on the roof of the cow shed. Lord knows it's needed mending these past six weeks or more."

"I would imagine things have been rather neglected around the farm, with your husband working for Sir Stanley at Camlet Moat."

She turned to walk along the path, Sebastian beside her. "I told him he was going to need to give up that nonsense for the harvest. But . . ."

"He was reluctant to quit?"

"He said he could hire Jack Williams to take his place around here for half what he was making with Sir Stanley. But a farm needs more than hired men. It's one of the reasons I—" She broke off and bit her lip.

It's one of the reasons I married him. The unsaid words hung in the air.

Pausing beside a rose-covered arch, she let her gaze drift to the slowly sliding waters of the stream. She was obviously better bred than her husband, her farm prosperous. She would have been quite a catch for a blacksmith's younger son.

Sebastian drew up beside her. "Sir Stanley has given up the excavations and filled in the trenches," he said. "So why would your husband go out to the moat this morning?"

She threw him a quick glance. Then her gaze skittered away, but not before he saw the leap of fear in her eyes.

"Did he go out to the moat last Sunday?" asked Sebastian.

"Rory? Oh, no. He was here with me, all night."

"He told you to say that, didn't he?"

She shook her head, her face pinched.

"You can't do your husband any harm by admitting the truth now. He's dead. But the more we know, the better chance we'll have of finding who killed him." Sebastian hesitated, then said again, "He went to the moat Sunday, didn't he?"

Her voice was a painful whisper. "He warned me not to tell anyone. Made me swear to keep his secret."

And probably threatened to beat her if she let the truth slip, Sebastian thought. Aloud, he said, "What time did he leave the farm last Sunday?"

She pressed a tight fist against her lips. "Not long before sunset. Even though it was Sunday and there wasn't likely to be anyone about, he still thought it best to wait till late."

"Do you know why he went?"

Her lip curled. "On account of the treasure, of course. He was mad for it. Much rather dig useless holes in the dirt out there than dig the new well we needed here."

"What time did he come home?"

"About midnight, I suppose. All wet, he was. Said he'd lost his footing and slipped into the moat. I was that put out with him. But he told me to shut up. Said we were going to be rich—that I was going to have fine silks and satins, and my own carriage, just like Squire John's lady."

"Do you think he actually found something?"

"If he did, he didn't come home with any of it; I can tell you that much." A faint hint of color touched her cheeks. "I checked his pockets, you see, after he fell asleep. Of course, he could've hid it someplace again, before he came in." She paused, then added, almost bitterly, "And now he's gone and got himself killed."

"Had you noticed him behaving in any way out of the ordinary these last few days?"

She thought about it a moment, then shook her head. "Not unless you count going into London yesterday."

"Did he often go to London?"

"Never knew him to do it before."

A shout drew Sebastian's attention to the stream, where Chien could be seen advancing on the geese in a low crouch, his tail tucked between his legs, his eyes fixed and focused.

Sebastian said, "Did he tell you why he went?"

"No. Although he was in a rare good mood when he came home. I hadn't seen him in such high spirits since the days when he was courting me." At the memory, a softness came over her features, then faded.

Arceneaux's voice drifted up from the banks of the stream. "Chien."

Sebastian asked quickly, "Is there anything else you can tell me that might help?"

She shook her head just as Arceneaux shouted, "Chien! *Mon dieu.* No!"

⁂

The message from Molly O'Keefe reached Hero late that afternoon.

She returned to Covent Garden just as the slanting, golden light of early evening was beginning to flood the mean, narrow streets. The residents of Molly's lodging house were already stirring.

"What have you found?" Hero asked Molly as a raucous trill of laughter floated from somewhere on the first floor above and two blowsy women pushed past them toward the lodging house door. The lodging house was not a brothel, although there was no denying that many of its occupants were Cyprians. But these women took their customers elsewhere, to establishments known as "accommodation houses."

One of the Cyprians, a black-haired woman in feathers and a diaphanous silver-spangled gown, smacked her lips and cocked one hip provocatively at Hero. "Shopping for a bit o' muslin to raise yer old sod's flag, are ye, me lady? Bet I can do the trick. Do you like to watch?"

"Thank you, but no," said Hero.

"Lizzy, ye foulmouthed trollop," hissed Molly, flapping her apron at the woman. "Ye mind yer bloody manners and get out o' here."

Lizzy laughed and disappeared into the night with a jaunty backward wave of one white hand.

"I've a girl by the name of Charlotte Roach waiting for ye in me sitting room," said Molly, drawing Hero toward the rear of the house. "Although if truth be told, I'm not certain a gently bred lady such as yerself should be hearing wot she's got to say."

"Nonsense," said Hero. "You should know by now that I am not so easily shocked."

Molly paused outside the closed door, her broad, homely face troubled. "Ye ain't heard wot she's got to say yet."

※

Charlotte Roach couldn't have been more than fourteen or fifteen years old. She had a thin, sharp-boned face and straw-colored hair and pale, shrewd eyes rimmed by short, sparse blond lashes. Her tattered gown of pink and white striped satin had obviously been made for someone both older and larger, and then cut down, its neckline plunging to expose most of the girl's small, high breasts. She sat in an unladylike sprawl on a worn settee beside Molly's empty hearth, a glass of what looked like gin in one hand, her lips crimped into a tight, hard line that didn't soften when Hero walked into the room. She looked Hero up and down in frank appraisal, then glanced over at Molly. "This the gentry mort ye was tellin' me about?"

"I am," said Hero.

Charlotte brought her gaze back to Hero's face, one grubby finger reaching out to tap the sketch of Childe lying on the settee beside her. "'E yer Jerry sneak?"

"If by that you mean to ask if the man in that sketch is my husband, then the answer is no." With slow deliberation, Hero drew five guineas from her reticule and laid them in a row across the surface of the table before her. "This is for you . . . *if* you tell me what I want to know. But don't even think of trying to sell me Grub Street news, for I'll know a lie if I hear it."

A flash of amusement shone in the girl's pale, hard eyes. "What ye want to know, then?"

"When was the last time you saw this gentleman?"

The girl took a long swallow of her gin. "That'd be goin' on two years ago, now. I ain't seen 'im since I was at the Lambs' Pen, in Chalon Lane."

Hero cast a quick glance at Molly. She had heard of the Lambs' Pen, a discreet establishment near Portland Square that catered to men who liked their whores young—very young. Two years earlier, Charlotte Roach couldn't have been more than thirteen. Even though the girl was only confirming what Hero had already

suspected, she felt her flesh crawl. With effort she said,
"Go on."

"'E used t'come into the Lambs' Pen the first Monday
o' the month. Always the first Monday, and at nine
o'clock exactly. Ye coulda set yer watch by 'im. A real
rum duke, 'e was." Charlotte sucked her lower lip between her teeth, her gaze drifting back to the shiny guineas laid in a row across the top of the table. "Anythin'
else ye want t' 'ear?"

Swallowing the urge to simply give the girl the money
and leave, Hero went to sink into the broken-down chair
opposite her. "I want to hear everything you know about
him."

Chapter 35

Hero paused at the entrance to the Reading Room of the British Museum, her gaze sweeping the rows of clerics, physicians, barristers, and antiquaries hunched over their books and manuscripts. The room was dark, with rush matting on the floor and a dusty collection of stuffed birds that seemed to peer down at her from above.

Bevin Childe was not there.

"Miss. I say, *miss*." A bantam-sized, plumpish attendant in a rusty black coat and yellowing cravat bore down on her, his hands raised in horror, his voice hushed to a hissing whisper. "This room is not part of the museum tour. Only registered readers are allowed in the library. You must leave. Leave at once."

Hero let her gaze sweep over the little man with a look that not only stopped him in his tracks, but also caused him to stagger back a step. "I am Lady Devlin," she said calmly. "Lord Jarvis's daughter."

"Lord J—" The man broke off, swallowed, and gave a shallow titter. "Oh ... Lady Devlin, of course!" He bowed so low his bulbous nose practically touched his knees. "How—how may we assist you?"

"I require a word with Mr. Bevin Childe."

"I'm afraid Mr. Childe is in one of our private research rooms."

"Then if you would be so kind as to direct me to him?"

"I'm afraid Mr. Childe does not like to be disturbed when— I mean, of course, Lady Devlin. This way, please."

He led her down a cramped corridor and around a dogleg to pause before a closed, peeling door. "Mr. Childe is here, my lady," he whispered, his somewhat prominent front teeth digging into his lower lip. "Shall I announce you?"

"Thank you, but I'll announce myself. You may leave us."

A wave of relief wafted across his lumpy features. "Yes, my lady. If you should require anything— *anything*— please do not hesitate to call."

Hero waited until he had bowed himself back down the corridor. Then she turned the door's handle and quietly pushed it open.

The room was small, lit only by a high dusty window, and hemmed in by piles of crates and overflowing shelves. Seated in a straight-backed chair, Bevin Childe had his head bent over the tattered pages of a manuscript held open on the table before him by a velvet-covered, sausage-shaped weight. He had a pen in one hand and was running the index finger of the other down a row of figures. Without even looking up, he said tartly, "You are disturbing my concentration. As you can see, this room is already engaged. Kindly remove yourself at once."

Hero shut the door behind her and leaned against it.

Childe continued frowning down at the figures, apparently secure in the assumption that he was once more alone. She walked across the room and drew out the chair opposite him.

"Did you not hear what I said?" His head jerked up.

His myopic gaze focused on Hero and he dropped his pen, the loaded nib splattering a blot of ink across the pages of his notes. "Good heavens. Not you again."

Smiling, she settled herself in the chair and leaned forward, her elbows on the table, her chin propped on her hands. "What a nice, private place for a comfortable little chat. How fortuitous."

He half rose to his feet.

"Sit down," said Hero.

He sank back into his seat, hands splayed flat on the surface of the table before him, lips puckering out in a scowl that clenched his eyebrows together. "When will you and your husband simply leave me alone?"

"As soon as you stop lying to us."

Childe stiffened. "I'll have you know that I am a respected scholar. A very respected scholar! Nothing I have told you is false. Nothing!"

"Really? You told me your argument with Miss Tennyson last Friday was a scholarly disagreement over her identification of Camlet Moat as Camelot. That certainly wasn't true. The quarrel was over the Glastonbury Cross."

His face reddened. "Miss Tennyson was a very contrary woman. After a point it becomes difficult to correctly separate these choleric episodes in one's mind."

"I might believe you if she hadn't ended that particular confrontation by hurling the cross into the lake. That strikes me as a comparatively memorable moment."

Childe pressed his lips into a tight, straight line and glared at her from across the table.

Hero settled more comfortably in her chair, her hands shifting to the reticule in her lap. "I can understand why you were selected to play the starring role in this little charade. Your skepticism toward all things Arthurian is well-known, which means that for you to be the one to step forward and present the Glastonbury Cross and a box of crumbling bones—particularly with the added fiction that they were found amongst Richard Gough's collection—would obviously help to make the discovery more believable."

"This is an outrage!" blustered Childe. "Why, if you were a man I would—"

"You would—what, exactly? Challenge me to a duel? I'm a very good shot, you know."

"To the best of my knowledge," said Childe through clenched teeth, "the cross I discovered in Mr. Gough's collection is the very same artifact presented to the world by the monks of Glastonbury in 1191. As it happens, the scholarly community will soon have the opportunity to judge for itself. The cross has been recovered from the lake and will be made available for inspection next week."

"Having a new one made, are you?"

Childe leaned back in his chair and folded his arms over his chest. "I see no reason to dignify that statement with a response."

Hero smiled. "But there's another reason you were selected for this charade; is that not so, Mr. Childe? You see, I kept thinking, Why would a respected scholar possessed of a comfortable independence lend himself to such a scheme? And then it came to me: because you have a deep, dirty little secret that makes you vulnerable to blackmail."

Childe shifted uncomfortably, his jaw set.

"That's why you killed Gabrielle, isn't it? Not because she somehow discovered the true origins of your so-called Glastonbury Cross, or because she spurned your suit, but because she found out about your taste for little girls."

He jerked, then sat very still. "I don't have the slightest idea what you're talking about."

"I'm talking about the Lambs' Pen. And don't even

think about trying to deny it. They keep very good records, you know. And—"

Childe came up out of his seat, his face purple and
twisted with rage, one meaty hand flashing toward her.
"Why you bloody little—"

Hero drew a small brass-mounted flintlock muff pistol from her reticule, pulled back the hammer, and
pointed the muzzle at his chest. "Touch me and you're
dead."

He froze, his eyes flaring wide, his big, sweaty body
suspended over the table, his chest heaving with his agitated breathing.

"If you will recall," she said calmly, "I did mention
that I am a very good shot. True, a weapon of this size is
not particularly accurate, but then at this distance it
doesn't need to be. *Now, sit down.*"

He sank slowly, carefully back into his chair.

"You, Mr. Childe, are a fool. Did you seriously think
that I would closet myself in private with a man I believe
could be a murderer and not come armed?"

Having been red before, his face was now pasty white.
"I did not murder Miss Tennyson."

"You certainly had a motive—several, actually. You
have just displayed a shocking propensity for violence
toward women. And last Sunday, you were at Gough
Hall in the afternoon and in your rooms in St. James's
Street that night. You could easily have killed Gabrielle
and her young cousins while traveling between the
two."

"I wouldn't do that! I would never do that!"

"And why, precisely, should I believe you?"

Childe swallowed.

Hero rose, the gun still in her hand. "Stand up, turn
around, and put your hands on the boxes in front of
you."

"What are you going to do?" he asked, throwing a

quick glance at her over his shoulder as he moved to comply.

"Keep your eyes on the wall."

"But what are you going to *do*?"

Hero opened the door behind her. "That depends largely on you, does it not?"

"What does that mean?"

She heard him repeat the question again when she was halfway down the hall.

"What are you going to do?"

※

By the time Sebastian made it back to London, the setting sun was casting long shadows through the streets.

He found Hero seated at the bench before her dressing table. She wore an elegant, high-waisted evening gown of ivory silk with tiny slashed puff sleeves and an inset of rose silk laced with a crisscross of ivory down the front, and she had her head bowed as she threaded a slender ribbon of dusty rose through her crimped hair. He leaned against the doorframe of her dressing chamber and watched as the flickering candlelight played over her bare shoulders and the exposed nape of her neck. And he knew it again, that baffling swirl of admiration and desire combined with a troubling sense that he was losing something he'd never really had. Something that was more than passion and far, far different from obligation or honor or duty.

She finished fastening the ribbon in place and looked up, her gaze meeting his in the mirror. Whatever she saw there caused her to nod to the young abigail waiting to assist her. "That will be all, Jane; thank you."

"Yes, miss," said the woman, dropping a curtsy.

Sebastian waited until Jane left; then he came into the room and closed the door. "Rory Forster is dead. I found him floating in Camlet Moat."

"Good heavens." Hero swung around to stare at him. "What happened to him?"

"He was shot point-blank in the chest. Sometime this morning, I'd say. Gibson should have the body by now, although I'd be surprised if he's able to tell us much more."

"But . . . why was he killed?"

"I had an interesting conversation with Rory's widow, who owns a prosperous farm to the east of the old chase. She married the man just last year, and if you ask me, she was well on her way to regretting the bargain. Forster might have been a handsome devil, but he seems to have been far more interested in searching for buried treasure than in taking care of things around the farm. I suspect he also wasn't above using his fists on his wife when she angered him . . . and his kind anger easily and often."

"Maybe she's the one who shot him."

Sebastian huffed a surprised laugh. "I confess that thought hadn't occurred to me. But I think it more likely Rory was trying to blackmail someone and ended up getting his payment in the form of a bullet."

"You think he knew who killed Gabrielle? But . . . how?"

"According to the Widow Forster, Rory took his shovel out to Camlet Moat at sunset on Sunday and came back later that night soaking wet and full of big talk about buying her silks and satins and a carriage to rival the Squire's lady. At the time she seems to have thought he must have found some of the island's famous treasure."

"When in fact he'd witnessed the brutal murder of a woman and two children?"

"I suspect so. The first time I spoke to him, he laughed at the men out looking for the Tennyson boys. He said no one was going to find 'them nippers.'"

"Because he knew they were already dead," said Hero softly. "Dear God."

"His wife says he made a trip into London yesterday, which may have been when he confronted the killer and offered his silence in exchange for gold."

"With the payment to be made this morning at Camlet Moat." Hero pushed up from her dressing table. "Interesting choice of locales—and telling, perhaps?"

"It might be more telling if it weren't for the fact that Sir Stanley and his wife both happen to be in London at the moment."

"I know." She went to select a pair of long ivory gloves from her glove box. "My father has invited them to a dinner party tonight at Berkeley Square."

"Ah. So that's where you're going."

She looked over at him. "You are invited as well, if you'd like."

He let his gaze rove over her face. She looked as calm and self-possessed as ever. Yet he was coming to know her better, and he was uncomfortably conscious of a sense of artifice, of concealment about her. And it occurred to him that in her own way she was as gifted an actress as Kat Boleyn.

As if aware of the intensity of his scrutiny, she gave a sudden laugh and said, "What? Why are you looking at me like that?"

"There's something you're not telling me."

She tipped her head to one side, a strange smile lighting her eyes. "And would you have me believe that you have been entirely open with me?"

He started to tell her that he had. Then he remembered the folded paper that lay in his pocket, a note he had received just moments earlier that read, *I have some information you might find interesting. Come to the theater before tonight's rehearsal. K.*

The words of assurance died on his lips.

He watched her eyes narrow. She had her father's eyes: a pale silvery gray at the outer rim with a starlike burst of sooty charcoal around the pupil and a gleam of intelligence almost frightening in its intensity. She said, "I don't imagine there are many couples who find themselves thrown into a murder investigation within days of their marriage."

"No. Although I suppose it's appropriate, given how we met."

She turned away. "Am I to take it that you're declining my father's dinner invitation?"

"I have an appointment with someone who may be able to provide me with information about Jamie Knox."

She waited for him to tell her more, and when he didn't, he saw the flare of some emotion her eyes, although whether it was hurt or suspicion or a gleam of malicious satisfaction, he couldn't have said.

Chapter 36

*W*ar was very much the topic of conversation that evening in the reception rooms of Lord Jarvis's Berkeley Square residence. War in Europe, war on the high seas, war in America.

Hero discussed Wellington's successes in Spain with Castlereagh, the depredations of those damnable upstart Americans on British shipping with Bathurst, and Napoléon's newest rampage against Russia with Liverpool. Most of the members of Liverpool's government were in attendance, along with the city's premier bankers, for war was very much a financial enterprise.

She found the night almost unbearably hot and close, the air in the crowded rooms unusually stifling. The hundreds of candles burning in the chandeliers overhead only added to the heat, and she could feel her cheeks start to burn. Ignoring the discomfort, she was working her way through her father's guests to where she could see Sir Stanley Winthrop in conversation with her mother, Lady Jarvis, when the Earl of Hendon stopped her.

"I'd hoped I might find my son here with you tonight," said Devlin's father, his intensely blue St. Cyr eyes narrowed with a combination of anxiety and hurt. She did not understand the obvious estrangement that had grown between father and son, yet at the same time she didn't feel quite right inquiring into it.

"I fear it will take more than a mere wedding to affect a rapprochement between Devlin and my father," she said lightly.

"But he is well?"

"Devlin, you mean? He is, yes."

"I heard he was set upon the other night in Covent Garden."

"A minor wound. Nothing serious."

Hendon sighed. "I'll never understand why he continues to involve himself in these murder investigations. Is it boredom? Some quixotic delusion that he can somehow make all right with the world?"

"I don't think Devlin suffers from any such delusions." She tipped her head to one side. "Who told you of the attack on Devlin in Covent Garden?"

An uncharacteristic softness stole over his features. "A mutual friend," he said, then bowed and moved on, leaving her staring thoughtfully after him.

She was brought out of her preoccupation by a woman's voice saying, "My dear Lady Devlin, please allow me to offer my felicitations on your recent marriage."

Hero turned to find herself being regarded by Sir Stanley Winthrop's wife, who was looking hot and vaguely sweaty in a gown of pink tulle and satin made high at the neck and with long sleeves.

It was the knowledge that Lady Winthrop would be at tonight's dinner that had inspired Hero to attend.

"Why, thank you," said Hero, smiling as she drew the banker's wife a little to one side. "I'm so glad you were able to come tonight; I've been wanting to talk to you about Gabrielle Tennyson."

Lady Winthrop's own somewhat ingratiating smile vanished, her gaze darting anxiously from left to right as if she were embarrassed by the thought that someone might have overheard Hero's remark. "But ... do you think this is quite the proper place to discuss—"

"Did you know her well?" Hero asked, ignoring the woman's discomfiture.

Lady Winthrop cleared her throat and swallowed. "Not well, no."

"But you are an intimate of Miss Tennyson's cousin, Mary Bourne, I believe."

"I don't know if I would describe myself as an *intimate*, precisely—"

"No? I thought someone told me you frequently study the Bible together with the Reverend Samuel at Savoy Chapel."

"We do, yes. God's chosen ones may be saved by his irresistible grace, but with God's grace comes an imperative to examine and consider the wisdom and beauty of his teachings. *Particularly* in these dangerous times, when so many are tempted by the blandishments of Satan and the lure of those ancient pagan beliefs so hostile to God."

"Ah, yes; I'd heard Mrs. Bourne is the author of a pamphlet warning of the dangers of Druidism—written under a pseudonym, of course. Is she familiar, I wonder, with the legends associating Camlet Moat with the ancient Celts?" Hero let her gaze drift, significantly, to where Sir Stanley, looking splendid in silk knee breeches and tails, stood in conversation with Liverpool.

Lady Winthrop followed her gaze, her jaw hardening; something very like hatred flashed in her eyes as she stared across the room at her tall, handsome husband. "I'm not certain I understand precisely what you mean to imply, Lady Devlin," she said, her voice low.

"Only that it's fascinating, don't you think, the subtle linkages that can connect one person to the next?"

"We are all joined together in sin."

"Some more so than others, I suppose," said Hero wryly.

Lady Winthrop's nostrils flared on a quickly indrawn breath. "Gabrielle Tennyson was a woman separated from God. St. Paul tells us that it is a woman's place to receive instruction with utter submission. The Lord does not allow women to teach or exercise authority over men, but enjoins them to remain quiet. Eve was created after Adam, and it was she who was deceived and fell into transgression. That is why a godly woman does not seek to go forth into the world and challenge men, but submits herself to a husband and devotes herself to the care of her household. I sometimes find myself wondering, if she had lived, what Miss Tennyson would have done, once her brother married. I don't imagine his recent betrothal sat well with her."

"What recent betrothal?"

A slow, unpleasant smile slid across the other woman's features. "Oh, dear; have I betrayed a confidence? I knew the betrothal was being kept quiet due to the death of Miss Goodwin's maternal grandmother, but I had assumed that as an intimate of Miss Tennyson's, you would have known. Did she not tell you?"

"No," said Hero. "She did not. How came you to know of it?"

"Emily Goodwin's mother is a dear friend of mine."

※

Kat Boleyn was wiggling a heavy costume of purple velvet trimmed with gold braid over her head when Sebastian slipped into her cramped dressing room at Covent Garden Theater and closed the door behind him.

"I was beginning to wonder if you were going to make it before rehearsal," she said, turning her back to him and lifting the heavy fall of auburn hair from her neck. "Here. Make yourself useful."

It was a natural request, for she was pressed for time and they were old friends. As his fingertips brushed against her warm body, he tried to think of her as an old friend—as a sister, although he knew only too well that she was not.

"You've learned something?" he asked, his voice strained.

She busied herself clasping a bracelet around her wrist. "You were right about Jamie Fox. He is indeed involved with a group of smugglers plying the Channel. They work out of a small village near Dover, running mainly French wine and brandy." She hesitated a moment, then added, "But there's something more going on . . . something I can't tell you about."

He swung her around to face him, his narrowed gaze studying the gentle curve of her cheek, the childlike upturned nose, the full, sensuous lips. "I thought you knew you could trust me—that nothing I learn from you will ever go any further, no matter what it is."

"This confidence is not mine to betray." Her familiar blue eyes narrowed with some emotion he could not name. "The only thing I can tell you is that what's going on here is dangerous—very dangerous. Jamie Knox is dangerous. He's loyal to no one except himself—and perhaps to his friend, a fellow rifleman named Jack Simpson."

"I've met him."

She touched his arm lightly. "I heard you were set upon the other night and hurt. Are you all right?"

"Where did you hear that?"

She gave him a jaunty smile. "Gibson told me."

"Gibson has a big mouth. It's just a scratch."

"Uh-huh."

A warning bell sounded in the distance. He hesitated a moment, then took her hand in his and kissed her fingers. "Thank you," he said, and turned toward the door.

"Sebastian—"

He paused to look back at her.

"They say Jamie Knox's hearing, eyesight, and reflexes rival yours. And we both know he looks enough like you to be your brother—or at least your half brother. What's going on here?"

All the noise of a theatrical troupe about to begin a dress rehearsal echoed around them—quickly stifled giggles, a hoarse shout for some missing prop, the thump of hurrying feet on bare floorboards. Sebastian said, "I don't know. He claims his father was a cavalry captain."

"But you don't believe him?"

"I don't know what to believe. Amanda told me once that my father was probably a groom."

Kat's lip curled. "That sounds like something Amanda would say, just to be hurtful." Sebastian's sister, Amanda, had hated him from birth—for being male, for being eligible to inherit their father's title and riches, and, as Sebastian had learned recently, for being living evidence of their mother's endless, indiscriminate infidelities.

He said, "That doesn't mean it couldn't be true."

❧

Sebastian was standing before the empty hearth in his library, a booted foot on the cold grate, a glass of brandy in his hand, when he heard a carriage draw up before the house and Hero's quick steps mount to the front door. A single brace of candles burned on the mantel; the rest of the room lay in shadow. He listened to her low-voiced consultation with Morey. Then she appeared at the entrance to the library, one gloved hand raised to release the throat catch of her evening cloak.

"You're home early," he said, straightening as he turned toward her.

"I'm glad I found you," she said, advancing into the room. "I've just learned the most astonishing information."

In spite of himself, Sebastian found himself smiling. "Really? What?"

She swung off her cloak and draped it over the back of a nearby chair. "Hildeyard Tennyson isn't just courting this Miss Goodwin; they're betrothed!"

"I know."

Hero stared at him, dawning indignation chasing incredulity across her features. "You knew!"

"Tennyson mentioned it when he first arrived back in London. He said the betrothal was arranged shortly before he left for Kent, but was never formally announced due to the sudden death of Miss Goodwin's grandmother in the midst of the settlement negotiations."

"But if you knew, why didn't you tell me?"

"I thought I did."

"No. You told me he'd formed an attachment to the daughter of one of his colleagues; you said nothing of a betrothal."

"I beg your pardon. I suppose I didn't consider it significant. You obviously disagree; why?"

"Think about it. Gabrielle was still in the schoolroom when she took over the management of her father's household after her mother died. She was mistress of the Tennyson town house in the Adelphi and their small estate in Kent for something like thirteen years. Can you imagine a woman like Gabrielle meekly turning over to her brother's new eighteen-year-old bride the reins to two houses she'd considered hers for years, and then continuing to live there in any kind of comfort?"

Sebastian took a slow sip of his brandy. "To be honest, I never gave a thought to the effect his marriage would inevitably have on his domestic arrangements."

The look on Hero's face said so clearly, *Men,* that he almost laughed out loud.

He said, "So tell me exactly what all I've missed by being so, well, male about this."

She jerked off her long gloves and tossed them on the chair beside her cloak. "The thing is, you see, if Gabrielle were penniless, she would have had no option but to continue living at the Adelphi with her brother and his new bride. But Gabrielle wasn't penniless; her father had left her an independent income. It might not have been excessive, but it was enough to enable her to live on her own, or—"

"Or with the man she loved," said Sebastian. "And under the circumstances, I can't see his qualms about being seen as a fortune hunter stopping him." The inclination to laugh was gone.

Hero walked to where she had left the book of English Cavalier poets lying on the table beside the chair. "I was thinking about that poem Arceneaux gave Gabrielle, the one by Robert Herrick. He copied out the last three stanzas to give to her. But it's the first three that I think may be important." She flipped through the book. "Here it is; listen:

> *Bid me to live, and I will live*
> *Thy Protestant to be:*
> *Or bid me love, and I will give*
> *A loving heart to thee.*
>
> *A heart as soft, a heart as kind,*
> *A heart as sound and free*
> *As in the whole world thou canst find,*
> *That heart I'll give to thee.*
>
> *Bid that heart stay, and it will stay,*
> *To honor thy decree—*

Sebastian recited the poem from memory along with her, his gaze locked with hers, their voices blending together, tenor and contralto. "'Or bid it languish quite away, / And't shall do so for thee.'"

"Bloody hell," he said, and drained his brandy to set the glass aside with a snap.

Chapter 37

*A*rceneaux's lodgings lay in a dark, narrow lane not far from the church of St. Clements. While not exactly a slum, the once genteel area had long ago begun the slow slide into poverty. As Sebastian paused on the footpath, his gaze scanning the old house's dusty windows and crumbling facade, a bedraggled woman well past her youth, her face gaunt and haunting, separated herself from the shadows of a nearby archway to hiss at him invitingly.

He shook his head and pushed open the street door.

The atmosphere inside the house was hot and close and filled with the smells of cooked cabbage and dry rot and the faint but inescapable odor of uncollected night soil. He climbed the worn, darkened stairs to the attic, trying to imagine Gabrielle's gentle, scholarly French lieutenant in this place. From behind one door came a man's hoarse, angry shouts and a woman's soft weeping; from the next, the wail of a babe went on and on. Someone somewhere was coaxing a sad melody from a violin, the bittersweet notes mingling bizarrely with the yowl of mating cats in the back alley.

There were only two doors at the very top of the stairs. Neither showed any trace of light through their cracks, but Sebastian knocked on both anyway and stood listening for some hint of movement.

Nothing.

Under the terms of his parole, Arceneaux should have been in his lodgings by now. Sebastian turned back toward the stairs, hesitating a moment with one hand on the battered newel post. Then he headed for the Angel on Wych Street.

He found the coffeehouse nearly empty in the heat. Tobacco smoke and the smell of freshly roasted coffee hung heavy in the pale flickering light. As he closed the door quietly behind him, the barman looked up questioningly. Sebastian shook his head, his gaze drifting slowly over the desultory groups of men hunched sullenly around their tables, their conversations low voiced.

Arceneaux was not amongst them. But in a corner near the empty hearth, the big blond hussar captain, Pelletier, was playing chess with a gaunt infantry officer in a tattered blue coat. At Sebastian's approach, the hussar lifted his head, the gold coins at the ends of his love knots winking in the candlelight, the fingers of one hand smoothing his luxurious mustache as he watched Sebastian cross the room toward him.

"Come to ruin another of my games, have you?" he said when Sebastian paused beside the table.

"Has Arceneaux been here tonight?"

The hussar pursed his lips and raised one shoulder in a shrug.

"Does that mean you haven't seen him? Or that you don't know where he is?"

"It means he is not here now."

"Do you know where I might find him?"

The man's lips parted in an insolent smile. *"Non."*

"I thought under the terms of your parole you were confined to your lodgings after eight p.m."

"Our lodgings are here," said the infantry officer when the hussar remained silent. "We've rooms upstairs."

Sebastian glanced down at the chessboard. "Interesting. Whose move?"

"Mine," said the infantry officer, plucking at his lower lip with one thumb and forefinger, his brow knit in a puzzled, hopeless frown.

"Try queen to F-seven," said Sebastian, turning away.

"*Casse-toi,*" hissed the hussar with an angry growl, half rising from his seat.

"Not a wise idea," said Sebastian, turning back with one hand on the flintlock in his pocket.

For a moment, the hussar's fiery eyes met his. Then the Frenchman sank back into his seat, his jaw set hard, his chest rising and falling with his rapid breathing.

Sebastian was aware of the man's angry gaze following him to the door.

Outside, the night had taken on a strange, breathless quality, the air hot and heavy and oppressive. He stood on the flagway, aware of a rising sense of frustration. Where the *hell* was Arceneaux? For a paroled officer to be found outside his lodgings after curfew meant the revocation of his parole and consignment to the same hell holes as men from the ranks.

Sebastian felt the faintest suggestion of a breeze wafting through the streets, carrying with it a coolness and the promise of a change. He smelled the river and the inrushing tide and a touch of brine that hinted at faraway lands.

And he knew where the French lieutenant had gone.

✢

Only ten months into its building, the new Strand Bridge rose from the bank of the river at the site of what had once been the Savoy, the grandest palace on the Thames.

But the Savoy had long since degenerated from its days of glory, first into an almshouse, then a prison and barracks. Now it was only a shattered, half-demolished ruin that stretched between the Strand and the riverbank below, a wasteland scattered with rubble and piles of dressed stone and brick and timber that extended out onto the rising bridge itself. As Sebastian worked his way down the darkened slope, he could see the curving stone foundations of a small medieval guard tower and a long brick wall pierced by empty mullioned arches. Beyond the ruins, the jagged, looming bulk of the new bridgehead stood out pale against the blackness of the sky.

The first four of the bridge's vast arches were already complete, although the wooden forms at their centers were still in place and a rope-suspended walkway and scaffolding ran beneath the beginnings of what would eventually be an entablature, cornice, and balustrade above. When finished, the bridge's carriageway would rise even with the level of the Strand. But now it lay some feet below it, a rough, unpaved grade that stretched out toward the opposite bank only to end abruptly over the rushing water.

As he walked out onto the bridge, Sebastian could hear the tide splashing against the cofferdams at the base of the piers, feel the unexpected coolness of the breeze wafting against his sweat-sheened face. He kept his gaze focused on the solitary figure of a man that showed against the sliding expanse of the Thames beyond. The man sat at the jagged end of the bridge, his legs dangling over the water hundreds of feet below, one hand resting companionably on the brown and black dog at his side.

"How did you know where to find me?" Arceneaux asked when Sebastian paused some ten feet away from him.

"I remembered what you told me, about liking to come here."

The Frenchman tilted back his head, the wind off the water ruffling the hair around his face. "Are you going to turn me in?"

"No."

Arceneaux took a long breath, eyes closing, nostrils flaring, lips pressed into a tight smile as he drew the air deep within him. "Do you smell it? It's the sea. The same sea that at this very moment is swelling the estuary of the Rance and battering the stone ramparts of Saint-Malo."

Sebastian stood very still, the growing wind tugging at the tails of his coat.

"Sometimes I wonder if I'll ever see any of it again," said Arceneaux. "We have the illusion of being free here, but we're not really. Whatever happened to all the prisoners of the Hundred Years' War? Do you know? What happens to the prisoners of a war that never ends? Is this my destiny, I wonder? To live out my life alone in a dusty, dark garret, scrabbling for a few shillings here and there, teaching bored little boys to speak French and—" His voice cracked and he shook his head.

Sebastian said, "Two weeks ago, Mr. Hildeyard Tennyson asked the daughter of one of his associates for her hand in marriage. Word of the betrothal was kept private due to the intended bride's recent bereavement. But I can't believe Miss Tennyson didn't tell you, her dear, beloved friend."

For a moment, Arceneaux sat motionless. Then Chien nuzzled his head against his friend's side. The Frenchman ran one hand down the dog's back, his attention seemingly focused on his companion. "She told me, yes."

"I'll admit the significance of Tennyson's betrothal escaped me at first. But as my wife—far more acute in such matters than I—pointed out, a woman of Miss Tennyson's temperament and independent ways would never have continued living as a mere sister-in-law and hanger-on in the houses where she herself had been mistress for more than a decade."

Arceneaux continued to stare silently out over the river, his hand running up and down the dog's back.

Sebastian said, "She must have been upset and in need of comfort. You had already declared your love for her. Yet you would have me believe that you still didn't ask her to marry you? That you didn't press her to marry you?"

"No." The word was a soft, halfhearted lie nearly lost in the wind.

Sebastian quoted,

> *Bid that heart stay, and it will stay,*
> *To honor thy decree*
> *Or bid it languish quite away,*
> *And't shall do so for thee.*

He paused, then said, "Were you thinking about violating your parole and going back to France?"

"No!"

"I think you were. I think you changed your mind because Gabrielle Tennyson finally agreed to marry you." Sebastian suspected that was probably when the two lovers had first lain together, but he wasn't going to say it.

Arceneaux scrambled to his feet and took a hasty step forward, only to draw up short. "All right, damn you! It's true. I thought about escaping. Do you imagine there is a prisoner of war anywhere who doesn't sometimes dream of breaking his parole and escaping? Who isn't tempted?"

Sebastian stared at the young French lieutenant. In

the fitful moonlight his face was pale, his eyes like sunken bruises in a pain-ravaged face. The wind ruffled the fine brown hair around his head, flapped the tails of his coat. Sebastian had the impression the man was holding himself together by a sheer act of will. But he was coming dangerously close to shattering.

"Did she agree to marry you?"

Rather than answer, the Frenchman simply nodded, his gaze turning to stare out over the wind-whipped waters of the river.

I'm half sick of shadows, thought Sebastian, watching him. He said, "There's something you're still not telling me. God damn it, Lieutenant; the woman you loved is dead. Who do you think killed her?"

Arceneaux swung to face him again. "You think if I knew who killed her, I wouldn't make them pay?"

"You may not be quite certain who is to blame. But you have some suspicions, and those suspicions are weighing heavily on you. It's why you're here now, risking your parole. Isn't it?"

The wind gusted up, stronger now, scurrying the tumbling dark clouds overhead and obscuring the hazy sickle of the moon.

"Who do you think killed her?" Sebastian demanded again.

"I don't know!" The Frenchman's features contorted as if the words were being torn from him. "I lie awake every night, wondering if I might somehow be responsible for the death of the woman I loved."

"Why?" pressed Sebastian. "What makes you think you might be responsible?"

Chien rose to his feet, his gaze fixed on the rubble-strewn bank, ears at half cock as he trotted a few steps toward the bridgehead and then stopped.

Arceneaux went to rest a hand on the dog's neck. "What is it, boy? Hmm?"

Sebastian was aware of an inexplicable but inescapable intimation of danger that quickened his breath and brought a burning tingle to the surface of his skin. He scanned the ruins of the ancient palace, his eyes narrowing as he studied the piles of stone and timber, the long line of broken wall with its empty windows a dark and melancholy tracery against the stormy sky.

"Arceneaux," he said warningly, just as a belching tongue of flame erupted from the foundations of the old guard tower and the crack of a rifle shot echoed across the water.

Chapter 38

"*G*et down!" Sebastian shouted as he dove for cover behind the half-built cornice.

Looking back, he saw Arceneaux stagger, a bloom of shiny dark wetness spreading high across the center of his waistcoat.

"*Arceneaux!*"

The Frenchman's knees buckled slowly, his head tilting back, his face lifted as if he were looking at the sky.

Sebastian scrambled into the open to grab the man as he fell and dragged him into the protective lee of the stonework. "Bloody hell," swore Sebastian, clutching the shuddering man to him.

Chien crouched beside them, his harsh barks splitting the night.

The entire front of the Frenchman's waistcoat was wet with blood, his mouth open and gasping in great sucking wheezes that blew little bubbles in the wet sheen on his chest.

Sebastian knew only too well what that meant.

He ripped off his cravat anyway and rolled it around his fist to form a thick pad.

"No . . . point . . ." Arceneaux whispered as Sebastian pressed the cloth against the gaping, oozing wound in his chest. Then he choked and blood poured from his mouth and nose.

"You're going to be all right," Sebastian lied, hauling the wounded man up so that his back lay against Sebastian's own chest in a desperate attempt to keep Arceneaux from drowning in his own blood.

Arceneaux shook his head, his eyes rolling back in his head. "Gabrielle . . ."

"Talk to me, Philippe," shouted Sebastian, the Frenchman's warm blood pouring over his hand as he desperately pressed the padded cloth to Arceneaux's shattered, jerking chest. "Who would want to kill you?"

The jerking stopped.

"Philippe? *Philippe!*"

Beside him, the dog whined, his nose thrusting against the Frenchman's limp hand.

"Damn," said Sebastian on a hard expulsion of pent-up breath.

Despite the coolness of the rising wind, he was sweating, his breath coming in quick pants. Shifting carefully, he eased the Frenchman's weight off his own body. He could smell the acrid pinch of burnt powder, see the drift of gun smoke as he slewed around to peer cautiously over the edge of the stone wall.

Nothing.

He focused his gaze on the remnants of the old medieval tower that lay to the right and just below the broken stretch of palace wall. Most of the tower's superstructure was long gone, leaving only a curving section of stone foundation perhaps four feet high. Studying it, Sebastian estimated that the shooter's position lay some two hundred yards from where he crouched, possibly three. It would have been a difficult shot to make in good light on a calm day. At night, with clouds obscuring the moon and a wind kicking up, most men would have said it was impossible.

But not a trained rifleman who could bring down a running rabbit at three hundred yards in the dark.

Sebastian swiped the back of his hand across his forehead. The problem was, why would Jamie Knox want to kill Gabrielle Tennyson's French lieutenant? It made no sense....

If the shooter was indeed Jamie Knox, and if his intended target was actually Arceneaux and not Sebastian himself.

A faint flicker of movement showed above the jagged top of the tower wall, then stilled. The shooter was still there.

Sebastian considered his options. He was essentially pinned down. He had a flintlock in his own pocket, but the pistol was small, its range limited. Against a rifle over any distance, it was useless.

Right now, he was protected by the solid length of the half-constructed cornice that ran along the edge of the bridge. But if the shooter were to shift—or if he had a confederate who could come in from the west— Sebastian would be as exposed at the end of that long, open bridge as a target in a shooting gallery.

He needed to move.

Shifting his gaze, he assessed the distance from where he lay to a stack of dressed stone that stood perhaps a third of the way back toward the bridgehead. Sebastian had heard enough Baker rifles in his day to know exactly what was shooting at him. The Baker was a single-shot weapon. But a good rifleman could reload and fire four times in a minute.

An exceptional rifleman could make it to five.

Sebastian had no doubt that the man shooting at him was an exceptional rifleman.

That meant that if Sebastian could lure the rifleman into firing, he would have at most twelve seconds to make it to the safety of that pile of stones before the shooter finished reloading and was able to fire again.

He was trying to figure out how he could trick the rifleman into firing—without actually getting shot—when Chien, who had been lying stretched out whining beside Arceneaux's still body, suddenly stood up.

"Down, boy," whispered Sebastian.

The dog hunkered into a lowered stance, eyes alert and fixed as it stared at the near bank.

"Chien," cautioned Sebastian. Then he shouted, "Chien! No!" as the dog tore into the night, a black and brown streak against the pale stone length of the bridge.

He watched, helpless, as the dog raced up the slope. Chien was nearly to the guard tower when the rifle cracked again, spitting fire into the night.

The dog yelped, then fell silent.

"Bloody son of a bitch," swore Sebastian, and took off running.

He could feel the wind off the water whipping at his coattails, the rubble of the roadway shifting dangerously beneath the soles of his boots as he mentally counted off the seconds since the last shot.

. . . six, seven . . .

He swerved around a pile of broken stone—*eight, nine*—and leapt a small chasm—*ten, eleven*—to dive behind the looming stones just as the next rifle shot reverberated across the open waterfront.

A cascade of pulverized grit exploded beside his face.

"Hell and the devil confound it," he swore, wiping his sleeve across his bloody cheek. Then he was up and running again, this time for the pile of timbers he could see near the bridgehead.

. . . seven, eight . . .

He could hear the inrushing tide slapping against the cofferdam at the base of the first pier, the rumble of what sounded like distant thunder.

. . . ten, eleven . . .

The timbers were farther than he'd realized. He skittered the last ten feet flat out on his stomach, the rubble of roadway tearing at his clothes as he braced himself for the next shot.

It never came.

Clever bastard.

Sebastian lay stretched out prone behind the pile of timbers, his heart pounding, the blood rushing in his ears. The rifleman had obviously figured out exactly what Sebastian was doing. Rather than wasting his shot, the man now had a loaded weapon; all he needed to do was wait for Sebastian to fully show himself again, and then calmly squeeze the trigger.

He can shoot the head off a running rabbit at three hundred yards in the dark.

The wind gusted up, bringing with it the smells of the river and the creaking of the suspended walkways that ran along both sides of the partially built bridge, just above the summit of the arches. Sebastian hesitated for a moment, his gaze fixed on the darkened ruins, his ears straining to catch the least sound.

Nothing.

Rolling quickly to the far side of the bridge, he lowered himself carefully over the edge until he hung suspended, his fingers digging into a gap in the stonework, feet dangling in space above the narrow suspended walkway, the river rushing far below.

Then he let go.

He landed lightly on the boards of the walkway, the suspension ropes swaying dizzily as the structure took his weight. Then, with the massive stone bulk of the bridge now between him and the shooter, Sebastian sprinted for the riverbank, the walkway dancing and swaying beneath him.

The last arch of the bridge soared high above the tidal

mudflats of the riverbed to butt into the rubble-strewn
bank. He reached solid ground and paused for a moment, his senses straining to catch any movement, any
sound. He scanned the dry, rutted slope of the bank, the
matted half-dead weeds, the looming wreck of the ancient palace. He found himself remembering other nights
in what seemed like a different lifetime, when death
waited in each dark shadow and around every corner,
when the rumble in the distance was artillery, not thunder, and the broken walls were Spanish villages blackened by the stains of fires not yet grown cold.

He drew a deep breath, suddenly aware of a powerful,
raging thirst. He swallowed hard, his throat aching. Then,
hunkering low, he darted across the open ground and
ducked behind the broken fragment of the old palace
wall.

Once, this section of the palace had overlooked the
river, an elegant facade pierced by high, pointed windows and supported by massive buttresses. Now only the
one wall remained, stretching eastward to end abruptly
just above the small round tower where the shooter
waited. Moving as quietly as possible, Sebastian crept
through the ruins, painfully aware of the rustle of the
long, dry weeds, of each broken stone that shifted beneath the soles of his boots. He passed the yawning
opening of what had once been a massive medieval fireplace, an empty doorway, a spiral of steps going nowhere.
Through the gaping windows he could see the massive
works of the new bridge, the dark, sliding shimmer of the
river, the low curve of the old guard tower's stone foundations.

Pausing at the jagged end of the wall, he slipped his
flintlock pistol from his pocket and quietly eased back
the hammers on both barrels. He could hear the distant
clatter of the carriages on the Strand up above, feel the
powerful thrumming of his own blood in the veins of his

eck. He took a deep breath. Then he burst around the
end of the broken wall, his pistol pointing down into the
foundations of the guard tower, his finger already tightening on the first trigger.

But the tower was empty, the weeds within it matted
and scattered with debris. The shooter had vanished into
the night, leaving only the Baker rifle leaning mockingly
against the worn, ancient stones.

Chapter 39

Sir Henry Lovejoy was not fond of heights.

He stood well back from the jagged edge of the bridge's last, half-constructed arch, his legs splayed wide against the powerful buffeting of the growing wind. He could see the river far below, the dark waters churning and frothing against the rough temporary cofferdams. The air was thick with the smell of the inrushing tide and the damp mudflats of the nearby bank and the coppery tang of freshly spilled blood.

"What did you say his name was?" Lovejoy asked, his gaze on the dead man sprawled in the lee of the bridge's half-built cornice.

Devlin stood beside him, his evening clothes torn and dusty and soaked dark with the dead man's blood. In one hand he gripped a Baker rifle, his fingers showing pale against the dark forestock. "Arceneaux. Lieutenant Philippe Arceneaux, of the Twenty-second Chasseurs à Cheval."

Grunting, Lovejoy hunkered down to study the French officer's fine-boned features, the sensitively molded lips and lean cheeks. In death, he looked shockingly young. But then, Lovejoy thought, by the time a man reaches his mid-fifties, twenty-four or -five can seem very young indeed.

Pushing to his feet, he nodded briskly to two of the men he'd brought with him. Between them, they heaved the Frenchman's body up and swung it onto the dead-house shell they would use to transport the corpse through the city streets.

"You've no idea of the identity of the shooter?" Love-joy asked Devlin.

"I never got a good look at him. He was firing from the ruins of the old guard tower. There, to the right."

"Want I should go have a look?" asked Constable Leeper, a tall beanpole of a man with an abnormally long neck and a badly sunburnt face.

Lovejoy nodded. "Might as well. We'll see better in the daylight, but we ought to at least do a preliminary search now."

As the constable turned to go, Devlin stopped him, saying, "The Lieutenant had a medium-sized brown and black dog that the rifleman shot. I've searched the river-bank for him myself without success. But if you should happen to come upon him—and if he should still be alive—I would like him taken to someone capable of caring for his wounds."

"Aye, yer lordship," said the Constable, his torch filling the air with the scent of hot pitch as he headed back down the bridge.

Lovejoy squinted into the murky distance. From here, the near bank was only a confused jumble of dark shapes and indistinct shadows. "Merciful heavens. The ruins of that tower must be three hundred yards away."

Devlin's face remained impassive. "Very nearly, yes."

"If I hadn't seen the results myself, I would have said that's impossible. In the daylight it would be phenomenal; how could anyone even *see* a target over such a distance at night, let alone hit it?"

"If he had good eyesight, good night vision, and a steady finger, he could do it. I've known sharpshooters who could hit a man at seven hundred yards, if the man is standing still and it's a sunny day."

Something in the Viscount's voice drew Lovejoy's gaze to him. He stood with his back held oddly rigid, his face stained with blood and dust and sweat.

Lovejoy said, "Are you certain Arceneaux was the shooter's intended target? He did continue firing at you, after all."

"He did. But that was only to keep me pinned down long enough for him to get away. I think he killed the man he came here to get."

With a succession of grunts, the two men from the parish lifted the shell to their shoulders and headed back toward the riverbank. Lovejoy picked up the lantern and fell into step behind them, the rubble of the half-constructed bridge crunching beneath his feet. "Am I to take it this Lieutenant Arceneaux is the young Frenchman who befriended Miss Gabrielle Tennyson?"

"He is," said Devlin. "Only, I gather they were considerably more than friends."

"Tragic."

"It is, yes."

"And you have no notion at all who could have done this, or why?"

Devlin paused beside the ruins of the ancient palace, his strange yellow eyes glinting in the fitful light from Lovejoy's lantern as he stared into the darkness.

"My lord?"

Devlin glanced over at him, as if only suddenly reminded of Lovejoy's presence. "Excuse me, Sir Henry," he said with a quick bow and turned away.

"My lord?"

But Devlin was already gone, his long legs carrying him easily up the dark, rubble-strewn bank, the rifle in his hand casting a slim, lethal shadow across the night.

※

Sebastian strode into the Black Devil with the Baker rifle still gripped in his fist. His shirt front and waistcoat were drenched dark red with Arceneaux's blood; his cravat was gone. His once elegant evening coat hung in dusty tatters. He'd lost his hat, and a trickle of blood ran down one side of his dirty, sweat-streaked face.

"Jesus, Mary, Joseph, and all the saints," whispered the buxom, dark-haired barmaid as Sebastian drew up just inside the door, the Baker propped at an angle on his hip, his eyes narrowing as he scanned the smoky, low-ceilinged room.

"Where's Knox?" he demanded, his words carrying clearly over the skittering of chairs and benches, the thumps of heavy boots as the tavern's patrons scrambled to get out of his way.

The girl froze wide-eyed behind the bar, her lips parted, the half-exposed white mounds of her breasts jerking and quivering with her agitated breathing.

"Where the bloody hell is he?" Sebastian said again.

"You do favor the dramatic entrance, don't you?" said a sardonic voice from a doorway that opened off the back of the room.

Sebastian turned. His gaze met Knox's across the now empty expanse of the public room, twin pairs of yellow eyes that shared an ability to see great distances and at night with an accuracy that struck most normal men as inhuman.

Or evil.

Sebastian laid the Baker on the scarred surface of the bar with a clatter. "I'm returning your rifle."

A faint smile curled the other man's lips. "Sorry. Not mine. Did someone lose it?"

"Where were you an hour ago?"

Jamie Knox advanced into the room, still faintly smiling. He wore his usual black coat and black waistcoat and black cravat, his face a dark, handsome mask. "Here, of course. Why do you ask?"

"Ever meet a Frenchman named Philippe Arceneaux?"

"Arceneaux?" Knox frowned as if with the effort of concentration. "Perhaps. It's rather difficult to say. I own a tavern; many men come here."

"Lieutenant Philippe Arceneaux."

"Does he say I know him?"

"He's dead. Someone shot him through the heart tonight from a distance of some three hundred yards. Know anyone who could make a shot like that?"

"It's a rare talent. But not unheard of."

"Your friend tells me you can shoot the head off a running rabbit at more than three hundred yards. In the dark."

Knox glanced over to where the wide-eyed girl still stood behind the bar. "Leave us."

She let herself out the front door, pausing on the threshold to throw him a last, questioning glance that he ignored. The public room was now empty except for the two men.

Knox sauntered behind the bar and reached below the counter for a bottle of brandy. "You've obviously been talking to my old mate, Jack Simpson." He eased the stopper from the brandy. "He'll also tell you that I can catch a will-o'-the-wisp out of the air and hear the whispers of the dead. But just between you and me, I wouldn't be believing everything he says."

Sebastian wandered the room, his gaze drifting over the low-beamed rafters, the massive old stone fireplace, and broad hearth. "I've heard it said you won this place at the roll of the dice—or that you killed a man for it. Which was it?"

Knox set the bottle and two glasses on the counter beside the Baker. "Like I said, you don't want to be believing everything you hear about me."

"I also hear you were at Corunna. Lieutenant Arceneaux was at Corunna, as well. Is that where you met him?"

"I never met your Lieutenant Arceneaux, God rest his soul." Knox poured brandy into the two glasses and tucked the bottle away. "Here. Have a drink."

"Thank you, but no."

Knox laughed. "What do you think, then? That I'm trying to do away with you?" He pushed both glasses across the bar. "There. You choose one; I'll drink the other. Will that allay your superstitions?"

Moving deliberately, Sebastian came to select one of the glasses of amber liquid.

His yellow eyes gleaming, Knox lifted the other to his lips and drank deeply. "There. Now, shall we wait to see if I drop to the floor and start thrashing about in my death throes?" He took another sip, this time letting the brandy roll around on his tongue. "It's good stuff, this. Comes from a château just outside Angoulême."

"And how did it make its way into your cellars?"

Knox smiled. "Would you have me believe you've no French brandy in your cellars, then?"

"Arceneaux hailed from Saint-Malo, another wine region. He told me once his father owned a vineyard. Perhaps that's how you met him."

Knox was no longer smiling. "I told you. I never met him."

"I'll figure it out eventually, you know."

"When you do, come back. But as it is, you've nothing against me but conjecture."

"So sure?"

"If you had anything you thought might begin to pass as proof, I'd be down at Bow Street right now, talking to the magistrates. Not to you."

"Thanks for the brandy." Sebastian set his glass on the bar and turned toward the street.

"You're forgetting your rifle," Knox called after him.

"Keep it. You might need it again."

The tavern owner laughed, his voice ringing out loud

and clear. "You remember how I told you my father was a cavalry officer?"

Sebastian paused with one hand on the doorjamb to look back at him.

Knox still stood behind the bar. "Well, I lied. My mother never knew for certain which of the three bastards she lay with had planted me in her belly. She was a young barmaid named Nellie, you see, at the Crown and Thorn, in Ludlow. According to the woman who raised me, Nellie said her baby's da could've been either an English lord, a Welsh captain, or a Gypsy stableboy. If she'd lived long enough, she might have recognized my actual sire in me as I grew. But she died when I was still only a wee babe."

Sebastian's skin felt hot; the abrasions on his face stung. And yet he knew the strangest sensation, as if he were somehow apart from himself, a disinterested observer of what was being said.

Knox said, "I saw the Earl of Hendon in Grosvenor Square the other day. He looks nothing like me. But then, it occurs to me, he don't look anything like you either. Now, does he?"

Sebastian opened the door and walked out into the warm, wind-tossed night.

Chapter 40

The storm broke shortly before dawn, with great sheets of rain hurled through the streets by a howling wind and thunder that rattled the glass in the windowpanes with all the savage power of an artillery barrage.

Sebastian stood on the terrace at the rear of his Brook Street house, his outstretched arms braced against the stone balustrade overlooking the garden. He had his eyes closed, his head tipped back as he let the rain wash over him.

When he was a very little boy, his mother used to take him for walks in the rain. Sometimes in the summer, if it was warm, she'd let him out without his cap. The rain would plaster his hair to his head and run off the tip of his nose. He'd try to catch the drops with his tongue, and she wouldn't scold him, not even when he waded and splashed through every puddle he could find, squealing as the water shot out from beneath his stomping feet.

But his favorite walks were those they took in the rain in Cornwall, when the fierce winds of a storm would lash the coast and she'd bundle him up and take him with her out to the cliffs. Together they would stand side by side, mesmerized by the power of the wind and the fury of the waves battering the rocks with an awe-inspiring roar.

She'd shout, *Oh, Sebastian; feel that! Isn't it glorious?* And the wind would slam into her, rocking her back a step, and she'd laugh and fling wide her arms and close her eyes, surrendering to the sheer exhilaration of the moment.

So lost was he in the past that he failed to mark the opening of the door behind him. It was some other sense entirely that brought him the sudden certainty that he was no longer alone.

"Devlin?"

He turned to find Hero standing in the doorway. She still wore the ivory gown with the dusky pink ribbons, and he wondered if she had awakened and dressed to come in search of him, or if she had not yet made it to her bed.

He had stripped off his torn, blood-soaked coat and waistcoat, but he still wore his ruined shirt, his collar askew. "My God," she said, her eyes widening when she saw him. "You're covered in blood."

"It's not mine. Philippe Arceneaux is dead."

"Did you kill him?"

"Why would I kill him? I liked him."

She walked out into the rain, the big drops making dark splotches on the fine silk of her dress as she reached up to touch his cheek. "You're hurt."

"Just scratched."

"What happened?"

"Whoever killed Arceneaux shot him from a distance of three hundred yards. In the dark."

"Who can shoot accurately at such a distance?"

"A Bishopsgate tavern owner and ex-rifleman named Jamie Knox, for one."

"Why would a tavern owner want to kill Arceneaux?"

"I don't know." He stared out over the wind-tossed garden, a jagged flash of lightning splitting the sky. The rain poured about them. "There's too much I don't know. And because of it, people keep dying."

"It's not your fault. You're doing everything you can."

He looked at her again. "It's not enough."

She shook her head, an odd smile hovering about her lips. In the darkness, her eyes had a strange, almost luminous quality. The rain ran down her cheeks, dripped off the ends of her wet hair, soaked the bodice of her gown so that her high, round breasts showed clearly through the thin silk of her gown.

His voice hoarse, he said, "You're ruining your dress. You need to go inside."

"So do you."

Neither of them moved.

Slowly, she slipped her hand behind his neck, her thumb flicking across his throat in a soft caress, her gaze tangling with his. Then, her eyes wide-open, she tilted her head and touched her lips to his.

He opened his mouth to her, drank deeply of her kiss, swept his hands up her back. He felt her tremble. But before he could pull her to him, she slipped away from him.

She paused at the door to look back. He saw a succession of raw, naked emotions flash across her face—guilt and regret and a fierce, hopeless kind of longing. She said, "When this is all over, we need to . . . begin again."

The rain pounded down on him, the wind billowing his wet, bloodstained shirt and plastering his hair to his head. He was aware of the lateness of the hour, the fullness of her lips, the unexpected raw wanting that surged through him for this woman who was his wife, the mother of his unborn child . . . and his enemy's daughter.

He said harshly, "And what if it's never over?"

But she had no answer, and long after she had gone, the question remained.

※

Friday, 7 August

The next morning, the rain was still falling out of a gun-metal gray sky when Sebastian climbed the steps of the elegant Mayfair town house of his sister, Amanda, Lady Wilcox.

The door was opened by Lady Wilcox's well-trained and normally stoic butler, who took a step back and said, "My lord Devlin!" in a voice pregnant with consternation and a touch of fear.

"Good morning," said Sebastian, handing his hat, gloves, and walking stick to the butler before heading for the stairs. "I assume my sister is still in the breakfast room?"

"Yes, but . . . My lord—"

Sebastian took the steps two at a time. "Don't worry; I'll announce myself."

He found his sister seated at a small table overlooking the rain-washed rear gardens, an empty plate before her. She'd been reading the *Morning Post* but looked up at his entrance, a delicate pink floral teacup arrested halfway to her puckered lips.

"Good morning, Amanda," he said cheerfully.

She set the cup down with enough force to send its contents sloshing over the rim. "Good God. You."

The first child born to the Earl of Hendon and his beautiful, errant countess, Amanda had never been a particularly attractive woman. She had inherited her mother's slim, elegant carriage and striking golden hair. But there was a bluntness to her features that she owed to Hendon, and at forty-two she had reached an age at which her disposition showed quite clearly on her face.

She wore a simple morning gown of dove gray made high at the waist and edged along the neckline with a dainty ruffle of lace, for she had been widowed just eighteen months and was not yet completely out of mourning.

The role Sebastian had played in the death of her husband was a subject brother and sister did not discuss.

She reached for her tea again, her lips turning down at the corners as she took a sip. "What do you want?"

Without waiting for an invitation he suspected would not be forthcoming, Sebastian drew out the chair opposite her and sat. "And I'm delighted to see you too, dear sister."

She gave a delicate sniff. "I've heard you're doing it again—that you've involved yourself in yet another murder investigation, this time of some mere barrister's sister, of all things. One might have hoped that your recent nuptials would put an end to this plebeian nonsense. But obviously such is not the case."

"Obviously not," said Sebastian dryly.

She sniffed again but said nothing.

He let his gaze drift over the familiar features of her face, the tightly held lips, the broad, slightly bulbous nose that was so much like her father's, the piercing blue St. Cyr eyes that had come to her, too, from her father. He was her brother—or at least, her half brother, her only surviving acknowledged sibling. And yet she hated him with a passion so raw and visceral that it could at times steal his breath.

As Hendon's firstborn child, she would have inherited everything—land, wealth, title—had she been a boy. But because she was a girl, she had been married off with only a dowry—a handsome one, to be sure, but still a mere pittance compared to all that would someday pass to Sebastian. Her two children, Bayard, the new Lord Wilcox, and Stephanie, his eighteen-year-old sister, were Wilcoxes; by the laws of male primogeniture, they had no claims on the St. Cyr estates.

It was the norm in their society. And yet for some reason, Amanda had always felt cheated of what she still somehow stubbornly believed in her heart of hearts should by rights have been hers. Even Richard and Cecil, Hendon's first- and second-born sons, had earned her resentment. But her true hatred had always been reserved for Sebastian. For she had known—or at least suspected—from the very beginning that this last son born to the Countess of Hendon had not in truth been begotten by the Earl.

She set her teacup down again. "Whatever it is you are here for, say it and go away so that I can read my paper in peace."

"I'm curious about the December before I was born; how well do you remember it?"

She twitched one shoulder. "Well enough. I was eleven. Why do you ask?"

"Where did Mother spend that Christmas?"

She thought about it for a moment. "Lumley Castle, near Durham. Why?"

Sebastian remembered Lady Lumley quite well, for she'd been one of his mother's particular friends, nearly as gay and beautiful—and faithless—as the Countess herself.

He saw Amanda's eyes widen, saw the faintly contemptuous smile that deepened the grooves bracketing her mouth, and knew that she understood only too well his reason for asking. "I can do sums, Sebastian. You're trying to figure out who her lover was that winter. Well, aren't you?"

Pushing up, he went to stand at the window overlooking the garden, his back to her. In the rain, the daylight was flat and dim, the shrubbery a sodden green, the slate flagstones of the terrace dark and shiny wet. When he didn't respond, she gave a sharp laugh. "An understandable exercise, given the circumstances, but unfortunately predicated upon the assumption that she took only one lover at a time. She could be quite shameless, you know."

Her scornful words sent a surge of raw fury through him. It startled him to realize that no matter how much Sophie had lied to him, no matter how cruel and destructive her betrayal and abandonment, the protective urge he'd felt for her as a boy still flared in him.

"And that Christmas?" he asked, keeping his voice level with difficulty, his gaze still fixed on the scene outside the window.

"I actually can't recall."

He watched the long canes of the arbor's climbing roses bend in the wind, watched the raindrops chase each other down the window glass.

Amanda rose to her feet. "You really want to know who begat our mother's precious little bastard? Well, I'll tell you. It was her groom. A lowly, stinking *groom*."

Turning, he looked into her familiar, pinched face and didn't believe her. Refused to believe her.

She must have read the rejection of everything she'd said in his eyes, because she gave a harsh, ringing laugh. "You don't believe me, do you? Well, I *saw* them. That autumn, on the cliffs overlooking the sea, in Cornwall. He was lying on his back and she was riding him. It was the most disgusting thing I've ever witnessed. Jeb, I believe his name was. Or perhaps Jed, or something equally vulgar."

He stared into his sister's hate-filled blue eyes and knew a revulsion so intense as to be physical. "I don't believe you," he said out loud.

"Believe it," she sneered. "I see him every time I look at you. Oh, his hair might have been darker than yours, and he might not have been as tall. But there has never been any doubt in my mind."

A sudden gust of wind blew rain against the window with a startlingly loud clatter.

He wanted to say, *Was the groom a Gypsy?* But he couldn't so betray himself to this cold, angry woman who hated him more than she'd ever hated anyone in her life. So instead he asked, "What happened to him?"

"I neither knew nor cared. He went away. That was all that mattered to me."

Sebastian walked to the door, then paused to look back to where she still stood, her hands clenched at her sides, her face red and twisted with hatred and some other emotion.

It took him a moment to recognize it, but then he knew. It was triumph.

※

Sir Henry Lovejoy hesitated at the entrance to the Bow Street public office, his face screwing into a grimace as he stared out at the ceaseless torrent driven sideways by the force of the wind. Water sluiced in sheets from the eaves, swelled in the gutters, pinged off the glass of the building's tall windows. Sighing, he was about to unfurl his umbrella and step out into the deluge when he became aware of a gentleman crossing the street from the Brown Bear toward him.

A tall, military-looking gentleman, he seemed oblivious to the elements, the numerous shoulder capes on his coat swirling about him as he leapt the rushing gutter. "Ah, Sir Henry, is it not?" he said, drawing up on the flagway. "I am Colonel Urquhart."

Swallowing hard, Lovejoy gave a jerky bow. The Colonel was well-known as Jarvis's man. "Colonel. How may I help you?"

"I'm told you are heading up the search for the killer of the Tennyson family."

"I am, yes. In fact, I was just about to—"

Urquhart tucked his hand through Lovejoy's elbow and drew him back into the public office. "Let's find someplace dry and private where we can have a little chat, shall we?"

Chapter 41

It had become Kat Boleyn's habit of late to frequent the flower market on Castle Street, not far from Cavendish Square. She'd discovered there was a rare, elusive peace to be found amidst the gaily colored rows of roses and lavender and cheerful nosegays. Sometimes the beauty of a vibrant petal or the faintest hint of a familiar scent was so heady it could take her far back in time to another place, another life.

The morning's rain had only just eased off, leaving the air cool and clean and smelling sweetly of damp stone. She wandered the stalls for a time, the handle of her basket looped casually over one arm. It wasn't until she paused beside a man selling small potted orange trees that she became aware of being watched.

Looking up, she found herself staring at a tall gentlewoman in an exquisitely fashioned walking gown of green sarcenet trimmed in velvet. She had her father's aquiline nose and shrewd gray eyes and a surprisingly sensuous mouth that was all her own.

"Do you know who I am?" asked Devlin's new Viscountess in a husky voice that could have earned her a fortune on the stage, had she been born to a less elevated position in society.

"I know."

By silent consent, the two women turned to walk toward Oxford Market, pushing past a Negro band and shouting costermongers hawking everything from apples to fried eels. After a moment, Kat said, "I assume you have sought me out for a reason."

"I wonder if you know someone nearly killed Devlin last night."

Kat felt a quick stab of fear that left her chest aching, her breath tight. "Is he all right?"

"He is. But the man who was standing beside him is dead, shot through the heart from a distance of some three hundred yards."

Kat knew of only one man with the ability to make such a shot. Two, if she counted Devlin. But she kept that knowledge to herself.

The Viscountess said, "I believe you are familiar with a tavern owner named Jamie Knox."

"I have heard of him," Kat said warily.

The Viscountess glanced over at her. "I should tell you that I know quite a bit about Russell Yates and his various . . . activities." She paused, then added, "My information does not come from Devlin."

Kat understood only too well what that meant. Kat's own encounters with this woman's father, Lord Jarvis, had been brutal, terrifying, and nearly fatal. He had promised her torture and a heinous death, and while that threat had abated, it had not disappeared. Kat knew he was simply waiting for the right opportunity to strike. She had to call upon all of her years of theatrical training to keep her voice sounding calm. "And?"

"I gather this Knox is one of your husband's . . . shall we call them 'associates'?"

Kat drew up abruptly and swung to face her. "Exactly what are you trying to say?"

The Viscountess met her gaze. "I think Knox is a danger to Devlin. I also think you know more about the man than you are willing to let on—even to Devlin."

Kat was aware of the darkening clouds pressing down on them, promising more rain. She could feel the dampness in the breeze, smell the earthy scent of the vegetables in the market stalls.

When she remained silent, the Viscountess said, "I can understand the problems that are created by divided loyalties."

Kat gave a startled laugh and turned to continue walking. "Well, I suppose that's one more thing you and I have in common, is it not?"

"My father at least is not trying to kill Devlin."

Kat glanced over at her. "Can you be so certain?"

Something flared in the other woman's eyes, quickly hidden. They continued along the side of the square for a moment; then the Viscountess said, "I don't know exactly what happened to cause the estrangement between you and Devlin last winter. But I believe you still care for him—at least enough not to want to see him hurt. Or dead."

"I think you underestimate your husband."

"He's mortal."

Kat stopped again. The wind was flapping the draping on the market stalls, scuttling handbills across the wet cobbles. She said, "Why did you come here?"

A gleam of unexpected amusement shone in the woman's eyes. "I should have thought that was rather obvious."

"My God," whispered Kat as understanding suddenly dawned. "You love him."

Rather than respond, the Viscountess simply tilted her head and turned away.

"Why are you so afraid to admit it?" Kat called after her. "You don't want to acknowledge it even to yourself, do you?"

She thought the woman would keep walking. Instead, the Viscountess paused to look back at her. "I would have expected you to understand that better than anyone."

"He is no longer my lover," said Kat, knowing exactly what the other woman meant. "He hasn't been, for nearly a year."

"No. But that doesn't mean he isn't still in love with you . . . as you are with him."

"Devlin will always love me," said Kat. "No matter who else he comes to love. He doesn't love easily, but once he lets someone into his heart, they are there forever. It's simply the way he is. It's the same reason he will always love Hendon, however much he might wish it were otherwise."

Kat saw the puzzlement in the other woman's eyes, and she thought, *Oh, Sebastian; you haven't told her. Why haven't you told her?*

Aloud, Kat said, "Have you ever seen Jamie Knox?"

"No; why?"

Because if you were to see him, thought Kat, *you would know.* But all she said was, "You're right; he is dangerous. For your sake as well as Devlin's, you would do well to stay away from him."

With any other woman, the warning might have worked. But this woman was Jarvis's daughter. Kat watched a thoughtful gleam light the Viscountess's eyes.

And knew she'd just made a terrible mistake.

❧

Sebastian left his sister Amanda's house and drove through the slackening rain to the Strand.

He paused at a butcher shop near Villers Street to buy a side of ham, then continued on to the half-cleared stretch of land that fell away steeply from the street to the site of the new bridgehead. The river was running

swollen and sullen with the rain, a pockmarked expanse
of muddy water that frothed and boiled around the new
piers. Against the dull gray sky, the soaring arches of the
bridge itself stood out pale and stark.

Reining in, he let his gaze drift over the work site. Far
to the left rose the massive neoclassical elevation of the
new Somerset House, bustling now with its usual assortment of functionaries; to the right lay the Savoy Chapel
and its burial ground, the sole surviving relics of the vast
medieval palace that had once stood here. In the dreary
light of day, the rain-washed expanse of churned mud,
sodden weeds, and broken walls looked forlorn and
empty.

The night before, in the hour or more that had elapsed
between when he sent word of Arceneaux's shooting to
Bow Street and the arrival of Sir Henry, Sebastian had
scoured these ruins in an increasingly wide but ultimately futile search for a certain scruffy black and brown
dog with a white blaze down his nose and a weakness for
ham. He wasn't entirely certain what he thought he
could do today that he hadn't done the previous night,
but he felt compelled to try.

"If you were an injured dog," he said to Tom, "where
would you go?"

The tiger screwed up his face with the labor of
thought, his gaze, like Sebastian's, studying the rain-
drenched riverbank. After a moment, he said, "Ain't we
just downriver from the Adelphi?"

"We are."

"Well, if that Frenchy lieutenant used to 'ang around
Miss Tennyson and them two boys, then I reckon maybe
'is little dog'd go there—if 'e could make it that far.
Plenty o' places to 'ide in them vaults under the terrace."

Sebastian reached for the ham. "Tom, you are a genius."

Chapter 42

*I*gnoring the curious stares and ribald comments that followed him, Sebastian plunged deep into the dank, shadowy subterranean world of the Adelphi.

"Chien," he called, unwrapping the ham. "*À moi*, Chien. Chien?"

He tromped through the warehouses of the wine merchants, their owners' angry shouts and threats following him; he scrambled over dusty coal piles and penetrated deep into the dank recesses of the wharf's vast stables.

"Chien?"

He stood with one hand on his hip, watched the dust motes drift lazily in the gloom, breathed in the odor of manure and moldy hay. "Chien!" he bellowed, his voice echoing through the cavernous, high-vaulted space.

Blowing out a long, frustrated breath, he turned to leave . . .

And heard a faint, plaintive whimper.

🌿

"Can you help him?" Sebastian asked.

Paul Gibson stared down at the dog that lay stretched out and panting on the table in the front room of his surgery. "Well, I don't suppose dogs are *that* much different from people, when it comes right down to it." He probed the bloody wound in the dog's shoulder with gentle fingers and frowned. "Leave him with me. I'll see what I can do."

"Thank you," said Sebastian, turning toward the door.

"But if word of this ever reaches my esteemed colleagues at St. Thomas's," Gibson called after him, "I'll never forgive you."

※

The ancient, soot-stained church of St. Helen's Bishopsgate squatted like a ragged wet hen in the midst of its swollen graveyard.

Wearing a plain cloak with the hood drawn up against the drizzle, Hero wandered amongst the overgrown churchyard's gray, lichen-covered headstones and broken tombs, her gaze narrowing as she studied the yard of the gable-ended public house that backed onto the ancient priory grounds. The sky had taken on the color of old lead, the leafy boughs of the elms overhead hanging heavy with the weight of the day's rain. She could easily trace the line of the Roman wall that Gabrielle had once come here to examine; it ran from the rear of the churchyard along the inn's court to disappear between the Black Devil and the decrepit structure beside it.

So absorbed was she in her study of the ancient masonry that it was a moment before she became aware of a tall gentleman dressed all in black walking toward her. He wore black trousers tucked into high black boots, a black coat, and a black waistcoat. Only his shirt was white, the high points of his collar standing out stark against the darkness of his cravat. He had the lean, loose-limbed carriage of a soldier and the grace of a born athlete. His hair was dark, darker even than Devlin's, although he had Devlin's high cheekbones and fine facial structure. But it was his eyes that instantly drew and held her attention.

And she knew then why Kat Boleyn had warned her away from this man—understood exactly what the actress had been trying to keep her from seeing—and guessing.

"I know who you are," he said, pausing some half a dozen feet before her.

"Then you have the advantage of me."

He swept her a bow tinged with just a hint of mockery. "I beg your pardon. Please allow me to introduce myself. Mr. Jamie Knox, at your service."

His accent was not that of a gentleman.

"Ah," she said noncommittally.

He straightened, his gently molded mouth curving into a smile that did not touch those strange yellow eyes. "Why are you here?"

"What makes you assume I am here for any reason other than to study the architecture and monuments of St. Helen's? Did you know it was once the parish church of William Shakespeare?"

"No. But I don't think you're here because of some long-dead scribbler. Are you spying on us, then?"

"And if I were to do so, would I see anything interesting?"

His smile broadened unexpectedly, a genuine if somewhat sardonic smile, and for a moment he looked so much like Devlin that the resemblance nearly took her breath. He said, "I see you left your carriage up the lane. That was not wise."

She raised one eyebrow in a deliberately haughty expression. "Are you threatening me?"

He laughed. "Me? Ach, no. But the neighborhood's not the best. You never know what might happen to a young gentlewoman such as yourself, all alone on a wet, gloomy day such as this."

She slipped her right hand into the reticule that hung heavily against her. "I am better able to defend myself than you may perhaps realize."

A gust of wind swelled the canopy of the trees overhead, loosing a cascade of raindrops that pattered on the aged tombstones and rank grass around them.

"That's good to know," he said, his gaze locked with hers. He took a step back and tipped his head. "Do tell your husband I said hello."

And he walked away, leaving her staring after him and wondering how he had known who she was when she herself had never seen him before that day.

※

Sebastian was stripping off his bloody, coal-stained shirt in his dressing room when he heard the distant pounding of the front knocker. Reaching for the pitcher, he splashed hot water into the washbasin.

An angry shout drifted up from the entry hall below, followed by a scuffle and the thump of quick feet on the stairs.

"Sir!" came Morey's outraged cry. "If you will simply wait in the drawing room, I will ascertain if his lordship— *Sir!*"

Sebastian paused, his head turning just as Charles Tennyson d'Eyncourt, the honorable member from Lincolnshire, came barreling through the dressing room door.

"You bloody interfering bastard," d'Eyncourt shouted, drawing up abruptly in the center of the room. His face was red from his run up the stairs, his hands curled into fists at his sides, his cravat askew. "This is all your fault. You've ruined me! Do you hear me? You have positively *ruined* my hopes of having any significant future in government."

Sebastian nodded to the majordomo hovering in the open doorway. "It's all right, Morey; I can handle this."

The majordomo bowed and withdrew.

Sebastian reached for a towel. "Tell me how, precisely,

am I supposed to have injured you?" he said to
d'Eyncourt.

Gabrielle's cousin stared at him, his nostrils flaring, his
chest lifting with his agitated breathing. "It's all over town!"

Sebastian dried his face and ran the towel down over
his wet chest. "What is all over town?"

"About Gabrielle and her French lover. This is your
fault—you and your damnable insistence on pushing
your nose into other people's private affairs. I've been
afraid this would come out."

Sebastian paused for a moment, his head coming up.
"You knew about Lieutenant Philippe Arceneaux?"

Suddenly tight-lipped and silent, d'Eyncourt stared
back at him.

Sebastian tossed the towel aside. "How? How did you
know?"

D'Eyncourt adjusted the set of his lapels. "I saw them
together. Indeed, it was my intention to alert Hildeyard
to what was happening as soon as he returned to town.
Not that anyone ever had much success in curbing Gabrielle's wild starts, but still. What else was one to do?"

"When did you see them together? Where?"

"I fail to comprehend how this is any of your—"

Sebastian advanced on him, the pompous, arrogant,
self-satisfied mushroom backing away until his shoulders
and rump smacked against the cupboard behind him.
"I'm going to ask you one last time: when and where?"

D'Eyncourt swallowed convulsively, his eyes going
wide. "I first came upon them quite by chance in the
park, last—last week sometime. They were so nauseat-
ingly absorbed in each other that they didn't even see
me. I thus had the opportunity to observe them without
being perceived myself. It was quite obvious what direction the wind was in with them."

Sebastian frowned. "You said that was the first time
you saw them. When else?"

D'Eyncourt's tongue slipped out to moisten his lower lip. "Thursday. He was there, you know—when she had that confrontation with the tavern owner I was telling you about, at the York Steps. The two men nearly came to blows."

"Arceneaux was with her when Gabrielle quarreled with Knox?"

"If Knox is the rogue's name, then, yes."

"And when you told me about the incident, you left Arceneaux's presence out—why?"

"I should think my reasons would be self-evident. My first cousin—my *female* cousin—involved in a sordid affair with one of Napoléon's officers— Do you have any idea what this is going to do to my political career?"

Sebastian was aware of a bead of water from his wet hair running down one cheek. "A man is dead because of you, and you stand there and bleat about your bloody political career?"

D'Eyncourt put up a hand to straighten his cravat, his chin lifting and turning to one side as if to ease a kink in his neck. "What man are you suggesting is dead because of me?"

"Arceneaux!"

D'Eyncourt looked dumbfounded. "I don't know how you think you can hang his death on me, but who cares if he is dead? The man killed Gabrielle and my nephews. Or hadn't you heard?"

Sebastian swiped the back of his arm across his wet cheek. "What the devil are you talking about?"

A condescending smirk spread over d'Eyncourt's self-satisfied face. "Seems that the night before he died, Arceneaux confided to one of his fellow French officers that he killed Gabrielle and the boys." D'Eyncourt's tight smile widened. "What's the matter? Did Bow Street forget to tell you?"

Chapter 43

Sir Henry Lovejoy paused beneath the protective arches of the long arcade overlooking the market square of Covent Garden. The rain had started up again, sweeping in great windblown sheets over the shuttered stalls and lean-tos in the square. He was not a man prone to profanity, but at the moment the urge to give vent to his anger against Charles Tennyson d'Eyncourt was undeniably powerful.

He swallowed hard and said to the man who stood beside him, "I would like to apologize, my lord. I had not intended for you to learn of this development in such a manner."

"Never mind that," said Devlin. "How did this come about?"

"A gentleman approached us this morning with word that Arceneaux's death had inspired one of his fellow French officers to come forward with the information."

"What's this officer's name?"

"Alain Lefevre—an infantry captain, I believe, taken at Badajos. He says Arceneaux confessed whilst in his cups to having stabbed Miss Tennyson in the midst of a lover's quarrel."

"And the two boys, Alfred and George?"

"He says Arceneaux claimed at first to have been overcome with remorse for what he'd done, so that he set out to drive the boys back to London. Only, he panicked and decided to kill the boys too, in an attempt to cover up his guilt. The children's bodies are hidden in a ditch or gully somewhere. We've set men out searching the routes between the moat and the city, but at this point it's becoming doubtful the poor lads' bodies will ever be found."

Devlin kept his gaze focused on the square, where loose cabbage leaves fluttered in the wind. "I'd be interested to speak with this Lefevre."

"Unfortunately, the man is already on his way back to France."

Devlin swung his head to stare at him. "He what?"

"As a reward for his cooperation. I understand they thought it best to get him out of the country quickly, for his own protection."

An eddy of wind blew a fine mist in their faces. Lovejoy removed his spectacles and wiped them with his handkerchief before carefully fitting them back on his face. "His information does fit the facts as we know them."

"Only if one were unacquainted with Philippe Arceneaux."

When Lovejoy remained silent, the Viscount said, "What was the basis of Arceneaux's quarrel with Miss Tennyson supposed to have been?"

"Lefevre did not know. But there are some recent developments that may shed light on the subject. Earlier today, four paroled French officers were captured attempting to escape to France. One of the men retaken—a hussar captain named Pelletier—was reputedly one of Arceneaux's intimates."

Devlin frowned. "Is this Pelletier a big bear of a man with blond lovelocks and a long mustache?"

"That sounds like him, yes. Do you know him?"

"I've seen him. When did the escaping men leave London?"

"Sometime before dawn this morning, we believe. They were found hidden in the back of a calico printer's cart that had been fitted out with benches on the inside. The speculation is that there were originally to have been six men involved in the escape attempt, with Arceneaux being one of the missing men, and the other being the French officer you killed when he attacked you in Covent Garden the other night. There appears to have been some sort of falling out amongst the conspirators, which is doubtless why Arceneaux was killed—for fear that he meant to betray them."

"Does this hussar captain, Pelletier, confirm that?"

"All of the fugitives taken up are refusing to speak to anyone about anything. One of the constables attempting to retake the men was shot and killed, which means they'll all now hang for murder." Lovejoy shook his head. "Shocking, is it not? For officers to go back on their sworn word . . . It displays such an utter want of all the feelings and instincts of a gentleman."

Lovejoy expected Devlin, as a former military man himself, to be particularly harsh in his condemnation of any officer who so dishonored himself. The Viscount was silent for a moment, his eyes narrowing as he stared out at the rain. But when he finally spoke, his voice was oddly tight. "I suppose they were homesick and despaired of ever seeing France again. Sometimes it does seem as if this war will never end."

"I suppose so, but—"

Devlin turned toward him suddenly, an arrested expression on his face. "Did you say a *calico printer's* cart?"

Lovejoy blinked. "Yes. Although I fear we may never determine precisely which calico printer is involved—if indeed one is. You find that significant for some reason, my lord?"

"It just may be."

⁂

Jamie Knox was supervising the loading of a dray in the rain-washed courtyard of Calvert's Brewery in Upper Thames Street when Sebastian came to stand under the arch. Propping one shoulder against the rough bricks, he crossed his arms at his chest and watched the tavern owner at work.

The air was heavy with the yeasty smell of fermenting hops, the tang of wet stone and brick, the odor of fish rising off the nearby rain-churned river. Knox threw him one swift glance but continued barking orders to the men lashing barrels to his wagon's high bed. He conferred for a moment with his driver. Then he walked over to stand in front of Sebastian, rainwater running down his cheeks, his yellow eyes hooded.

"You're obviously here for a reason; what is it, then?"

Sebastian stared into the lean, fine-boned face that was so much like his own. "I know why you killed Philippe Arceneaux."

Knox let out a bark of laughter. "That's rich. So tell me, then; what reason would I have for killing this young French—ah, lieutenant, was he not?"

"He was." Sebastian stood back as a cart piled with sacks of hops and drawn by a bay shire horse turned in under the arch, steam rising from the animal's wet hide, hooves clattering over the cobbles. "I noticed there's a calico printer's shop across the lane from your tavern."

"So there is. But there must be several dozen or more calico printers scattered across London. So if you're thinking there's any connection between the calico printer's cart I hear those four escaping French officers were taken up in and my tavern, then let me tell you right now, you're fair and far out."

"I might have believed you if I hadn't discovered that Philippe Arceneaux was present at that little set-to you had with Miss Tennyson last Thursday at the York Steps. I'm thinking there's a reason you left that detail out, and this is it."

Knox stood with his hands on his slim hips, his cheeks slightly hollowed, a faint smile dancing around his mouth as if he were amused.

Sebastian said, "You see, I'm thinking there were originally supposed to be six Frenchmen in that cart, with Arceneaux being one of them. Only, somehow the woman he loved—that would be Miss Tennyson, by the way—found out he was planning to escape and begged him to stay. So he backed out."

"An interesting theory, to be sure. Although I fail to see what the hell any of this has to do with me."

Sebastian watched the team of heavy dapple grays hitched to Knox's beer wagon lean into their collars. "I'm told that six hundred and ninety-two paroled French officers have escaped—or attempted to escape—from England in the past three years. That's an extraordinary number of men. Is that how you pay for the French wine and brandy you smuggle in? With escaped prisoners of war?"

The rain drummed around them, pounding on the puddles in the courtyard and sluicing off the brewery's high roof. Knox stared back at him, silent, watchful.

Sebastian said, "It's a clever, lucrative rig you're running, but it's also dangerous. Did Gabrielle Tennyson discover what you were doing? Is that why you were quarreling with her by the York Steps last Thursday? Because there's some men who might consider that kind of threat a good motive for murder, if they thought a woman was going to give their game away.

Did Arceneaux accuse you of killing her, I wonder? Did you decide to kill him before he could cause you any trouble?"

A cold, dangerous light glittered in the depths of the rifleman's eyes. "And the two lads? Am I to have killed them too, just for the sport of it?"

"In my experience there's a certain kind of man who can turn decidedly lethal when he's feeling cornered. Maybe you saw an opportunity to strike against her and you didn't let the fact that the boys were there, too, stop you."

"And what was I doing out at that moat with Miss Tennyson and the two brats? Mmm? You tell me that. You think she drove out there with me? Her in love with Arceneaux and thinking me a smuggler and all-around degenerate character?"

It was the one inescapable flaw in Sebastian's theory, and he'd known it when he decided to approach the rifleman. "I don't know why she went out there with you. Maybe you followed her. Maybe she wasn't even killed at the moat. Maybe that's why the two lads' bodies have never been found, because you killed and buried them someplace else."

The tight smile was back around Knox's lips. "Someplace such as St. Helen's churchyard, perhaps? Now, there's a clever place to hide a couple of bodies, don't you think? In a graveyard full of moldering corpses?"

"Perhaps," said Sebastian. "Then again, it's always possible you didn't kill Miss Tennyson at all—that someone else killed her for a different reason entirely. But Arceneaux would have no way of knowing that, would he? Something he said to me the other day suggested he was afraid he might be responsible for what had happened to her. So maybe he accused you of killing her, even when you hadn't. Maybe he threatened to expose you once his friends escaped. The timing of his death is curious, wouldn't you agree?"

All trace of amusement had drained from the rifle-man's face, leaving it hard and tight. "I've killed many men in my day; what soldier hasn't? But I've never killed a woman or a child, and I've never murdered a man in cold blood."

The two men stared at each other. The rain poured around them, loud in Sebastian's ears. He settled his hat lower on his forehead. "If I find out you shot Philippe Arceneaux, I'll see you hang for it."

Brother or no brother, he thought. But he didn't say it.

Chapter 44

Sebastian stood at the top of the Cole Harbour Steps, the storm-churned waters of the Thames slapping the ancient masonry at his feet. Behind him loomed the soot-covered brick walls of the brewery and the steel-yard beyond that. Dark clouds pressed down on the city, heavy with the promise of rain.

More and more, he was beginning to think there was something in Gabrielle Tennyson's life that he was missing, something that would explain the puzzle that was her death and the mysterious disappearance of her two young cousins. He had pieced together much of it—her love for the scholarly young French lieutenant, the conflicts swirling around her work on the legends of King Arthur and Camelot, the ill-fated escape attempt by Arceneaux's fellow officers. But something still eluded him. And he couldn't shake the growing conviction that the missing children were the key.

Had Gabrielle and the two boys driven up to Camlet Moat in the company of their killer? Or was her body simply planted there for reasons Sebastian could only guess at? Why would the killer leave Gabrielle at the moat and then take her young cousins elsewhere to kill or bury them? *Had* the cousins been killed, or were they even now out there, somewhere, alive?

Sebastian turned, his gaze narrowing as he stared up the river. From here he could look beyond the soot-blackened expanse of Blackfriars Bridge to the distant bend marked by the rising arches of the new Strand Bridge. Farther beyond that, lost in the mist, lay the imposing facade of the Adelphi. An idea was forming in his mind, a scenario that made more sense as the different possibilities he was looking at spiraled narrower and narrower.

Swinging away from the river, he darted through the rain to Upper Thames Street, where he flagged down a hackney and directed the driver to Tower Hill.

"Come to collect your dog, have you?" asked Gibson, limping ahead of Sebastian down his narrow hall.

Sebastian swung off his wet cloak and swiped his sleeve across his dripping face. "Is he going to be all right, then?"

Gibson led the way into his tattered, cluttered parlor, where the little black and brown dog raised his head, his tail thumping against the worn rug in welcome. But Chien made no effort to get up, and Sebastian could see blood still seeping through the thick bandage at his shoulder.

"It might be better if you left him with me a wee bit longer, just so I can keep an eye on him." Gibson rasped a hand across his chin, which from the looks of things he hadn't bothered to shave that morning. "Although there's no denying he's a sore trial."

"What have you been doing, Chien? Hmm?" Sebastian went to hunker down beside the dog. "Stealing the ham Mrs. Federico had intended for our good surgeon's dinner?"

"As a matter of fact, he tried. But that's not the worst

of it. I let him out in the yard to answer nature's call, and what does he do but bring me back a bone. Thankfully, he wasn't chewing on it—just presented it to me like he'd found something precious and expected a reward."

"Did Mrs. Federico see it?" Gibson's housekeeper, Mrs. Federico, was both extraordinarily squeamish about her employer's activities and blissfully ignorant of what lay buried in his yard.

"Fortunately, no. But if he starts digging holes out there, I'm going to be in trouble." Gibson eyed Sebastian darkly. "Go on, then, laugh if you want. But if you're not here for the dog, then why are you here?"

"Do you still have the clothes Gabrielle Tennyson was wearing when she was murdered?"

"I do, yes. Why?"

"Something's been bothering me."

※

Sebastian found Hero sipping a hot cup of tea in the drawing room. She wore a sarcenet walking dress and her hair was damp, as if she had just come in out of the rain. He set a brown paper–wrapped bundle on the table beside her and said, "I'm beginning to think it's more and more likely that Gabrielle Tennyson was actually murdered in London and then taken up to Camlet Moat."

Hero looked at him over the rim of her cup. "I thought Gibson said there was no evidence that she'd been moved after death."

"He did. But just because he found no evidence of it doesn't mean it didn't happen." He untied the string holding the bundle together. "This is what Gabrielle was wearing when she was killed. Is it the sort of thing she would be likely to put on to go up to Enfield?"

She reached out to touch one of the gown's short puffed sleeves, a quiver passing over her features as she studied the bloodstained tear in the bodice. "The material is delicate, but it is a walking dress, just the sort of thing a woman might wear for a stroll in the country, yes." She turned over the froth of petticoats to look at the peach half boots. Then she frowned.

"What is it?" asked Sebastian, watching her.

"Is this everything?"

"Yes. Why?"

"She had a pretty peach spencer with ruched facings and a stand-up collar I would have expected her to be wearing with this. Only, it isn't here."

"Sunday was quite hot. She might have left the spencer in the carriage. The shade in the wood is certainly dense enough that she wouldn't have needed to worry about protecting her arms from the sun."

"True. But I wouldn't have expected her to take off her bonnet, as well. She had a lovely peach silk and velvet bonnet she would have worn to pick up the color of the sash and these half boots. And it's not here, either."

"Would you recognize the spencer and bonnet if you found them in her dressing chamber?"

Hero met his gaze. Then she set aside her tea and rose to her feet. "I'll get my cloak."

※

"Hildeyard could have already directed Gabrielle's abigail to dispose of her clothes," said Hero as they drove through the rain, toward the river.

"I doubt it. His energy has been focused on the search for the missing children. And even if he did, the woman will surely remember what was there."

Hero was silent for a moment, her gaze on the wet streets. "If you're right, and Gabrielle was killed here in London, then what do you think happened to the children?"

"I'd like to think they're in the city someplace, hiding—that they ran away in fear after witnessing the murder. But if that were true, I think they'd have been found by now."

She turned to look at him. "You think it's d'Eyncourt, don't you? You think he killed George and Alfred over the inheritance and hid their bodies someplace they'll never be found. And then he drove Gabrielle up to Camlet Moat to make it look as if her death were somehow connected to the excavations or her work on the Arthurian legends."

Sebastian nodded. "I keep going back to the way he was just sitting there, calmly reading *The Courier* in White's. What kind of man wouldn't be out doing everything he could to search for his own brother's children? He's either more despicable than I thought, or—"

"Or he knew they were already dead," said Hero, finishing the thought for him.

They arrived at the Adelphi to find Hildeyard Tennyson still up at Enfield.

Rather than attempt to explain their mission to the servants, Hero claimed to have forgotten something during her previous visit and ran up the stairs to Gabrielle's room, while Sebastian asked to see the housekeeper and returned George Tennyson's poem to her.

"Oh, your lordship, I'm ever so grateful for this," said Mrs. O'Donnell, tearfully clasping the paper to her ample bosom. "I thought sure you must've forgotten it, but I didn't feel right asking you for it."

"My apologies for keeping it so long," said Sebastian with a bow.

Looking up, he saw Hero descending the stairs. Their gazes met. He bowed to Mrs. O'Donnell again and said, "Ma'am."

He waited until he and Hero were back out on the pavement before saying, "Well?"

Hero was looking oddly flushed. "All her things are

still there; Hildeyard obviously hasn't had the will to touch any of it yet. I found the spencer and bonnet immediately. In fact, it looked as if Gabrielle had worn them to church that morning and hadn't put them away properly because she was planning to wear them again."

The mist swirled around them, thickening so fast he could barely see the purple skirt and yellow kerchief of the old Gypsy fortune-teller at the end of the terrace. Sebastian said, "Well, we can eliminate Sir Stanley from the list of suspects; he would never have taken Gabrielle's body to the one place certain to cast suspicion on him. And while I wouldn't put it beyond Lady Winthrop to cheerfully watch her husband hang for a murder she herself committed, the logistics—" He broke off.

"What?" asked Hero, her gaze following his.

Today the Gypsy had a couple of ragged, barefoot children playing around her skirts: a girl of perhaps five and a boy a few years older. "That Gypsy woman. I noticed her here on Monday. If she was here last Sunday as well, she might have seen something."

"The constables questioned everyone on the street," said Hero as Sebastian turned their steps toward the Gypsies. "Surely they would have spoken to her already."

"I've no doubt they did. But you can ask a Rom the same question ten times and get ten different answers."

The Gypsy children came running up to them, bare feet pattering on the wet pavement, hands outstretched, eyes wide and pleading. "Please, sir, lady; can you spare a sixpence? Only a sixpence! Please, please."

"Go away," said Hero.

The boy fixed Hero with a fierce scowl as his wheedling turned belligerent and demanding. "You must give us a sixpence. Give us a sixpence or I will put a curse on you."

"Don't give it to them," said Sebastian. "They'll despise you for it."

"I have no intention of giving them anything." Hero

tightened her grip on her reticule. "Nor do I see why we are bothering with this Gypsy woman. If she lied to the constables, what makes you think she will tell you the truth?"

"The Rom have a saying: *Tshatshimo Romano.*"

Hero threw him a puzzled look. "What does that mean?"

"It means, 'The truth is expressed in Romany.'"

Chapter 45

"*Sarishan ryor,*" Sebastian said, walking up to the fortune-teller.

The Gypsy leaned against the terrace's iron railing, her purple skirt and loose blouse ragged and tattered, her erect carriage belied by the dark, weathered skin of a face etched deep with lines. Her lips pursed, her eyes narrowing as her gaze traveled over him, silent and assessing.

"*O boro duvel atch pa leste,*" he said, trying again.

She snorted and responded to him in the same tongue. "Where did you learn your Romany?"

"Iberia."

"I should have known." She turned her head and spat. "The Gitanos. They have forgotten the true language of the ancients." She eyed him thoughtfully, noting his dark hair. "You could be Rom. You have something of the look about you. Except for the eyes. You have the eyes of a wolf. Or a *jettatore.*" She touched the blue and white charm tied around her neck by a leather strap. It was a *nazar,* a talisman worn to ward off the evil eye.

Sebastian was aware of Hero watching them, her face carefully wiped free of all expression. The entire conversation was taking place in Romany.

He said to the Gypsy, "I want to ask you about the lady who used to live in the second house from the corner. A tall young woman, with hair the color of chestnuts."

"You mean the one who is no more."

Sebastian nodded. "Did you see her leave the house last Sunday?"

"One day is like the next to the Rom."

"But you know which day I mean, because the next day the *shanglo* came and asked you questions, and you told them you had seen nothing."

She smiled, displaying tobacco-stained teeth. "And what makes you think I will tell you anything different? Hmm?"

"Because I am not a *shanglo*."

No one was hated by the Rom more than the *shanglo*—the Romany word for police constable.

"Did you see the woman and the two boys leave the house that day?" Sebastian asked.

The light had taken on an eerie, gauzelike quality, the mist eddying around them, wet and clammy and deadening all sound. He could hear the disembodied slap of oars somewhere unseen out on the water and the drip, drip of moisture nearer at hand. Just when he thought the Gypsy wasn't going to answer him, she said, "I saw them leave, yes. But they came back."

He realized she must have seen Gabrielle Tennyson and the two children leaving for church that morning. He said, "And after that? Did someone come to visit them? Or did they go out again?"

"Who knows? I left soon after." The Gypsy's dark gaze traveled from Sebastian to Hero. "But I saw her."

Sebastian felt his mouth go dry and a strange tingling dance across his scalp.

The old woman's lips stretched into a smile that accentuated the high, stark bones of her face. "You didn't want to hear that, did you? But it's true. She came here not that day, but the day before, in a yellow carriage pulled by four black horses. Only, there was no one home and so she went away again."

As if aware that she had suddenly become the topic of conversation, Hero glanced from him to the Gypsy, then back again. "What? What is she saying?"

Sebastian met the old woman's dark, unblinking eyes. "I want to know the truth, whatever it might be."

The old woman snorted. "You just heard it. Now the question becomes, what will you make of it?"

※

They walked along the edge of the terrace, the sound of their footsteps echoing hollowly in the white void. Sebastian could feel the mist damp against his face. The opposite bank, the wherries on the river, even the tops of the tall brick houses beside them had all disappeared behind the thick white blur of fog.

It was Hero who broke the silence, saying, "Where did you learn to speak Romany?"

"I traveled with a band of Gypsies for a time, in the Peninsula."

She stared at him, her gaze solemn. "And are you going to tell me what the woman said?"

"She says you came to see Gabrielle on Saturday. And don't even think about denying it because she described your carriage and horses. Did you not notice her? Or did you simply assume she wouldn't recognize you?"

He watched as her lips parted on a suddenly indrawn breath. Then she said, "Ah," and turned her head away to gaze out at the fog-choked river.

He studied her tense profile, the smooth curve of her cheek, the faint betraying line of color that rode high along the bone. "There's only one reason I can come up with that would explain why you've kept this from me, and that's because Jarvis is somehow involved. Am I right?"

"He says he didn't kill her."

"And you believe him?"

She hesitated a moment too long. "Yes."

He gave a sharp bark of laughter. "You don't exactly sound convinced."

The figure of a man materialized out of the mist and walked toward them, a workman in rough clothes with what looked like a seaman's bag slung over one shoulder.

Sebastian saw the flush along her cheekbones darken now with anger. He said, "Tell me what's going on."

"You know I can't."

He gave a ringing laugh. "Well, I suppose that answers the question about where your loyalties lie."

"Does it?" She brought her gaze back to his face. "You think I should betray my father to you? So tell me, would you expect me to betray you to him?" She laid her hand on the soft swell of her belly. "And twenty years from now, if this child is a girl, would you think it right that she betray *you* to whatever man she marries?"

When he remained silent, she said, "Have you been so honest with me, Devlin? Will you tell me why you can't even bear to be in the same room with your father? And will you tell me about Jamie Knox? Will you tell me why a common ex-rifleman and tavern owner looks enough like my husband to be his brother? Neither one of us has been exactly open with the other, have we?"

"No," said Sebastian, just as the man passing them pivoted quickly, his bag slumping to the pavement as he raised a cudgel and brought it down hard across Sebastian's back.

The breath left his body in a huff, the pain of the blow dropping him to his knees.

Sebastian fumbled for the dagger in his boot, fought to draw air back into his lungs. He saw the man raise his club to strike again, was aware of Hero beside him, her hands at her reticule.

Then she drew a small walnut-handled pistol from her reticule, pulled back the hammer, and fired point-blank into the assailant's chest.

"Jesus Christ," yelped Sebastian as the man staggered back and went down, hard. He gave a jerking kick with one leg, the worn heel of his boot skittering over the wet paving.

Then he lay still.

"Is he dead?" Hero asked.

His dagger held at the ready in his hand, Sebastian went to crouch beside the man.

He looked to be somewhere in his thirties or early forties, his body thick and hard, his face darkened by the weather, his hair a light brown, badly cut. A thin trickle of blood ran from the corner of his mouth; his eyes were already glazing over. Sebastian dropped his gaze to the pulverized mess that was the man's chest.

"He's dead."

"Are you all right?"

He twisted around to look at her over his shoulder. She stood straight and tall, her face pale but composed. But he could see her nostrils flaring with her rapid breathing, and her lips were parted, as if she were fighting down an upsurge of nausea. "Are you?"

She swallowed, hard. "Yes."

His gaze dropped to the pistol in her hand. It was a beautiful if deadly little piece, a small muff flintlock with a burnished walnut stock and engraved gilt mounts. "Where did you get that?"

"My father gave it to me."

"And taught you to use it?"

"What would be the point in my having it otherwise?"

Sebastian nodded to the dead man. "Is he one of your father's men?"

"Good heavens, no. I've never seen him before."

Sebastian drew in an experimental deep breath that sent a white flash of pain shooting across his back and around his side, so that he had to pause with one arm propped on his bent knee and pant for a minute.

She watched him, a frown drawing her brows together. "Are you certain you're all right? Shall I get one of the footmen to help you up?"

"Just give me a moment." He tried breathing again, more cautiously this time. "Are you going to tell me about the connection between Childe and your father?" he asked when he was able. "That is how Jarvis comes into this, isn't it?"

She met his gaze. "You know I can't do that. But I see no reason why you can't ask him about it yourself."

Sebastian grunted and reached out to grasp one of the dead man's arms and haul the lifeless body up over his shoulder.

She watched him. "Is that wise, considering you are hurt?"

He pushed to his feet with another grunt, staggering slightly under the dead man's weight.

"What are you doing?" she asked.

"Taking your father a present."

He thought she might object.

But she didn't.

Chapter 46

Sebastian's knock at the house on Berkeley Square was answered by Jarvis's butler, who took one look at the bloody corpse slung over Sebastian's shoulders and staggered back with a faint mew of horror.

"Good afternoon, Grisham," said Sebastian, pushing past him into the elegant entrance hall.

"Good gracious, Lord Devlin; is that . . . is that man *dead*?"

"Decidedly. Is his lordship home?"

Grisham stared in awful fascination at the dead man's flopping arms and blue-tinged hands. Then he seemed to recollect himself, swallowed hard, and cleared his throat. "I fear Lord Jarvis is not at present—"

A burst of male laughter filtered down from the floor above.

"In the drawing room, is he?" Sebastian headed for the delicately curving staircase that wound toward the upper floors, then paused on the first step to look back at Grisham. "I trust there are no ladies present?"

"No, my lord. But—but— My lord! You can't mean to take that—that corpse into his lordship's drawing room?"

"Don't worry; I suspect Bow Street will want to come

collect it. Perhaps you could dispatch someone to advise them of the need to do so?"

Grisham gave a dignified bow. "I will send someone right away, my lord."

꒜

Charles, Lord Jarvis stood with his back to the empty hearth, a glass of sherry in one hand. "The Americans have shown themselves to be an abomination," he was telling the gentlemen assembled before him. "What they have done will go down in history as an insult not only to civilization but to God himself. To attack Britain at a time when all our resources are directed to the critical defense against the spread of atheism and republican fervor—"

He broke off as Viscount Devlin strode into the room with a man's bloody body slung over his shoulders.

Every head in the room turned toward the door. A stunned silence fell over the company.

"What the devil?" demanded Jarvis.

Devlin leaned forward and shrugged his shoulder to send the slack-jawed, vacant-eyed corpse sprawling across Jarvis's exquisite Turkey carpet. "We need to talk."

Jarvis felt a rare surge of raw, primitive rage, brought quickly under control. "Is this your version of a brace of partridges?"

"The kill isn't mine. He was shot by an elegant little muff pistol with a burnished walnut handle and engraved brass fittings. I believe you're familiar with it?"

Jarvis met Devlin's glittering gaze for one intense moment. Then he turned to his gawking guests. "My apologies, gentlemen, for the disturbance. If you will please excuse us?"

The assemblage of men—which Sebastian now noticed included the Prime Minister, the First Lord of the

Admiralty, and three other cabinet members—exchanged veiled glances, and then, murmuring amongst themselves, filed from the room.

Sebastian found himself oddly relieved to notice that Hendon was not one of them.

Jarvis went to close the door behind them with a snap. "I trust you have a damned good explanation for this?"

"Actually, that's what I'm here to ask you. I want to know why the hell my wife and I were attacked by—"

"*Hero?* Is she all right? My God. If my daughter has been harmed in any way—"

"She has not—with no thanks to you."

"I fail to understand why you assume this has anything to do with me. The world must be full of people only too eager to put paid to your existence."

"He's not one of your men?"

"He is not."

Devlin's gaze narrowed as he studied Jarvis's face. "And would you have me believe you didn't set someone to follow me earlier this week?"

Jarvis took another sip of his sherry. "The incompetent bumbling idiot you chased through the Adelphi was indeed in my employ—although he is no longer. But I had nothing to do with"—he gestured with his glass toward the dead man on the carpet—"this. Who is he?"

"If I knew, I wouldn't be here."

Jarvis went to peer down at the dead man. "Something of a ruffian, I'd say, from the looks of him." He shifted his gaze to the dead man's torn, bloody shirt. "Hero did this?"

"She did."

Jarvis looked up, his jaw tightening. "Believe it or not, until my daughter had the misfortune of becoming involved with you, she had never killed anyone. And now—"

"Don't," said Devlin, one hand raised as if in warning. "Don't even think of laying the blame for this on me. If

Hero was in any danger this afternoon, it was because of you, not me."

"Me?"

"Two days before she died, Gabrielle Tennyson stumbled upon a forgery that involved someone so ruthless and powerful that she feared for her life. I think the man she feared was you."

Jarvis drained his wineglass, then stood regarding it thoughtfully for a moment before walking over to remove a crumpled broadsheet from a nearby bureau and hold it out. "Have you seen these?"

Devlin glanced down at the broadsheet without making any move to take it. "I have. They seem to keep going up around town faster than the authorities can tear them down."

"They do indeed, thanks to certain agents in the employ of the French. The aim is to appeal to—and promote—disaffection with the House of Hanover. I suspect they've succeeded far better than Napoléon ever dreamt."

"Actually, I'd have said Prinny does a bang-up job of doing that all by himself."

Jarvis pressed his lips into a flat line and tossed the broadsheet aside. "Dislike of a monarch is one thing. The suggestion that he sits on his throne as a usurper is something else again. The Plantagenets faced similar nonsense back in the twelfth century. You might think people today wouldn't be as credulous as their ancestors of six hundred years ago, but the idea of a messianic return has proved surprisingly appealing."

"It's a familiar concept."

"There is that," said Jarvis.

"I take it that like the Plantagenets before you, you've decided to deal with the situation by convincing the credulous that King Arthur is not, in fact, the 'once and future king,' but just another pile of moldering old bones?"

"Something like that, yes."

"So you—what? Approached a scholar well-known for his skepticism with regards to the Arthurian legend—Bevin Childe, to be precise—and somehow convinced him to come forward with the astonishing claim of having found the Glastonbury Cross and a box of ancient bones amongst Richard Gough's collections? I suppose a competent craftsman could simply manufacture a copy of the cross from Camden's illustrations, while the bones could be acquired from any old churchyard. Of course, history tells us the cross was separated from the relevant bones long ago, but why allow details to interfere with legend?"

"Why, indeed?"

"There's just one thing I'm curious about: How did Miss Tennyson realize that it was a forgery?"

Jarvis reached into his pocket for his snuffbox. "I'm not certain that's relevant."

"But she did quarrel with Childe and throw the forgery into the lake."

"Yes. A most choleric, impetuous woman, Miss Tennyson."

"And determined too, I gather. Which means that as long as she was alive, your plan to convince the credulous that you had King Arthur's bones was not going to succeed."

Jarvis opened his snuffbox with the flick of one finger. "I am not generally in the habit of murdering innocent gentlewomen and their young cousins—however troublesome they may make themselves."

"But you would do it, if you thought it necessary."

"There is little I would not do to preserve the future of the monarchy and the stability of the realm. But in the general scheme of things, this really wasn't all that important. There would have been other ways of dealing with the situation besides murdering my daughter's troublesome friend."

"Such as?"

Jarvis lifted a small pinch of snuff to one nostril and sniffed. "You don't seriously expect me to answer that, do you?"

Devlin's lips flattened into a thin, hard line. "Last night, someone shot and killed a paroled French officer named Philippe Arceneaux. Then, this morning, one of Arceneaux's fellow officers supposedly stepped forward with the information that before his death, Arceneaux had confessed to the killings. As a reward, our conveniently community-minded French officer was immediately spirited out of the country. The only person I can think of with the power—and the motive—to release a French prisoner that quickly is you."

Jarvis closed his snuffbox. "Of course it was I."

"And you had Philippe Arceneaux shot?"

"I won't deny I took advantage of his death to shut down the inconvenient investigation into the Tennysons' murders. But did I order him killed? No."

"The *inconvenient investigation*? Bloody hell. Inconvenient for whom?"

"The Crown, obviously."

"Not to mention you and this bloody Glastonbury Cross scheme of yours."

When Jarvis remained silent, Devlin said, "How the devil did you convince Childe to lend his credibility to such a trick?"

"Mr. Childe has certain somewhat aberrant tastes that he would prefer others not know about."

"How aberrant?"

Jarvis tucked his snuffbox back into his pocket. "Nothing he can't indulge at the Lambs' Pen."

"And did Gabrielle Tennyson know about Childe's aberrations?"

"Possibly."

"So how do you know Childe didn't kill the Tennysons?"

"I don't. Hence the decision to shut down the investigation. It wouldn't do to have this murder be seen as linked in any way to the Palace." Jarvis straightened his cuffs. "It's over, Devlin; a murderer has been identified and punished with his own death."

Devlin nodded to the dead man before them. "Doesn't exactly look over to me."

"You don't know this attack was in any way related to the Tennyson case. The authorities are satisfied. The populace has already breathed a collective sigh of relief. Let it rest."

Devlin's lip curled. "And allow the real murderer to go free? Let those boys' parents up in Lincolnshire live the rest of their lives without ever knowing what happened to their children? Let Arceneaux's grieving parents in Saint-Malo believe their son a child killer?"

"Life is seldom tidy."

"This isn't untidy. This is an abomination." He swung toward the door.

Jarvis said, "You're forgetting your body."

"Someone from Bow Street should be here for it soon." Devlin paused to look back at him. "I'm curious. What exactly made Hero think you killed Gabrielle Tennyson?"

Jarvis gave the Viscount a slow, nasty smile. "Ask her."

Chapter 47

Rather than return directly to Brook Street, Sebastian first went in search of Mr. Bevin Childe.

The Cheese, in a small cul-de-sac known as Wine Office Court, off Fleet Street, was a venerable old eating establishment popular with antiquaries and barristers from the nearby Temple. A low-voiced conversation with a stout waiter sent Sebastian up a narrow set of stairs to a smoky room with a low, planked ceiling, where he found Childe eating a Rotherham steak in solitary splendor at a table near the bank of heavy-timbered windows.

The antiquary had a slice of beef halfway to his open mouth when he looked up, saw Sebastian coming toward him, and dropped his fork with a clatter.

"Good evening," said Sebastian, slipping into the opposite high-backed settee. "I was surprised when your man told me I might find you here. It's my understanding you typically spend Fridays at Gough Hall."

The antiquary closed his mouth. "My schedule this week has been . . . upset."

"How distressing for you."

"It is, yes. You've no notion." Very slowly, the antiquary retrieved his fork, took a bite of steak, and swallowed, hard. "I . . ." He choked, cleared his throat, and tried again. "I had hoped I'd explained everything to your wife's satisfaction yesterday at the museum."

Sebastian kept his face quietly composed, although in truth he didn't know what the bloody hell the man was talking about. "You're quite certain you left nothing out?"

"No, no; nothing."

Sebastian signaled the waiter for a tankard of bitter. "Tell me again how Miss Tennyson discovered the cross was a forgery."

Childe threw a quick, nervous glance around, then leaned forward, his voice dropping. "It was the merest chance, actually. She had made arrangements to drive out to Gough Hall on Friday to see the cross. I'd been expecting her early in the day, but as time wore on and she never arrived, I'd quite given up looking for her. Then the craftsman who'd manufactured the cross showed up." Childe's plump face flushed with indignation. "The scoundrel had the unmitigated gall to come offering to make *other* artifacts. I was in the stables telling him precisely what I thought of his suggestion when I turned and saw her standing there. She . . . I'm afraid she heard quite enough to grasp the truth of the situation."

"How did she know Jarvis was involved?"

Childe's tongue flicked out nervously to wet his lips. "I told her. She was threatening to expose the entire scheme, you see. So I warned her that she had no idea who or what she was dealing with."

"The knowledge didn't intimidate her?"

"Unfortunately, no. If anything, it only enraged her all the more."

Sebastian let his gaze drift over the stout man's sweat-sheened face. "Who do you think killed her?"

Childe tittered.

"You find the question amusing?"

Childe cut another bite of his steak. "Under the circumstances? Yes."

"It's a sincere question."

He paused in his cutting to hunch forward and lower his voice. "In truth?"

"Yes."

The antiquary threw another of his quick looks around. "Jarvis. I think Lord Jarvis killed her—or rather, had her killed."

"That's interesting. Because you see, he rather thinks you might have done it."

Childe's eyes bulged. "You can't be serious. I could never have killed her. I loved her! I've loved her from the moment I first saw her. Good God, I was willing to marry her despite knowing only too well about the family's fits."

Sebastian stared at him. "About the what?"

Childe pressed his napkin to his lips. "It's not something they like to talk about, I know. And while it's true I've never seen any indication that either Hildeyard or Gabrielle suffered from the affliction, there's no doubt it's rife in the rest of the family. Their great-grandfather had it, you know. And I understand the little boys' father—that Reverend up in Lincolnshire—suffers from it dreadfully."

Sebastian stared at the man across the table from him. "What the devil are you talking about? What kind of fits?"

Childe blinked at him owlishly. "Why, the falling sickness, of course. It's why Miss Tennyson always insisted she would never marry. Even though she showed no sign of it herself, she feared that she could somehow pass it on to any children she might have. She called it the family 'curse.' It quite enraged d'Eyncourt, I can tell you."

"D'Eyncourt? Why?"

"Because while he'll deny it until he's blue in the face, the truth is that he suffers from it himself— although nothing to the extent of his brother. When we were up at Cambridge, he half killed some sizar who said he had it." Childe paused, then said it again, as if the implications had only just occurred to him. "He half killed him."

Chapter 48

Sebastian found Hero at the library table, one of Gabrielle Tennyson's notebooks spread open before her.

The pose appeared relaxed. But he could practically see the tension thrumming in every line of her being. She looked up when he paused in the doorway, a faint flush touching her cheeks. He was aware of a new sense of constraint between them, a wariness that hadn't been there before. But he couldn't think of anything to say to ease the tension between them.

She said it for him. "We haven't handled this situation well, have we? Or perhaps I should say, I have not."

He came to pull out the chair opposite her and sit down. The raw anger he'd felt, before, along the Thames, had leached out of him, leaving him unexpectedly drained and weighed down by a heaviness he recognized now as sadness.

He let his gaze drift over the tightly held lines of her face. "I'd go with 'we.'"

She said stiffly, "I might regret the situation, but I can't regret my decision."

"I suppose that makes sense. I can admire you for your loyalty to your father, even if I don't exactly agree with it."

He was surprised to see a faint quiver pass over her features. But she still had herself under rigid control. Only once had he seen her self-control break, in the subterranean chambers of Somerset House when they faced death together—and created the child she now carried within her.

He said, "I spoke to Jarvis. He said to ask you how you came to know of his involvement with Gabrielle. Did she tell you?"

"Not exactly. I was visiting my mother Friday evening when I heard angry voices below. I couldn't catch what they were saying—" A hint of a smile lightened her features. "We aren't all blessed with your hearing. But I thought I recognized Gabrielle's voice. So I went downstairs. I'd just reached the entrance hall when she came out of my father's library. I heard her say, 'I told Childe if he attempts to go ahead with this, I'll expose him—and you too.' Then she turned and saw me. She just . . . stared at me from across the hall, and then ran out of the house." Hero was silent for a moment, her face tight with grief. "I never saw her again."

"Did you ask your father what it was about?"

"I did. He said Gabrielle was an overly emotional and obviously imbalanced woman. That she'd had some sort of argument that day with Childe but that it was nothing that need concern me."

"He doesn't know you well, does he?"

She met his gaze; the smile was back in her eyes. "Not as well as he likes to think." She closed the notebook she'd been reading and pushed it aside. He realized now that it was Gabrielle's translation of *The Lady of Shalott*. She said, "I went to the Adelphi the next day to try to talk to her. Unfortunately, she was still out at the moat."

"What time was that?"

"I don't know, precisely. Midafternoon sometime. I left her a message. Later that evening, I received this

from her." She withdrew a folded note from the back
cover of Gabrielle's book and pushed it across the table
to him.

He flipped open the paper and read,

> Hero,
> *Believe me, I would be the last person to blame
> anyone else for the actions of their family. Please do
> come up to see the excavations at Camlet Moat on
> Monday, as we'd planned. We can discuss all this
> then.*
>
> > *Your friend,*
> > *Gabrielle*

Sebastian fingered the note thoughtfully, then looked
up at her. "Did Gabrielle ever tell you why she was so
determined never to marry?"

His question seemed to take Hero by surprise. She
looked puzzled for a moment, then shook her head. "We
never discussed it. I always assumed she'd decided marriage wasn't compatible with a life devoted to scholarship."

"Bevin Childe claims it was because there is epilepsy
in her family and she feared passing it on to her own
children."

Hero's lips parted, her nostrils flaring as she drew in a
quick breath. "Epilepsy? That's the falling sickness, isn't
it? Do you think Childe knows what he's talking about?"

"I'm not certain. I went by the Adelphi to try to ask
Hildeyard, but he's still out searching for his cousins.
There's no denying it makes sense of a number of
things—all the strange statements made about the Reverend Tennyson's health, d'Eyncourt being made his father's heir, even some of the things said about the two
boys."

"You think the children could suffer from it?"

"I don't know. You never saw any sign of it?"

"No. But the truth is, I know almost nothing about the affliction. Do you?"

"No." Sebastian pushed to his feet. "But I know someone who does."

※

"The falling sickness?"

Paul Gibson looked from Sebastian to Hero and back again. They were seated on the torn chairs of the Irishman's cluttered, low-ceilinged parlor, the black and brown dog stretched out asleep on the hearth rug beside them.

Sebastian said, "It's the more common name for epilepsy, isn't it?"

Gibson blew out a long breath. "It is, yes. But . . . I'm not sure how much I can tell you about it. I'm a surgeon, not a physician."

"You can't know less about it than we do."

"Well . . ." Gibson scrubbed one hand down over his beard-shadowed face. "It's my understanding no one knows exactly what causes it. There are all sorts of theories, of course—one wilder than the next. But there does seem to be a definite hereditary component to it, at least most of the time. I suspect there may actually be several different disorders involved, brought on by slightly different causes. Some affect mainly children; others don't seem to start until around the age of ten or twelve."

"The age at which the Old Man of the Wolds disinherited his firstborn son and changed his will to leave everything to d'Eyncourt," said Sebastian.

Hero looked at Gibson. "There's no treatment?"

"None, I'm afraid. The usual advice to sufferers is to take lots of long walks. And water."

"Water?"

"Yes. Both drinking water and taking soaking baths or going for swims is said to help. Sufferers are also—" Gibson looked at Hero and closed his mouth.

"What?" she said.

The Irishman shifted uncomfortably and threw Sebastian a pleading look. "Perhaps you could come with me into the kitchen for a wee moment?"

"You may as well say it; I'll just turn around and tell her."

Gibson shifted again and cleared his throat. "Yes, well . . . There are indications . . . That is to say, many believe that the attacks can be brought on by certain kinds of activities."

"What kind of activities?"

Gibson flushed crimson.

Hero said, "I gather you're referring to activities of a sexual nature?"

The Irishman nodded, his cheeks now darkened to a shade more like carmine.

Sebastian said, "I suspect that belief is a large part of why there is such a stigma attached to the affliction."

"It is, yes. Smoking and excessive drinking have also been identified as bringing on seizures. The interesting thing is, when we think of epilepsy, we tend to think of full seizures. But the malady can also manifest in a milder form. Sometimes sufferers will simply become unresponsive for a few minutes. They appear conscious, but it's as if they aren't there. And then they come back and they're totally unaware that anything untoward has occurred."

Sebastian noticed Hero leaning forward, her lips parted. "What?" he asked, watching her.

"Gabrielle used to do that. Not often, but I saw it happen twice. It was as if she'd just . . . go away for a minute or so. And then suddenly she would be all right."

Gibson nodded. "Sometimes the malady progresses

no further. But occasionally a moment of great stress or excitement or something else we don't even understand can trigger a full seizure."

Hero glanced over at Sebastian. "If you think this is the key to Gabrielle's murder, I still don't understand it."

"I keep thinking about something Childe said to me, that Charles d'Eyncourt half killed one of the poor scholars at Cambridge who suggested he suffered from it. Most people see epilepsy as something shameful, a family secret to be kept hidden at all costs, like madness."

"And no one is more ruthless and ambitious than d'Eyncourt," said Hero. "So what are you suggesting? That young George started showing signs of epilepsy? And that when Gabrielle refused to bundle the child back up to Lincolnshire, d'Eyncourt killed her? Her and the boys, both?"

Chien lifted his head and whimpered.

"It wasn't George and d'Eyncourt I was thinking about," said Sebastian, going to hunker down beside the dog. "There's no doubt the man is an arrogant, unprincipled liar, but he's also a coward. I'm not convinced he has what it takes to haul his cousin's dead body ten miles north of London to some deserted moat he's probably never heard of and surely never seen. And I suspect if someone like Rory Forster tried to blackmail him, he'd pay the bastard off—he wouldn't arrange to meet him in a dark wood and shoot him in the chest."

Hero watched him pull the dog's ears, her eyes widening. "Good lord. You can't think *Hildeyard*— Because of Gabrielle?" She shook her head. "But that's impossible. He was in Kent."

"He was. But his estate is only four hours' hard ride from London. He could conceivably have left Kent early Sunday morning, ridden up to London, killed Gabrielle, driven her body up to Camlet Moat, and then ridden back to Kent late that night. We know he was there when he messenger arrived from Bow Street on Monday with word of Gabrielle's death, but I seriously doubt the man inquired into Mr. Tennyson's movements the previous day."

A flicker of lightning showed outside the room's nar- row window, illuminating Hero's face with a flash of white that was there and then gone. "But why? Why would he do such a thing?"

"I think Gabrielle had a seizure—one much worse han anything she'd ever had before. It was probably provoked by the emotional turmoil of learning the man she loved was thinking about escaping to France, or per- haps by their lovemaking, or maybe even by the fear and anger she experienced when she discovered the truth about Childe's deception. I think she wrote her brother about it and told him he needed to warn his betrothed that there was epilepsy in the family. And that's when he rode up to London."

Thunder rumbled in the distance. "To kill her? I don't believe it."

"I don't think he came here with the intention of kill- ing her. I think he came here to argue with her. Then he lost his temper and stabbed her in a rage."

"And murdered the children too?" Hero shook her head. "No. He's not that . . . evil."

"I seriously doubt he sees himself as evil. In fact, I suspect he even blames Gabrielle for driving him to do it. In my experience, people kill when their emotions overwhelm them—be it fear, or greed, or anger. Some are so stricken afterward with remorse that they end up destroying their own lives too. But most are selfish enough to be able to rationalize what they've done as necessary or even justified."

"The problem is," said Gibson, "you've no proof of any of this. Even if you discover Tennyson did leave his estate on Sunday, that would only prove that he could have done it, not that he did. D'Eyncourt could have done it too. Or Childe. Or Arceneaux."

"What I don't understand," said Hero, "is if you're right—and I'm not conceding that you are—then why would Hildeyard hide the children's bodies someplace else? D'Eyncourt would have a clear reason—to shift the investigation away from the children's deaths onto Gabrielle. But not Hildeyard. He's been up at Enfield every day, looking for them."

Sebastian let his hand rest on his thigh. "Has he? We know he went up there on Tuesday and made a big show of organizing a search for his cousins. But do we know for certain he's actually been there all day, every day since then?"

She thought about it, then shook her head. "No."

"For all we know, he could have been spending the bulk of his time scouring London in the hopes of finding the children—and silencing them."

"But if they're not dead, then where are they?"

Chien nudged Sebastian's still hand, and he moved again to stroke the brown and black dog's silken coat. He was thinking about a nine-year-old boy telling Philippe he should have called his dog "Rom." Not Gypsy, but "Rom." He had a sudden image of a blue and white *nazar* worn on a leather thong around the neck of an old Gypsy woman, and an identical talisman lying on a nursery table beside a broken clay pipe bowl and a horse chestnut.

"What?" said Hero, watching him.

He pushed to his feet. "I think I know where the children are."

"You mean, you know where they're buried?"

"No. I don't think they're dead. I think they've gone with the raggle-taggle-Gypsies-oh."

Chapter 49

They drove first to the Adelphi Terrace in hopes the Gypsy woman might still be there. But the angry clouds roiling overhead had already blotted out much of the light from the setting sun. The windows in the surrounding houses gleamed golden with lamplight, and the terrace lay wet and deserted beneath a darkening sky.

"Now what do we do?" asked Hero, shouting to be heard over the din of the wind and driving rain.

Sebastian stared out over the rain-swollen river. Lightning flashed again, illuminating the underbellies of the clouds and reflecting off the choppy water. A charlie on his rounds came staggering around the corner, headed for his box. He wore an old-fashioned greatcoat and had one hand up to hold his hat against the wind; his other hand clutched a shuttered lantern.

"Sure, then, 'tis a foul night we're in for," he said when he saw them.

"It is that," agreed Sebastian. "We were looking for the Gypsy woman who's usually here reading palms. Do you know where we might find her?"

"Has she stolen something from you, sir? Nasty thieving varmints, the lot of 'em."

"No, she hasn't stolen anything. But my wife"—

Sebastian nodded to Hero, who did her best to loo
credulous and eager—"my wife here was desirous o
having her palm read."

The charlie blinked. But he was obviously inured t
the strange ways of quality, because he said, "I think sh
belongs to that band what camps up around Nine Elm
this time of year. I seen her leaving once or twice b
wherry." The hamlet of Nine Elms lay on the south sid
of the river, beyond Lambeth and Vauxhall in a low
marshy area known for its windmills and osier stand
and meadows of rue and nettle.

"Thank you," said Sebastian, turning to shout direc
tions to his coachman and help Hero climb into the car
riage.

"Funny you should be asking about them," said th
charlie.

Sebastian paused on the carriage steps to look bacl
at him. "Why's that?"

"Mr. Tennyson asked me the same thing," said th
charlie, "not more'n a couple of hours ago."

※

They found the Gypsy camp in a low meadow near ;
willow-lined brook, where some half a dozen high
wheeled caravans were drawn up in a semicircle facin;
away from the road. Wet cook fires burnt sluggishly i
the gloaming of the day, their blue smoke drifting u
into the mist, the penetrating smell of burning wood an
garlic and onions carrying on the wind. At the edge o
the encampment, a herd of tethered horses sidled ner
vously, their heads tossing, their neighs mingling wit
the thunder that rolled across the darkening sky.

As Sebastian signaled to his coachman to pull up, ;
motley pack of lean yellow dogs rushed barking fron
beneath the wagons. A tall man wearing a broad
brimmed black hat and a white shirt came to stand be

ide the nearest caravan, his gaze focused on them. He
made no move to approach, just stood with one hand
cupped around the bowl of his clay pipe, his eyes hidden
by the brim of his hat as he watched the dogs surround
them.

"Now what do we do?" asked Hero as the pack leapt
snapping and snarling around the carriage.

"Stay here." Throwing open the door, Sebastian
jumped to the ground to scoop up a rock and hurl it into
the pack. They all immediately drew back, ears flattened,
tails low.

"Impressive. Did you learn that in Spain too?" Hero
dropped down behind him. But he noticed she kept one
hand in her reticule.

"Even if you don't have a rock, all you need to do is
reach down and pretend to throw one, and the effect is
the same."

"I'll try to remember that."

They crossed the waterlogged meadow toward the
camp, the tall, wet grass brushing against their clothes. They
could see more men, and women in full, gaily colored skirts,
crouched around the fires, pretending not to notice their
approach. But the children hung back in the shadows, still
and quiet as they watched with dark, sullen eyes.

"O boro duvel atch pa leste," called Sebastian to the
lone man standing beside the nearest caravan.

The man grunted, his teeth clenching down on the
stem of his pipe, his eyes fierce. He had weathered, sun-
darkened skin and a bushy iron gray mustache and curly
dark hair heavily laced with gray. A pale scar cut through
his thick left eyebrow.

"The woman who tells fortunes near the Adelphi and
the York Steps," said Sebastian, still in Romany. "We
would like to speak to her."

The Gypsy stared at Sebastian, not a line in his face
moving.

"I know you have two Gadje children here with you," said Sebastian, although the truth was, he didn't know if he was still only working on a hunch. "A boy of nine and a younger child of three."

The Gypsy shifted his pipe stem with his tongue. "What do you think?" he said in English. "That we Rom are incapable of producing our own children? That we need to steal yours?"

"I'm not accusing you of stealing these children. I think you've offered them protection from the man who killed their cousin." When the Gypsy simply continued to stare at him, Sebastian said, "We mean the children no harm. But we have reason to think that the man who murdered their cousin now knows where they are."

Hero touched Sebastian's arm. "Devlin."

He turned his head. The old woman from the York Steps had appeared at the front doorway of the nearest caravan. She held by the hand a small child, his dark brown hair falling around his dirty face in soft curls like a girl's. But rather than a frock he wore a blue short-sleeved skeleton suit. The high-waisted trousers buttoned to a tight coat were ripped at one knee, the white ruffle-collared shirt beneath it grimy. He stared at them with wide, solemn eyes.

"Hello, Alfred," said Hero, holding out her arms. "Remember me, darling?"

The Gypsy woman let go of his hand, and after a moment's hesitation, he went to Hero. She scooped him off the platform into her arms and held him tight, her eyes squeezing shut for one betraying moment.

Sebastian said, "And the older child? George?"

It was the woman who answered. "He went down the river with some of our boys to catch hedgehogs. They were coming back to camp along the road when a man in a gig drove up behind them and grabbed the lad."

"How long ago?" said Sebastian sharply.

"An hour. Maybe more."

Hero met his gaze. "Dear God," she whispered.

Fishing his engraved gold watch from his pocket, Sebastian turned back to the mustachioed Gypsy. "I'll give you four hundred pounds for your fastest horse and a saddle, with this standing as security until I can deliver the funds. And to make damned certain you give me your best horse, I'll pay you another hundred pounds if I catch up with that gig in time."

"But we don't know where they've gone," said Hero.

"No. But I can guess. I think Hildeyard is taking him to Camlet Moat."

Chapter 50

*T*he Gypsies sold him a half-wild bay stallion tha danced away, ears flat, when Sebastian eased the saddl over its back.

"I don't like the looks of that horse," said Hero. Sh had the little boy balanced on her hip, his head on he shoulder, his eyelids drooping.

"He's fast. That's what matters at this point." He tight ened the cinch. "Lovejoy should still be at Bow Stree Tell him whatever you need to, but get him to send me out to the moat, fast."

"What if you're wrong? What if Hildeyard isn't takin George to Camlet Moat?"

"If you can think of anyplace else, tell Lovejoy." Se bastian settled into the saddle, the stallion bucking an kicking beneath him.

"Devlin—"

He wheeled the prancing horse to look back at her.

For one intense moment their gazes met and held Then she said, "Take care. Please."

The wind billowed her skirts, fluttered a stray lock o dark hair against her pale face. He said, "Don't worry; have a good reason to be careful."

"You mean, your son."

He smiled. "Actually, I'm counting on a girl—a daughter every bit as brilliant and strong and fiercely loyal to her sire as her mother."

She gave a startled, shaky laugh, and he nudged the horse closer so that he could reach down and cup her cheek with his hand. He wanted to tell her she was also a part of why he intended to be careful, that he'd realized how important she was to him even as he'd felt himself losing her without ever having actually made her his. He wanted to tell her that he'd learned a man could come to love again without betraying his first love.

But she laid her hand over his, holding his palm to her face as she turned her head to press a kiss against his flesh, and the moment slipped away.

"Now, go," she said, taking a step back. "Quickly."

Sebastian caught the horse ferry at the Lambeth Palace gate. The Gypsy stallion snorted and plunged with fright as the ferry rocked and pitched, the wind off the river drenching them both with spray picked up off the tops of the waves. Landing at Westminster, he worked his way around the outskirts of the city until the houses and traffic of London faded away. Finally, the road lay empty before them, and he spurred the bay into a headlong gallop.

His world narrowed down to the drumbeat of thundering hooves, the tumbling, lightning-riven clouds overhead, the sodden hills glistening with the day's rain and shadowed by tree branches shuddering in the wind. He was driven by a relentless sense of urgency and chafed by the knowledge that his assumption—that Hildeyard was taking his young cousin to Camlet Moat to kill him—could so easily be wrong. The boy might already be dead. Or Hildeyard might be taking the lad someplace else entirely, someplace Sebastian knew nothing about, rather than bothering to bury him on or near the island in the hopes that when he was eventually found the authorities would assume he'd been there all along.

A blinding sheet of lightning spilled through the storm-churned clouds, limning the winding, tree-shadowed road with a quick flash of white. He had reached the overgrown remnant of the old royal chase. The rain had started up again, a soft patter that beat on the leaves of the spreading oaks overhead and trickled down the back of his collar.

The Gypsy stallion was tiring. Sebastian could smell the animal's hot, sweaty hide, hear its labored breathing as he turned off onto the track that wound down toward the moat. He drew the horse into a walk, his gaze raking the wind-tossed, shadowy wood ahead. In the stillness, the humus-muffled plops of the horse's hooves and the creak of the saddle leather sounded dangerously loud. He rode another hundred feet and then reined in.

Sliding off the stallion, he wrapped the reins around a low branch and continued on foot. He could feel the temperature dropping, see the beginnings of a wispy fog hugging the ground. As he drew closer to the moat he was intensely aware of his own breathing, the pounding of his heart.

The barrister's gig stood empty at the top of the embankment, the gray between the shafts grazing unconcernedly in the grass beside the track. On the far side of the land bridge, a lantern cast a pool of light over the site of Sir Stanley's recent excavations. Hildeyard Tennyson sat on a downed log beside the lantern, his elbows resting on his spread knees, a small flintlock pistol in one hand. Some eight or ten feet away, a tall boy, barefoot like a Gypsy and wearing only torn trousers and a grimy shirt, worked digging the fill out of one of the old trenches. Sebastian could hear the scrape of George Tennyson's shovel cutting into the loose earth.

The barrister had set the boy to digging his own grave.

Sebastian eased down on one knee in the thick, wet humus behind the sturdy trunk of an ancient oak. If he'd been armed with a rifle, he could have taken out the barrister from here. But the small flintlock in his pocket was accurate only at short range. Sebastian listened to the rain slapping into the brackish water of the moat, let his gaze drift around the ancient site of Camelot. With Hildeyard seated at the head of the land bridge, there was no way Sebastian could approach the island from that direction without being seen. His only option was to cut around the moat until he was out of the barrister's sight, and then wade across the water.

Sebastian pushed to his feet, the flintlock in his hand, his palm sweaty on the stock. He could hear the soft purr of a shovelful of earth sliding down the side of George's growing dirt pile. The fill was loose, the digging easy; the boy was already up to his knees in the rapidly deepening trench.

Moving quietly but quickly, Sebastian threaded his way between thick trunks of oak and elm and beech, the rain filtering down through the heavy canopy to splash around him. The undergrowth of brush and ferns was thick and wet, the ground sloppy beneath his feet. He went just far enough to be out of sight of both boy and man, then slithered down the embankment to the moat's edge. Shoving the pistol into the waistband of his breeches, he jerked off his tall Hessians and his coat. He retrieved his dagger from the sheath in his boot and held it in his hand as he eased into the stagnant water.

Beneath his stocking feet, the muddy bottom felt squishy and slick. A ripe odor of decay rose around him. He felt the water lap at his thighs, then his groin. The moat was deeper than he'd expected it to be. He yanked the pistol from his waistband and held it high. But the water continued rising, to his chest, to his neck. There was nothing for it but to thrust the pistol back into his breeches and swim.

Just a few strokes carried him across the deepest stretch of water. But the damage was already done; his powder was wet, the pistol now useless as anything more than a prop.

Streaming water, he rose out of the shallows, his shirt and breeches smeared with green algae and slime. He pushed through the thick bracken and fern of the island, his wet clothes heavy and cumbersome, the small stones and broken sticks and thistles that littered the thicket floor sharp beneath his stocking feet. Drawing up behind a stand of hazel just beyond the circle of lamplight, he palmed the knife in his right hand and drew the water-logged pistol from his waistband to hold in his left hand. Then he crept forward until he could see George Tennyson, up to his waist now in the trench.

He heard Hildeyard say to the boy, "That's enough."

The boy swung around, the shovel still gripped in his hands. His face was pale and pinched and streaked with sweat and dirt and rain. "What are you going to do, Cousin Hildeyard?" he asked, his voice high-pitched but strong. "The Gypsies know what you did to Gabrielle. I told them. What do you think you can do? Shoot all of them too?"

Hildeyard pushed up from the log, the pistol in his hand. "I don't think anyone is going to listen to a band of filthy, thieving Gypsies." He raised the flintlock and pulled back the hammer with an audible click. "I'm sorry I have to do this, son, but—"

"Drop the gun." Sebastian stepped into the circle of light, his own useless pistol leveled at the barrister's chest. "Now!"

Rather than swinging the pistol on Sebastian, Tennyson lunged at the boy, wrapping one arm around his thin chest and hauling his small body about to hold him like a shield, the muzzle pressed to the child's temple. "No. You put your gun down. Do it, or I'll shoot the boy," he added, his voice rising almost hysterically when Sebastian was slow to comply. "You know I will. At this point, I've nothing to lose."

His knife still palmed out of sight in his right hand, Sebastian bent to lay the useless pistol in the wet grass at his feet. He straightened slowly, his now empty left hand held out to his side.

Hildeyard said, "Step closer to the light so I can see you better."

Sebastian took two steps, three.

"That's close enough."

Sebastian paused, although he still wasn't as close as he needed to be. "Give it up, Tennyson. My wife is even as we speak laying information before Bow Street."

The barrister shook his head. "No." His face was pale, his features twisted with panic. He was a proud, self-absorbed man driven by his own selfishness and a moment's fury into deeds far beyond anything he'd ever attempted before. "I don't believe you."

"Believe it. We know you left Kent at dawn on Sunday morning and didn't return to your estate until long past midnight." It was only a guess, of course, but Tennyson had no way of knowing that. Sebastian took another step, narrowing the distance between them. "She wrote you a letter, didn't she?" Sebastian took another step forward, then another. "A letter telling you she'd had an epileptic seizure."

"No. It's not in our side of the family. It's not! Do you hear me?"

"Did she think you owed it to your betrothed, Miss Goodwin, to warn her that you might also share the family affliction? Is that why you rode into town to talk to her? And when you told her you wanted her to shut up and keep it a secret, did she threaten to tell Miss Goodwin herself?" Sebastian took another step. "Is that when you killed her?"

"I'm warning you, stay back!" Hildeyard cried, the gun shaking in his hand as he swung the barrel away from the boy, toward Sebastian. "She was going to destroy my life! My marriage, my career, everything! Don't you see? I had to kill her."

For one fleeting moment, Sebastian caught George Tennyson's frightened gaze. "And the boys?"

"I forgot they were there." Hildeyard gave a ragged laugh, his emotions stretched to a thin breaking point. "I forgot they were even there."

Sebastian was watching the man's eyes and hands. He saw the gun barrel jerk, saw Hildeyard's eyes narrow.

Unable to throw his knife for fear of hitting the boy, Sebastian dove to one side just as Hildeyard squeezed the trigger.

The pistol belched fire, the shot going wide as Sebastian slammed into the raw, muddy earth. He lost the knife, his ears ringing from the shot, the air thick with the stench of burnt powder. He was still rolling to his feet when Hildeyard threw aside the empty gun and ran, crashing into the thick underbrush.

"Take the gig and get out of here!" Sebastian shouted at the boy, and plunged into the thicket after Hildeyard.

Sebastian was hampered by his heavy wet clothes and stocking feet. But he had the eyes and ears of an animal of prey, while Hildeyard was obviously blind in the darkness, blundering into saplings and tripping over roots and fallen logs. Sebastian caught up with him halfway across the small clearing of the sacred well and tackled him.

The two men went down together. Hildeyard scrabbled around, kicked at Sebastian's head with his boot heel, tried to gouge his eyes. Then he grabbed a broken

stone from the well's lining and smashed it down toward
Sebastian's head. Sebastian tried to jerk out of the way,
but the ragged masonry scraped the side of his face and
slammed, hard, into his shoulder.

Pain exploded through his body, his grip on the man
loosening just long enough for Hildeyard to half scramble up. Then Sebastian saw George Tennyson's pale face
looming above them, his jaw set hard with determination, the blade of his shovel heavy with caked mud as he
swung it at his cousin's head.

The flat of the blade slammed into the man's temple
with an ugly *twunk*. Tennyson went down and stayed
down.

Sebastian sat up, his breath coming heavy. "Thank
you," he said to the boy. He swiped a grimy wet sleeve
across his bloody cheek. "Are you all right?"

The boy nodded, his gaze on his cousin's still, pros-
trate body, his nostrils flaring as he sucked in a quick
breath of air. "Did I kill him?"

Sebastian shifted to rest his fingertips against the
steady pulse in Hildeyard's neck. "No."

Stripping off his cravat, Sebastian tied the man's
hands together, then used Hildeyard's own cravat to
bind his ankles, too. He wasn't taking any chances. Only
then did he push to his feet. His shoulder was aching, the
side of his face on fire.

George Tennyson said, "I still don't understand why
he killed her. She was his sister."

Sebastian looked down into the boy's wide, hurting
eyes. He was aware of the wind rustling through the
leaves of the ancient grove, the raindrops slapping into
the still waters of Camelot's moat. How did you explain
to a nine-year-old child the extent to which even seemingly normal people could be blindly obsessed with ful-
filling their own personal needs and wants? Or that there
were those who had such a profound disregard for

others—even their closest family members—that they were willing to kill to preserve their own interests?

Then he realized that was a lesson George had already learned, at first hand; what he didn't understand was how someone he knew and loved could be that way. And with that, Sebastian couldn't help him.

He looped an arm over the boy's shoulders and drew him close. "It's over. You're safe, and your brother's safe." Inadequate words, he knew.

But they were all he had.

Chapter 51

*G*ustav Pelletier sat on the edge of his hard bunk, his laced fingers tapping against his mustache.

"You're going to hang anyway," said Sebastian, standing with one shoulder propped against the prison cell's stone wall. "So why not tell the truth about Arceneaux?"

The tapping stopped. "You would like that, yes? So that you can make all tidy?" The hussar's lips curled. *"Casse-toi."* Then he turned his face away and refused to be drawn again into conversation.

Lovejoy was waiting for Sebastian in the corridor outside. "Anything?" he asked as the turnkey slammed the heavy, ironbound door closed behind him.

Sebastian shook his head.

They walked down the gloomy passageway, their footsteps echoing in the dank stillness. "If he did shoot Philippe Arceneaux," said Sebastian, "he's going to take the truth of it to the grave."

Sebastian had already identified one of the recaptured French officers, a Lyonnais by the name of François LeBlanc, as the second of the two men who had jumped him that night in Covent Garden. The man confessed that he and his fellow officer had attacked Sebastian out of fear the Viscount's persistent probing might uncover their escape plan. But the Frenchman swore he knew nothing about Arceneaux's death.

Lovejoy sighed. "You think Arceneaux abandoned his plans to escape with his comrades for the sake of Miss Tennyson?"

"I think so, yes."

"But then, why, once she was dead, didn't he reconsider?"

"Perhaps he'd come to regret the decision to break his parole. Although I think it more likely because he suspected his comrades of killing the woman he loved. He said as much to me right before he was shot, only at the time I didn't know enough to understand what he was saying."

They walked out the prison gates into the brilliant morning sunlight. The rain had cleared the dust and filth from the city streets to leave the air blessedly clean and fresh. Lovejoy said, "I'm told the children's father, the Reverend Tennyson, has arrived from Lincolnshire. Fortunately, Hildeyard provided us with a full confession, so young George shouldn't need to testify against him."

"Thank God for that," said Sebastian. The previous night, while they were waiting for Bow Street to reach Camlet Moat, Sebastian and the boy had sat side by side in the golden light of the lantern, the rain falling softly around them. In hushed tones, George had told Sebastian of how they'd been playing hide-and-seek that morning after church. Gabrielle was "it" and the two boys were hiding behind the heavy velvet drapes at the dining room windows when Hildeyard came barging into the house. Much of the argument between brother and sister had gone over George's head. But the confrontation had ended in the dining room, with Hildeyard grabbing the carving knife from the table in a fit of rage to stab Gabrielle.

The boys had remained hidden, silent and afraid, until Hildeyard stormed from the house—probably to fetch a gig. Then George grabbed Alfred's hand and ran to his friends the Gypsies.

Lovejoy said, "To think the man went out every day looking for his young cousins—even posted a reward! I was most impressed with him. He seemed such an admirable contrast to the boys' uncle."

"Well, unlike d'Eyncourt, Hildeyard sincerely wanted to find the boys—and silence them. He might have made a great show of hiring men to comb the countryside around the moat, but he advertised the reward he was offering here in London—and set up a solicitor in an office in Fleet Street to screen any information that might come in."

Lovejoy nodded. "The solicitor has proved most anxious to cooperate with us, for obvious reasons. Seems he received a tip yesterday from a wherryman who'd seen the two lads with the Gypsies. Of course, he claims he was utterly ignorant of Tennyson's real reason for wanting to find the boys."

"I suspect that he's telling the truth."

"One would hope so. He also admits to having put Tennyson in contact with the ruffian who attacked you beside the Thames yesterday—once again claiming no knowledge of Tennyson's purpose in hiring such an unsavory individual."

"A most incurious gentleman, if he's to be believed."

"He claims it's an occupational hazard."

"I assume he'll hang?"

"Tennyson, you mean? I should think so." Lovejoy paused to look back at the prison's grim facade. "Unfortunately, he insists he knows nothing about the death of the French lieutenant. I'd like to believe Pelletier or one of the other escaping officers was responsible. But I don't know. I just don't know. . . ."

He glanced over at Sebastian, the magistrate's brows

drawing together in a frown as if he knew there was something Sebastian was keeping from him.

But Sebastian only shook his head and said, "I wonder if the boys would be interested in a dog."

※

He came to Hero in the quiet of the afternoon, when the sun streamed golden through the open windows of her bedchamber and the breeze wafted clean and sweet.

She was watching a small boy and girl roll a hoop along the pavement, their joyous shouts and laughter carrying on the warm breeze. She didn't realize she was crying until he touched his fingers to her wet cheeks and turned her to him.

"Hero," he said softly. "Why now?"

The night before, she had insisted on driving out to Camlet Moat with Lovejoy and his men. The magistrate hadn't wanted her to come, but she had overridden his objections, impatient with every delay and tense but silent until they arrived at the old chase. Then, for one intensely joyous moment, her gaze had met Devlin's across the misty dark waters of the moat. But she had turned away almost at once to focus all her attention on the comfort and care of her dead friend's nine-year-old cousin.

And she hadn't shed a tear.

Now she laid her head against his shoulder, marveling at the simple comfort to be found in the strength of his arms around her and the slow beat of his heart so close to hers. She said, "I was thinking about Gabrielle. About how she felt as if she were missing out on all the joys and wonders that make life worth living. And so she gave in to her love for Lieutenant Arceneaux. And then she died because of it."

"She didn't die because she loved. She died because she was noble and honest and wanted to do the right thing, whereas her brother wanted only his own pleasure. Her choice didn't need to end in tragedy."

"Yet it did."

"It did, yes."

A silence fell between them. And she learned that the silence of a shared sorrow could also bring its own kind of comfort.

His hand shifted in a soft caress. She sucked in a shaky breath, then another, and raised her head to meet his gaze. His lips were parted, the sunlight glazing the high bones of his cheeks.

"Did you close the door behind you?" she asked, her voice husky with undisguised want.

"Yes."

Her gaze still locked with his, she brushed her lips against his. "Good."

She saw the flare of surprise in his eyes, felt his fingers tug impatiently at the laces that held her gown. He said, "It's not dark yet."

She gave him a wide, saucy smile. "I know."

🌶️

Later—much later—Sebastian lay beside her in a shaft of moonlight spilling through the open window. She raised herself on one bent arm, her fingertips skimming down over his naked chest and belly. He drew in his breath with a quiet hiss, and she smiled.

"Is the offer of a honeymoon still open?" she asked.

He crooked his elbow about her neck. "I think we deserve one, don't you?"

She shifted so that her forearms rested on his chest, her hair falling forward to curtain her face, her eyes suddenly serious. "We can do better than this, Sebastian."

He drew her closer, one hand drifting to the small of her back. "In the end I'd say we worked quite well together." He brought up his free hand to catch her hair away from her face. "But I think we can do better, yes."

And he raised his head to meet her kiss.

Author's Note

This story was inspired by Alfred, Lord Tennyson's haunting poem "The Lady of Shalott," first published in 1833, then revised and republished in 1842. Tennyson himself was inspired by a thirteenth-century Italian novella, *La donna di Scalotta*.

Gabrielle and Hildeyard Tennyson are fictional characters of my own invention, but the family of Alfred Tennyson was indeed plagued by epilepsy, alcoholism, and insanity. The poet's own father, a brilliant but troubled reverend from Somersby, Lincolnshire, was severely afflicted with epilepsy, and two of Alfred's brothers spent most of their lives in mental institutions. Alfred feared the family affliction his entire life, although to my knowledge I am the only one to suggest that this is the "curse" referenced in his poem. Alfred did indeed have an older brother named George, although he was born in 1806 and died in infancy.

Alfred's uncle, Charles Tennyson d'Eyncourt, is much as depicted here; however, while he attended Cambridge and sent his sons to Eton, there is no actual record of him having attended Eton. Six years younger than Alfred's father, he was nevertheless named the heir of the "Old Man of the Wolds" when his elder brother began exhibiting signs of severe epilepsy at puberty. The animosity between the two households was intense, with the wealthy Charles ironically coming to look down upon his older brother's family as "poor relations." Although he always denied it, Charles, too, suffered from a milder form of epilepsy. He did serve many years as a member of Parliament, although not until after the end of the Napoleonic Wars, and he did indeed change his name to d'Eyncourt, although his repeated attempts to do so were frustrated until 1835. I have moved the date of that name change up to avoid the confusion of too many Tennysons in the story. Later in life, d'Eyncourt bitterly resented his nephew's literary fame and was especially incensed when Alfred was made a lord (d'Eyncourt did finally achieve that honor himself, but much later in life). Charles's sister, Mary Bourne, is also a real figure, a dour, unhappy woman who found singular solace in the conviction that she would go to heaven while the rest of her family—particularly the Somersby Tennyson branch—suffered the everlasting torments of hell. I am indebted to Robert Bernard Martin for his groundbreaking study of the Tennyson family in *Tennyson: The Unquiet Heart*.

Epilepsy, once also known as "the falling sickness," was little understood in the nineteenth century and considered something shameful, to be kept hidden.

In 1812, archaeology was still in its infancy, although some of the first excavations at Stonehenge were undertaken as early as the seventeenth century. Further work was carried out there in 1798 and 1810 by William Cunnington and Richard Colt Hoare.

The legend that Arthur is not actually dead but will someday return to save England in her hour of need is real, hence his sobriquet "the once and *future* king." For obvious reasons, this legend was the bane of unpopular British monarchs, who were repeatedly driven to try to convince their subjects that Arthur really was dead. The lack of a grave site complicated this effort, which may have led to the "discovery" of Arthur's burial site at Glastonbury Abbey in the twelfth century.

Camlet Moat, once called Camelot, is a real place whose history is much as described here. It is now part of Trent Park, a country park open to the public, although the original eighteenth-century estate was named Trent Place. Over the years Trent Place went through many owners, several of whom instituted extensive remodeling projects. The amateur excavations on the island described here were actually carried out by two later owners, the Bevans during the 1880s and Sir Philip Sassoon in the early twentieth century. Curiously, the findings of those excavations are not reflected on the local council's information board currently in place at the site.

The island has long been reputed to have an association with the grail maidens of old, and yes, Sir Geoffrey de Mandeville's ties to the site also are real, as are his strange relationship with the Templars and the tales of his treasure. The story that he drowned in the well on the island and still haunts it, protecting his treasure, is indeed a local legend, although he actually died from an arrow in the head. Even the tales tying the highwayman Dick Turpin to the site are real; he frequently hid out at Camlet Moat during the course of his brief, ill-fated career. The numerous legends associated with the island can be found in various nineteenth-century works on the environs of London, including Jerrold's *Highways and Byways in Middlesex*, Thorne's *Handbook to the Environs of London*, and Lysons's *The Environs of London*. For a modern, more fanciful interpretation of the site, see Street's *London's Camelot and the Secrets of the Holy Grail.*

The antiquarian Richard Gough was a real figure who did indeed live at Gough Hall near Camlet Moat. He left his library to Oxford, but not his collections, which were sold.

In the 1990s, a local man named Derek Mahoney claimed to have found the leaden cross from Arthur's Glastonbury grave amongst mud dredged from an ornamental lake near Gough Hall. The local council claimed the find; Mahoney went to jail rather than surrender it, and then committed suicide. The cross, seen only briefly by the British Museum, again disappeared. It is assumed but has never been proven to be a modern forgery.

The system of billeting paroled French and allied officers around England is as described, albeit slightly more complicated. Although the concept of a gentleman's "word of honor" might seem strange to many today, paroled officers—as gentlemen—were given a startling amount of freedom. Many began businesses, married British women, and had children. The British government even allocated them a half-guinea-a-week allowance. Their restrictions were few: a curfew, a circumscribed location within which movement was allowed, an injunction to obey the laws of the land and to communicate with France only through the agent appointed by the Admiralty. From 1809 to 1812, nearly 700 paroled officers tried to escape, of whom some 242 were recaptured. The calico printer's cart described here (basically a closed cart of a type typically used by tradesmen who printed designs on cloth) was one of the ruses used in an escape attempt in the summer of 1812.

Although the waltz was not allowed at Almack's in London in 1812, it was danced elsewhere in England well before that date. The family wedding Mary Bourne prattles about to Hero in chapter 17 actually took place in 1806; her letters about the event mention the waltz.

Although we tend to think of neo-Druidism as a modern phenomenon, it was actually quite popular in the eighteenth and nineteenth centuries as part of the Romantic movement, which identified the Druids as national heroes. An Ancient Order of Druids was formed as early as 1781. Among the writers associated with the movement were William Stukely (who incorrectly believed Stonehenge was built by the Druids) and Iolo Morganwg (born Edward Williams), a Welsh nationalist with a deep admiration for the French Revolution. A form of spiritualism that stressed harmony with nature and respect for all beings, eighteenth- and nineteenth-century Druidism also drew on the teachings of the Enlightenment. Lacking any written texts, a rigid dogma, or a central authority, neo-Druidism was basically a philosophy of living that located the divinity within all living creatures.

The foundation stone for what was then known as the Strand Bridge was laid in October of 1811, at the site of the old Savoy Palace. By the time the bridge opened nearly six years later, it had been renamed the Waterloo Bridge.

Although women were not a common sight in the British Museum's Reading Room, they were allowed to become registered readers. According to the museum's records, three were listed as registered readers for the years 1770 to 1810, and five were listed in 1820 alone. The museum closed in August and September, but for the sake of my story I have allowed it to remain open a few extra days.

When Kat Boleyn's husband is arrested for murder, Sebastian and Hero work together to find the real killer, in a mystery involving a rare blue diamond, the theft of the French Crown jewels, and impoverished children who sweep the streets. Don't miss the next Sebastian St. Cyr Mystery,

WHAT DARKNESS BRINGS

Available now in hardcover and e-book, and in March 2014 in paperback.

London
Sunday, 20 September 1812

*T*he man was so old his face sagged in crinkly, sallow folds and Jenny could see pink scalp through the thin white hair plastered by sweat to his head.

"The irony is delicious; don't you agree?" he said as he slid a big, multifaceted piece of blue glass down between the swells of her breasts. The glass felt smooth and cool against her bare skin, but his fingers were as bone thin and cold as a corpse's.

She forced herself to lie still even though she wanted desperately to squirm away. She might be only seventeen, but Jenny Davie had been in this business for almost five years. She knew how to keep a smile plastered on her face when inside her guts roiled with revulsion and an exasperated urge to say, *Can't we just get this over with?*

"Think about it." He blinked, and she noticed he had no lashes fringing his small, sunken eyes, and that his teeth were so long and yellow they made her think of the ratty mule that pulled the dustman's cart. He said, "Once, this diamond graced the crowns of kings and nestled in the silken bosom of a queen. And now here it lies . . . on the somewhat grubby breasts of a cheap London whore."

"Go on wit' you," she scoffed, squinting down at the pretty glass. "Jist because I'm a whore don't mean I'm stupid. That ain't no diamond. It's *blue*. And it's bigger than a bloody peach pit."

"Much bigger than a peach pit," agreed the old man as the glass caught the flickering light from a nearby brace of candles and glowed as if with an inner fire. His dark eyes gleamed, and Jenny found herself wondering what he needed a whore for since he seemed more excited by his big chunk of blue glass than he was by her. "They say that once, this stone formed the third eye of a heathen—"

He broke off, his head coming up as a loud pounding sounded at the distant front door.

Before she could stop herself, Jenny jerked. She was lying on her back on a dusty, scratchy horsehair sofa in the cavernous, decrepit parlor of the old man's house. Most men took their whores in the back rooms of coffeehouses or in one of the city's numerous accommodation houses. But not this man. He always had his whores brought here, to his cobweb-draped old mansion in St. Botolph-Aldgate. And he didn't take them upstairs, either, but did his business here, on the couch—which suited Jenny just fine, since she never liked being too far from a way out of trouble.

He muttered something under his breath she didn't understand, although from the way he said it she figured it was some kind of curse. Then he said, "He wasn't supposed to be here this early."

He reared up, straightening his clothes. He'd had her strip down to her stockings and shift, which he'd untied so that it gaped open nearly to her waist. But he hadn't taken off any of his own clothes, not even his fusty, old-fashioned coat or shoes. He glanced around, the blue chunk of glass held tight in one fist. "Here," he said, gathering her stays, petticoat, and dress and shoving them into her arms. "Take these and get in—"

The knocking sounded again, louder this time, as she slid off the couch with her crumpled clothing clutched to her chest. "I can leave—"

"No." He moved toward the looming, old-fashioned chimneypiece that stood at one end of the room. It was a fantastical thing of smoke-darkened wood carved into tiers of columns with swags of fruit and nuts and even animals. "This won't take long." He pressed something in the carving, and Jenny blinked as a portion of the nearby paneling slid open. "Just get in here."

She found herself peering into a dark cubbyhole some six or eight feet square, empty except for an old basket and a couple of ironbound trunks lined against one wall. "In there? But—"

His hand closed around her bare upper arm tight enough that she squealed, "Ow!"

"Just shut up and get in there. If you let out a peep, you won't get paid. And if you touch anything, I'll break your neck. Understood?"

She supposed he saw the answer—or maybe just her fear—in her face, because he didn't wait for her reply but thrust her into the little room and slid the panel closed. Whirling around, she heard a latch click as a thick blackness swallowed her. She choked down a scream.

The air in the cubbyhole was musty and old smelling, like the man and the rest of his house, only nastier. It was so dark she wondered how the blazes he thought she was going to steal something when she couldn't see anything but a tiny pinprick of light about level with her head. She went to press one eye against the speck of light and realized it was a peephole, contrived to give a good view of the room beyond. She watched as he nestled his pretty piece of glass inside a velvet-lined red leather box. Then he shoved the box in the drawer of a nearby console and yelled, "I'm coming, I'm coming," as the knocking at the front door sounded again.

Jenny took a deep, shaky breath. She'd heard about some old houses having hidden cupboards like this. Priests' holes, they called them. They had something to do with Papists and such, although she'd never quite understood what it was all about. She wondered what would happen to her if the old goat never came back to release her. And then she wished she hadn't wondered that, because it made the walls seem to press in on her, and the blackness became so thick and heavy it felt as if it were stealing her breath and sucking the life out of her. She leaned her forehead against the wooden panel and tried to breathe in sucking little pants. She told herself that if Papists used to hide their priests in these cubbyholes, then they must have contrived a way for the panel to be opened from the inside. She began feeling around for the catch, then froze when she realized the voices from the front hall were coming closer.

Pressing her eye to the peephole again, she watched as the nasty old codger backed into the room. He had his hands raised queerly, sort of up and out to the side, like a body trying to ward off a ghost or something. Then she saw the pistol in the hands of the old man's visitor, and she understood.

The old cove was talking fast now. Jenny held herself very still, although her heart thumped in her chest and her breath came so hard and fast it was a wonder they couldn't hear it.

Then she heard a new pounding on the front door and someone shouting. The visitor holding the gun jerked around, distracted, and the old goat lunged.

The gun went off, belching flame and pungent smoke. The old man staggered back. Crumpled.

Jenny felt a hot, stinging gush run down her legs and realized she'd just wet herself.